Trouwerner

S. Pitt

Firsthale

Contents.

Author's Note.

This is a work of fiction inspired by the history of Tasmania. I have attempted to represent the period 1792-1835 as accurately as possible but I have not tried to recreate the manner of speech of aboriginal Tasmanians or Europeans of the time, or the actual words of historical figures featured. Truganana, Woorady, Dray, Robinson and Manalargenna were real people whose role was pivotal in the fate of the indigenous Tasmanians but they have been used fictitiously. Robinson's eulogy for Manalargenna in *'The Coming of Night'* is based on Arthur Papers, **28**, MSS A1771148-A1171161 (State Library of NSW). Touami, his kin and the Meelayginnee clan are all fictional.

Where relevant, the calendar month (or season), and year, in which each story begins has been inserted beneath the title. Readers unfamiliar with the Southern Hemisphere should note that in Australia, the summer solstice is 21st December.

Aboriginal words are from: Plomley, N.J.B. (1976) *A word-list of the Tasmanian aboriginal languages*. Published by N.J.B. Plomley in association with the Tasmanian State Government.

Glossary.

ballawiné: red ochre
comenner: beard
darwalla: fan-tail synonym. 'small bird'
ebenook: the sea
kannenner: thylacine, Tasmanian Tiger
karteila: seal
koonah: bettong
korerenner: brown hawk
korunah: wedge-tail eagle
larener: male wallaby
layngana: firetail finch
liapota: river
loinah: black snake
lueena: blue wren
lunna: brown quoll
lyner/ lyenah: raven
menuggana: black cockatoo
monagunarrah: sickness
narrar: white cockatoo
noné: louse
noonah: goods synonym 'objects'
nowhummer: lightning
num: white man/men
ny rae num: good white man
nymenner: father
parner: aboriginal man/men
Pygeewar: ' long time ago'
pynener: 'native bread' fungus
ragae: evil spirit syn. demon/devil
runnawehnah: brown skink
ruwah: sandlark
tarner: Forester kangaroo (male)
tarrabah: Tasmanian devil
tienna: bandicoot
tirurar: seagull synonym 'skua'
Trouwerner: Tasmania/the world
yolla: mutton-bird (Shearwater)

Trouwerner

1. Rites of Passage 1.

(Southern Tasmania, December 1791).

Not a leaf stirred as the boy made his way along the narrow trail. He moved with great care, alert to every sound and movement. The charcoal on his skin rendered him almost invisible in the dappled light and shade.

Touami was thirteen years old. Never before had he ventured so far from his hearth-group. The unaccustomed solitude made the scents of the forest, familiar for as long as he could remember, seem sharper, more exciting. And he knew that today the great trees, silvery swamp gums soaring like mighty pillars through lesser growth of myrtle, sassafras and blackwood, stood witness. A successful hunt would set him on the path to manhood.

A wallaby was browsing a little way from the path. It sat upright and the boy froze. After a few moments, the animal relaxed again. It scratched its ribs with a black forepaw and blinked. It was *larener*, a young male: a legitimate target. Touami held his breath, tried to steady the pounding of his heart. A flock of blue wrens fluttered in the bushes but he was oblivious to their chatter.

Slowly, Touami flexed and raised his spear-arm. His weapon was a simple finely-balanced javelin of tea-tree. Everything depended on the power and accuracy of a single throw. The wallaby's ears twitched. It snuffed the air then scratched again. Its dark liquid eyes reflected the overhanging trees and mirrored the boy but it did not see him.

Another wallaby grunted from within a clump of ferns to the left. This one was downwind of Touami, could catch his scent at any moment. If he delayed any longer, it might sense him and thump the ground in warning as it leapt away: he would lose his chance. And though no-one would blame him if he failed on his first solo hunt (even his father often came home empty-handed), it would have been his fault.

His arm was now stretched to its limit but before he cast, the boy jogged his hand up and down, sending a resonance along the length of the shaft. As he did so, his whole being focused on the throw, the muscles tensing from the soles of his feet to his fingers. The spear became an extension of his body, his will.

He threw: the wallaby bounded too late. Its eyes rolled white in terror as the boy sprang after. The spear had sunk deep in its flank but if it was knocked out or broken in the animal's flight, Touami knew he would be lucky to make a kill.

A flock of rosellas flew up in a tumult of screeches and flapping wings; every time the boy came close, the wounded wallaby leapt away. But he must have hit something vital because the animal tired rapidly. It stopped and watched him. Its tongue protruded pinkly at every breath; the spear shook with its panting.

Touami's fingertips grazed the shaft: the wallaby lurched to one side and tried to burrow into a clump of cutting-grass too dense to admit more than its head and shoulders. His ribs pumping almost as fast as his quarry's, the boy grasped the spear and drove it into the shuddering, cringing body. The point stuck for a moment so he pulled back, altered the angle slightly, then thrust hard.

The wallaby grunted and heaved; a feeble cry came from its throat; its feet twitched and stretched. Blood bubbled from its mouth and nose. It died.

Touami waited. He wanted to laugh or shout in triumph but alone in the forest he did not dare. He pulled the spear out, crouched and touched the eyeball to make sure the animal was truly dead.

Fleas jumped as his hand brushed the dense fur and he scratched at the thatch of his own hair. Then he grasped the wallaby's tail and bent it over his shoulder. That was how the men carried home their kills, slung casually so that the head dangled behind their buttocks and the hind-legs stuck up to frame their faces. Now all he had to do was stand. It was a long walk to camp and he had to carry his kill back alone. Otherwise it would not count.

Though skinny and pot-bellied, Touami was strong for his size. But the dead wallaby seemed to weigh almost as much as he did and, stretched from nose to tail-tip, was almost as long as he was tall. Each time he managed to hoist it over one shoulder, the carcass slid to the ground when he tried to stand.

The third time this happened, he let it lie and squatted to rest. As his triumph in the kill ebbed beneath the problem of transporting it, he felt tired. Already there was a slight slant to the sun's rays. If he did not reach camp by nightfall, his hearth-group would search for him at first light.

And the thought of being treated like a lost child lent Touami the strength he needed. He propped his spear against a tree and managed to struggle upright with the wallaby on his back. Holding the tail with one hand, his spear with the other, he found he could manage though he was forced to walk lop-sided to keep the carcass from slipping.

Staggering a little under his burden, leaning on his spear, the boy made his way back along the narrow trail. Now he felt the silent presence of the trees as a tangible force, his passing a fleeting instant in the long years of their growth. The wallaby's head bumped behind his knees, at times almost tripping him. His footsteps were heavy now: he saw no creatures except birds and insects.

This was not Touami's first kill: waterfowl especially had fallen prey to his skilfully flung stones, but no other could be so significant. As the dead weight bore down on him he realized that the taking of life was not a trivial matter. He remembered the wallaby's bright eye, the flick of its ears in the moment before he cast: it too had had its place in the world. And he thought he understood the air of power possessed by the best hunters in the band. To them the act of killing was a serious, almost sacred undertaking, something not to be abused or taken lightly but as the enactment of a pact made at the beginning of all things, the embodiment of the law by which Trouwerner existed.

Now, on the threshold of joining that elite, of becoming one in a continuum that stretched back over uncounted generations,

Touami shivered. If he succeeded in bringing the wallaby into camp, he would be judged fit to begin his proving. He would be driven out, exiled from his hearth-group and while, if he chose, he could make his own camp close to theirs, he would be denied a share of their meat, their fires. For a whole year he would have to survive apart from his family, conversing only with other tyros and wise-men, and at the end of it he would undergo the final test of initiation. From that he would emerge a man, his lineage cut into his skin, and thereafter the spirit of his totem, be it animal, bird, tree, rock or water, would be known to all the band and he would be given his true name, the one he would be called by until he died.

So daunting was this prospect that for an instant, the time it took for a bee-eater to swoop across the path, the boy's resolve faltered. He thought of his mother and sisters who, at meal-times, always made sure he got a choice portion once his father and grandfather were replete; how last winter, when he was ill, the women had carried him between camps though to do so was forbidden. (His mother and grand-dam had been punished for their contempt of the law but the beating hardly marked them: in gratitude that his only son was still alive, Touami's father, Umara, had been lenient.)

Once he began his trial, such security would be lost. And when he became a man, he would be given a wife from a different skin-group: the responsibilities of providing for his family dictating the pattern of his life. At the end, his body would be burned and his name would never be spoken again. The start of his proving marked the end of boyhood.

Yet as Touami knew, it was still within his power to delay that moment. All he had to do was abandon the dead wallaby a little way from the path. Within a night the scavengers, *kannenner* and *tarrabah* would have devoured it. Without proof of the kill, he could remain a child.

But barely had this thought crystallised when another picture sprang to his mind: Niama, his foster-brother, swaggering into camp with a dead pademelon slung over his shoulder. Niama was older than Touami by two seasons but the death of his father and the kidnapping of his mother in a tribal dispute had left him insecure and ashamed before his kin, feelings he concealed behind a kind of proud diffidence and an unusual competitiveness which, to Touami, often made him seem more rival than friend.

Niama had left the group: pride would not allow Touami to give up now. He hoisted the carcass a little higher and trudged on. A green gloom was spreading beneath the canopy. It lent a verdant lambency to the mosses and ferns which festooned forest floor and fallen trees but he knew the twilight would thicken swiftly once the sun had set. He gritted his teeth and increased his pace. It seemed to him that he had been struggling with his burden for half a lifetime.

When at last the red glow of campfires appeared ahead, Touami was close to exhaustion, unsure whether it was the wavering firelight which made the trees and their shadows sway and shudder or his own weariness. But when he came to the edge of the glade, he gathered what remained of his strength to heft his kill higher on his shoulder, to straighten his back and hold his head high before stepping forward.

Like all his people's camps, this was a temporary one, consisting of a few simple shelters fashioned from sticks and bark, little more than wind-breaks. The hearth-group comprised Touami's parents, his four sisters, his grandparents on his father's side and his maternal grandmother, Wagarulepu. His uncle, Tumara, was with them also, having come to invite the group to a corroboree at which his daughter would be initiated and betrothed.

As was customary, the men sat on one side of the largest cooking fire, with the women opposite. Touami's mother, Tealana, sat suckling her youngest child, a little girl of eighteen months while Toualena, his twin, served the men portions of a possum that had been baking in the ashes. His other sisters squabbled over one of the hind legs; the elders ate with quiet, fierce, concentration, Wagarulepu mumbling her food in an almost toothless mouth. Touami walked towards them, his heart beating fast.

'Yah! Here he is at last!' Umara did not stop eating but his eyes glinted in the firelight as he watched his son. The boy stopped a few paces from the fire in the gap between the men and the women. All eyes were upon him as he let the wallaby fall to the ground where it could be seen and admired. He was trembling with weariness and his mouth watered at the smell of food but he waited proudly, in silence, allowing the significance of his achievement to sink in.

'Aiee, that it should come so soon . . .' Touami heard his mother's lament though she was careful to keep her voice low lest the elders hear. Contempt for her weakness, her inability to understand his new-found power, made the boy tighten his lips. This made him appear even younger than before yet there was something of his father's fierceness in his expression and Wagarulepu chuckled and shook her head in appreciation: 'See: he thinks he is a man already!'

'The thinking is one thing, the being another.' Touami's grandfather, Meelangana, a grim old man with a burn scar disfiguring his body from where he had been trapped in a bush fire, looked penetratingly into the boy's face. 'Tonight is the last of his boyhood: he is ready to start his proving.' He broke off abruptly to stare at Tealana, who had begun to wail. 'That is the law: it is how it has always been. Mourn when the time comes, woman: for now give the boy something to eat.'

Never before had the women been so attentive: they made Touami sit and gave him possum ribs to take the edge off his hunger while the wallaby, his wallaby, was covered with hot ashes and set to bake at the edge of the fire. The stench of burning hair and fat filled the glade but though he would normally have moved away from the foul smoke, this time the boy endured, even savoured it. His whole being craved the meat of his first real kill: crisp, fire-blackened skin; blood-oozing flesh, rich marrow to be sucked from the bones.

'Eh, look how proudly he sits.' Umara's tone was half-mocking, half-admiring. 'But was it by chance or skill that *larener* ran onto his spear?'

Touami sensed that he was being tested so instead of rising to the insult as he longed to do, he bent his head and tried to let the chuckles of his grandfather and uncle pass over him like rain.

'Ay, it's almost as big as he is: maybe he fell over it when he went to shit!' Uniala, Umara's mother, hugged herself and rocked with glee. 'If he has such luck again, you men can lay aside your spears and sleep all day.'

'Quiet, woman,' Umara growled but the mood had been set and soon even Tealana joined in the goading which was meant to determine a boy's maturity: if he reacted with anger or violence he would be mocked and refused his trial until he learned humility. Touami sat quietly, enduring the provocation with as much patience as he could muster until at last Umara took pity on him and called for silence.

'Small he may be but he is my son and soon he will be a man,' he said and these words rewarded each dragging step of the boy's journey home and renewed his sense of triumph. 'Niama has already left: when the pepper berries are ripe again they will return or else we will set free their spirits.'

Touami felt suddenly afraid for an odd, guarded look had come into his father's eyes and a faint moan escaped his mother's lips. But his grandfather snorted disparagingly.

'First let us see if this is a real wallaby he's brought back or a sewn-up skin full of bones and earth,' he said. 'Like Wyerkartenner when he tried to trick Storm into giving him fire, leaving the children of Tarner to eat their meat raw! Though – ' his teeth glistened as he drew back his lips in a smile akin to a snarl, '- it smells good enough!'

The wallaby was barely more than seared on the outside but they began to eat anyway, in part to acknowledge Touami's achievement but mainly because these people were, like all hunter-gatherers, opportunists and gorged when the chance arose. The women divided the carcass and, as was proper, the choice pieces, liver, kidneys, heart were shared between the elders. Touami ate eagerly of the haunch he was given and even when his belly felt tight and full, he continued to eat, in part because it seemed to him that while the group feasted he was still secure, part of them. The blackness at the edge of the glade looked threatening, almost impenetrable by contrast with the homely circle of firelight illuminating the camp.

Inevitably, the time came when no-one could eat any more. Touami felt that if he tried to swallow another mouthful, he would vomit. He belched loudly and noticed that his father was watching him with a kind of sardonic amusement. As soon as he realized the boy had seen, Umara yawned and stretched then tilted his head meaningfully at the others. 'Time to sleep.'

There was nothing unusual in the manner in which the women roused the drowsing children or the elders clambered stiffly to their feet and made their way slowly to the shelters, yet Touami thought he detected an odd tension in the air, an atmosphere of suppressed expectancy. It seemed to him that the men were careful not to look him in the face and the women's surreptitious glances betrayed a mixture of pride and pity. By chance or design he was last to leave the fireplace and he felt inordinately self-conscious as he made his way to the shelter he had formerly shared with Niama because he knew he was being watched.

The lean-to seemed large and empty without his foster-brother and though Touami mounded up the pile of leaves that served as a bed and laid his spear within reach, he could not get comfortable. He watched smoke spiral up towards the stars until weariness gradually overcame his apprehension. He snuggled deep into the dry leaves, savouring the smells of eucalypt and earth. Whatever they had planned for him, he was no child to be caught unawares: he would face his trial like a great hunter … a fighter … a man …

Silently, as if stalking the shyest wallaby, the men converged on the sleeping boy. Their faces, rib-cages and wiry limbs were daubed with white clay. This contrasted so sharply with their charcoal-darkened bodies that even in the faint, ruddy light from the embers, they appeared unearthly, like creatures from ancient times, the Pygeewar, when only ancestral beings walked the earth. Indeed, it was as if the pigments possessed some magical power of transfiguration because as they stepped across the short grass the men felt the power of those they represented possess them in the touch of the earth against their feet, the caress of the cool night air against their skins. And their movements took on an eerie fluidity, more akin to the flowing of mist or shadows than the action of living beings.

For the millennia that this ritual had been enacted, no female or uninitiated boy had set eyes on the spirits conjured to claim a new candidate's boyhood. When the men left their shelters, the women turned to face the wall and concentrated on keeping the younger children quiet, terrified of witnessing the forbidden. And yet they also had their part to play in the ceremony: as the men raised their spears, the women felt the tension which seemed to make the very air quiver and drew breath for the mourning cry that would accompany the boy's flight.

Touami was jerked from sleep by an ear-splitting shriek. He sat up, heart pounding, as the cry was repeated, rising to a series of appalling howls. The noise came from all directions, worse than anything he had ever heard before or imagined, even exceeding the screams of a woman in childbirth or the squabbling of *tarrabah* over a carcass. He groped for his spear, thinking the camp must be under attack. Then he saw the first apparition.

A scream swelled in his chest and died there. It did not occur to him that these could be anything but supernatural beings, ghosts or things that had never been human: Raegeowrapper and his kind who hungered after the warmth of living creatures. The power of movement forsook him as he stared at the foremost of the figures, skeletal, immeasurably tall, hissing as it bent towards him. The coldness of death seemed to seep from its mouth: he thought to hear his own name come from its lips, distorted and drawn-out like a curse.

They were sorcerers then, come to steal his spirit. Terror lent the boy strength to grasp his spear. Though earthly weapons were useless against magic, on the day he had killed his first wallaby he would not give up without a fight. With an immense effort, he drew himself into a crouch, then launched himself at the apparition. To his surprise, it twisted away with a grunt that sounded oddly familiar but it was not alone. He was beyond the safety of the shelter and they surrounded him: the hissing became a chant.

Touami knew he must not listen to the spell designed to weaken and bind him but in the time, measured in heartbeats, that he stood poised between running and fighting, it seemed to him that the words coalesced out of the night, coiling around him like mist, stroking his skin with a touch both seductive and deadly. He felt the power of the spell seep into him with every breath, spreading a slow poison through his blood: his fingers opened as if obeying some will other than his own. In another moment he would drop his spear.

Then another sound pierced the night. Mournful, heart-rending, the women's lament for a lost child vied with the ghost-chant. Touami shuddered for he knew the wailing was for him but it broke the evil spell. The slim spear-shaft was solid and real again against his palm: he gripped it with desperate strength and, with an incoherent shout, leapt towards a gap that opened between the nightmare figures.

He was through: the forest loomed ahead, no longer a threat but sanctuary from the dark magic conjured all around him, the frenzied howling that marked him as one already dead. He heard the ghosts shriek in frustration and anger, felt their hands clutch air behind him as he ran. Though the voices of the women faded quickly from wild keening into silence, he thought to hear inhuman laughter mocking his flight and ran on.

When at last even that sound was swallowed by the forest, Touami stumbled to a halt, the breath sobbing in his throat. He waited, tensed to run again at the slightest indication of pursuit. His whole body lurched to the pounding of his heart.

The wind whispered softly through the branches overhead, a pademelon grunted nearby, something scratched claws on bark: most likely a bandicoot or quoll hunting grubs or beetles. Slowly, the boy relaxed. Although supernatural beings possessed the power to move silently, he was sure he would notice the approach of these: somehow they had seemed almost as substantial as living beings. Doubt began to surface in his mind but then he remembered their voices. He shivered at the memory of the hissed imprecations, tried to push them aside lest recollection increase their potency. And yet as he recalled them, he realized that the voices had not been wholly strange. They had mimicked those he knew: his father's, uncle's, grandfather's only horribly changed, as if malignant spirits were torturing those he loved.

As he thought this, a hot flood surged through Touami's blood: a mixture of shame and anger. He had believed himself a man because he had succeeded in hunting a wallaby (something the most worthless *parner* could do), yet at the first sign of danger he had fled like a scared child.

The quietness of the night now seemed ominous. The apparitions had not followed him but they might have preyed on the rest of the group, sucking the life-force from each of them, leaving only empty husks of flesh which breathed but were incapable of thought or feeling. Such things were common in the tales his grandfather, Meelangana, told and there were other evil beings in the forest: the giant man-like creature Yowee who could tear the strongest man limb from limb; little poteroo-like spirits with long fangs which fed on blood, returning night after night until, in the end, their victims died.

Touami shivered, remembering a little girl who had been bitten and became helpless as a suckling babe. Her kin had carried her with them until the elders decreed that she must be outcast lest the creatures attack again. She had been left behind in the forest and her whimpering had haunted Touami all that day though in truth it could not have been audible for more than a spearthrow. That night, the women wailed until dawn, drowning the shrieks of carrion-eaters but the event had sunk deep in Touami's memory. It had been his first conscious recognition of the law that governed not only the life of the tribes but the whole of their world.

Now, despite his terror, because of it, he knew he must retrace his steps, to discover what had happened to his kin even if he were powerless to help them. If he did not, he would always carry the guilt of cowardice deep within and, if his hearth-group were dead, the rest of the band would look upon him as one unworthy of initiation: he would never be a man.

Slowly, gripping the spear with both hands, he crept back along the wallaby trail. His shadow was thrown sharply ahead of him where moonlight drenched the forest floor and his dread mounted with every step: on such a night the slightest ill-portent seemed momentous. All his senses strained for any untoward sound or movement but apart from a startled pademelon which broke from cover almost beneath his feet, the forest was still. It seemed to the boy that all creation was in suspense, waiting.

It took far longer than he had expected before a point of red light between the trees betrayed the location of the camp. This late on any ordinary night the fire would have been banked over with ash while the people slept but from its brightness and the wavering of shadows, he could tell it was blazing. He wondered what horrors that flaring light would reveal, imagined his father's body lying asprawl with throat and ribs torn open or spears stuck through belly and groin as Niama's father had died, saw the blood glinting blackly in the red light, and a sob gathered in his throat so vivid was the picture in his mind.

Leaves clashed and whispered in a breath of wind. Mingled with it the boy caught the sounds of voices and laughter, the kind men make when a joke has been had at another's expense. Touami felt a chill run through him: it was true then – his father had been slain and the killers were celebrating their triumph – soon the women would scream. Despair rose through him in a suffocating wave: he almost turned and slunk away. But then the laughter sounded again and cold, clear hatred overtook him. A boy would flee, yes, but today he had stepped on the path to manhood. And he was armed: at least he could try to avenge his father, set his spirit free. If he failed, he would die in the attempt like a warrior.

His approach to camp was like a re-enactment of his stalk earlier in the day except that this time he was afraid. It was not the panic-fear that had possessed him earlier but something more profound, a dread lodged at his very heart: the fear of death. In the normal run of things the boy seldom contemplated how his life might end: there were too many ways to die by chance or accident - a falling branch, the bite of a black snake, a wayward step on a narrow cliff path – to waste time brooding on it. In any case, as the smallest child knew, the energy intrinsic to all things (even stones, though in these it was torpid and weak), never died. At the end of his life a man's spirit would join his daemon's while his body, whether consumed by fire or earth, would not vanish but be incorporated into other living things. Yet though he understood this, Touami did not want to die and as he crept forward he felt his own life-force surge powerfully though him. This made the possibility of dying before the sun rose even more daunting.

He was almost within full view of the camp, taking care to keep in deep shadow, when the laughter sounded again, freely as if a corroboree were in progress. As he listened, Touami's anger and dread dissolved in astonishment. Wondering, he edged even closer until he had a clear view of the fire and those that sat around it.

The ecstasy which had possessed the men during the ceremony was slow to dissipate for the intensity of the experience had acted like a drug. They had rubbed off most of the white clay but as they sat around the fire they were animated by the kind of wild energy that comes on the edge of exhaustion. With extravagant gestures and grotesque mimicry they related tales of past initiations: how one boy, long ago, had died of fright while another grappled with one of the 'spirits' and pushed it into the fire whereupon it turned into an angry father who had beaten the boy soundly though he had grown to be a famous wise-man.

'Yah! Who knows, my son may turn out the same: he would have had me if I'd been an instant slower,' Umara said, stretching out his arms until the muscles cracked. 'His foster-brother didn't wait so long.'

'Eh – don't be too proud.' The old man, Meelangana, shook his head. 'Perhaps Niama has more cause to be afraid. Your lad didn't linger once there was clear space in front of him.'

'There's a difference between courage and foolhardiness,' Tumara remarked dryly. 'Which of us did not flee? But,' he paused and a shrewd look settled on his features, 'maybe he has not gone far.'

'Ah – but did you see his face?' The elder was determined to have the last word. 'His eyes almost sprang from their sockets. Like a startled girl's!'

Hidden within the scrub, the boy clenched his teeth. He was too respectful of the law to burst from cover and challenge the men: that would be the behaviour of a spoilt child but he had been tricked and now they were making fun of him. The shame was almost unbearable.

For a moment Umara stiffened as if he, too, were pricked by the insult but then, to Touami's dismay, his face spilt in a wide grin. 'Yah – on her wedding night, when she sees how big her husband's thing's grown.' He mimicked staring eyes, a look of horrified anticipation, raised his hands and squeaked coyly, 'Oh don't, please!'

This had the others laughing uproariously but it was too much for Touami. Tears of resentment scorched his cheeks as he turned and ran. Wanting only to be free of those scornful voices, he blundered into trees, felt the lash of springing branches, heard dry twigs crack beneath his feet. Fearful of being injured, he eventually slowed to a jog-trot but, half-blinded by tears, he still made as much noise as a stampeded wallaby and from the burst of raucous laughter from the direction of the camp, he knew the men had heard and guessed the cause of it.

At last the quietness of the forest enveloped Touami: he was far beyond sight or sound of the camp. The sweat had grown chill on his skin and he shivered and began to look for somewhere to lie down and rest. His anger had been overtaken by a creeping, immeasurable weariness: he knew the humiliation he had suffered would have to be borne, then forgotten. He found a leaf-filled hollow and jabbed his spear into it to make sure there were no snakes there, then ruffled up the leaves: these simple actions did much to calm him. Thanks to his mother and sisters (and, he remembered proudly, his own hunting prowess), he had eaten well; the shock and bitterness of the night were passing. He curled up in the nest of dry leaves and sank into a dreamless slumber.

2. First Sighting.

(South West Cape, Tasmania, May 1792).

The seals were packed so tightly that from a distance the rock platform looked cobbled. Only close scrutiny and the noise revealed that the brown rounded objects were not stones but animals. And though at first sight the colony appeared rock-still, there was constant flux: seals slipping into the water at the edges or shoving through the mass of bodies after clawing their way onto the shelf; mothers turning onto their sides to nurse grey-pelted young. A cacophony of barks, growls and the calls of hungry pups (which was akin to the squalling of human babes), rose above the roar of the ocean; the stench, an oily mixture of fish, rotting seaweed and the reek of the males, wafted up the cliff face on the salt-laden breeze.

Oué-mala's nostrils widened as he breathed in the seal-smell. *Karteila* was the totem of his people, the Toogee; his skin glistened with seal-fat and he watched the animals with a kind of paternalistic affection for they were more than a source of food and warmth: deep at the very root of things they were kin. Thus as he noted the plumpness of the pups and their abundance he felt a mixture of pride and anticipation for soon the birthing season would be over and the animals could be hunted.

The number of pups meant this season would be a good one and Oué-mala sighed and pulled contentedly at his foreskin. The Toogee was one of nine tribes inhabiting Trouwerner, second only in numbers and prosperity to the Lairmairrener to the north-east. Living on the coast all year round with a source of red ochre, *ballawiné*, at the heart of their territory, the Toogee rarely went hungry and lesser tribes traded chert and kangaroo skins for their shells and pigment. And though they had a reputation as warriors, in reality Oué-mala's was a peaceful and happy people. It was simply that having so much that was good to protect, they responded fiercely to any perceived threat. To those who were respectful and generous with their gifts, the Toogee were welcoming and prepared to share the shore's bounty. A single beached whale could feed several hearth-groups for weeks and strandings were common on their coast.

Oué-mala grinned to himself for he had planned a great corroboree next autumn when Umara's hearth-group came. They belonged to the Meelayginnee clan of the Lairmairrener, and their territory lay in the forested valleys and highlands of the interior. For them the cold meant great hardship in their own lands so they over-wintered on the coast, alternating between the Toogee to the south-west and the Nuenone to the south-east. A meeting between the hearth-groups was always a cause for celebration but in the summer Oué-mala's daughter would come of age and he had chosen Touami, Umara's son, to be her husband. Among the Toogee the girl, Uné-mawa, was famed for her beauty while Touami could hold his own against any of his peers. And the union between the groups would be doubly cemented because his own son's wife had recently died in childbirth and Umara also had a daughter ripe for marriage.

'Eh, it'll be good for all of us,' Oué-mala thought and he straightened (he had been leaning at ease on his spear, right foot hooked around left calf), and stretched as a preliminary to setting off back to camp. But before leaving the cliff-top, he half-turned to scan the sea for to him, as all his people, the ocean was the prime source of food, of life itself if old tales were to be believed: a man ignored it at his peril.

On this section of the coast two great currents converged and there were many islets and skerries around which the surf foamed even when the sea was calm. Beyond the reefs a mighty swell ran, heaping the green water into massive rolling waves and troughs; the air between was ridden by grey gulls, albatrosses and gannets. A silver sheen of cloud covered the sky from horizon to horizon and where it was broken, the sun's rays illuminated irregular patches of sea, a surface that otherwise had the colour and lustre of struck flint. This shifting light played tricks on the eyes: lacking perspective, Oué-mala could not tell whether dark spots in the glittering water were seals, seabirds or simply pieces of storm-torn kelp.

He was about to turn away when something far out towards the horizon caught his eye. It flashed white like a gannet's wings yet as he stared he realized this was no bird for instead of gliding parallel to the crest and troughs, it was crossing them, so slowly it seemed hardly to move. A bright spot against the gleaming mass of grey and silver water, that was all, yet Oué-mala was disturbed by it. He lifted his free hand to shade his eyes from the glare but the clouds had moved and the thing had disappeared. Though he looked until his eyes ached, he did not see it again.

It was only when he had returned to camp that Oué-mala realized it was the shape and unnatural progress of the white spot over the sea that had disconcerted him. Unlike any bird or animal he knew, its form had been oddly regular, tall and straight-sided, more like something made by the hands of men than a living creature. Yet it could not have been a canoe-raft such as his people built for they were small, constructed of bark and reeds and would have been invisible at such distance had anyone been foolish enough to paddle out so far.

Frustrated by the impossibility of discovering more, afraid that the sighting might be an ill-omen (for among the Toogee white portended death), Oué-mala was troubled for weeks afterwards. Whenever he was by the sea he scanned the waters uneasily yet he did not confide in his hearth-group, thinking they would scorn him. After all, there was no proof it had been anything but sunlight catching a large breaker or the splash of a breaching whale. But as winter passed and nothing unusual happened, Oué-mala dismissed what he had seen. It was clearly of no significance to him or his people: nothing had changed.

3. The Wise-man.

(Southern Tasmania, Spring 1792).

Aged nearly fifty, Meelangana, Touami's grandfather, was an old man. His hair and beard were grizzled and his skin wrinkled, the flesh slack where once there had been hard muscle. But he was not, by any means, the most ancient of the Meelayginnee nor had age diminished his wits. Indeed the years had taught him that guile served better than physical prowess when it came to getting his own way though it was rarely that his will was contested. In his youth he had travelled the length and breadth of Trouwerner learning the natures and speech of the nine tribes; the Ochre and Chert trails were well-known to him and there was no-one who understood the concerns and beliefs of the different peoples of the island with so much compassion. And because of his reputation as a wise-man, the elders of the southern bands sent their boys to him for instruction.

Meelangana was at once flattered and annoyed by this assumed trust. It was the sacred duty of every man to instil understanding and respect in his children (for the law governed not only their lives but all that existed), yet each year it seemed to the elder that the boys were harder to teach, more wilful yet also lazier. Every spring he vowed to himself that this would be the last year he would instruct the youths but he knew in his heart that to give up would be to relinquish his status and then the powers bestowed upon him by his daemon might vanish. And if that happened, if he could no longer heal and comfort the sick, predict and guide the weather, sometimes even see into the future, it seemed to him that he might as well give up life itself. For those abilities had set him apart even before his initiation and made him famous across the whole of Trouwerner: some of those he had helped in the past still sent gifts of ochre and shells in gratitude. To become simply another old man, maundering over past glories until some sickness struck him or he grew too weak to keep up with the rest, he could not countenance: pride and a sense of his own place in the world would not allow it.

Thus it was that this time, when the hearth-group moved on, Meelangana did not go with them. It was late spring, the silver wattle flowers were fading and the swallows had flown from the north, diving and swooping with flashing wings: soon the first of his pupils would arrive. And it was his secret hope that they would bring news of Touami and his foster-brother, Niama, who was also undergoing his trial.

Days passed and no-one came yet Meelangana was not dismayed. The camp was one of his favourites, situated in a glade on the banks of the Brown River. The trees, mainly blackwood interspersed with wattles, provided shade in the heat of the day yet the clearing was large enough that sunlight fell into it in the early morning where the old man could enjoy its warmth. Food was plentiful while there was only himself to feed: crayfish dwelt in the shallows and there was a well-used watering-place close by where he could ambush animals that came to drink; the tributaries of the river were crowded with tender man-ferns and fungi; grubs and roots were always to be found by anyone with the patience to collect them. So he waited, content in his solitude, idling warm afternoons by the river by watching the obsidian-dark water swirl past and, at night, conversing with his daemon, *Lyenah*, in dreams.

When he thought back on it, Meelangana knew he should have heeded the appearance of a flock of black cockatoos one morning. With their unearthly screeches, slow, deliberate wingbeats and destructive nature the birds were an ill omen, minions in their spirit form of the deceiver, Wyerkartenner. At the time he had thought little of it, even though their shadows had passed right across the camp: he was hungry for fresh meat and his mind was focused on getting it. But afterwards he wondered if things might have turned out differently had he heeded the warning and, instead of going hunting, had moved on.

As it was, he returned as the sun's rays had begun to slant steeply between the branches, picking out gyres of insects, shining on spider's webs suspended high between the trees. He walked carelessly because his hunt had been successful: a fat lyrebird dangled from his right hand and he carried his waddy against his left shoulder. Pleased with his catch and looking forward to a full belly, it was only after he had entered the clearing that he saw a figure sitting cross-legged by the fire. In his surprise Meelangana stopped in his tracks and stared for this was not one of the boys he had expected but a man he did not know.

Although he was seated, it was clear that the stranger was tall: his body was lean and scarred as the trunk of an ancient tree. Suspended from a thong about his neck was a little bag almost identical to that worn by Meelangana during ceremonies but the cicatrices on his chest, belly and upper arms were different from any the old man had seen before: long vertical slashes separated by lines of dots. His hair was shorn at the front like a woman's but he had tied the long, grease-laden hanks at the back into an elongate bun. He looked at the elder and his eyes conveyed a kind of sardonic amusement, but he did not move except to tilt his head slightly, waiting as if this were his hearth and Meelangana the trespasser.

The old man was profoundly disconcerted by the stranger's rudeness. It was customary among the tribes for a traveller to acknowledge those generous enough to share their fire: that this man did not do so was enough to turn the elder's astonishment to anger. He stood motionless, staring, aware that every moment of indecision betrayed his weakness while rage swelled within him, pressing like a fist against his throat. But, with an effort, he restrained it. He was a famous wise-man, not a youth needing to prove himself. With studied dignity he paced forward to the fireplace though he felt more than a little ridiculous with the dead bird hanging from his hand.

'What do you want?' So direct a demand was discourteous but in Meelangana's eyes the stranger had already forfeited the right to be treated with respect. He let the lyre-bird fall in the ashes at the edge of the fire but remained standing, still gripping his waddy. Having spoken, he was bound to look at the man to see the effect of his words but meeting dark, mocking eyes set in a face that was like something carved from wood, he felt an unaccustomed and unwelcome thrill of fear. There was something in the effrontery of the other's gaze that was deeply disquieting: noting the talisman-bag, the strange skin-marks, Meelangana realized that here was one who assumed a power equal to his.

'I expected to find Umara,' the man said slowly: it was clear Meelayginnee speech was unfamiliar to him. 'Finding myself in your lands I wanted to make peace. For I am respectful of the law, whatever you may think.'

In an effort to conceal his discomfiture at being so easily read, Meelangana squatted and laid his club carefully on the ground before settling himself, cross-legged, opposite the stranger.

'I am Meelangana, the wise-man,' he said. 'The rest have gone on. But I can speak for them and sanction your presence.' He hesitated, then added meaningfully, 'If it is rightful, that is.'

There was challenge in his tone and gaze but instead of rising to it, the man smiled.

'I know who you are,' he answered. 'I met two boys. They told me to come here.'

Fear leapt like a flame to the old man's throat lest the stranger should have harmed the two though youths undergoing their trial were generally regarded as sacred personages. And yet he did not ask after them because he sensed that was exactly what the man wanted. Instead, to hide his concern, he poked at the fire with a half-burnt stick.

'Then it's good you met me and not my son,' he remarked at last. 'He's quicker to anger than I, though it was a different story in my youth.'

'For us all.' The stranger bent his head with a wry expression and began to knead a great pitted scar on his thigh. 'One day our bones too will go to the fire.'

'Ay.'

They sat in silence for a while until Meelangana could no longer ignore his hunger. He threw twigs onto the embers and threads of smoke spiralled into the still air. Then he raked out a hollow in the thick ash at the edge of the fire, laid the dead bird in it and covered it with glowing charcoal from the centre. A foul-smelling smoke filtered out as the feathers smouldered but neither man heeded it.

They knew it would soon be followed by the delicious odour of roasting fowl and their mouths watered in anticipation.

According to the law, those with food were bound to share it: by his action Meelangana had, unwillingly, demonstrated acceptance of the stranger at his hearth. And while he still seethed inwardly at the arrogance of this unknown man, he forced calmness on himself, vowing that he would not speak again until the other at least vouchsafed his name.

The sun's rays slipped horizontally between the trees. It set and green shadow spread across the forest floor though the sky above was still light, a thin layer of cloud lending it a silver sheen like the surface of the sea. Meelangana dug the roast bird from the fire with the handle-end of his waddy and brushed the ashes off with his fingers. But, as was proper, he held back from breaking the carcass open. Time-honoured custom dictated that the guest should eat first. And mindful of his promise to himself, he invited the man to begin not with words but by gesture.

Either because he had eaten earlier in the day or from politeness, the stranger ate sparingly. Once he had finished, Meelangana felt free to satisfy the lust for meat that had set him on the hunting trail and he gorged until only the bones, bowels and crop of the bird remained. Then he cracked the bones and sucked out the marrow while the stranger gathered fuel and built the fire to a bright blaze. A kookaburra called loudly to its mate and a feeling of contentment stole over the old man: that sound had been a part of nightfall for as long as he could remember. He belched loudly and stretched out upon his side so that the whole length of his body was warmed by the fire.

The stranger, having piled up dry branches to use later, returned to his former place and reclined on his elbows, staring fixedly into the blaze. Now, with a full belly and a pleasant torpor spreading through his blood, Meelangana softened towards the man and regretted his decision not to speak. Discourse with another wise-man was something not to be spurned lightly yet it was a more basic social need to talk and, in turn, be entertained, that wore at the old man's resolve.

'Those boys,' he said at last, trying to make his voice sound casual. 'Were they together? And well?'

'Eh now . . .' the stranger drawled. 'They were well enough I think. Niama I met first, at the end of the hot season. And Touami, your grandson, soon after. He was angry because he had broken his best spear. I left him trying to make another.'

His apparent indifference infuriated the old man. 'Ach useless ones!' he exploded. 'What kind of men will they make? They were free enough with their names it seems: did you tell them yours?'

'They did not ask,' came the laconic reply. 'They were too eager to hear my tale. Anyway,' he hesitated and an odd, guarded look settled on his features, 'they are only boys.'

These words, calculated to arouse Meelangana's curiosity, inflamed the old man. It took a huge effort of will for him to keep control, to hold his face impassive, allowing his rage no outward expression other than the clenching of his hands. Yet all the time he sensed that the other was aware of, and enjoying, his struggle.

'And what are you?' he thought furiously, feeling the horny rims of his fingernails bite deep into his palms. 'I am no green youth to dance according to your song. I will choke before I beg for your tale.' And he said nothing.

The silence that now stretched between the two men had nothing in common with the quiet companionship they had shared during and immediately after their meal. It was tense with latent hostility and every time the fire hissed or spat they glanced at each other surreptitiously. Meelangana's desperation for tidings of his grandson betrayed itself in movements so small as to be almost imperceptible in the wavering firelight: a slight twitch of his hand, tightening of his thick, purplish lips, creasing of his brow but stubborn pride would not allow him to give in. And his certainty that the stranger was aware of and enjoying his discomfiture only hardened his resolve.

Yet unbeknownst to, and unsuspected by, Meelangana, his adversary was undergoing a struggle intense as his own. In the face of the old man's intransigence, the stranger's desire to tell his story had become a burning need. At any moment Meelangana might rise and go to one of the shelters to sleep and then the chance would be lost. Daylight would lessen the impact of the tale: in any case, it was not in his nature to linger long in any place. Thus his frustration was compounded by the knowledge that he was caught in a situation of his own making, having deliberately antagonised the old man.

The call of a tawny frogmouth sounded hauntingly from far away and a light breeze stirred the branches overhead as if in answer. The air was moist and cool, presaging rain, and Meelangana gazed searchingly into the sky. The starlight was already diffused by a thin layer of cloud and the old man grunted, hunched his shoulders and swung his head slowly from side to side, easing the tension in his neck and shoulders.

'Wait!' The stranger could no longer bear the possibility that his tale might remain untold. Thus his cry betrayed the passion he had tried to keep secret, giving Meelangana victory in their unspoken battle of wills. The old man stared, so he said quickly: 'My name is Ouniaga. I come from the coast of long lagoons. Forgive my discourtesy, O wise man: one who has enemies he has never met is slow to trust strangers.'

A deep frown made the folds of Meelangana's face appear as gashes in the red glow from the sinking fire.

'Whatever shame hangs on a man's name, while he lives he has the power to redeem himself,' he observed. 'Having enemies is no cause for pride, much less an excuse to disrespect those who offer goodwill.' He paused then added with studied emphasis, 'Unless of course your purpose is to cause mischief.'

'Is that what you think?' Ouniaga's face screwed up in an expression of disdain yet his eyes slewed away from the elder's steady gaze. 'Our ancestors have returned from the dead and all your care is for two boys undergoing their trial? Eh, but perhaps you are right: maybe your precious grandson is lying helpless in the forest, pierced by spears or struck down from behind. Or a branch has fallen on him or he has been bitten by a black snake. Many misfortunes can befall a lad alone in the woods, not least chance encounters with travellers he does not know.'

Meelangana bared his teeth in an effort to counter the malign force he felt gathering in the darkness all around and all his muscles tightened until they stood out like strings beneath the wrinkled skin.

'If any harm has come to them, tell me now,' he hissed. 'And if you are the cause of it, I'll give you another scar to match the one you earned long ago. Where are they and why are you here?'

Ouniaga took a deep breath, held it a moment then expelled it in a great sigh of satisfaction. He lifted his head and his eyes glinted like wet stones in the firelight.

'Eh, old man,' he said softly. Meelangana shuddered. There was a caressing quality to the other's tone that confused and frightened him: he could not tell whether the stranger meant to threaten or reassure. 'Listen well,' Ouniaga continued, 'and you will begin to understand why one of your charges has run away towards the sunrise while the other lingers on Meelayginnee land, torn between fear and envy.'

The tale he told was so fantastical that at first the old man was ready to scoff but so skilful was Ouniaga in the telling that before long Meelangana was ensnared. Against his will he leaned forward, pressing the palms of his hands together in his eagerness to gather every nuance of meaning from the stranger's words while in his mind he saw a great white bird-like creature glide majestically over the sea until it reached the bay of white lagoons where it stopped and furled its wings with the help of little figures akin to men who swarmed over it fearlessly as fleas.

'It was when we saw them that we were drawn onto the beach,' Ouniaga said. 'For we began to wonder whether this thing was indeed alive as we had first thought, or some kind of great raft. Then the figures lowered smaller rafts from the sides of the winged one and came ashore and we saw that though they possessed the form of men their skin was white and many had pale eyes of blue or green. And they had covered their bodies with coloured stuff so that only their hands and faces were visible. At first we were much afraid, thinking they must be already dead - perhaps the spirits of our ancestors returned- for what living man seeks to hide his skin? But they called out to us with the voices of men in words we did not understand and then it was like the meeting of any group of strangers: they offered gifts and we gave them food and spears in return for we were confused still and did not wish to antagonise them. And there was something in their manner that made us uneasy: after a little while they split up and began to walk around as if we, the keepers of the place, did not exist. We did not like it so we watched without trying to intervene for we were wary of their power and uncertain as to their true nature. And that night they returned to the raft with wings though they did not go away but returned next morning and began to build a camp.'

In Meelangana's mind, men like his own kind but with oddly bleached skins swarmed on the shore while their white bird floated in the bay and because clothes were beyond his power to visualise he imagined them wrapped in coloured bark, stiff figures removed from his own reality, remote and untouchable as Tarner, the first man. Eager to hear more, he reached out towards the storyteller and demanded, 'What next?'

Ouniaga evaded the old man's touch and a sardonic smile twisted his lips. 'Eh, do not trouble yourself – they kept close by the shore. They made huts and collected all kinds of things, many of which could not be eaten, and they were glad to exchange their own *noonah* for spears and woven baskets though they used none of them and their gifts to us were like pebbles seen underwater: bright and wondrous at first sight but useless. And we continued to watch them and wait, for it seemed to us that they were ignorant of the law or else had their own from the place they came from. They caught and ate fish and then our doubts returned that they only pretended to be alive. But they continued to be friendly though day by day our uneasiness increased for by then we had seen their magic and were afraid.'

'What magic?' A clammy hand seemed to stroke Meelangana's spine for he sensed that it would take something both powerful and terrible to frighten Ouniaga.

'Some among them carried sticks. At first we thought they were poorly made waddies for they were too thick and short for spears, too flimsy to make good clubs. But when they put them to their shoulders the things made darting flame with a noise like thunder and whatever they were pointed at fell down dead. Kangaroos, swans, all kinds of animals and birds succumbed to the spell: we wondered what would happen if these death-sticks were pointed at a man. And though we offered ochre and shells, the strangers would not be parted from them, any more than a man will part with the bone of an ancestor, lest their magic turns against him.'

'Humph.' Meelangana was prepared to accept the tale of the white bird and pale men but that they ate fish, taboo to all the tribes, and possessed magic sticks which pointed death was too much to believe. And yet beneath his scepticism was a nagging fear because unless he went to see for himself, he might never know the truth unless the boys returned having witnessed the wonder. And this thought exacerbated his anxiety for Ouniaga had failed to mention them since beginning his tale.

'And then?' Had he been younger, Meelangana would have struck the stranger for his patience was at an end and in anger he was impetuous and rash. But as he raised his fist he became sharply aware of the weakness of his muscles, the pathetic picture he must present. He lowered his hand and hissed between his teeth: 'You promised to tell me about my grandson!'

'Did I?' Ouniaga's face was in shadow but the old man felt his gaze keenly as if two fingers were pressing on his brow. 'Do you not want to see these things with your own eyes?'

'No.' Meelangana growled. 'I am no child or fool to go running after traveller's tales. And who can say whether these white men and their bird-raft will still be there? If they are more than a wild dream, that is!'

Now it was the younger man who stiffened and his right hand, which had come to rest on the scar on his thigh, clenched. And yet so forceful was the elder's anger, Ouniaga found himself answering, 'Well, then, I shall tell you: what have I to lose? The swallows had just flown when I met Niama. He I brought from the scrub with the smell of roasting wallaby for he was very hungry. And yet when he had heard my tale, he displayed the courage, ay, and recklessness of a great man: he set out at once to see the wonders for himself. But the other, your grandson, whom I came across later, was more wary: timid, I should say. He listened avidly but he was afraid, both of what he might find and what his father would think if he had dealings with the white ones without knowing their true nature. Ach – he was clumsy and slow in all he did - a girl could have fashioned better spears. Although' he added grudgingly, 'he at least had food to share.'

'Yah! So your belly welcomed a meal while your heart despised the host?' Meelangana scoffed. 'Because my grandson has respect for the law, the ways of his people, you set him below a fosterling with no more sense than to scamper off on a stranger's word – one who is not of his skin or even known to his band. Come back when the pepper berries are ripening again and see which of the two is more deserving of manhood!'

Ouniaga did not reply but he leant forward and his face was hard as rock in the dull red glow of the embers. So frightening was his expression, an inhuman mixture of anger and contempt, and so fierce his stare that the old man's heart quailed and he wished he had not been so flippant though he was wise enough not to try and undo his words.

'Listen, dotard!' The stranger's voice had changed to match his appearance. It was low and menacing yet oddly toneless as if, Meelangana thought uneasily, a spirit were using him as its mouthpiece. 'Of the two, only one will be initiated. And he will live long, long enough to see his people diminish to such a condition that the spirits of their ancestors will spurn them. Yet none of this is my doing: I saw it in a dream.'

The old man shuddered. Only pride prevented him scrambling to his feet and running to dig up his talisman to ward off the curse. And a growing sense of outrage made him grind his teeth and say with an effort, 'If anyone should dream the truth for those two, it will not be a stranger chance-met in the forest. Something bad follows you like a shadow: what do you want?'

Ouniaga laughed softly and Meelangana seemed to feel icy fingers trail down his spine though in reality it was a trickle of fear-sweat that made him writhe and shiver.

'From you, *Lyenah*, nothing,' Ouniaga hissed. 'Perhaps all this' - he waved to take in the forest, the night, the dying fire – 'is a dream and the visions which come in the sacred trance are all that is real.'

At the naming of his daemon, Meelangana shrank. 'This stranger is trying to frighten me,' he thought distractedly, 'and he is succeeding. How can he know my daemon if he is not in league with spirits?'

Summoning all his will-power, he raised his right hand and

stretched it out, fingers stiffly extended towards the stranger in a gesture of defiance and denial though he knew that against the supernatural any such action was futile. But after a while, when the old man's hand began to tremble with the effort of holding it out, Ouniaga's face changed as if the warmth of the fire had softened it, melting away all the aggression.

'Eh, Meelangana, forgive me,' he said and his voice was easy and full of friendliness. 'I forgot to whom I was speaking. Truly, it is through my sound leg that I deserve your spear. Forget my words concerning Touami: there was much spite and little truth in them. He will come to manhood and flourish, have no doubt.'

This unexpected capitulation, the change from hostility to obsequiousness made the old man, if possible, more suspicious than before. And yet with the sudden easing of tension, Meelangana felt tired to his very bones. His outstretched hand dropped to his lap simply because he lacked the willpower and strength to hold it up and when he sighed, his lungs felt heavy in his chest.

'I am too old for games,' he muttered. 'Go and sleep, Ouniaga. Wherever you are from, whatever your purpose, you may pass freely through Meelayginnee land. But do not name my daemon again until my bones have gone to the fire.'

The other bent his head in apparent acknowledgement and Meelangana scrambled to his feet because it seemed to him that if he did not move now, he might never possess strength to do so: it was as if the warmth of his blood, the very substance of his muscles, were leaching into the darkness of the night. He stood swaying slightly then bent to pick up his waddy but the stranger sat as if turned to stone.

'Ach, if that's how he wants it!' The old man snorted disgustedly then made his way to his bark humpy, determined not to waste any more time on Ouniaga and his tale.

Once inside, however, all Meelangana's misgivings returned. He lay down on the leaf bed but he could not get comfortable, nor would his mind give him peace. He tossed and turned, stared through the narrow door-frame to the lean figure of the stranger, starkly silhouetted against the dying fire. So still was Ouniaga that after a while the old man was tempted to call out but he dared not disturb the quiet of the forest. And gradually a feeling of horror settled upon him that this was no man he was watching but one of the ghosts that haunted the forest at night, creatures neither living nor wholly dead whose mere touch could suck the soul out of a man and whose faces were death to look upon.

'Aie, *Lyenah*, help me!' he whispered and with an effort that seemed to sap all his willpower and the last of his strength, he raised himself on his hands and knees, crawled to the back of the shelter and began to dig with fingers so chilled they possessed no more feeling than sticks of bone. All the time he seemed to feel icy fingers trace the line of his spine but he did not pause to look behind.

At last his fingers jarred against stone. It was the flat slate for grinding ochre which he had laid over the kangaroo-skin containing his most precious possessions: a knife made from volcanic glass; a human tarsal bone; a lump of red ochre and another of white clay. He moved the stone and lifted out the bundle, then unwrapped it with trembling hands. The longer his back was towards the stranger, the more his dread increased and he moaned with relief as he picked out the little bone, a relic of his father. Muttering words of propitiation he stroked it, waiting for the strength of his ancestor to flow into him but instead, an unearthly screech from behind tore the trembling silence apart.

Cold with terror, Meelangana twisted to face the sound. It was as he imagined the voice of an evil spirit might be, a shriek both agonised and triumphant, and his hand closed round his talisman with such force he felt the bone bite into the palm. He stared out and the view framed by the doorway was empty. The deserted heap of embers seemed to pulsate like the still-throbbing heart of a badly butchered wallaby: he did not realize that the pounding of his own heart, which shook his whole body, was causing the illusion.

The cry died away but the silence that followed was so complete, Meelangana wondered if he had been deafened. He strained his ears for any sound other than the soughing rush of blood in his ears but it seemed an age before he heard the growl of a quarrelling wallaby close by followed by a thud as its antagonist leapt away.

The old man went weak with relief: he was still in the world and the spirits had not harmed him. The fear-sweat chilled on his skin and the wild beating of his heart steadied. He relaxed his hold on the knob of bone which he had gripped so tightly, it stuck to the skin when he opened his hand. And now, as he recalled it, he realized that the blood-curdling scream had been more like *tarrabah's* than anything else he had ever heard or imagined.

'What am I but a doddering old fool!' he berated himself. 'To come to such a state because of a stranger's wild tales and a scavenger's ill temper!' He looked at the bone lying on his palm. 'Oh my father, forgive me if I have disturbed you this night. Age must excuse my foolishness!'

A hawk-owl's plaintive call echoed in the darkness and Meelangana's bitterness dissolved in a wave of sorrow. 'What is the point of living longer than most men if the reward of experience is not wisdom but witlessness?' he wondered. 'No doubt my guest has simply gone into one of the shelters to sleep or is by the fire where I cannot see him. All I have to do is go and look.'

He felt carefully around the hard-packed earth floor until he found the objects he had dug up, intending to bury the bone with them. But as soon as he let go the relic, he felt horribly vulnerable as if it alone, his faith in his father's wisdom, was keeping the forces of evil at bay. He groped frantically to find the talisman again and gripped it tightly as before, vowing not to let go until dawn.

Thus it was that Meelangana remained awake all night, too afraid of what he might find to seek out the stranger. Only once had he known the darkness last so long: in the Bad Year when his father lay dying. That winter the snow had come down to meet the sea and the shore-folk refused access to the beaches because no whales had been stranded and they too were hungry. Meelangana remembered how, as a small boy, he had resented the food given to the hunters, though it was his efforts to bring in meat that had exhausted his starving father. But the horror of what was happening then had been dulled by hunger: what he felt now was a sharper, more immediate fear. Every time the wind moaned in the branches or an owl called, he was jerked to heart-thumping wakefulness though when he peered outside to where the embers had sunk to a dull red glow there was nothing to see but trees.

When at last dawn came the old man had sunk into a stupor, his mind so bemused by fatigue he hardly knew whether he was dreaming or waking. But then as kookaburras and rosellas greeted the day with their calls and the grey-green gloom beneath the trees slowly receded, he realized that the night was truly over. With a mixture of relief and shame, he wrapped his treasures carefully in the kangaroo skin and buried them, pulling the mass of matted leaves and grass that served as his bed over to hide the place. Then he went outside.

Despite his misgivings as to the stranger's true nature, Meelangana was convinced he would find Ouniaga sleeping beside the fire or in one of the shelters. But he was not there, nor had he left the slightest trace. It was as if he had vanished into thin air. Even with a lifetime's experience of tracking, of reading the faintest scuff in the earth, Meelangana could not find a single footprint. Even when he went over the ground where the visitor had sat, he could not be certain of the marks he found and of the bones they had flung into the fire after their meal nothing remained.

A raucous laugh startled the old man: he glanced up to find a kookaburra perched on an overhanging branch. Seeing that he was watching, the bird tilted its head and called again and this time it seemed to Meelangana that it was mocking him. Annoyed more by his disappointment in finding Ouniaga gone than the kookaburra's jeering, he bent to pick up a stone but by the time he straightened, the bird had flown. And the old man was overwhelmed by an unexpected sense of futility, of powerlessness. He let the stone drop and stood staring at the place where the bird had been. At first the branch and leaves shook with the violence of its launch, then the movement grew so slight as to be almost imperceptible. For a moment the whole forest was still.

'What if Ouniaga's tale is true?' Meelangana murmured. Deep within himself he felt a profound and immovable dread. It was not fear of anything tangible, more a prescience of impending change, a threat to the law he had assumed was inviolate. If the dead were walking, could bind a bird beautiful and great as one of the ancestors and kill merely by pointing a stick, anything was possible.

And thinking of the danger Touami and Niama might be exposed to if, entranced by the stranger's words, they came face to face with the white ones, he ground his teeth in frustration. In the end, what could an old man whose strength was failing do against the impetuosity of youth?

'Yah! It is not for me to interfere: they will become men or they will die,' he muttered at last. 'As for me, I must sleep. What need have I of children's tales when before long my bones will be ash?'

With that he turned and went back inside his shelter. Within moments of stretching out on the leaf bed he was asleep.

4. The Talismans.

(Southern Tasmania, November 1792).

The moon waxed and waned many times before Niama, the fosterling, returned to his hearth-group among the Meelayginnee. After hearing Ouniaga's tale of the living dead and their giant bird, he had journeyed to the Place of Wide Lagoons to see the wonders for himself. And having seen, he stayed awhile. Umara's group often over-wintered with Nuenone people and so they knew and welcomed his foster-son though as he was undergoing his proving, they left him to fend for himself. Since life on the coast was far easier than in the forest, he was in no hurry to leave until summer.

During his stay he had seen enough of the white-skinned ones to satisfy himself that they were not spirits but men. Yet compared with an elder like Meelangana, they seemed woefully ignorant of Trouwerner. He was still curious as to who they were and where they had come from when, inexplicably, they dismantled the camp they had made in the woods, paddled their rafts (which they called *bateaux*), to the great one (whose wings flapped impatiently in the breeze), climbed onto it and sped away. Like his hosts, Niama was secretly glad because the latest encounters with the strangers had been tense. But the question of why they had come at all remained.

With the novelty of the white ones gone, the groups camped around the lagoons dispersed for they had already lingered in one place more than was usual: the camping grounds were befouled and food scarce even on the beaches. As each family left, Niama felt a yearning to see his foster-brother Touami and all his hearth-group again. And this was not simply nostalgia but the need to boast of all he had seen, to show the gifts he had been given to those who would be most envious of his daring. Even Umara and Meelangana had never encountered the white strangers: they would listen in awe and be forced to hide their jealousy in silence. For what he had achieved would, he was sure, mitigate for the fact that by staying so long on the coast, he had missed much of the teaching deemed necessary for initiation.

It took longer than he had expected to find those he sought. On the coast, where the rhythms of life were dominated by the tides, he had lost track of the forest's seasons and where Umara's group was most likely to be (though they migrated according to a pattern inexorable as the movement of stars). When at last he found them they were camped on a sky-rimmed plateau, so high that snow still lingered in shadowed crevices. Yet Niama did not walk straight into camp but waited, constrained by a complex and unexpected mixture of guilt and embarrassment. And this awkwardness made him angry, in part because in the scant cover of heath and thorny bushes surrounding the camp he was afraid of being spotted before he was ready, but mainly because as he watched the women tending the young children while the old man, Meelangana, told a tale, he realized that during his absence the life of the hearth-group had continued as if he had never been part of it, never even been born.

So bitter was this knowledge that Niama was tempted to rise out of his hiding place and stalk away so that they could see him leave, spurning them as they had, apparently, rejected him. But then the longing that had compelled him to return swelled within him so powerfully that he felt like weeping. All he had missed since the loss of his parents crystallised at the sight of the camp: the women, children and old man interacting happily together; the smoke spiralling from the cooking fires; the shelters, low and humped like the backs of animals, barely visible above the heath clumps yet promising warmth and security. He clutched the little bag containing the white one's gifts which hung from a thong about his neck and rocked back and forth in an access of grief, oblivious to all else, silent and blind behind clenched lips and eyelids.

'Yah! Who's this, skulking like *kannenner* in the bushes?' The unexpected voice, the heavy, jeering tone of Toualena, Touami's twin sister, so startled the boy that he snatched up his spear, leapt to his feet and stood glaring at her, the weapon held defensively before him.

'What are you doing here?' The girl, who was herself on the

cusp of puberty, planted hands on hips and her ripening breasts seemed suddenly strange and threatening to Niama. He stared and the rage that had taken the place of his initial fright was swamped by a confusing mixture of sensations: a gathering heat in his loins; an urge to grasp and dig his fingers into that flesh which looked so pliant; to taste that smooth, coppery skin and plunge the warm depths of her mouth and secret cleft. And she, recognising the effect she was having on him, tilted her head provocatively and pouted before demanding, 'Have you lost your tongue, boy?'

Niama swallowed hard, not trusting his voice. A light sweat had broken out all over his body. As if it had a will of its own, his left hand stole down to his quivering penis while his right gripped the spear so hard it hurt.

'You'd better come and explain yourself to the elders.' There was something hard and calculating in her voice that made the boy instantly defensive. He raised his head and stood rigidly still, aware that he had put himself in his foster-sister's power and she was enjoying every moment.

'Wait!' As she began to turn, he reached out and caught her upper arm. Her skin was softer than he had expected, the underlying flesh firmer and a thick dizziness clouded his senses. He pulled her towards him, dropping his spear to use both hands upon her.

She squealed – he did not know whether in anger, dismay or delight – and writhed in his arms: their legs tangled and they fell together. His nostrils were full of the smell of her, pungent sweat mixed with rancid grease, all underlain by a musky scent that emanated from deep within her pores, an odour fecund and moist that made his head reel.

Initially she giggled as they struggled together. He grunted and gasped, trying to hold onto her and she slapped him, playfully at first then in earnest as his efforts became more urgent and she realized his intent. When, at last, he managed to pin her down, she yelled in protest, heaving beneath him like a speared wallaby: that having no effect she screamed, a sound so piercing it hurt the boy's ears.

The blow from behind caught Niama completely by surprise.

He lurched forward, half-stunned, and Toualena squirmed away, managing to kick him in the crotch as she did so. The boy writhed, clutching at himself, moaning and retching in turn, his ears ringing with the girl's laughter which was raucous as a kookaburra's. Then, abruptly, it was cut off. Niama's pain subsided a little and his vision cleared. He saw who had intervened.

Umara stood over his foster-son and there was no trace of pity or compassion in his features as he stared down. Looking into that implacable face, Niama realized how deeply he had offended against custom. A cold, heavy feeling settled in his stomach.

'I didn't mean – ' he stammered and the rush of heat to his face made his cheeks and temples feel swollen and uncomfortable. He swallowed bile and got shakily to his feet, head bowed and hands crossed over his groin in an attitude of abasement.

'Why are you here?' Umara's tone was as grim as his expression. 'What's this?' He plucked the little bag from the boy's neck, jerking with such force that the thong snapped. 'You think you're a wise-one though you're not even a man?'

'Yah – he's a great one indeed - that's why he was sneaking around,' Meelangana, drawn like the rest of the group by Toualena's scream, looked with distaste upon the cringing boy. 'So wise you're above the law, eh Niama? Perhaps the Great Ones, Moinee or Droémadeener, will make you a man themselves.'

'Please –' The strength seemed to leach from Niama's legs; he felt they would give way at any moment and wished with all his heart that the earth might open and swallow him or a creek burst its banks and sweep him away. Instead Umara, who had torn open the soft wallaby-skin pouch to see what it contained, reached out with the sudden swiftness of an eagle stooping and grasped the boy's shoulder. His fingers gripped to the bone.

'What are these?' He pulled Niama close then thrust his free hand under the boy's nose. On his broad, dirt-ingrained palm lay a shard of clear glass and a brass button.

'The white ones gave them to me!' Eyes fixed on his foster-father's face, Niama was oblivious to the look of horror which spread over Meelangana's. The old man, who alone amongst the group understood the significance of these words, craned his head to see and his right hand went to his chest, automatically seeking his bone talisman. The merest glance sufficed to tell that the objects were magical and his mind went to Ouniaga and the evil that had hung about him like a shadow.

'Out! Out!' Meelangana's cries startled everyone save Toualena who had retreated to the other side of the camp where she lay snivelling, her nose and lips swollen from the blow that had silenced her. 'These *noonah* will bring death!. Aiee! – did *Menuggana* steal your wits or bewitch you that you come to us like this? Go now, before it's too late and never show your face to us again!'

He had drawn himself to his full height and stretched out his hands: the fingers, rigid and knobbly as a skeleton's, pointed straight at Niama. So focused was his whole being on driving out the enemy, the old man's body shook, his mouth twitched and a high-pitched whine escaped his throat. Sensing that some spirit was taking hold, the women and children recoiled. Even Umara took a step backwards though he did not drop the objects nor close his hands upon them. But Niama was transfixed. He stared into Meelangana's bulging, bloodshot eyes as if the powers of speech and movement had deserted him.

For what seemed like a lifetime the two remained thus, the boy petrified, the old man possessed by a power which drew on the awe and fear of his audience. The children pressed close to each other, staring; their toes kneaded the gritty earth while their hands stole to their mouths. Then a raven cawed, directly overhead. For an instant, the space between one heartbeat and the next, the boy felt the wise-man's concentration waver. He grabbed the objects from Umara's outstretched hand, spun on his heel and fled.

'Aie . . .' A murmur of astonishment arose from the women and children but Umara leapt in pursuit with a shout of outrage, snatching up Niama's spear. His trance shattered, Meelangana reeled and put out a hand to stop his son but too late. Although the boy was running with the strength born of desperation, it was so clear he would be overtaken that the women began to keen the lament for a dead child for none doubted that once caught, he would be killed.

'Wait – come back!' Meelangana blinked and stared after the

running figures like one awoken from deep slumber. His cry seemed to hang in the air but neither heard it.

His ears full of the pounding footsteps and panting breath of his pursuer, Niama forced himself on. The air seared his lungs; every step was an effort. So tightly was he gripping the sacred objects, his talismans, that his right hand dripped blood from where the glass had sliced into the palm but he felt nothing.

'Huh!' Umara grunted as he cast: the boy swerved and felt a whiffle as the spear flew past and stuck harmlessly in the ground. And then his foot snagged in a root and he fell sprawling.

'Now I have you!' As he rolled over, his foster-father planted one foot each side of the boy's waist. 'Give me the things!'

So certain had he been that Umara, the mighty hunter and fighter meant to slay him, Niama stared dumbly into that glowering face where rage had been overtaken by a kind of lust. Involuntarily his fist tightened even closer on the objects and for the first time he felt the pain of his cut palm.

'I can't.' Before his return Niama would have handed over his treasures to any of the elders, reluctantly but without question because as an untried boy he had no choice. Now, gauging their true worth from the need in his foster-father's eyes, he understood that for the first time in his life he, the fosterling, held the power. And he vowed that whatever happened, he would not give it up easily.

'You dare defy me, boy?' Umara asked in a terrible voice, bending low so that his face filled Niama's vision. 'You think anyone cares if you live to be a man?'

Niama did not answer but he clutched the objects close, relishing the sting across his palm and the warmth of fresh blood between his fingers. Beneath the fear stamped in his face was a kind of defiant stubbornness and recognising this, Umara seized his shoulders, pulled him up and began to shake him violently as *tarrabah* worrying a corpse.

'Father!' Niama gasped the word through clenched teeth and attempted to twist free but it was like trying to fight some elemental force, a wild torrent or storm wind: he was powerless against Umara's rage. Spots whirled before his eyes: he slumped, felt his foster-father's kicks slam into his ribs, head, back. In his mind he begged for it to stop and yet he kept his hand closed around the sacred objects: it seemed to him that to give them up would be like relinquishing his soul.

Hands like talons grasped Niama's arm. He was jerked up then thrown down. A mixture of blood and bile flooded his mouth. He was sure he must be dying and, fleetingly, felt a kind of glee in his refusal to submit: that in itself was a kind of triumph. But then, astoundingly, the assault stopped. Instead of blows there were angry voices but they seemed oddly blurred and far away. He moved his head and black wings seemed to beat about him: his mind swooped into darkness.

When Niama awoke it was night. There were furtive rustlings in the undergrowth and a rank stench: carrion-eaters drawn by the smell of blood. He was curled into a tight ball but when he tried to straighten, such agony shot from his groin that he moaned and curled up again. His right hand stung and ached, the fingers welded by dried blood. He waited while his mind struggled from dull acknowledgement of pain to coherent thought, listening to the snuffling of *kannenner* and *tarrabah*. The human smell beneath the blood was holding them back so far but he knew that if he did not move soon, they would grow bold and attack.

Painfully, the boy levered himself upright. The night was clear and starlight made clumps of heath loom like menacing figures. He looked for a stone, a stick, anything he could use to defend himself but there was nothing. Yet it seemed that the simple act of sitting had deterred the carrion-eaters for he heard and saw nothing more of them. And as his eyes adjusted to the semi-darkness, he recognised the bushes for what they were. In any case, if there had been other people nearby, the animals would never have come so close.

As his fears subsided, Niama felt thirsty. He tried to remember whether he had crossed water on his way up to the plateau but the most obvious source was the pool beside the camp. He clambered to his feet and stood irresolute for a while but with every heartbeat his thirst intensified. And it was late: by now everyone in camp should be asleep.

Even on the hunting trail, Niama had seldom moved with such care. The stiffness of his muscles eased as he walked but he held himself back. Every-so-often he stopped to look all about and listen but there was no untoward movement and no sound other than a soft soughing that might have been the resonance of the night itself. As he drew closer to the camp he became aware of a watchfulness, a tension in the air that he did not attribute to his own apprehension but to the omnipresent guardians, the ancient spirits. He clutched the objects in his hand and the pain of his cut palm reassured him, anchored him in the present. He would drink and leave Meelayginnee lands until the time of his proving was over. Then, on his return, he was sure the terror of this day would have been forgotten: Umara would welcome him, seeing in his defiance the true nature of a warrior. And, as men, Touami and he would still be like brothers: nothing had changed.

But when he entered the camp, he stood staring, stricken. The shelters were empty and the fires had been extinguished. The only sound was the lapping of the tarn, loud and hard in the stillness but Niama did not heed it. His thirst had been overwhelmed by a terrible realization.

'Where are you?' In his distress he called aloud. His voice, plaintive, despairing, was lost in the vastness of the night. His injured hand throbbed, seeming to drag him down. He sank to his knees in the still-warm ashes of a cooking-fire and bent over, cradling his hand to his chest, whimpering like a sick child. They had deserted him in fear and loathing: deemed unworthy of initiation, he would be mocked and reviled all his life; tribeless, he would be forced to travel from one territory to another; would never know the tenderness of a wife's hands nor father children to keep his memory alive. And when he died, without a daemon to guide it, his spirit would wander forever: along with the right to manhood he had forfeited his chance of peace. The only certainty now was that he was alone.

'Aiee!' Distractedly, he rubbed his hands and forehead in the ashes; smeared them all over until his body glimmered in the starlight like a ghost. For, like death, his loneliness had no ending.

5. Rites of Passage II.

(South Coast of Tasmania, January 1793).

When the black pepper-berries were ripe again, Touami joined his hearth-group in the sacred place at the heart of Meelayginnee territory. After more than year away, fending for himself and conversing only with wise-men and other boys undergoing their proving, he had matured in body and mind but when his sisters asked teasingly if his experiences had included sex, he became confused and, in his shyness, looked for his friend, Niama. And when he was told that his foster-brother was gone, he wept for him. He assumed Niama must be dead because the others referred to him only as 'the fosterling', never by name: that he had been outcast after defying Umara, was kept secret. And this was because Meelangana, the wise-man, was afraid that if he knew the truth, Touami might try to find his foster-brother and bring him back. The old man feared that the talismans the white ones had given Niama would bring evil upon all who came in contact with him.

Three days after Touami's return, the same ghostly figures that had driven him from camp came for him again. This time he mastered his fear and went with them quietly. He knew now that they were simply men of the band in disguise but his awe was great because their personalities had been subsumed by those of the spirits they represented: possessed, they were both more and less than the men he had known all his life. There followed a night removed from time, where pain and ecstasy melded into dreams more wonderful and terrible than anything he had ever imagined. The content of those visions he would keep to himself all his life but, as was customary, he danced the essence of them in the corroboree following his initiation so that everyone would know which daemon had chosen him.

Fan-tail was the creature that had reached to his spirit, the little bird, *darwalla*, which hung about the camp when the women were pounding grass seed; whose song warned when ravens and hawks were close; brave in defence of its young and nest, joyous and quick in its actions. And though he might have been disappointed had he known the identity of his daemon before his initiation, (having hoped secretly for something fierce like *korunah* or *kannenner*), now he recognised his own nature in Fan-tail's and was content. It was not, in any case, for a person to choose their daemon: the spirit cleaved to that closest to its own and a person who was not satisfied was incomplete and would never belong anywhere.

The incisions on Touami's upper arms, shoulders and breast, which defined his skin-group and marked his full initiation into manhood, had not fully healed when the group left the sacred place. Already the season had turned towards winter. The trees and grasses were sere in the lowlands and on the plateaux where it was driest, and great pillars of smoke marked where migrating groups had set the bush to burn behind them. Fire, the gift of Moinee, destroyed the rank undergrowth so that grass would grow with the winter rains, providing plentiful feed for the wallabies and kangaroos which were staples for all the people of Trouwerner. And yet it was not a gift to be used rashly. Umara's group was especially careful to note the wind strength and direction before firing the scrub: the scars disfiguring Meelangana's body attested to what could happen when fire turned on those who set it free.

With smoke billowing behind, they set off towards the sunset, the women and girls bowed under woven grass bags containing all their possessions, the men walking a little ahead, spears and clubs balanced on their shoulders. Touami strode proudly at his father's side, a fresh wallaby skin draped around his shoulders. The pelt had been crudely cleaned and the smell of decay attracted flies to his wounds but he did not care: it was another symbol of his transition from boy to adulthood.

A well-marked track through Trouwerner connected ochre-rich cliffs in the south with quarries in the distant north. This Ochre Trail crossed the territories of several bands and many different clans and it was the responsibility of each group to look after their section, keeping it clear of fallen vegetation and tending the sacred stones and trees along the way. The getting of *ballawiné*, which represented the life-force by which all things existed, transcended tribal and family hostilities: those upon the Trail were protected by sacred law. And while on this occasion the gathering of ochre was not their main purpose, Umara's group still felt safer when they reached it. They were not in open dispute with any neighbours but it was still wise to be careful, especially in autumn when game was beginning to grow scarce and many people were on the move. Upon the sacred path even Meelangana relaxed.

From then on, the journey was easy: as was their wont, they did not hurry. When autumn gales lashed the trees and sleet brought a stinging foretaste of winter, they simply built up the fires, huddled together in their wind-breaks, and told stories or slept until the weather changed. The women especially were glad of the chance to rest for they had to carry the smaller children as well as their woven bags. But gradually they drew nearer to the coast.

During the journey Touami became reconciled to Niama's death but he sensed that something momentous had happened during his absence. At times he caught Meelangana and his father watching him thoughtfully and his twin sister, Toualena, became awkward and self-conscious on the rare occasions the fosterling was mentioned. But as a young man it was not for him to question the elders, nor did he associate their preoccupation with his foster-brother's absence. And as for Toualena, she was on her way to her betrothal and exploring the bounds of her newly awakened sexuality: towards boys she was either cruelly provocative or painfully coy.

They came to the great lichen-encrusted boulder which marked the beginning of Toogee territory. The trees all about were carved with sign for this was a sacred place. Tealana took the children out of sight and for the first time Touami stayed with the elders as Meelangana and Wagarulepu conducted ceremony to acknowledge the boundary and arrange free passage from the guardian spirits of that land. Upon the stone they left a little pile of ground ochre on a scrap of wallaby-skin with some carefully broken sticks laid across it, each one representing an adult member of the group. This would warn any passing Toogee that a Meelayginnee hearth-group had entered their territory peacefully.

Two days after passing the marker stone, the nature of the forest began to change. The trees grew more scrubby, wind-tortured into fantastic shapes: tea-tree and she-oaks took the place of swamp gums, myrtle and blackwood. The creeks ran dark-red, as if the earth's blood were streaming towards the sea; beyond the murmur of leaves overhead and the rippling of rivulets was a constant deep roaring: the voice of the great ocean as it pounded the rocks and sands of the south-western coast. They followed a river to the head of a long lake and there were many cormorants and other seabirds on its dark water as well as black swans. A great mountain loomed on the opposite side: it was sacred to the Toogee and others were forbidden to tread there. At the far end of the lagoon was a line of dunes: beyond that a white haze marked the sea.

When they tasted salt in the air, the same visceral excitement gripped them all. They hurried over the marshy ground, splashed across muddy creeks and the ridges of sand loomed high as they approached. The noise of the ocean was muffled as they climbed; sand dragged at their feet, then they reached the crest of the dune and the roar of surf battered their ears: they stood in a line and gazed joyfully upon the sea.

A wide beach spread before them. It was bounded on one side by great red and black cliffs that fell in jagged steps to the churning water. Seabirds wheeled and cried there for the cliffs were their home. To the left of where the Meelayginnee stood, the lagoon poured its dark waters out through a narrow channel; beyond that, a rock platform stretched to the base of the cliffs. It was packed so closely with seals that they looked more like brown boulders than animals.

'Ah . . .' A sigh came from the group at this sight for such bounty was unsurpassed in their experience though the Toogee imposed strict quotas. Yet one animal could provide enough meat and blubber to feel all Umara's family for a week so the women grinned and hugged their children close. Here there was no need to go hungry and it was impossible to starve: the supply of food was limitless.

'We must find Oué-mala,' Umara decided and he ran down the

seaward slope of the dune onto the beach. The others followed, leaping and sliding in the loose sand for the sight of the sea meant journey's end was close and a sense of holiday affected them all. But they still had to traverse the low, rocky headland that formed the western side of the beach for the Toogee camp lay on the other side.

They followed a narrow path which led over the promontory before splitting, one fork leading to a deeply indented bay, the other to the Toogee camp which was set in the forest next to a freshwater creek. The huts were more substantial than those traditionally built by the Meelayginnee, comprising low humpies made from thick layers of closely woven bark with grass and moss packed between to keep out the cold and wet. Each hut was large enough to house several people and there were many of them for Oué-mala's hearth-group was three times the size of Umara's. One hut, however, was bigger than the rest: the skin of a huge bull elephant seal was stretched over the roof. This was the home of Groua, the Toogee's wise-man and the place where the elders gathered in council when the weather was too bad to meet outside. But though hearth-fires burned outside each hut, the camp appeared empty.

'We'll go to our own camp then,' Umara said, for at the other end of the bay was a cluster of shelters used by visitors. The women hoisted their bags onto their backs again and the whole group followed him down along the creek and onto the beach for the sand made easier walking than the bush. None of them looked back and therefore they were unaware of the figure that came out of the trees and stood watching, an ancient man whose eyes were pale with age and contrasted sharply with his charcoal-darkened skin, who instead of the talisman-bag borne by most wise-men, wore round his neck a fine cord of woven grass from which, incongruously, a single brass button was suspended.

'There they are!' Uniala, Meelangana's wife, stopped in her tracks and pointed. A group of people was standing on the rocks at the far end of the bay. Some were fossicking in the rock-pools, others were watching something in the sea. Touami stared but though he could make out black heads bobbing in the water, he could not tell whether they belonged to people or seals.

'Good.' Umara walked forward a few paces, laid down his spear-bundle, cupped his hands to his mouth and gave a piercing cry: 'Ou-eee!' At that, all the figures, even those in the water turned abruptly to stare. Then they made their way swiftly onto the beach and hurried to meet the visitors. Even from a distance it was clear that most were women for they carried mesh bags and short, pointed waddies but the foremost figure was, unmistakeably, the Toogee leader, Oué-mala, recognisable by his build and the pride of his bearing. At the sight of him, Touami was filled with apprehension. If her father was there, then Uné-mawa could not be far away. He scanned the approaching figures eagerly. One lagged far behind but it was too skinny to be his betrothed so he dismissed it and concentrated on the women and girls. They had closed together as they walked, laughing and giggling as they recognised the newcomers. He guessed she was in their midst and they were trying to conceal her from his eyes as long as possible, to tease and provoke him.

As was proper, when they came to within a few paces, the Toogee women stopped and their chatter became more subdued though every-so-often one would nudge another and they would chuckle together. Knowledge that he was the likely target of their mirth made Touami uncomfortably self-conscious but there was nowhere he could hide for Umara touched him on the arm, indicating that he should follow, and walked forward to meet the Toogee leader.

Oué-mala was a formidable, heavily built man, a renowned hunter and fighter who wore a band of seal-skin about his spear-arm as symbol of his authority. Unlike Meelayginnee men who wore their hair loose, his was tied in a tight knot at the back of his head, the front half of his scalp being shaved. He looked at Touami with a critical eye, then hawked and spat. Neither Umara not Touami moved but they sensed the other's latent hostility and were perplexed by it.

'So, the children of Tarner have come out of the forest,' Oué-mala said. His gaze went to Toualena who stood nearby and the grimness of his expression eased a little. 'My son will be glad. But as to my daughter . . .' His voice trailed into silence and he looked penetratingly into Touami's face. Then, without looking round, he shouted, 'Noné, come here!'

So loud and unexpected was that shout, Touami started and was instantly ashamed: from the flicker in his eyes, he knew Oué-mala had seen and thought he was afraid. The Toogee women murmured together and some glanced over their shoulders. As he waited, Oué-mala's face darkened and his body seemed to swell with impatience: the women fell silent.

'Noné – do I have to come and fetch you?' the Toogee leader shouted in a terrible voice, then as no answer was forthcoming, he turned on his heel and strode back, the women parting before him like grasses under a blast of wind. Within a few moments he was back, dragging a boy with him. The boy was small and skinny and he writhed and cringed as he was pulled along for Oué-mala was tugging him by the hair. As soon as he reached the watching Meelayginnee, the Toogee leader yanked the boy to a halt then thrust hard so that he fell on his hands and knees before them. It was only at that moment, when they saw him close, that they recognised Niama.

Unlike the rest of the Toogee who were well-fed, their flesh smooth and plump from a diet rich in seal-meat, Niama was so thin his ribs stuck out and his limbs were like sticks, making him appear younger than when he had left his hearth-group to begin his proving. His body was coved in scars and bruises, no honourable marks of manhood but the legacy of many beatings and his hair hung in matted hanks past his shoulders. He did not raise his head to look at his former foster-kin but shrank, hunching in on himself until he was huddled in the sand like a crab.

'This nothing,' said Oué-mala disgustedly, 'claims to be one of you. And, indeed, I thought I saw it when you were last here. Were it not that Groua uses it, we would have sent it away. If it is yours, you are welcome to it. But not my daughter. I will not wed her to a Meelayginnee man and have nothings for grandsons.'

With these words the mood changed abruptly. Umara's group went swiftly from astonishment to outrage while the Toogees' amusement altered to a kind of tense expectancy. Touami especially was affected by Niama's degradation. Pity, anger and sheer disbelief vied within him for it was a shock to know that his foster-brother was still alive. But with an effort, he controlled himself and instead of looking at the pathetic figure at his feet, gazed past the women to the distant rocks though his face betrayed his feelings.

Umara frowned, considering. Trapped between the two men he feared more than anything except, perhaps, death itself, Niama began to shake and a thin stream of urine dribbled between his legs into the sand. The stink of it was unmistakeable and Oué-mala smiled grimly, then nudged the boy hard with his foot so that he fell onto his side. Niama made no attempt to escape but hugged his knees to his chest, whimpering softly.

'Once he lived with us,' Umara said at last, 'but he is a fosterling, an orphan. When he failed his proving, he was outcast. His skin is unmarked: he has no clan, no kin. You need not fear for your grandchildren, Oué-mala: he is none of ours. If your wise-man wants him, why should we care?'

'Why indeed?' Oué-mala said but his gaze was now bent on Touami. 'And yet I must be sure before I hand over my daughter. Would you kill this thing if I asked it as a wedding gift?'

Revolted by the suggestion, Touami shuddered and looked down. His father's words had shaken him to the core and yet Niama's abasement somehow distanced him: it seemed impossible that this cringing boy could be the companion with whom he had shared his childhood, who had been as much rival as friend. Then, as Niama's whimpering ceased and he began to weep, Touami looked away and saw Uné-mawa among the young women. She was watching him expectantly and Touami felt a swooping sensation through his loins for there was a ripeness to her beauty that Meelayginnee women lacked: young though she was, her flesh was sleek, her breasts full and her thighs smooth and rounded. She tilted her head and smiled provocatively, daring him to accept the challenge and when he looked again at Niama, his pity hardened to contempt. It seemed to him that it would be merciful to slay this creature, a thing so wretched and degraded it could never be a man. Then no-one could dispute his, Touami's, right to Uné-mawa.

'I'll do it.' The words were half-formed in Touami's mind when Umara put a hand unexpectedly on his shoulder, signalling restraint.

And though it was unclear what his father intended, Touami was at once relieved and disappointed for something ugly and insidious had awoken in him: the idea of killing someone as the means to an end.

Yet instead of Umara, it was Wagarulepu who spoke. She had been standing beside Meelangana: when the wise-man did not react, she shook her head disgustedly and stepped forward. Beside the two leaders she appeared diminutive, her figure squat and bent, yet her very antiquity demanded respect and both stepped back to give her room.

'Yah! Have you no sense?' she asked and her eyes, deep-set and piercing, glanced from Umara's face to Touami's, resting at last on Oué-mala's. 'What kind of grandchildren would come after such a deed? Noné, Niama, whatever his name: whoever kills him will be cursed for he has no daemon. Is that what you want? Drive him out if you will but unless you want his ghost haunting your dreams, let him live. There's only one kind of blood should be seen at a wedding and that comes through love-making, not death!'

A ripple of laughter spread through the women but Touami cringed with embarrassment and the two leaders continued to stare at one another. Then Umara's eyes crinkled and he also began to laugh. And his laughter was not sarcastic or meant in mockery of the other's hostility but was easy and full of good humour.

'Ah, Oué-mala,' he said at last. 'What has changed between us? My son has already proved himself a man: what woman has need of more? We have brought gifts of wallaby-skin and chert; my daughter is ready for the marriage-bed. Why should we let a nothing turn a time of joy to distrust and bloodshed? He has no lineage, no kin: he is as much yours as ours.' He paused, then added deliberately: 'His skin proves it.'

Oué-mala thought a moment, his face grim and it seemed that he would try to argue further. He glanced down to where Niama lay sobbing and shaking and then at Touami who stood erect, watching Uné-mawa with hungry eyes, his hair ochred and the scars of his initiation proud against his skin. And the Toogee leader smiled and relaxed for no-one in their right mind would connect the two.

'Eh, yours is a wise people for all that they live in the forest,' he said. 'Let Noné remain Groua's boy for it is not clever to cross a sorcerer. Come on, we too have gifts to exchange.'

At these words all the women, Meelayginnee and Toogee, raised their hands to the sky in token of peace and then the two groups flocked together, laughing and chattering as if nothing had happened. Only Touami remained aloof for he was shy of meeting his bride face to face. And although he tried to maintain the feelings of contempt and disgust that distanced him from Niama, he could not keep his eyes from that huddled, snivelling figure, nor stay an upwelling of pity.

'Eh, Touami – are you coming?' The others were already walking away towards the Toogee camp where great plumes of smoke marked where Groua had built up the fires to mark the start of celebrations. Slowly Touami turned and followed, wondering at the chances that had brought him and Niama to such different states, disturbed by how close he had come to killing his former foster-brother. And when, on reaching the place where the path left the beach, he paused to look back and saw that Niama had not moved although white foam now washed around him, Touami was overwhelmed by a sense of grief he did not understand but which wrenched him to the core. It was as if something infinitely precious had been lost forever.

6. Contact.

(South Coast of Tasmania, Summer 1799).

It was midsummer, a time of ease and plenty for the Toogee. Even the sea was flat calm as if it shared their indolence. While the gathering of food and the care of children were still ceaseless tasks, in such a season and on a day when the sky was clear, cloudless blue from horizon to horizon, the women were affected by a sense of holiday. Leaving the men in camp to sleep, tell tales or make spears as the mood took them, they gathered the children and headed for the beach, ostensibly to harvest shellfish but in truth because they yearned to splash and frolic in the cool, glittering water. And hearing their shrieks and laughter in the distance, the men frowned, Groua the wise-man muttering darkly that the laughter of women meant grief for men.

The others were too accustomed to the old man's grumbling to heed it but Oué-myehny, whose young wife was constantly teasing and playing tricks on him, took the remark personally. He threw aside the spear he had been straightening in the fire, sprang to his feet and stalked away, taking the path by the rivulet which led to the sea. The men guffawed but he ignored them and strode swiftly between the running water and groves of twisted she-oaks and tea-trees, his bare feet soundless on the sandy ground. When he reached the beach and saw the women and children splashing in the tide-pools towards the far end, he waded the river (which here was wide but shallow, the channels splitting and splaying like a bird's foot), and hurried towards them, filled with a kind of righteous anger.

'Eh – look who's coming!' The approaching figure was stark against the white sand and Toualena, looking up and following the speaker's pointing finger, felt her heart contract as she recognised her husband. In the years they had been together she had come to understand every nuance of his mood from his tone of voice, the manner in which he looked at her, even the way he moved. Now, from the swiftness of his stride and the set of his head, she could tell he was angry. She glanced to where their four-year-old daughter was pulling at a long strand of kelp and thrust the infant she was carrying into the arms of her mother-in-law, Coopehmyenna. She did not know who his rage was directed towards but she could, at least, deflect it from their children.

'See – he can't get enough of you!' Coopehmyenna laughed and pinched Toualena's upper arm whilst expertly settling the child in the crook of her elbow. 'Most men lay off once the children start coming but he's just like his father. Eh – sometimes I thought Oué-mala would eat me alive – insatiable he was, like a bull seal!'

By now everyone had stopped to watch Oué-myehny. Under their scrutiny he became acutely self-consciousness. Although he was too far away to hear what they were saying, from their grins and the joggling of their breasts he knew the women were laughing at him. But to turn back now or to ignore them would mean losing face and he was a proud man. So although his pace slowed slightly, he held his head high and kept his gaze fixed on his young wife, who being of the Meelayginnee, was more slenderly built than Toogee women and therefore easy to pick out.

'Yah! If he wants me, he'll have to catch me!' Oué-myehny's presence, his obvious displeasure, had spoilt the day for Toualena. A mixture of annoyance and fear inspired a reckless mood in her. She snatched her arm from the older woman and sprinted away through the shallows towards a rocky headland at the end of the beach.

Silence fell as the women and children waited for Oué-myehny to reach them. He was quick-tempered and passionate by nature and no-one wanted to attract his wrath. And because none of them would have dared defy their own husbands, they wanted to see what he would do. Already Toualena was far away, running with such long, effortless strides it seemed to the watchers that if she wished, she could leap into the sky and fly like the albatross-woman, Lowa-Tarrim.

With the half-mocking, half-apprehensive eyes of the women

upon him, Oué-myehny felt bitterly ashamed. His lack of control over Toualena would be interpreted as weakness and this knowledge exacerbated his anger. His former wife, being Toogee-born (though of a clan who lived beyond the great Bay of Islands), had been properly respectful, compliant and eager to please. Never had he needed to raise a hand to her but she had died in childbirth one spring. By contrast when, within a few days of marriage, Toualena had defied him and he had threatened her, she had simply walked away, leaving him open-mouthed, confounded. Now, humiliated by her wilfulness once again, he promised himself that this time he would make no allowances for her youth and inexperience but beat obedience into her. And the thought of her flesh yielding under his fists, her voice pleading instead of jeering, turned his blood to fire. Heedless of the watching women and children, the spectacle he was making of himself, he sprang in pursuit.

Afterwards when they told the tale of Grey Gull, the women maintained that his wife, Fan-tail, slowed and looked back to goad him to greater efforts for she was strong to endure as he and fleeter. But the truth was, Toualena paused in the hope that pride would constrain Oué-myehny for she was flagging, her breasts sore and the wet sand proving treacherous to run on. Also, she was beginning to regret her defiance for she understood how close he had already come to violence: further intransigence would only provoke him. And yet, although she knew that as a married woman her first duty was to her husband, that she should wait or even go to meet him and accept her punishment without complaint, something at her very core balked at such submission. She thought of her grandmother, Wagarulepu who, so the tale went, had picked up a cudgel when her husband's brother set upon her and given him such a beating that he kept to his shelter for three days, too broken and ashamed to face anyone. And while she had grown to love Oué-myehny and did not wish to hurt him, neither was she ready to relinquish what remained of her independence for therein lay much of her self-respect. Therefore, seeing that the distance between them was diminishing rapidly, for he was running fast, she turned again and fled.

With the instinctive sense of sea and weather possessed by most coast-dwellers, Oué-myehny was sharply aware that the tide was on the turn and he berated the ignorance and foolhardiness of his wife as he followed her round the promontory. On the other side of the headland lay a series of deeply indented bays and inlets where the Toogee rarely ventured for the cliffs were loose and treacherous and it was easy to be tide-trapped in the bays and drown. For an instant he was tempted to turn back, for he was certain she would eventually return, contrite. But the fire that had awoken in him could not be so easily assuaged, nor did he want to face the elder's questions and his father's wrath if, through accident or wilfulness, she was lost. He looked all about and, seeing no sign of her, clambered down into the first narrow inlet, noting with dismay that surf was already swirling in to fill it.

The inlet marked a fault-line which ran straight through the cliff. It had been eroded into a wide, cave-like fissure. Faint light filtered in from the top and the floor was sandy save for where water had entered from the other end, cutting down to bare rock. A single line of footprints led inside.

Cursing, Oué-myehny followed. It was many years since he had explored this area and he could not remember whether the cleft was blind and he risked drowning by going in. But by now, surely, if that were the case Toualena would have turned back. And the sand and broken shells beneath his feet were dry and powdery: it was long since the tide had reached so far.

About a hundred paces in, the sand abutted against a rock shelf but the cleft had widened and there was daylight ahead, marking an opening. The brightness dazzled Oué-myehny: when he put out a hand to steady and guide himself, his fingers encountered grooves and circles carved into the wall in a time beyond Toogee myth. Then he reached the opening and saw Toualena.

She was squatting to drink from a deep brown pool, one of a number linked by a small rivulet like shells on a string. The level of the water was below that of the cave-mouth where he stood and she seemed oblivious to his presence because having slaked her thirst, she sat down and dabbled her feet. The pools were surrounded by rushes; further up, the valley floor was thicketed with fern-trees.

On the opposite side the land sloped gently upwards and was crowded with tea-trees and she-oaks. To the left, the creek drained into the sea: the roar of surf was loud from that direction. But Ouémyehny had ears only for the trickle of water as Toualena lifted and dipped her feet and the murmur of her voice. She was singing a lullaby of the Meelayginnee.

For a moment a kind of pity held Oué-myehny in thrall. He stood staring, amazed that having fled, she should so quickly have forgotten him. And then as, absently, she lifted one hand to a milk-swollen breast and began to tease the nipple, he remembered how she had mocked and humiliated him. A hot tide suffused him: he leapt towards her.

The thud of bare feet on rock broke Toualena's reverie. One glance at her husband's face was enough to send her scrambling away but she was barely upright before he caught her, grabbing her arms and jerking her to a standstill with such force that the eyeballs jolted in her head.

'Why did you run, worthless one?' His voice was harsh: his fingers dug into her flesh (which was soft and yielding as he had imagined it). Then his lust and anger fused. The breath caught in his throat: he pulled her close and when she tried to twist away, raised his hand to strike her.

A twig cracked.

So sharp and intrusive was the sound, they turned their heads in the same instinctive movement and Toualena cried out in terror. All other emotion swept away, they grabbed one another for reassurance, child-like in their need of physical contact. Having nothing to prepare them for what was standing at the edge of the trees (except fantastic tales told by Toualena's grandfather, Meelangana, and the pariah, Noné), they stared with the amazement of anyone encountering the unimaginable.

The thing resembled a man in size and shape, having a forked body with two arms and two legs on which it stood upright. Its head too was like a man-like, only hairier. The hair was the colour of a wallaby's fur. It had two eyes, a nose pointed like a beak and a mouth, barely visible. But unlike any living person's, the face, neck and hands and feet were pale and the eyes blue as the sky. The rest of the creature's skin hung about it in course, coloured folds and was devoid of marks denoting lineage or clan. Nor was there any sign of genitalia.

The creature opened its mouth, a glistening pink hole in the matted beard, and sounds came out but not in any form of speech the two recognised. They stared, transfixed, as it left the trees and clambered down the river bank. It stood in the water and looked at them, then delved in a fold of its skin. It brought out something that flashed in the sunlight and held it towards them, like someone offering a gift. And all the while it kept talking. The utterances were incomprehensible but the wheedling tone of voice needed no interpretation.

'Let's go,' Oué-myehny hissed and he tugged Toualena's wrist to pull her towards the cleft, forgetting that the rising tide would have made that way back impassable.

'No, wait!' She pulled against him, her initial terror subsiding as the man-thing began to wade towards them. Its steady speech and clumsy movements convinced her it would not harm them and she was fascinated by the object in its hand which was long and leaf-shaped and reflected the sunlight like water. She longed to touch and play with it, to find out if she could see herself in its surface as she had sometimes done when bending over a still pool to drink or glimpsed in someone's eyes when they were very close. And for Oué-myehny also, dread vied with curiosity, only he wished he had a spear to hand. Unarmed, he felt vulnerable despite the stranger's benign appearance.

But the creature was, apparently, as wary of them as they were of it. Halfway across the creek it stopped. It looked from Oué-myehny to Toualena and let out a nervous laugh. The shiny object shook slightly in its hand.

That laughter, as incongruous against the rippling of the water and the roar of the ocean as the very presence of its author in this narrow valley with its tangled forest and tumbling rocks, affected the two in profoundly different ways. For Toualena it broke down the last barrier of suspicion: however outlandish its appearance, she no longer doubted that the creature was a real person. But Oué-myehny, for whom the object that had entranced the woman held no interest, sensed danger. It was a feeling so intense that his skin prickled. His toes loosened a smooth river stone embedded in the damp soil where he stood: a poor enough weapon but better than nothing. As the stranger began to move again, Oué-myehny bent to pick it up.

In that instant, the creature's eyes flicked away. Too late, Oué-myehny realized they had been tricked: it was not alone. Another had crept up behind while their attention was on the first. Before he could shout a warning he was struck down with such force that he crashed onto the rocks and lay still. A dark stain blossomed beneath his head.

Toualena gasped, then she was grabbed from behind, her arms wrenched back so brutally her spine bowed. She gave a piercing scream and the first man-creature struck her across the mouth with the hand holding the knife which had so fascinated her. Shocked into silence, blood streaming down her chin, she was half-dragged, half-carried across the creek and along the bank towards the sea.

The two sealers had followed the creek from a little bay they had entered in search of water: now, as they dragged Toualena back, they could hardly contain their lust for it was months since either had had a woman. When they reached the narrow inlet where the stream spilled into the sea, the tide was high, their skiff pitching and tossing wildly against its moorings, but there was a little patch of dry sand above the debris-line, soft as a feather mattress. Toualena barely had time to realize that there was no camp, that the boat was the man-creature's destination, before they threw her to the ground. One held her down while the other delved at his crotch: there was no doubt then that these were men. She struggled against them, rolling and twisting in a desperate effort to escape while they grasped handfuls of her flesh, clutching so roughly at her breasts that she cried out with the pain, grabbing whatever they could reach until at last her strength was utterly exhausted. And then, for Toualena, the assault took on the detached unreality of a dream. She was numb: her consciousness hovered hawk-like above, watching as they mauled and raped her: it was as if it were happening to someone else. For all the reaction they got from her, they might as well have rutted on a still-warm corpse.

When they were done, they left her on the sand and sat on a couple of boulders next to the water casks they had filled before venturing upstream. The elder of the two, a man in his mid-twenties whose beard was already grizzled and face tanned to leather by the sea, took out a tobacco pouch. They filled stubby black pipes and smoked, their eyes on the swirling water.

Below them, Toualena lay spread-eagled under the blazing sun. Flies crawled greedily over her swollen, bloodied lips; they buzzed and swarmed over her leaking nipples and the secretions glistening on her crotch and thighs. Her mind floated far away, soothed by the inrush and backwash of the waves. She wanted the cool quiet of the forest but the desire was not strong enough to make her move. The heat pressed her into the sand like a heavy, remorseless hand: when she smelled smoke she thought it was her burning, that she must have died without realizing it. And then all desire left her save for a fleeting regret that her daemon, Fan-tail, had not come. But her twin brother, Touami, was far away: *darwalla* must be looking after him. She breathed deeply and let darkness overtake her.

When the sealers judged the tide was right they hauled in their boat and loaded the casks. These were heavy and unwieldy but even the sound of the men's cursing did not wake Toualena who had sunk into a stupor of shock and exhaustion. Her breasts rose rhythmically as the sea and her hands, which had formerly been clenched, lay loose and open on the sand.

'My God – will you look at that!' Liam O'Grady, the younger of the two, who had enticed the woman with his knife, clucked his tongue and rolled his eyes appreciatively. 'Not a bleedin' care in the world. How'd'ye like to set up here, John?'

The other cast a critical eye round the little bay, the jutting headlands and looming cliffs; the blood-coloured rivulet and scrubby trees and it seemed to him that the whole landscape was hostile, full of unseen eyes.

'Nah – too quiet.' He jerked a thumb at Toualena. 'What about her? Take her along? The old man won't like it.'

O'Grady considered for a moment, his eyes cold. Then he grinned, broken teeth glinting wetly against full, purplish lips. 'So what? We'll tie her up and chuck her over if he's not agreeable. Plenty more where she came from.'

The other looked hard at him, trying to gauge if he were serious, then shrugged. Should there be trouble, he could always say he had agreed to the kidnapping because of O'Grady's temper. The Irishman was well-known for his violent outbursts: he was tolerated on board because, when sober, he could kill and skin a full-grown seal with a swiftness and efficiency that was the envy of the whole crew.

Having decided what to do, the men worked quickly. They untied one of the lines from the boat and crept up on the sleeping woman. No speech was required, just a nod and a wink and between them they had her trussed neatly as a market-bound goose.

As they hoisted her up and flung her unceremoniously into the boat, Toualena cried out. It was a wail of despair that for an instant gave her captors pause, O'Grady from a kind of malignant satisfaction, John Bayliss from horror, not at what they were doing but something more visceral. Once, long ago, he had heard a woman make such a noise and though he could not recall the circumstances, the sound sent a chill through him.

'Will you shut your lip?' O'Grady sprang into the skiff as the woman struggled to rise and dealt her a blow that drove her back. Her head struck one of the strakes and she collapsed, stunned, into the pool of water swilling in the bottom of the boat.

'C'm'on.' Having dealt with the woman, the young man was suddenly nervous. By now the body of the native they had struck down might have been discovered: the woman's cry could attract an avenging war-band. And Bayliss, seeing near-panic in the other's eyes, was gripped by the same urgency. He threw the painter into the bows, pushed off and clambered in, the skiff tipping alarmingly as he did so.

By now tide and current were running strongly. By the time the two men had the oars settled, the little boat had been borne beyond the rocks which had made the inbound journey hazardous. Their ship, *The Advantage*, was anchored a good hour away, sheltered from south-westerlies behind a jutting headland but they settled easily into the rhythm of rowing. Every-so-often they glanced shorewards, half-expecting to see a line of naked, spear-waving figures silhouetted against the sky but the cliff-tops and dunes appeared empty. When the woman began to moan and stir, struggling futilely against her bonds, they grinned at one another and jabbed her with their feet. Her eyes bulged with terror like those of a trapped animal: she bit frenziedly at the rope around her wrists until the hemp was stained with blood and then the two licked their own lips in anticipation of pleasures to come.

Oué-myehny shuddered and woke. Flies buzzed and swarmed all around: they crawled on his eyelids and lips. His skull felt as if it would burst. When he opened his eyes, the sunlight stabbed deep into his brain so that he flinched. Even to think was an immense effort. In a voice that was like a death-gasp he whispered, 'Toualena?'

There was no reply, only the sounds of water and the call of a distant seabird. Levering himself into a sitting position his hands encountered something wet and sticky: he had been lying in a pool of his own blood. Painfully, head reeling, he got to his feet and looked around, shading his eyes with one hand. The man-creatures must have gone away, otherwise they would surely have knocked him down again. But Toualena?

A few paces from where he had fallen were more blood splotches. Oué-myehny crouched to study them, using his hands to steady himself. Fear of what might have happened to Toualena and shame at how easily he had been tricked enabled him to force his pain aside and concentrate on the bloodstains but they told him nothing except that someone else was hurt. The water was within reach: he scooped some up and drank though it tasted brackish, fouled by the tide which had raised the level of the creek to the top of the banks. He realized that wherever they had taken her, it could not have been through the cleft.

A long wavering cry penetrated the background noises of creek, surf, the sough of the wind through the trees. To Oué-myehny it was as if a hand had reached down his throat to grasp his entrails: he recognised Toualena's voice. He plunged into the water, waded across, hauled himself out on the other side. He had no idea of what he would do, injured, weaponless and alone, he knew only that he must reach her quickly. As he staggered blindly through the scrub, a calmer, clearer part of his mind warned that he would do better to go back and fetch Oué-mala and a war-band but he ignored it.

When he reached the beach at last Oué-myehny stood gasping, hands pressed to his waist to aid his lungs. Unaware that the man-creatures possessed a boat he did not look out to sea but studied the sand and rocks. The beach was deserted but the sand was scuffed and pitted: he could read the marks upon it easily as a book-learned man could comprehend a newly written page.

The imprint of Toualena's body he recognised at once though it was marred by footprints and surrounded by holes gouged by the men's knees, feet and hands: he knew then that they had raped her. A groan escaped him and he dropped to his knees. Her shoulder-blades, buttocks and head were so deeply moulded that he laid his hands gently in the imprint as if by doing so he could bring her back. The sand was warm and crumbled beneath his fingers, blurring her outline as if to emphasise the fact that she was gone. And grief overwhelmed his anger and the physical pain wrenching his body: he sat back on his heels, stricken, and saw the boat far out across the bay, heading away from Toogee lands.

Oué-myehny leapt to his feet and plunged into the sea, governed by the same recklessness that had impelled him to follow the man-creatures instead of going for help. The water was shockingly cold and stung his thorn-torn skin but the creek's outflow swept him swiftly out. Then the rocks fell behind and the water became more broken: he could only see the boat intermittently. The man-creatures were dark humps, rowing with a steady, seemingly tireless rhythm and there was no sign of Toualena but he knew she must be with them. None of her tracks had led off the beach.

'Hah – look there!' O'Grady, who was sharp-eyed as a gannet (and as voracious), had spotted the figure, tiny with distance, kneeling on the beach. They watched as he ran into the sea but never for an instant did their pull on the oars falter: it was an action they were inured to, unconscious as breathing. And it was so clear that their pursuer would never catch them, they began to laugh and shout taunts and insults to spur him to greater efforts though had he been able to understand the words it would have made no difference. He was deaf to everything save the thudding of his heartbeat and a low, constant resonance all around him, the murmuration of the deep.

'Perhaps her voice'll do it.' The Irishman's nature was not such as to be satisfied by the shouting of obscenities. He stopped rowing and John Bayliss paused also and rested on his oars. The woman, exhausted by her struggles, lay quiet though her eyes were still fixed on her abductors. O'Grady picked up a wet rope and lashed her viciously to make her cry out. But though she writhed and heaved, unable to escape, she clamped her teeth shut and made no sound other than short gasps as purple welts spread across her breasts, belly and thighs. It was as if, Bayliss thought uneasily, she had guessed the Irishman's purpose. And the fear in her eyes had been replaced by a terrible unreadable blankness: he could not tell whether it masked hatred, defiance or indifference.

Toualena's stubbornness drove O'Grady to frenzy. He lurched to his feet and tried to stamp on her but the boat rolled so violently he was thrown to one side and only the other's quick hands saved him from going overboard. Like most sailors, the Irishman could not swim and the instant of icy terror when he saw the green water rise to meet him brought him to himself. He sat back on the bench and gripped the oars with such force his knuckles stood out white. Without a word, he began to row.

Oué-myehny was tiring rapidly though he refused to admit it even when the wavelets running over the surface of the swell slapped him repeatedly in the face. Among his people, women were the most accomplished swimmers: Toogee men took to the water only when there was no choice, to ford a river or reach a reef where seals congregated. But even in those circumstances, it was customary for men to use a canoe-raft for they did not share their women's easy relationship with the sea. Thus lurking in Oué-myehny's mind was a profound dread of deep water. The ocean could swallow a man so completely, his daemon might never find him: then his spirit would wander the roaring wet darkness forever.

When the current caught him he was not, at first, aware of what was happening. Cold water snaked up his body, spiralling round his legs, engulfing his hips and torso. The sensation was so immediate and physical he thought he must have blundered into a pod of whales or dolphins and they were nudging him or else a frond of kelp had wrapped him round. He faltered and felt the drag on his body: an inexorable, irresistible force was pulling him down. He flailed, panic-stricken, his arms weak and heavy but the current tugged him under. As he sank, he clawed desperately at the water but it slipped through his fingers, resistless as air. Beneath the pounding of his heart, the murmur of the ocean had changed to a mighty roar: it was overwhelming him, its power inescapable. He could hold his breath no longer. Bubbles burst from his mouth and nose. They streamed to the surface, glittering like fish, and disappeared.

The men in the boat scanned the sea. There was a spot over which birds wheeled and called but there was no sign of their pursuer. They rowed on. At their feet Toualena lay tense and still. She heard the rush of water and the crying of gulls and her whole being wailed though she uttered not a sound.

7. The Estranging.

(South Coast of Tasmania, Autumn 1800).

It seemed that the ancestors approved of the union between Touami and Uné-mawa for within a year of their marriage a healthy boy was born to them. And though the following season was one of the coldest in living memory, mother and infant thrived. On the coast, where the hearth-group over-wintered, no-one starved that year. The bond between Meelayginnee and Toogee seemed inviolable.

But in that time there was death as well as life among Touami's kin. Uniala, his grandmother, died suddenly one morning. A rime of frost had made the surface of the beach slippery and she fell on her way to gather mussels from the reef. She had got up, telling those who rushed to help that there was nothing wrong but the oyster-catchers, which had flown up with plaintive cries as the women approached, had barely cleared the foam-whitened rocks when Uniala jerked and staggered as if she had been speared, then fell face down on the sand. The women's wails brought the men running but by the time her husband, Meelangana, reached them, she was dead.

They had burned her body later that same day but the ashes had been collected, every scrap of bone saved, to take back to Meelayginnee territory in the spring. And there the ancient blackwood that was her totem was carved with sign so others would know the tree was already taken, and her ashes were laid reverently in a hollow between the roots. These were covered with a layer of grass on which sticks were arranged in the pattern of her skin. From that moment, her name was never spoken again.

Five winters on, Touami was in the prime of his strength and his reputation as a hunter had spread beyond his own hearth-group so that he found a welcome wherever he went. Yet he knew he had much to learn before he could become an elder and so, despite his prowess, he remained humble. Every time he visited his wife's hearth-group and saw Noné, the pariah who had once been his foster-brother Niama, he was reminded how easily chance could turn good fortune to bad.

Now as they came to the camp where they would spend the winter (it was a little further down the coast from where he had been married), Touami felt a rush of satisfaction, a sense of homecoming. His first-born had earned the title Cuckana ('little boy'); his second child, a girl, was learning to walk (her Toogee grand-parents had not yet seen her), and Uné-mawa's belly was already rounded with a third. As he checked the huts (which were stoutly built, Toogee-fashion, to withstand the wild weather), Touami pictured his father-in-law's face when he saw his daughter and her family again. In their eyes she was the most handsome of both their peoples and now, in the bloom of pregnancy, she exhibited a well-being which, Touami knew, attested as much to his prowess as a hunter and provider as to her fecundity.

Having made sure that the shelters were empty, Touami gave his firestick to Wagarulepu and began to climb the huge hump-backed dune that protected the camp from storms. The sand slid beneath his feet and he did not hurry but listened with pleasure to the noises coming from behind: his sisters laughing and chattering as they played with Cuckana; the infant, Cottruluttyé grizzling because she was hungry and Uné-mawa was too busy to suckle her; Umara and Meelangana talking quietly as they lit fires outside each hut, glad that the journey was over. Once they were settled in, they would all go to the beach to find food but Touami was eager to see whether some of Oué-mala's people were already there. There was a Toogee camp not far away.

The day had been overcast but as Touami reached the crest of the dune, a shaft of dazzling sunlight broke through the cloud cover. At the same time the sound of the ocean (which had been a constant murmur in the background), became a deafening roar and wind-driven spume hit him: he tasted salt and his mouth and nose became gritty with sand borne by the blast. Sheltered up till then by the bulk of the dune, he was unprepared for the fierceness of that wind and he turned his face away to look up the beach towards the rocks where the best shellfish were to be found and seals congregated. With the sea this wild he knew none of Oué-mala's people would be in the water but they might still be on the beach in search of seabirds broken in the storm or, if they were lucky, a beached dolphin or whale.

The wide, shining expanse of sand was deserted but though he had begun to shiver in the bitter wind, Touami continued to stare. There was something deeply disturbing in the emptiness of the beach with its tide-heaped debris and surf-washed rocks, enough to compel him to kneel in the sand and continue looking. A gust rocked him and he regretted leaving his wallaby-skin below but still he stayed. The calls of seabirds caught his attention: their wings flashed in the sunlight as they rode the air between great green rollers. Then the clouds closed and they were lost to view.

Touami sighed and prepared to rise knowing that Meelangana and Umara would wonder why he was lingering so long. But as he glanced again towards the far end of the beach, he realized suddenly what he missed. In former years the seals had been packed so tightly there had been no room to see the rocks: now there were so few, he could mark them off on his fingers. And then he noticed white streaks in the numerous sand mounds between the high-tide line and the dunes. He had assumed these to be buried heaps of the usual detritus to be found on beaches: kelp tangle, branches, the trunks of fallen trees washed down the rivers after winter rains but as he stared, his eyes mere slits against the driving sand, a dreadful certainty grew upon him that they were bones.

Shouting at the others to stay where they were (his father and grandfather shook their heads and muttered together but obeyed), he half-slid, half-ran down the dune face. What he found made the gorge rise in his throat and the cold that assailed him was no longer due wholly to the blasting wind.

The sand mounds contained seal corpses and the bones he had glimpsed were mostly skulls for flesh still clothed the skeletons though it had dried to a texture like wood. All were skinless, the tough hide that withstood all but the sharpest spears stripped cleanly as if the animals had been peeled. This perplexed Touami greatly though the cause of death was easily ascertained: most of the skulls were cracked as if from waddy blows. As he wandered between the high tide line and the base of the dunes, zig-zagging from mound to mound, Touami's bewilderment increased for the scale of the slaughter was beyond comprehension. And from their state of decay he guessed all the animals had died at the same time.

The gale buffeted him: realizing he was unlikely to find anything different further along the shore, he turned, filled with a growing sense of outrage. Whoever, whatever, had done the killing, not one of the animals had been butchered. Such waste violated the very law by which life was possible: no man he knew was capable of such an act. Yet the damaged skulls indicated that the seals had been killed deliberately.

His foot banged against something hard. It was another seal-skull, a round hole punched between the eyes, a huge section missing from the back. He bent to pick it up but his fingers had only grazed the smooth, wind-polished surface, when he jerked his hand back. Clearly as if a voice had spoken, he realized that the bones were witness to something new and terrible, some power beyond the law which governed all he knew. And since it had destroyed the seals, there was no reason why it might not prey on people also. The Toogee, for whom *Karteila* was both ancestor and totem, might already have succumbed. There was, after all, no sign of them.

As this thought crystallised, Touami was overtaken by such terror that he began to run. His feet sank in the loose sand but he was loth to step where the tide washed lest *Ebenook* detect his presence and alert the thing that had caused so much death. (It was inconceivable to him that the evil could have come from the land). By the time he reached the rivulet that wound past the dune and spilled into the sea, his skin was wet with sweat despite the cold and the breath rasped in his throat.

Splashing through the shallow blood-red water he wondered how to break the news, whether he should demand they return to their own lands at once. But the chill of the stream brought him to himself and restored his sense of propriety: he could not blurt his tale like a frightened child and expect Umara and Meelangana to take it seriously. He scooped water in his palms and drank and the familiar, slightly bitter taste calmed him. Whatever had happened here could not reach the forest, refuge and sanctuary of the Meelayginnee: there was safety far beyond the sea's reach, insatiable though its hunger might be.

A little comforted by this thought, Touami stepped up onto the sandy bank and made his way into the camp. Here, in the shelter of the massive dune, all was homely and peaceful. Fires burned brightly before each doorway and the women and children were busy repairing the shelters with strips of bark and handfuls of grass and moss while Meelangana and Umara sat by the largest fire, sharpening spears. They looked up at his approach and, seeing his expression, rose and came to meet him.

'What is it?' Because of his age, Meelangana could be direct without causing offence. He watched Touami with deep concern for the young man's face was taut with worry, as if he expected something terrible to happen at any moment.

'I don't know.' As he spoke, Touami became aware of Unémawa's gaze and he hesitated. His news would, he knew, affect her more profoundly than any of them and he wished he could go to her and tell her quietly, away from the others. But having begun, he was bound to go on while she continued with her task, listening from a distance because as a young woman she was not permitted to join in a conversation between men.

In stumbling words, unable to express the full magnitude and horror of it in speech, Touami described what he had found and he saw his own perplexity mirrored in the faces of his father and grandfather. When he had finished they were silent for a while. Then Umara said uneasily, 'Oué-mala will know.'

'If he is here.' Meelangana grimaced and pulled distractedly at his foreskin. 'But you saw no sign of Toogee on the beach, Touami?'

'The wind would have destroyed any footprints and the sea was too rough for swimming,' Touami replied. 'But men could not have done this thing. The seals had been skinned, all of them, yet the flesh was not cut: no animal or person had eaten them. It was the work of some evil spirit from the sea, something outside the law.

Most likely Oué-mala has taken his people inland to safety.'

'Nonetheless, tomorrow we'll visit their old camp,' Umara decided. 'And for now we shall avoid the beach. Come on, let's get some food.'

The group went hungry that night for they found nothing to eat except some fungi and the pig-face that straggled over the lee-side of the dune. Touami and Uné-mawa were unable to sleep and lay in each others arms listening to the roar of wind and sea, haunted by thoughts of what lay on the beach and what it might portend. During the night the gale eased but that made the noise of surf seem even louder and Cuckana grizzled unbearably until, in desperation, Uné-mawa put him to her breast. Then at last he fell asleep but as if realizing her rightful dues had been usurped, the infant awoke and began to scream and her mother did not have enough milk left to satisfy her. Thus the night seemed endless: long before dawn, Touami tied his wallaby skin about his shoulders and crept out to watch for first light.

To his surprise, he found his grandfather sitting in the ashes at the edge of the central fire, still and silent as a tree-stump. They kept vigil together and when at last a grey bar appeared behind the forest, Touami returned to his hut, thankful that the night was over but the old man remained where he was. Meelangana was deeply worried. Throughout his long life he had encountered little that could not be explained by his own experience or myths, the tales handed down through uncounted generations. Once, for example, when men had begun to trap and kill more fish than they could eat, the angry spirits turned the sea into blood and made the flesh of sea-creatures poisonous to punish the greedy children of Tarner. But these deaths of *karteila* were, the old man sensed, unprecedented, and so he was afraid with the kind of nameless fear that had assailed him when he first heard about the great white bird and the pale-skinned men who had bound and commanded it.

'Aie, that such times should come upon me and my sons,' the old man sighed. 'These things did not happen when I was strong enough to bear them.' And he pulled his worn, stinking fur closer about his shoulders and fell into a stupor while a pearly light spread across the sky.

For the next two days the Meelayginnee avoided the beach. The women and children foraged in the woods while the men went in search of the Toogee, carrying their spears in the hope of disturbing a wallaby or other prey. But the land seemed empty of people and animals: a single female pademelon with young joey in pouch was all they came across and that was taboo.

Though they did not tell the women, the men had visited the old Toogee camp at the far end of the bay on the first day. They found it abandoned, the roofs of the huts broken in as if they had been deliberately destroyed, and this turned their worry to gnawing anxiety. And on the way back to their own camp, each had been assailed by a growing uneasiness, a prickling between the shoulder-blades as if unseen, hostile eyes were watching though every time they stood still or swung round to look, there was nothing there.

On the second night as they sat around the central fire, hungry and depressed, Umara told them that next day, if the sea was calm, they would all go to the beach, to get food and, if possible, discover the truth of what had happened there. Touami was reluctant and Meelangana opposed to this but they knew they had little choice: even if they returned to their own lands, they would have to eat first.

The harsh croak of a raven rent the air as the group filed along the narrow path between dune and rivulet next morning. Meelangana shuddered and looked up but the sky was empty of even a cloud. It was so still that the screech of sand grains beneath their feet seemed loud. Cuckana jumped and kicked to make the sand squeak even more but to the old man the sound seemed ominous, as if the beach itself was voicing pain.

The tide was out, exposing the grey and black rocks of the reef and slippery tangles of kelp; the wet sand gleamed in the sunlight while above the high tide line, mica glittered. Yet the gale had exposed many of the seal carcasses which had been buried when Touami was there and Uné-mawa stopped in her tracks and put one hand to her mouth, letting out a low cry of distress.

Tealana, her daughters, and Wagarulepu hurried onto the wet flats, knowing they did not have long to gather food before the tide turned. The little boy followed, stopping to investigate empty shells, worm casts, piles of sand balls left by tiny crabs which burrowed into the sand as he tried to catch them. But although she should have been collecting shellfish with the other women, Uné-mawa trailed after the three men who had gone to inspect the dead seals and when she saw the crushed skulls and mummified flesh, she clutched Cottruluttyé to her breast and sank weeping to her knees.

Touami's heart was wrenched by his wife's grief but though he guessed what she must be thinking, that her hearth-group had met the same fate as the animals which were their totem, he did not go to her. Meelangana, who still missed Uniala, glanced sternly at his grandson but it was not for him to intervene so he contented himself with a snort of disapproval. Yet it was not hardness that kept Touami away but the feeling that to acknowledge his wife's loss would somehow validate her fears. Umara was already striding along the beach towards another pile of seal carcasses so the young man hurried after and soon Uné-mawa rose and walked out to join the other women though her head was bowed and her tread heavy and slow.

'Ah!' Umara, who was not afraid to touch the corpses, delved into a small hole in the side of a huge bull seal and extracted what seemed to be a kind of pebble. He squatted in the sand and sniffed the thing then weighed it in his hand with a look of astonishment. The other two did not understand until each of them had examined it in turn and then they too wondered at the heaviness of it. It was similar in size and shape to a gum-nut, shiny and solid as a wet stone but how it had come to lodge deep in the flesh of an animal was not something they considered: it was a curiosity, ominous in context but not, in itself, threatening.

'Do you feel anything?' Meelangana was suspicious of the lead ball as something unnatural for he had never encountered anything like it before but if it had caused the seal's death, he assumed they would sense it. Umara grimaced and tilted his hand so that the thing dropped. It sank instantly into the loose sand, leaving a slight circular indentation like the mouth of a spider's trap.

'Yah – leave it,' he said. 'If it is magic, its power is spent. Let's get some food: no good will come of lingering here.'

He set off across the wet sand towards the rocks where the

women were although it was almost unprecedented for the men to join in so menial a task as gathering shellfish. Touami watched him go with an expression of such amazement that Meelangana chuckled. 'A wise man, your father: he doesn't voice his fears,' he said and then he went after, Touami following reluctantly. He did not find it so easy to dismiss the mystery of the dead seals, perhaps because he understood their significance to the Toogee more deeply than the others, nor could he shake off the feeling that they were being watched all the time. But though he looked carefully along the line of scrub-dotted dunes, he saw nothing untoward and in the end he smoothed over the place where the strange pebble was and made his way to the rock platform, already washed by the incoming tide.

The work of gathering shellfish restored some sense of normality even though the participation of Umara and Touami made the harvesting a special event. Meelangana waited on the beach on the pretext of watching out for freak waves and no-one criticised though the sea was flat calm. Little wavelets lapped the rocks and sand with a soft plashing sound and even Cuckana was able to dabble in the water without fear of being swept out and drowned.

Inevitably though as the tide rose the group was forced back towards the shore and the heaped carcasses which, for a while, they had managed to forget. Uné-mawa, the little girl supported on one hip, walked with her head bent seawards, refusing to look at the carnage, but the others could not help staring. Meelangana was especially troubled. Standing at the water's edge, eyes dazzled by the sparkling water, he had remembered that one of the Niama's talismans, the things the boy claimed had been gifts of the white strangers, had been somehow akin to the black pebble lodged in the dead seal.

The old man tried to relax and dismiss his fears when at last they reached camp and settled down to cook and eat the shellfish. Away from the beach even Uné-mawa seemed to shrug off her despondency as she taught Cuckana how to open a mussel and eat without burning his fingers or scalding his mouth. Touami also felt better with food in his belly. It seemed impossible that only on the other side of the dune there was evidence of such evil.

They feasted late into the afternoon, slaked their thirst at the rivulet and lay down to sleep for they were sated and drowsy and the autumn sun was warm. When the rest were dozing, Touami rose and led Uné-mawa to a hollow filled with a soft bed of she-oak needles, leaving Cuckana asleep beside his great-grandfather. Touami was feeling too indolent for sex but he had been overwhelmed by a desire to be with his wife, to hold her and be held, offering comfort and receiving reassurance in return.

The scent of the trees mingled with the salt tang of the sea; they lay quietly together while the little girl amused herself by digging a hole in the sandy soil nearby. Touami closed his eyes and breathed deeply. For a while, at least, the horror receded. They slept.

A piercing scream shattered the dreaming quiet of the late afternoon. It was a child's cry, heart-rending and urgent. Touami, woken abruptly, pushed Uné-mawa aside and leapt to his feet for the voice was Cuckana's. Bursting from the scrub into camp, he looked desperately for his son and found him standing by the fire, pointing towards the crest of the dune.

'Bad men!' The little boy's face puckered then Uné-mawa ran past Touami and swept the child into her arms. A spear thudded into the sand, just missing her. It stuck there, quivering, and to Touami its movement seemed to echo her scream. Everything seemed to slow: he followed her gaze, saw the nightmare figures lined on the crest of the dune, felt his heart lurch. He could not believe what was happening.

Seven men stood staring down, their bodies painted red and white in a pattern signifying death. Strips of seal-skin were bound about their arms and thighs; their hair was thick with ochre. Six stood in a line, spears poised to throw; their leader stood a little in front and his hands were empty for he had already cast. His face, painted in crude representation of a skull was, like the others, rigid with hostility.

'Oué-mala: what is this?' Umara was the first of the Meelayginnee to recover from the shock. He strode forward until he stood between the base of the dune and the camp. He was naked, weaponless and Tealana let out a little cry of distress but in fact this was a shrewd move on his part. It was considered cowardly for any warrior to spear an unarmed man unless he was being punished.

'You're not welcome here.' A young man to his right handed Oué-mala another spear, heavier than those used by the Meelayginnee: it was designed for hunting elephant seals. 'The evil that has come upon us was brought by one of you. Go now or face death.'

By now the women and children were huddled together behind Umara as if his will alone could protect them; Touami and Meelangana stood uncertainly a little apart. But the Toogee remained still and tense and their gaze was fierce and unrelenting.

'Your daughter and grandchildren too?' Umara asked. 'We have given ochre to the guardian spirits, brought gifts as is fitting: do we not deserve at least to know how Toualena has so offended you?'

Up until that moment Oué-mala had looked pitilessly upon the weeping women and children, the three men, one of whom was almost a dotard, who stood at his mercy. But at the naming of his daughter-in-law, a shadow seemed to cross his face.

'It was not her,' he said and his voice was hard and expressionless. 'Are you leaving?'

Fear for his twin sister compelled Touami to move to his father's side though he had no clear idea of what to do.

'Niama – Noné, then?' Umara was puzzled. He sensed that Oué-mala was motivated by more than a simple desire to rid himself of unwanted guests, that there was fear at the root of his anger but it made no sense that any of the Meelayginnee could have anything to do with the carnage on the beach. Yet he knew it would be folly to underestimate the danger he and his hearth-group were in for the Toogee warriors shifted restlessly where they stood and looked down with a kind of grim expectancy.

'Eh, my son, don't waste time talking to these Toogee: as well try to reason with *tirurar* when he finds chicks alone and defenceless on the nest.' Meelangana shuffled forward and, to Touami's astonishment, took hold Umara's arm and pulled to lead him away. 'Let us go then, since Oué-mala and his people no longer recognise the law. No wonder *karteila* died: the ancestors have turned away in shame!'

Because of their long association, language was no barrier between these groups and the old man had spoken loudly and clearly enough for all those ranged upon the dune to hear him. Oué-mala's face contorted with rage and as the old man, his son and grandson turned their backs, he let out an incoherent yell and ran down the slope, his feet slipping and sliding in the loose sand. His men, perhaps because they felt that insult had been aimed specifically at him or else that he had given them no orders, remained where they were.

'Stand still so that I can ram my spear down your throat and kill those words, old man!' The shout rang in the ears of the three Meelayginnee but they did not stop until they had reached the women and children. Then, with a kind of studied deliberation, they turned. For all of them it was a relief to be facing their enemies though even as he thought this, Touami still could not quite believe this could be real. And seeing his father-in-law's face closely, it seemed to him that Oué-mala shared the same confusion for a perplexed look overtook his features, which were taut and strained beneath the war-paint, and he lowered his spear.

'We are kin: it is not fitting that we fight,' Umara said. He paused to survey the line of spearmen, stark against the sky. 'Tell us what has happened. Then we shall know what to do.'

There was pride in his tone and he stood straight and tall, looking his antagonist unflinchingly in the eye. Touami held his breath while the women moaned softly and the children whimpered in fear. The Toogee men muttered together but their words were inaudible to those below and Umara ignored them: his gaze was fixed on Oué-mala's face.

Then, despite his advantage, the Toogee leader's resolve faltered. With his fighters behind him he was invincible yet he could not match Umara's courage. It seemed to him that his hesitation had already given the Meelayginnee a kind of moral victory. But only a flicker in his eyes betrayed his disquietude for he dare not risk backing down before his men.

'Ach, this is *narrar's* talk!' Wagarelepu heaved herself to her feet with considerable effort and shook her head as if admonishing naughty boys. So unexpected was her intervention that all stared at her in astonishment. Undaunted, she pointed a thick, scarred finger at Uné-mawa who was sitting blank-faced as if in a trance, the little girl's face pressed between her breasts. 'Her belly is already rounded with another child, one that should have two grandfathers to teach him how to live, not a tale of how they slew each other to haunt him all his days!'

The warriors on the dune waited for Oué-mala's reaction and when he did not respond, they began to mock the Meelayginnee men, calling them cowards who were ruled by women, promising to cut them according to their natures if they survived the fight. But the crone tilted her head and asked loudly, 'Do you not know that each of you came bloody and squealing from between a woman's legs?' and then the jeering stopped for Wagarulepu possessed a power that transcended gender: the wisdom gained through age and experience. There was not one among them who had attained even half her years.

Umara was as surprised as any by his mother-in-law's boldness but he did not betray it by so much as the flicker of an eyelid. If Tealana had dared such audacity he would have beaten her but Wagarulepu was a respected elder and he knew she might have averted much grief. Therefore he smiled and inclined his head slightly in acknowledgement but his eyes did not leave Oué-mala's.

'Wagarulepu is right,' he said after a short, tense silence. 'What will be gained if we fight? Let us discuss the matter, then, if you still wish it, we'll leave. The Meelayginnee have no claim on this land: why should we quarrel?'

At this, Oué-mala's eyes narrowed and a spasm passed over his features, of anger or regret Touami thought. Then the Toogee leader sighed and as the tension of his muscles eased, he seemed to diminish. He waved the spearmen down and they reversed their weapons in token of peace and half-slid, half strode across the dune face. When Oué-mala squatted beside the rivulet and began to wash off the war-paint, they did likewise without complaint, changing instantly from figures of terror to ordinary men.

But as they made themselves comfortable around the central fire it became apparent that a dreadful change had overtaken the

Toogee. The sleek flesh and smooth skin that had formerly distinguished them seemed to have shrunk to their bones: they were gaunt and there was an odd tension about them, an almost febrile restlessness. Meelangana watched them carefully for it was as if something vital was missing from these men and they were no longer at ease with themselves, like people forsaken by their daemons.

Tealana and her daughters went to fetch bags of shellfish left from the morning's harvest from where they had been anchored near the mouth of the rivulet to keep fresh. No one spoke much until the food had been consumed and water brought by the women to the men in bark dippers: this was a special courtesy which acknowledged the Toogee warriors as honoured guests. Then Wagarulepu went to sit beside Meelangana (for as an elder she was privy to and instrumental in all the decisions affecting the hearth-group), while the other women went to their own fires to tend the children. Usually they would have danced to mark the start of corroboree but on this occasion everyone wanted to hear Ouémala's tale and so they feigned indifference while their ears strained to catch every word.

But the Toogee leader was silent. He sat cross-legged with his forearms resting on his knees and stared into the fire. His face had lost its fierceness and was grim and sad. His men sprawled around him and at first glance they appeared at ease but they also stared at the fire, the trees, the sky with unusual intensity, as if haunted by some horror they were trying, unsuccessfully, to forget.

Touami did not possess the patience of his father and grandfather. He looked surreptitiously from face to face and the impassivity of his kin, the reticence of the Toogee, exacerbated his anxiety for Toualena, his twin sister. And his fear required outlet in action since, as the youngest man there, it was not for him to speak first. He lunged to his feet and as the warriors started, he strode to the clear patch of flat ground near the rivulet, drew his hands towards his chest and tilted his head. These simple movements were the preliminary to a dance and the Toogee relaxed and settled down to watch.

Kangaroo was the totem of all Meelayginnee for the clan traced their lineage to Tarner, the first man. Now Touami danced the tale of his creation, his life among the other ancestral beings; his mutilation by Moinee, the Great Spirit; his healing by Droémadeener, the Kindly One; his awakening from kangaroo-spirit to man-spirit. And having observed the animals in his tale all his life, Touami emulated their movements with such accuracy and feeling that to his audience the story became real, as if they themselves had been transported to the Pygeewar and, at any moment, one of the ancestral beings might appear above the trees and leap onto the dune crest in a single bound. Indeed, so passionate was his performance that Umara soon joined in and Meelangana, his eyes bright and fierce, tapped two sticks together and chanted the ancient story with the others singing the refrains, swaying and clapping their hands in a kind of ecstasy.

At last the tale was done and the two dancers flung themselves down exhausted and panting. Twilight was gathering and the tide was in: the surge and backwash of the waves seemed loud in the sudden quiet around the fires.

'Our turn.' Tealana rose and went to help Wagarulepu to her feet, for the blood was running hot and high in the women after the strain of the afternoon. But Uné-mawa had been watching her father closely and she murmured something that made the elder pull back, shaking her head in warning. Then Tealana glanced towards the men and sat down again for Oué-mala had risen to his feet. His eyes swept the gathering with a look both terrible and compelling.

'*Karteila* does not live in the forest, nor *tarner* in the sea!' he cried, and the Meelayginnee glanced at one another in dismay, having no idea of what would follow. The Toogee leader sat down again but this in no way diminished the force of his presence which, like a spell, commanded the attention of all there.

'You all know how the boy, Noné, came to us and the tale he told,' he said at last. 'Even Groua, the wise-man could not out-do his story of the white-skinned, pale-eyed ones who had ensnared a great spirit in the shape of a white bird to bring them to Trouwerner. He himself, Noné said, had met the white ones and they had given him gifts. And when Groua saw the things, he coveted them, guessing they contained great power, magic which, used properly, would bring the strange ones to our shores. So instead of driving Noné out, we allowed him to stay, according to Groua's will. It is never good to upset a wise-man lest he turn his mind to curses.'

He paused and sighed heavily, his eyes bent on the red heart of the fire. 'Soon it was Groua who bore the talismans and Noné was his thing, a creature too debased to ever be a man. And the seasons passed. Groua often conducted ceremony to bring the white ones here, but they never came. At last he began to doubt the power of the things he had stolen and the tale of their origin, yet however much he was beaten, Noné would not change his story.'

Touami shuddered and his belly crawled clammily for Oué-mala's tone and the grim expressions of his companions boded ill for the rest of the tale. But Umara felt a kind of selfish relief for he was beginning to understand that by casting Niama out, he might have averted great evil from his own people.

'It was the hot season,' Oué-mala continued. 'The seals had whelped and were so thick upon the rocks that there was not room for all: they spilled over onto the beach and however many we killed (for we hunted according to custom, taking only what we needed), it seemed to make no difference to their numbers.'

His voice faltered while his eyes filled with tears. And Touami who, with a young man's arrogance, had always assumed weeping to be a sign of weakness, was amazed and a little daunted because the Toogee's leader's dignity was enhanced rather than diminished by this display of grief. Oué-mala made no move to wipe the tears away as they trailed down his hollow cheeks nor did he bow his head but, after a moment's silence, resumed speaking in a voice that occasionally shook with the intensity of the experiences he was reliving.

One day, he said, the women had gone to collect shellfish, leaving the men in camp. They teased Oué-mala's son, who was having trouble controlling his Meelayginnee wife: angry that she should cause him shame, he had gone onto the beach with the intention of punishing her. When she fled, he followed her. Over the far headland she led him and soon they were gone from view but they did not return.

'Aie, at first we thought they had found a place for love-making and would soon be back,' Oué-mala lamented, and Tealana wailed for this was the first she knew of her loss. 'But days passed and there was no sign of them. And when Groua did magic to find out what had happened, his dreaming made no sense save that he saw my son swallowed by the sea.'

The Toogee leader was rigid with the effort of keeping control: he stared at the trees to avoid seeing the stricken faces around the fire and a murmur of sympathy and grief arose from his comrades.

'Barely had we come to terms with that loss, for both were beloved by all, when a greater evil came upon us,' he continued. And then, although the main part of his audience was still stunned by the news of Toualena's disappearance, he told how doom had overtaken the Toogee and the animals upon which their very existence depended.

The sea was calm and the women were collecting shellfish from the rock-pools beneath the cliffs, he said, when a huge white bird glided into view. It was what Noné had spoken of and Groua had desired and the women ran back to camp with the tidings. Then the whole group hid in the dunes to watch. So majestic and unearthly was the sight, they were all afraid.

The creature's wings folded and the Toogee realized that what they had taken to be swarming insects were, as Noné had insisted, the figures of men, tiny with distance. They trussed the white bird with long ropes and lowered a small raft into the water. At this, Noné became frenzied with excitement and Groua had to knock him down to prevent him running onto the beach and betraying their presence: faced with the unknown, it was their instinct to remain concealed. Yet as men clambered into the raft and began to row they were reassured a little for their own craft, while made of bark and reeds, were paddled in similar fashion.

The tide was still low and so the strangers landed too far away for the Toogee to see the detail of their faces but their cumbersome body-coverings made them outlandish and their obvious excitement when they saw the seals made the watchers uneasy. Though the women's footprints were clearly marked in the sand, the strangers heeded them not: their attention was all on *karteila*. They pointed and shouted and some danced and skipped like grotesque, wayward children. Then they took from the boat a number of objects that looked like weapons: clubs and long sticks and things that gleamed and flashed with the brilliance of sunlight on water and began to walk purposefully towards the rocks.

What happened next, said Oué-mala in a voice that shook with emotion, was terrible beyond belief. The strangers approached to within spearthrow of the seals, moving carefully so as not to frighten them. When they were within spearthrow, some of the white ones stopped. They sighted along the sticks they carried, then sudden fire spat from the ends followed by a loud noise like the crack of thunder. Three of the closest cows jerked and heaved as if they had been speared: blood spouted onto the sand and the sound of laughter came to the appalled Toogee as the strangers moved in to club their victims' pups. The rest of the seals dived into the sea in a heaving, bawling mass.

That first day the white ones skinned and butchered the cows they had killed and put the hides and meat into the boat though they were wasteful and left much that could have been eaten to be washed away by the sea. But the pups they only skinned, leaving the raw carcasses where they lay. And then they boarded their craft and rowed back to the white bird which, the watchers now realized, was no living creature at all but a great raft with wings controlled by the strangers whom, the Toogee were now convinced, must be evil spirits in the shapes of men.

The women wailed all that night and the men danced, their bodies painted white to mourn and appease the spirits of *karteila*. And Groua did magic to make the strangers go away, smashing the talismans he had stolen, grinding the glass to dust between two stones and battering the brass button into a shapeless lump. Noné did not try to stop his master but he looked on with angry, bitter eyes and did not speak to the wise-man again.

Next morning the exhausted hearth-group slept late. They were roused by a series of sharp cracks like breaking branches. The sound came from the direction of the beach and they scrambled from their shelters to see what was happening. At length they stood in a line along the dune crest and the same emotion gripped them all: horror beyond anything they had felt before or imagined.

It was a bright, blustery day, the air clear, the sea sparkling in sunlight but the wise-man's efforts in the night had been futile. Two boats were drawn up on the sand and the white bird-craft rode close into shore so that the details of rigging lines and the ship's structure were clearly visible. But these the Toogee hardly noticed. Further down the beach the strangers had the seals surrounded. A small boat guarded the seaward side of the reef and though the craft was rocked and tossed by the waves, its crew were able to fire shots to frighten the seals into staying ashore. There they yelped and milled in terrified confusion while, working their way in from the edges, the rest of the sealers began their slaughter.

So practised were these men, they could kill and skin an adult seal in a matter of minutes. The exposed fat, marbled blue and red with blood vessels, gleamed in the sunshine so that the dead animals appeared ghost-like for they were not butchered but left to lie whole. And this added to the horror of the carnage because the seals that were still alive seemed incapable of recognising what was happening and sometimes a mother would nudge the clubbed and stripped body of her pup, so intent on identifying and reviving it that her own killer was able to approach unheeded.

The watching Toogee felt the deaths of *karteila* deep within themselves: it was as if something integral to their very being, their identity, was being torn out. Uncaring whether the white demons should hear, the women wept and wailed, flinging themselves down on the sand and rolling about in paroxysms of grief: frightened by the killing and its effect upon the adults, the children joined in. But the men stood rigid and silent, feeling a hardness encase the emptiness that had lodged in their hearts, the cold clear rage that may carry a man to feats beyond his strength. Their hands tightened on their spears as they breathed in the stench of seal-shit and sun-warmed blubber, waiting for the tension that was building in every fibre of their bodies to spill over into battle-frenzy.

Yet before they could yell their war-cries and run into the attack, the pariah, Noné, pre-empted them. He had sulked since the destruction of his talismans and, that morning, stayed behind in camp while they went to see what was happening. Now he pushed through the line and leapt down onto the beach before anyone could stop him, his face full of a strange, ecstatic joy, his right hand clenched so tightly that the knuckles stood out white. He carried no weapon, not even a stone and the Toogee watched in amazement as he ran towards the strangers. There was a fey wildness in his demeanour that filled them with dismay, as if he had been possessed by a malignant spirit.

So intent were the sealers on their work, they had not noticed the Toogee but as Noné ran across the beach he shouted to them. To him the words he used were sacred, the gift of the first white ones he had encountered, but to these they were unintelligible, for he had imposed the cadence of his own tongue on the French: 'Bon-jur-mess-yers-sa-va!' Startled by the clear, boyish voice coming so unexpectedly from behind, the sealers turned and, in doing so, saw the menacing, spear-bearing figures lined along the crest of the dunes. Then, as Noné, close enough to see the details of their faces, slowed, two of the strangers picked up weapons from where they had laid them on their coats to keep dry. They shouted at the young man, asking whether he had a sister and he, encouraged by their good humour, advanced, holding out his hand on which some small object gleamed dully in the bright sunshine.

There was a flash of fire, a crack like thunder, followed swiftly by another. The watching women screamed, more in surprise than understanding: only when Noné staggered did any of the Toogee realize he was hurt. He dropped to his knees and, almost languidly, pitched forward to lie face down in the sand, arms outflung. His legs twitched a little then he was still. Even from a distance his body had taken on the flaccid heavy look of death.

This time the women were silent and the men looked on, grim-faced and wondering as the killers strolled over to inspect the corpse. One nudged it with his foot then, apparently satisfied, they returned to their work overseeing the loading of the sealskins into the boats for the tide was on the flood. Once this was done they rowed back to the white bird-craft, leaving the dead to the sea.

'Ay – if that had been the end of it, the last we would see of them as Groua insisted that night, perhaps were could have made peace with *Karteila* and lived again,' Oué-mala said sadly. 'But it was not the end, it was only the beginning. The white demons came back day after day and when most of the seals were dead, their naked bodies left lying on the beach to reproach us, they looked landwards.'

'The bravest of us had, of course, gone to see what had happened to the Nothing: we owed that much to his spirit at least. And we found bloody holes in his chest as if he had been speared though the white ones had no spears, only the sticks that spat fire. Then we knew we had done right in holding back. Whoever they were, whatever their purpose, we lacked power to counter such magic. And so, uncertain what evil might be lurking in the dead to spring on us, we left him unburned and begged *Ebenook* to take him. And so it was: we did not see him again.'

He paused and sighed while the Meelayginnee looked askance at one another for this tale was more dreadful than any they had heard before. And Touami and Umara glanced uneasily towards the beach remembering the unnatural heaviness of the black pebble they had dug from the seal carcass, wondering if its evil had infected them.

'Eh, had it not been for our kinship with *karteila*, we would have gone far away,' Oué-mala continued. 'But though we were afraid to fight the strangers, we did not want to run: there were restless spirits enough in our land without angering them further. And so we stayed and every night Groua worked magic to bring death to the white demons and each morning they returned, ever ranging closer to our camp, and we could not prevent them.'

He lowered his gaze to stare unblinking into the fire and his face was anguished: all that saw it pitied him. But his voice, though low, did not waver as he told how one day the men returned from hunting to find the camp destroyed, Groua beaten senseless, the children crying. Only one woman remained, Oué-mala's mother who was older even than Wagarulepu: her face was battered and bruised and she sat wailing and scratching bloody furrows in the wrinkled flaps of her breasts. When she was calm enough to speak she told how the white demons had descended on the camp soon after the men left, how at first they seemed friendly and then, when they realized that Groua was the only man there, they beat him with clubs until he lay still and grabbed the women whom they raped with the savagery of *tarrabah*. After that they took them away: some of the young girls hardly able to walk.

The men had snatched up their spears and given chase but it was too late. Tracks on the beach marked where the strangers had drawn up their boats but these were long since gone. A distant gleam of white against the sea was all they saw: the bird-raft sailing away.

Stunned, defeated, the men returned to the ruined camp with dragging steps. The loss of the women was a disaster they could barely comprehend: beside it the deaths of *karteila* faded into insignificance. And yet, in their minds it was inconceivable that the two events could be unconnected: they had been punished for allowing the slaughter on the beach, therefore if they performed ceremony to acknowledge their failure, perhaps the women would come back. Groua, their wise-man lay in a deep trance, his body broken by the white demons, but he was not dead: this they took as a sign that they should wait. And so all that night the men howled and danced, their bodies covered in white clay which glimmered eerily in the starlight while the children shuddered and hid their eyes: they understood now why that colour stood for grief.

And, next morning, it seemed the ceremony had worked. One by one the women crept back into camp. They were quiet and subdued and their bodies bore the marks of violence: they were ashamed to meet the eyes of the men. Looking at them, the men felt their humiliation deep within themselves and their anger, having no outlet, turned in on itself. Some began to blame their wives and daughters for giving themselves too freely to the strangers and the women cringed and wept as more punishment was inflicted upon them.

The sun was high, clouds streaming on the wind when it was realized that two were still missing. One was an uninitiated girl, the other a young woman called Wyé-mawa. At once the group set off for the beach and this time everyone was armed, the men with spears and the women with waddies. Even the children bore stones to throw if any of the white demons was caught and the matriarch hobbled behind, muttering horrible curses upon her abusers. Only

Groua remained in camp for he was deep in dreaming. In fact he had sunk into a coma for he had been beaten so brutally about the head that his skull was fractured in several places.

When they reached the dunes a sudden reluctance took hold of the Toogee, a dread of what they would see beyond. But it was later than they had realized and the tide was sweeping in, driven by a westerly wind so that their faces were wetted with spume as they stood looking out. The surf rolled the seal carcasses back and forth and the stench of death rose with the salt smell of the ocean. Then they hesitated but Oué-mala shouted and ran down onto the beach where the waves were already eating at the base of the dunes.

The rest watched appalled as he caught hold of something brown and stick-like which flapped between two of the rolling seal carcasses. He pulled hard, his feet sinking into the wet sand, and the body of a young woman slowly emerged from the water. Her head lolled like a broken-necked bird's.

It was Wyé-mawa and the rest of the group hurried to help drag her above wave's reach. Water spilled from her mouth and nose and her body was swollen from its long immersion, the flesh soft and bruised-looking. But there were no holes like those made by the death-sticks and the hearth-group concluded that she must have drowned, most likely attempting to escape her abductors. Wailing, the women bore her back to camp while the men strung out along the dunes in search of the missing girl.

When they returned it was nearly nightfall and a thin, chill rain had begun to fall from clouds edged with a sunset like flame.

By then everyone was exhausted yet they burned and mourned the dead woman as was fitting while Groua lay unmoving in his trance. And in the morning they were calmer. Though the huts were still wrecked and the marks of their attackers' nails, teeth and fists were fresh upon their bodies, to the women it seemed somehow that the coming of the white demons had happened long ago: already the great bird-raft and the slaughter of *karteila* seemed remote, like a myth.

'Aye, after that,' said Oué-mala, 'we tried to continue our lives as before. Two more days we searched for the missing but in vain. Then, believing no good could come from lingering where such evil had come upon us, we moved further up the coast though it meant leaving our wise-man behind. He had not stirred since being struck down and his life was almost spent. Indeed it seemed that his daemon had already come for him: nothing we did could rouse him.

'It was our hope that having taken what they wanted, the white demons, *num* as we learned to call them, would never return. But as we travelled, we came upon other hearth-groups with the same tales to tell: *karteila* slaughtered and skinned; women raped and abducted, though the Nothing remained the only one slain outright: no-one else dared approach the white demons. And yet,' he hesitated and a thwarted, perplexed look settled on his features, 'and yet these were not the only hurts we were to suffer, woeful though they were. For soon many of our women and girls fell sick: foulness streamed from their vaginas, babes were still-born, and some grew lazy and dull-witted as if the spirits had been stolen from them. So thinking that the ancestors were still angry, we moved inland, though in our hearts we knew it would change nothing.'

Again he paused and sighed and this time his gaze swept his audience. Touami's face was full of anguish: the loss of his twin sister was like having part of himself torn out, leaving a raw, bleeding wound. And Uné-mawa sat with bowed head, keening softly while the rest, from respect, were looking not at the narrator but into the glowing heart of the fire.

'Life away from the sea was harder than we expected and the sickness of the women made it worse,' Oué-mala continued. 'Soon we were close to starving and as our weakness increased so did the hardship. And without a wise-man we were lost, adrift. It was as if the white ones had stolen something we had not even known existed: away from our own place our lives had no meaning. *Karteila* cannot live without ocean any more than *tarner* can dwell on the shore.

'So we returned and some hoped it had all been a bad dream, that we would find the reef thick with seals again and our lost ones would be waiting. But it was not so: the stripped carcasses were still piled on the shore, decaying under the ravages of wind and waves and what was left of our wise-man lay scattered about the camp: *tarrabah* and *kannenner* had been busy.

'We burned his remains as was fitting and built him a funeral-house but with the freeing of his spirit we remembered how it had all begun with the arrival of the Meelayginnee boy, how the wise-man had coveted the talismans he bore, the things he claimed had come from white-skinned strangers who had captured a giant bird. And it seemed to us then that those objects must have drawn *num* to Toogee lands after all, even as the wise-man had desired, though he had not intended the evil that had come with them.

'Not knowing what to do, we called a corroboree of all our people for often many find wisdom together. Three days and nights the meeting lasted but there was little joy. The deaths of *karteila* affected us all: even the children sensed the wrongness. And many folk were sick: there was little dancing and more painted their bodies with white clay in mourning than with *ballawiné*. As if to compound our woes, a great storm fell upon us, quenching the fires, and we knew then that our surmise was right and that the coming of the white demons was no chance event but part of a greater evil threatening the very foundation of our lives: the law formulated at the beginning of all things.'

The Toogee leader's voice trailed into silence and he seemed suddenly awkward and self-conscious as if reluctant to continue. Umara's eyes narrowed and the Meelayginnee exchanged uneasy glances. They had guessed what was coming: it had been inevitable from the moment Oué-mala had first spoken of the difference between *karteila* and *tarner*, but none was minded to make it easier for him.

'Long was the debate over what had happened and many agreed that the Meelayginnee boy was to blame: it was remarked also that your daughter had been the first to disappear and that she had enticed my son to follow her. And because of these things, it was argued that as our troubles had begun with the Meelayginnee, so also they might be ended by estranging ourselves from them. Even those of us who were loth to believe this could not deny the fear that gnawed our hearts: that the coming of the white demons heralded the demise of the Toogee, that the deaths of *karteila*, the sickness of our women were but the beginning and that by mixing our blood with a weaker, inland tribe, we would diminish from a fierce, strong people to a pitiful remnant until at last all memory of us, our lives, our stories, would be lost forever.'

Umara snorted angrily at this for it seemed grossly unfair that he and his people should be blamed for misfortunes of which they had neither first-hand knowledge nor control. But Meelangana listened with profound resignation. In this judgement of the Toogee he recognised the continuation of the tale begun by Ouniaga in the year of Touami's initiation; by recognising the evil in the talismans borne by the boy, Niama, and making him outcast, it seemed to the old man that he had set in motion the very events he had wanted to avoid.

Having finished, Oué-mala sat silent while his men shifted restlessly and muttered among themselves. It was the opinion of many Toogee that the balance of their world could only be restored by the shedding of Meelayginnee blood: respect for their leader alone had restrained them thus far. Ignorant of this (though mindful that if it came to a fight his group was hopelessly outnumbered), Umara gave a short, harsh laugh and said tightly: 'Is that it then? You're telling us to leave?'

'*Karteila* does not live in the forest, nor *tarner* in the sea,' Oué-mala repeated and his voice was hard and expressionless because he liked Umara and his kin and hated the necessity of what he was doing. 'Must we chase you away at spearpoint? This is our place: we do not want strangers here. Go!'

From the women came a stifled sob and at that sound a hard knot gathered beneath Touami's ribs. He rose to his feet and stared defiantly at his father-in-law. 'We too?' he demanded. 'Your own daughter and grandchildren? Are we no longer kin?'

A look of pain settled on the Toogee leader's face and he glanced to where Uné-mawa sat with her head bent over her little girl, rocking gently. As if aware of her father's gaze, she looked up and her eyes were filled with tears but she did not beg or plead: to her, his word was law.

'Even now another child grows in her belly,' Touami's voice shook and his fists clenched. 'Winter is almost upon us. You know how much harder life will be for her in Meelayginnee lands, for us all. Our peoples are bound to each other by more than words and gifts. Is your fear of the white demons so great that our agreements, our kinship mean nothing?'

'Quiet, my son.' Oué-mala's warriors had stiffened and Umara was anxious to promote calm, sensing their readiness for violence. 'It is for the elders to decide.' He looked again towards the Toogee leader and spread his hands in a gesture of conciliation. 'Will you give us time to discuss the matter?'

Oué-mala hesitated, torn between love for his daughter and the need to impose his authority: if he wavered he risked losing the esteem of his warriors. And, he reflected, these Meelayginnee were not suffering like his own people: they came and, whilst generous with their gifts and respectful of Toogee ways, they, like the white demons, took from the coast without belonging to it.

'Une-mawa must make her own choice,' he said at last, grimly. 'She may stay here with her own kind and take a new husband. Then, if the child in her belly lives, it will be sent to you for initiation for it is not of our skin. Her other children must go now, with the rest of you. There is nothing to discuss.'

'Aiee . . .' The young woman looked with anguish from her father to her husband and rolled her head from side to side like a wounded animal. Discomfited by her distress, the little girl scrambled from her lap and crawled to Wagarulepu who hugged her close.

'No!' Touami looked for his spear but it had been stacked with the other weapons behind one of the shelters. In his frustration he stamped his foot and the muscles stood taut beneath his skin so that he seemed almost to swell with rage. 'It's not fair!'

'Eh, a child is talking.' Meelangana reached out to touch the young man's thigh. His voice was low and compassionate yet firm. 'How will it help if these Toogee turn from words to spears? They have suffered greatly but unless Oué-mala's heart is made of stone, he will yearn to see his daughter and grandchildren again: who else will tell his tale when his bones are ash? One day he will welcome us back and all will be as it was before the white demons came. You'll see.'

There was much wisdom in these words and Umara grunted his agreement: beneath his anger he felt great sympathy for the Toogee leader. But Touami stood tense and still. The contempt and scorn of the warriors seemed to press upon him as a palpable force and though he understood the sense of his grandfather's speech, he longed to answer that silent challenge. But then the matriarch, Wagarulepu, hawked loudly and spat a great gob of phlegm into the fire. In her broad, age-seamed face her eyes gleamed like black pebbles.

'Yah! It's a foolish man who comes between a mother and her children,' she mocked. 'What kind of choice is that to lay upon a young woman? Have you not already seen the evils that may follow when children grow up bereft of kin and place, rootless, unsure whose skin they belong to? Do not forget: he whom you called Nothing was such a one!'

Oué-mala stared and his men muttered ominously together but the old woman was undaunted and returned his gaze without flinching. Yet after a moment the Toogee leader tilted his head dismissively and looked instead at Umara.

'It makes no difference,' he said sternly. 'You Meelayginnee are no longer welcome here. And if Uné-mawa forsakes those who gave her birth, then she is no longer one of us. That is final.'

'Aue . . .' Umara shook his head as if in disbelief but he did not argue. The warriors were watching him and the other Meelayginnee with a kind of grim anticipation. A choking sob came from Uné-mawa's throat and her father glanced in her direction then immediately looked away.

'Very well then,' Meelangana said at last, his voice grating in the sudden, tense silence. 'But from henceforth no Toogee may tread Meelayginnee land unless upon the Ochre Trail. Stray but a spearthrow from the track and we shall know of it.'

He stretched his right hand towards Oué-mala, the fingers pointing straight at the Toogee leader in a gesture of defiance and renunciation. Then, with impressive dignity, he stood up, turned his back on the warriors and paced slowly to his shelter which he entered without looking back.

'Meelangana speaks for us all,' Umara said resignedly. There was sorrow and pity in his eyes as he looked upon Oué-mala. 'We have no wish to fight but from now on we are no longer kin and if you venture into our forests we will watch you as the hawk-owl watches the mouse.'

'So be it.' Oué-mala rose to his feet. His gaze lingered long on the figure of his daughter who had gathered both children to her and sat with head bent over them. Then he turned abruptly, barked a command to his men. They collected their spears and he led them away along the narrow path beside the rivulet, heading towards the beach.

'How could they?' When the Toogee were out of sight, Touami strode to where Uné-mawa huddled weeping over the children. The little boy stared at him with wide accusing eyes so Touami crouched and pulled him close. Although the child resisted at first, he was reassured by the touch and smell of his father and was soon tugging at the long, greasy hanks of Touami's hair.

'He will relent,' the young man murmured, holding the little boy firmly while stroking his wife's head in an effort to comfort her. 'When the white demons do not return he will rue his hardness. He is not a bad man.'

The two remained together until Uné-mawa's grief was spent but the others began to dismantle the camp although the light was already failing. Wagarulepu wanted to wait until dawn but both Umara and Meelangana argued that while Oué-mala was perhaps prepared to be lenient, his men were spoiling for a fight and to delay would give them the excuse they wanted. There was no need to point out that against so many the Meelayginnee men stood no chance: the old woman shrugged and went grumbling away to gather her possessions.

The drizzle had turned to rain by the time they were ready to leave. The little boy was tired and reluctant but Uné-mawa was in no mood to accommodate his tantrums and dragged him roughly to his feet. She was bowed against the forehead-strap of the woven bag she bore and her movements were uncharacteristically slow and awkward. The weight of the child in her womb seemed to drag upon her like a stone.

'Eh, come on girl.' Wagarulepu lifted Cottruluttyé and it was unclear whether she was addressing her daughter-in-law or the child. 'Tomorrow the sun will rise again, on Toogee and

Meelayginnee both.'

'Come then.' Umara cast a last look round the camp. The rain-darkened dune reared ominously behind and steam rose hissing from the hearths: the place already looked desolate. He blew on the firestick in his hand until it glowed, then led the way into the scrub in the opposite direction to that taken by the Toogee. The women and children followed and Touami and Meelangana brought up the rear, walking warily with their spears ready. Gradually the roar of surf was swallowed by the rush of the wind through trees: they passed like shadows into the forest.

8. The Ochre Trail.

(Southern Tasmania, 1805).

The Ochre Trail ran through Trouwerner like a great artery. In some places it was straight as a spear-shaft; in steep terrain it wound so intricately that the first and last of a travelling hearth-group could almost touch fingers as they passed. Being sacred, the path was always kept clear of fallen branches, undergrowth, even rockfalls: according to myth, its course had remained unchanged since the Pygeewar. And, by tradition, those who travelled upon it were immune from attack even though they might pass through hostile territory.

The trail led to prime sources of earth-blood, *ballawiné*, the red pigment which symbolised the life-force connecting all that existed. Without *ballawiné* ceremonies would be meaningless; stories would lose their potency; children could never be initiated or the dead appeased: the land and its people would be estranged, leaving the tribes rootless and adrift. And so, every year, representatives of each clan were chosen to travel on the Ochre Trail and bring back enough to last their people five seasons.

Although the journey was long and arduous (and the time taken lengthened if another group was already at the quarry since only one clan was permitted entry at a time), there was fierce competition to be chosen. Sometimes the young men wrestled for the honour while in years when blood ran less high, the elders would decide after lengthy debate. But once made, the choice was irrevocable and the onus was upon the chosen and their hearth-group to complete the task ere winter so there was no danger of the precious *ballawiné* running out before they returned.

It was four winters after being exiled from Toogee lands that Touami was picked for the Ochre Trail. His hearth-group had suffered much during that time for news travelled swiftly along the coast and the Nuenone had also turned hostile, forcing them to stay in their own territory, land already hunted over during the warmer seasons. Meelangana, his grandfather, had become a bent old man, embittered by his decrepitude, blaming the white demons for all the group's misfortunes. When Uné-mawa's third babe was stillborn, he maintained it was part of the same evil. And he foretold that these events were only the beginning, that the very fabric of their world, the law which governed all things, was in danger and that if the evil were not stopped, Trouwerner would be destroyed.

Umara and the matriarch, Wagarulepu, tried to reassure the old man that in time the proper order of things would be restored, while Touami, now a man in the prime of his strength, argued that the *ballawiné* they brought back from the north would exorcise the badness in the south. But Meelangana would not be comforted, pointing out that there would have been no need to travel so far had the Toogee remained their friends for they were guardians of a prime source of *ballawiné* on the coast which the Meelayginnee had often quarried in the past. And when the others looked doubtful, he jerked his head towards Uné-mawa who had become thin and strained-looking since the loss of the babe, saying: 'Ask her if *num* are to be feared,' and to that they had no reply.

Meelangana's forebodings were, to some extent, substantiated by the stories of others who had encountered the strangers, for the white demons had not gone away. Their bird-rafts had been seen far up the Big River and they had camped upon its banks, hacking down trees and building huts on the cleared land. There were rumours of a great slaughter of Paradarerme people on the far side of the Big River: they had driven kangaroo into a cove as they had for generations and found *num* living there. And there were accounts of creatures outlandish as something made up to amuse or frighten children: four-legged grazers which strode on feet instead of hopping (of these there were two kinds, a large horned beast which mooed and a smaller, timid kind with fur like grey moss), and lean quick animals akin to *kannenner*. But strangest of all were the *num* themselves for instead of eating the alien grass-eaters, they preferred to go into the forest though their bush-craft was so inept that they killed little with their death-sticks and relied on the fierce creatures, which were swift enough to bring down a fleeing wallaby, to do their hunting for them.

Remembering the carnage on the beach, the doom that had overtaken the Toogee, Umara and his kin heard these tales with deep foreboding. One day, when Uné-mawa tried to persuade Touami to forsake the Ochre Trail and hide deep in the mountains, he did not argue but took her a little way into the bush where there was a secluded hollow, filled with leaves. Here he made love to her with unusual violence, leaving her bruised and bewildered. It was as if he were trying to assert himself in a world made suddenly uncertain and his intensity frightened her more than the rumours: she realized then that he also was afraid. And yet he would not be dissuaded from his purpose.

It was the storm season between summer and winter and lightning raked the sky as the group of five adults and four children set off upon the Trail. Initially Umara had wanted Meelangana and Wagarulepu to stay behind but they argued that since the pace of the group would be held to the children's, two elders would not delay them. And secretly Umara and Touami were pleased for they knew in their hearts that if half the rumours about the white destroyers were true, the wisdom of the old ones might prove invaluable.

The first days of the journey were uneventful. The path was clear before them, wending its way from valley to valley: whether in dense forest or marshy meadows it had been well kempt though they saw no other people. Game was plentiful and, as was their wont, they did not hurry. But on the fourth day they came upon a deserted camp, the windbreaks smashed and spears left lying on the ground as if the inhabitants had fled in sudden panic. Then all their fears returned: too much did the scene remind them of what had befallen the Toogee.

The wrecked camp was close to the trail and that night, as they sat around their fire, the group debated what to do. To Meelangana it seemed plain that the white demons were responsible for the destruction and once they found the open track they were bound to follow it. As the group had not yet encountered them, they must be ahead: it was inevitable that one day they would meet.

Thunder muttered in the hills and a few drops of rain splattered through the canopy and hissed in the fire as the rest considered the old man's words. They looked uneasily into the sky but there was no comfort to be had from the gathering clouds and growing darkness. At last Umara got to his feet. His face was grave and stern as he gazed upon his hearth-group.

'We are on the Ochre Trail,' he said. 'Touami and I at least must go on: without *ballawiné* there is no hope of countering the white ones' magic. But the rest should return to Meelayginnee country. We cannot fight these *num* and their death-sticks but we can evade them and two may travel more swiftly than many, especially when there are young ones to carry.'

At this, a wail escaped Tealana for she knew her husband was proud and strong and this speech seemed an admission of weakness. But the elders nodded sagely though Meelangana was assailed by a secret dread that if his son and grandson parted from the group, he would never see them again. And Uné-mawa sat tight-lipped with anxiety as she looked upon Touami, the husband for whom she had been exiled from her own people. Their children clung to her, sensing her dismay.

'Eh, don't worry: we'll return before the cold comes,' Touami said. 'And we'll travel easier knowing you are safe. Whatever these white demons do, they won't catch us!'

He spoke lightly, intending reassurance but at that moment an unearthly screeching rent the air as a flock of black cockatoos passed overhead. Meelangana shuddered and to avert the evil portent his right hand strayed to the little bag that hung at his breast.

'*Menuggana's* wings spread darkness across the sky but *darwalla* cocked his head and raised his tail and his song lent courage to Sun and Night fled at his rising,' Wagarulepu murmured, recalling a tale designed to comfort those scared by night-time shadows. 'So then, it is decided. Let us sleep well tonight, then we'll part. The more we delay, the greater the chance of meeting *num*. Yah! - the sooner the setting off, the sooner comes journey's end.'

Their parting next morning was accompanied with much wailing from the older women though Uné-mawa remained silent.

She watched Touami intently as he checked his spears and folded bark into tight wads for firesticks. There was an avid hunger in her eyes as if she wanted to imprint his very being into her memory and when the children pestered her she pushed them roughly away. Only when Wagarulepu scolded her for her laziness did she rise and gather her possessions: by that time the rest were ready to leave. Yet Umara and Touami, torn between their eagerness to start the journey and reluctance to leave their wives and children, lingered. In the end it was Meelangana who goaded them into action.

'Do you want the white demons to show you the way?' he demanded, his anxiety finding expression in anger. 'Go, then we can return to our own lands. What are you waiting for?'

'Are those the best words you can find for your son and grandson?' Umara asked and he touched Tealana briefly on the head in farewell, hefted his spear bundle onto his shoulder and strode away towards the trail without a backward glance. Touami crouched to light a firestick and, once satisfied it would not go out, followed but he could not avoid seeing Uné-mawa's expression as he rose. Her gaze struck him to the core and long after he must have passed from view he thought to feel her eyes bore into him, anguished and accusing. Yet like his father, he did not look back.

Without the others, the two men travelled fast though they walked warily, too apprehensive to relax their guard. Their caution was well-founded: before long they came across strange footprints. Most were the rough size and shape of a man's save that they lacked toes; these were intermingled with marks akin to *kannenner's* only longer and narrower. They led along the path to a watering place and here the tracks were clear, deeply incised in the mud. Inside some of them and scattered on the bank were fragments of scallop shells.

Touami watched anxiously as his father crouched to look though it was clear the shells had been broken deliberately. He knew no *parner* could be responsible: the shells were a gift from travellers on the sacred path to the stream which quenched their thirst. Whoever had done this was ignorant of the law, the very nature of things: it was desecration no less than the massive scale of slaughter on the Toogee beach. It was a simple matter to conclude that the white demons were to blame.

'Eh, what are they?' Umara murmured and the resignation of his tone shook Touami more than any angry outburst. 'What purpose is there in this?'

The young man did not answer for there seemed nothing to say. He shifted uneasily from foot to foot and tugged at his foreskin. At length Umara rose and sighed. '*Ballawiné*,' he muttered and he spoke not for his son's benefit but to himself: he gritted his teeth and waded across the creek and in his carriage and the set of his head there was defiance.

Rarely had Touami been so proud of his father as on that day for Umara neither hesitated nor faltered but kept resolutely to the trail even though, as they progressed, there were more signs that *num* had passed that way: vegetation hacked down to widen the path; strange-smelling ordure; blood and entrails where a wallaby had been killed. And always the tracks of the white ones were intermingled with those of the *kannenner*-like creature. This perplexed the two Meelayginnee greatly for they could not imagine any relationship between man and animal save that of hunter and prey unless the daemons of *num* walked upon the earth beside them, a prospect too terrible to contemplate.

In the late afternoon they veered a little way off the path to make camp for the night. Touami was kindling a fire and Umara gathering boughs for a wind-break when a faint barking, not unlike that of seals, echoed between the trees. Both men froze to listen and even the birds fell silent as if they also recognised the unnaturalness of such a sound in the forest.

'What is it?' Touami spoke more for reassurance than because he expected an answer: the outlandishness of hearing *karteilas'* voices so far from the sea was deeply disturbing.

Umara shrugged but the dismissiveness of the gesture was belied by his frown. 'Who knows? Perhaps *tarrabah* speaks differently in this part of the world: I have never been here before. Anyway, it's a long way off.'

They continued making camp but each was listening to the noise which continued spasmodically until the sun had almost set. For a meal it had been their intention to wait in ambush at a watering place but now, Umara grumbled, the animals would be even more wary than usual. But as it happened they were lucky: an echidna came bumbling towards them as they made their way to the creek. They clubbed it to death and carried it triumphantly back to the camp where they buried it in the ashes to cook. Such good fortune when they had least expected it heartened them both and as twilight spread beneath the trees and the smells of charring hair and roasting flesh mingled with the woodsmoke, they felt more at ease than at any time since discovering the ruined camp. As the darkness deepened and the first stars appeared they knew every sight or sound so intimately it was as if they, the forest and the night were a single entity. Indeed, so secure did they feel and so sated were they with echidna meat, they did not think to keep watch and soon fell asleep side by side in the scant shelter of the bark wind-break.

When they woke at dawn the two Meelayginnee were even more confident that the danger had passed. Both had slept well though Touami had woken once to the sound of stealthy footsteps: *tarrabah* on the prowl for an easy meal, having smelt fresh blood. But what remained of the echidna had been cached safely in the fork of a tree and the scavenger soon gave up for the scents of men and fire were strong and fear overcame its hunger. After that, nothing disturbed the young man's slumber save that he dreamt of Uné-mawa walking alone through the forest and woke with a lingering sense of loss and longing.

They ate as much meat as they could stomach, not knowing when the next meal would come. Umara watched his son carefully but he was in too good a humour to question Touami's troubled look which, in any case, faded as the light grew. No unusual sounds disturbed the usual forest hum of insects and birdsong and they were ready to rejoin the trail by the time the sun rose clear of the hills. It was a still, bright day and without women and children to impede them they looked forward to making swift progress.

It was mid-morning when they reached a lightly forested area of flat ground. Water glinted ahead and the smell of marsh was heavy in the air. Being thirsty, they hurried forward and then there was an outcry that stopped both in their tracks.

It was a kind of strangled yelping, frenzied, double-voiced and it varied in tone and volume so that it was impossible to tell whence it came. The two exchanged dismayed glances and Umara shifted his firestick from his right hand to his left then jerked his head at Touami who was carrying the spears. As he handed his father a weapon, Touami was assailed by a dread more powerful than he had ever felt before, even on the beach where he had discovered the murdered seals.

'Whatever comes,' Umara whispered hoarsely, 'make sure you escape. There is no shame in running from evil spirits. The tale of this thing must be told.'

The young man swallowed hard. He knew that in part it was Umara's own immortality, his place in Meelayginnee story, his father was thinking of, nor was it his, the son's, place to dissuade him. He gripped his spear tightly and icy sweat bathed him as he stared along the trail. The path skirted the marsh and plunged into denser forest through what now seemed like a dark tunnel, the maw of some terrible, unknown beast.

As they listened, the two discerned what sounded like men's voices mingled with the yelps. The noise subsided, then a howl shuddered through the air. Umara and Touami waited.

Nothing happened.

A white cockatoo screeched overhead and the two started and exchanged shame-faced glances. They were so tense, every breath was deliberate and beneath their lungs each felt his heart pounding.

They waited. A bee laden with pollen droned past; a flock of wrens fluttered and twittered in the scrub. There was no movement along the trail save the swaying of shadows as a slight breeze moved through the trees.

'Yah! It's gone,' Touami said at last. He stuck his spear-butt on the ground and used the weapon as a prop to lean on, letting his muscles slowly relax. But Umara frowned. He was staring down the line of the trail as if he expected the coming of Raegeowrapper or Rowra, the evil ones which haunted Meelayginnee myth.

'Raven flew on high and saw the Cunning One approach but foolish Fan-tail was dancing before his betrothed and did not heed the warning,' he said, referring to a fable beloved of children. 'If *karteila* has come to live in the forest, who knows what dangers lie ahead?'

'We are on the Ochre Trail,' Touami, stung by the reference to his daemon (an insult Umara had not intended), spoke with the recklessness of pride. 'What harm can befall us on the sacred path? Will you wait here all day or shall we seek the *ballawiné* we were sent for?'

Umara did not answer at once but he lowered his spear and breathed upon the firestick in his left hand until the end glowed red. His countenance was impassive but his anger was betrayed by the hardness of his muscles and the slight narrowing of his eyes.

'*Karteila* cannot live in the forest, so Oué-mala said, yet we have heard them,' he replied stubbornly. 'Perhaps the power has gone out of the land and the spirits have fled before the white demons.'

'You speak like an old woman!' Touami retorted. 'Will you then go back to the elders of all the Meelayginnee and say that because of your faintheartedness they must do without *ballawiné*: that no young people can be initiated, no dead ones given to the earth, no ceremony conducted: do you think the forest will still be bountiful, our women fertile? Is that how you want to be remembered: as the most cowardly of all *parner*, the man who heard a strange sound and fled the Ochre Trail like a joey running to its mother's pouch? Even the children will point at you and laugh!'

'A *narrar* is talking!' The flash of Umara's anger was so sudden, his expression so terrible that Touami took an involuntary step back. 'Who spoke of giving up? Go on then: rush down the trail spear in hand and perhaps all will be well. But if the white demons and their spirit-helpers are waiting, what happens then? They have magic sticks that spit death and they lust to kill like Rowra. We are men, children of Tarner: we will not run blindly into a trap like driven game. Do as you want, Touami: you are no longer a little boy. But for me, I shall take the path of caution, walk not upon the trail but beside it. If *num* are there I will pass them like a shadow and they will never know they have been tricked.'

'Eh . . .' Before his father's sagacity Touami was overcome by shame. He bowed his head like a guilty child and the spear dangled loosely from his hand. And the sight of his son brought from youthful pride to abasement dissolved Umara's ire in a rare rush of affection. Transferring the firestick to his spear-hand, he took Touami in a quick, hard embrace that surprised them both by its spontaneity and passion. Embarrassed, Umara soon pulled away but not before Touami had time to savour the gesture.

'Come then.' Umara checked the firestick was still alight, jerked his head and made his way into the scrub. Within a few paces they were all but invisible from the trail.

It was well they had taken cover for within moments the sound of voices came from further up the path. The two crouched instinctively and froze, waiting and watching the small section of the trail visible through the scrub. The voices grew louder, speaking a tongue so different from their own it barely sounded like human speech. And mixed with it was something neither Meelayginnee could identify: the chink of metal against metal for when travelling, the kangaroo-hunters' dogs were kept on chains to prevent them running off after bush-hens and pademelons.

'Aiee!' Touami's breath hissed between his teeth and his hand tightened convulsively on the slender spear-shaft. Even Oué-mala's tale had left them unprepared for their first sight of *num*. Clad in motley clothing of faded cloth and kangaroo skins, their feet shod in heavy boots, the white men appeared clumsy yet terrible. They were five in number and walked carelessly as if the forest was their domain and they had nothing to fear from it.

The first was tall, with a shaggy beard and hair that hung to his shoulders. He was unencumbered by any load and the two aborigines identified him instantly as the leader. Behind him walked a short man whose flesh hung loosely from the bones of his face: he was shaven like a woman. On his back a large bundle was tied and balanced against his shoulders he carried two muskets, the metal parts of which shone in the sun. These things, Touami guessed, were the dreaded death-sticks and he was amazed at the casualness with which objects of such power were borne.

Close on this man's heels came two brown and white dogs. They were lean and rough-coated, lurcher-like in build only a little heavier. Their tongues lolled between their teeth and their eyes were bright for they were alert to every sound and movement that might betray the presence of new quarry. Long chains led from their necks to the third man who seemed sick or exhausted for he stumbled as he walked and his head was downcast: the chains had been fastened round his waist lest he fail to keep hold. Upon his back a great number of kangaroo skins had been fastened and the stench of putrefaction was strong about him. Last came a pair walking one behind the other, a pole slung between them from which several gutted kangaroos hung, their tails looped up behind to prevent them dragging on the ground. Flies swarmed around the carcasses and the uncured hides so that the men flapped their hands constantly and cursed.

Alone, the men would have passed Umara and Touami by for they walked without any particular awareness of their surroundings. But a slight breeze arose and the dogs caught their scent. They raised their heads, ears pricked, and launched themselves towards their quarry for while it was the express wish of the Governor that natives should be treated with respect, it had become a sport among kangaroo hunters to set their hounds after any aborigine they chanced to meet.

There was pandemonium as the chains snapped tight, jerking the tether-man to his knees. The hounds, brought up short, bayed and yelped, leaping wildly as they struggled to free themselves while the men scrambled to haul them back, yelling as the dogs writhed and snapped in a frenzy of excitement.

Touami and Umara waited no longer. Terrified by the noise and ferocity of the strange animals, they broke cover and ran, crashing recklessly through the undergrowth, clutching their spears and the firestick with desperate strength. Only when the yelping had died down behind did they slacken pace.

'They're not following.' At last Touami stopped and turned to face back the way they had come. He was trembling in the aftermath of terror. Gradually the usual quiet of the forest settled around them and they relaxed a little though they still started at every cracking twig and sharp bird call. Umara squatted, leaning on his spear for balance. Sweat made runnels in the dust and ingrained charcoal on his skin and his breathing was quick and harsh.

'Are you sure?' The elder's voice was so low as to be barely audible. 'What are they, Touami? Those creatures: they are not from

Trouwerner. And the white demons: they walk along the Ochre Trail as if they, not we, belong here. How can this be? Something is happening I do not understand.'

Touami did not answer at once. There was a note of bewilderment and fear in his father's tone he had not heard before and it shook him to the core. Never had he known Umara to be afraid, much less admit it, and the fact that *num* were responsible made him hate them all the more.

'Touami?' Worried by the young man's prolonged silence, Umara rose stiffly to his feet. His sweat had cooled and he shivered as he put out a hand to touch his son's shoulder.

'They are not real people,' Touami said. 'They must be made to leave before they destroy everything. I think they are without daemons. They have no respect.'

Umara was not overly superstitious but at these words the chill that had come upon him seemed to sink through his flesh to freeze his blood. Of all the tales of the Meelayginnee those of the Lost, men and women who, through their own misfortune or the cunning of evil spirits, had been forsaken by their daemons, were most terrible to him. While they lived, such people were incomplete, adrift, lacking that vital part of themselves encapsulated in the totem spirit that should have helped and guided them and when they died, they were doomed to wander forever between being and non-being. Though their flesh might decay and be accepted by the earth, their spirits could never attain peace and that, to Umara, was the worse fate of all. He looked searchingly into his son's face and saw that while his own horror was reflected there, Touami had mastered his fear.

'We must follow them.' The young man's voice was fierce. 'Their evil must not be allowed to spread. But without knowing what they are, we cannot fight them.'

Before such passion Umara felt suddenly impotent and old. 'The *ballawiné* . . .' he protested weakly.

'Will you set off again knowing they are on the path between us and our kin?' Touami asked. 'Let us make sure of their purpose first. There is time enough to reach the quarries and return before the cold begins.'

Umara shook his head from side to side like a wounded animal. 'But the fanged ones?'

'The forest will shelter us,' Touami replied impatiently. 'This time we'll be more careful. They will never know we are there. Or has the heart shrunk within you at the mere sight of them?'

There was challenge in his tone and Umara sighed, knowing argument would be fruitless. 'Maybe,' he said quietly. 'Yet there is truth in what you say. We must know more of these *num* and their magic before we can decide how best to deal with them.'

Unencumbered as they were, the two moved more swiftly through the forest than the strangers did upon the trail. It was not long before the chink of metal came to their ears, followed by the tread of shod feet on the beaten earth of the path. A light breeze was blowing from the hills, making the leaves rustle, and this time they were careful to stay downwind.

The success of this strategy (for the dogs, whilst alert, were not aware of them), did much to reassure Umara and Touami that these were animals of flesh and blood rather than bloodthirsty spirits. And though the forest was drier and more open than the rainforest of Meelayginnee territory, there was enough cover to conceal them. This in itself gave them confidence for it seemed to justify their belief that no harm could befall them while they were on their quest. To them the Ochre Trail was more then a trackway, it was a state of mind, and the steadfastness of their purpose was as integral to it as the physical path.

It was late afternoon before the *num* stopped on the banks of a creek close to where the two Meelayginnee had spent the previous night. Touami pulled his father down into a slight hollow from which they could watch without being seen. So complete was their stillness and self-effacement it was as if they possessed the power of invisibility. If any of the hunters had looked in their direction, their eyes would have passed over the two for the streaks of dirt and charcoal on their skin assimilated perfectly with the patterns of light and shade cast by the trees.

This was not the first trip the party had made into the bush and they set about making camp with a quiet efficiency like that of

Meelayginnee women, each going about their task without need for speech. The dogs were tethered on one side of the camp while the pole from which the meat hung was wedged high between two trees, beyond reach of scavengers. The bearded leader undid one of the packs and took out a tin can for boiling water then set about kindling a fire from the wood gathered by two of the others (one of these passed within touching distance of Touami but did not see him). A fourth cut the larger branches with a small hatchet while the other spread out kangaroo skins and blankets to make beds. The sharp sound of the hatchet seemed to ring in the skulls of the watchers but their attention was focused on the leader who, having struck sparks into a little mound of dry duff, was nurturing the flame by sheltering it with his hands and blowing gently.

'Aue.' A faint groan escaped Umara as the kindling caught and smoke and flame spiralled into the air. The magic of the death-sticks (which had been laid carefully on one of the beds) was one thing, this making of fire was a different order of power. Fire was the gift of *Nowhummer* and therefore sacred: it seemed to Umara that any man who possessed the ability to create it on his own would forget his place in the order of things, the need for respect within the law. At last he began to understand the nature of the threat not only to him and his people but everything that was Trouwerner.

'We must leave!' His voice hissed no louder than the soft soughing of leaves overhead but it was enough to rouse the dogs. They had been lying flat on their sides, dozing in the late afternoon sunshine but now raised their heads to snuff the air and there was tension in every line of their bodies.

'No, wait!' Touami breathed. He laid a restraining hand on his father's shoulder, sensing that if they moved now, the dogs would alert *num* to their presence. They watched as the men gathered round the fire. A can of water had been set in the centre of the blaze and the two observed the preliminaries to tea-making, the setting out of tin mugs and undoing of little bags of tea and sugar, the careful shaking out of the black and brown powders into the steaming water, with profound apprehension, wondering what kind of ceremony would follow.

Once the tea was boiling, the shaven man lifted the can from the fire with a stick and poured the contents into the mugs. While he was thus occupied, the others settled themselves comfortably on their beds and took clay pipes and leather tobacco pouches from beneath their coats. But their leader, who had been first to take out his pipe, could not find his tobacco: he got to his feet, delved within the layers of his clothing and patted his legs though his trousers lacked pockets. Then he began to accuse the others of stealing his pouch, his voice loud and angry, his face reddening and his fists clenching as his fury rose.

It was obvious that the rest feared this man because they tried to mollify him, protesting their innocence and offering their own tobacco. When it became clear that no amount of blustering or force would restore the missing pouch, he sat down again, took a generous pinch from each of the others' and began to smoke in moody silence, his companions exchanging relieved glances that he had been so quickly appeased.

From their hiding place, Touami and Umara watched these proceedings with great consternation. For a man to breathe out smoke as if it were an ordinary and pleasurable activity was something so far beyond their experience they did not know what to make of it. As the men relaxed and drank their tea between puffing upon their pipes, the dogs also settled but though their eyes were half-closed, their ears were cocked.

'Come on!' Umara slowly raised himself into the half-crouching stance of a hunter and began to back out of the hollow, spear in one hand, the precious firestick in the other. His fear had intensified with every passing moment and it seemed to him that the longer they stayed the more certain the chance of being seen. But Touami, held by a kind of dreadful fascination, did not respond.

'Touami!' Umara's lips were dry. He licked them and tasted the acrid sweetness of tobacco-smoke in the air: the gorge rose in his throat. Then he was sure that despite the seeming lack of ceremony, this ritual of breathing smoke was a kind of *num* magic and Touami had been ensnared by it.

'*Darwalla!*' To call a person by their daemon was the only way Umara knew to counter an evil spell: he hissed the word as loudly as he dared. At last Touami raised himself and began to turn.

But perhaps because he was annoyed at being disturbed, Touami moved carelessly. His elbow brushed a hanging branch. He felt Umara grasp his arm and pull him out of the hollow as the dogs sprang to their feet then leapt against their chains, barking wildly.

The two ran. They knew now that the Ochre Trail would not protect them: they pounded along winding wallaby paths with no thought but to get away. Behind them they heard shouting and yelping as before but then the noise of the dogs changed tone as they were released. They were trained for hunting: they gave tongue when they found the scent of their quarry, and set off in pursuit.

Terror lent Umara and Touami strength. They flung away spear-bundle and firestick, keeping one spear each, and ran as fast as was possible in such rough terrain. By instinct they followed one another, taking turns to lead, crashing through the low scrub and all the while the baying grew louder. Soon they could hear the rapid beat of pursuing feet and hoarse panting breath. The dogs were less than a spearthrow behind.

As he ran, Touami's panic ebbed: with death on his heels his mind grew clear and cold. He looked for a tree to climb but he could hear men's voices in the distance and guessed that temporary escape from the fanged demons would only mean death or capture by the white ones: up a tree, he and his father would be trapped like possums. The only hope was to stand and face the beasts, to slay them and run again for from what he had seen so far, *num* alone were easily eluded.

Touami was in front and he never forgot his father's expression when he stopped, turning round to block the path so that Umara almost crashed into him. The elder was gasping for breath, his face and body glistened with sweat and he looked at his son with appalled, bulging, bloodshot eyes.

'Kill them!' Touami gasped and there was no time for more: even as Umara turned, the dogs were upon him. They leapt for his throat so ferociously he dropped his spear and fell backwards. In the confusion of snapping teeth and writhing bodies which followed, Touami, who had remained on his feet, managed to spear one dog straight through the chest.

The hound gave a jerk which snapped the light weapon, and fell dead: the point had pierced its heart. But the other was on top of Umara, its feet raking bloody furrows across his naked torso as it lunged for his face and throat. He managed to fasten one hand about its neck while with the fingers of the other he jabbed frantically at the frenzied, white-rimmed eyes but it shook free and its jaws closed on his right arm just above the elbow, puncturing skin and flesh, severing the artery, crunching the bone.

Umara's screams rang through the forest as the dog leapt aside and began to pull and worry the limb, growling fiercely all the while. Touami groped for his father's spear but even when he found it, the animal's movements were so quick he could not thrust properly. His tentative prods only maddened it further: it let go the mangled arm and sprang again for Umara's throat. In desperation, Umara wrapped his legs around to try and hold it off but as the dog twisted and jerked in its efforts to escape, it ripped his belly open.

'Father!' The anguish in Touami's voice roused Umara to one last effort. With a convulsive heave, using all his weight, he managed to throw the animal onto its side, pinning it with his body. It clamped his teeth deep in his shoulder but he was oblivious to the pain, his whole being focused on the need to hold the demon long enough for Touami to kill it.

It gave a shudder and was still: Touami had speared it between the ribs. Frantically he pulled his father away, half-lifting, half-dragging him off the wallaby trail into the trees. Umara was barely conscious, blood streamed from his wounds: with his good hand he pressed the injured arm against his torn abdomen. He staggered and almost fell as Touami guided him to the shelter of a massive, moss-covered tree trunk, the hulk of a fallen giant killed by fire years before.

'Quiet!' As terror gave way to shock, Umara began to moan. His face was grey beneath the layers of dirt and sweat and he rolled his head in agony as Touami forced him to sit with his back against the rotting trunk. The voices of the white demons were now very loud: to Umara, whose hearing seemed to sharpen as his sight dimmed, their approach seemed inevitable as that of the darkness rolling in from every side. He gritted his teeth and listened but with each passing moment it was harder to focus his mind.

From where he crouched, Touami watched the *num* approach. When they reached the dead dogs one gave a low whistle then they began to talk, their voices loud with outrage. The bearded leader crouched and probed the spearholes in the bodies with his fingers but his eyes searched the ground. When he spotted the heavy blood-trail leading off the path he rose slowly to his feet.

'Go!' Umara spoke weakly and with great effort. Blood spurted between his fingers; his eyes were glazed and sunken. '*Korerenner* is close. Get the *ballawiné* before it is too late.'

Touami did not answer. He sat down and took his father in his arms, pulling and cradling him against his chest, willing strength into Umara's failing body. At the same time he appealed to *darwalla* for help.

The *num* began to argue. Then the party split, the leader remaining while the others trudged back along the path. But once they were out of sight, the bearded man turned, breathing slowly and deliberately, the corpses at his feet, his musket held club-like across his body. His eyes surveyed the trees under which twilight was now spreading, the dark splotches and lines of blood on the red-brown earth. He sniffed the air. All was quiet. Leaves whispered overhead in a breath of wind and a currawong called, far away. His eyes followed the blood-trail to the fallen tree. He cocked his musket and the click of the mechanism was loud in the stillness. Then he stepped forward.

Umara's body had grown slack and heavy. It seemed to Touami that the weight of it was crushing him into the moss and rotten wood against which he leant, that the chill of the dying flesh was seeping inexorably into his. It took an immense effort of will to remain as he was, holding mind and body still while the sound of footsteps grew louder.

The *num* was close: the *num* could see him. Touami stared down the long tube of the musket barrel. He was looking straight at death. Suddenly he jumped to his feet and dashed away. His movements were so quick and agile he was gone from view before the flash and crack of the gun exploded into the space he had occupied. The ball ploughed deep into the tree trunk.

Umara had fallen sideways. Entrails bulged through the rips in his belly. The bearded man kicked him savagely, cursing. To shoot a corpse would be a senseless waste of ammunition: there was no satisfaction to be gained from it. But then he reflected that the head was whole and unmarked and there were those among the colonists who would pay handsomely for a native's skull, perhaps enough for another pair of kangaroo-dogs.

Propping his musket against the fallen tree, he unsheathed his knife. The blade was long, the edge so finely honed, it shone silver as he tested it against the ball of his thumb. Satisfied, he crouched and pushed the body over onto its back. Blood pulsed weakly from the lacerated arm. Umara was not quite dead.

Grinning to himself, the hunter prepared to cut. And then, in case the other was close, he lifted his head and yelled: 'If you're watching, this is what happens to any black who crosses Nat Skinner!'

Weeping as he ran, bowed with grief and shame, Touami heard the shout and slowed. His hands and body were sticky with his father's blood, his mouth and nostrils clogged with the taste and smell of it. For a moment he thought of going back, of stalking the white demon: he would never know what had struck him. But he had no weapon, not even a stone or club with which to smite the enemy. He jogged on until his weariness was such that he could drive himself no further and then he slunk into the shelter of a hollow tree, lay down and sank into a stupor of exhaustion.

The croaking of ravens sounded loud and harsh through the twilight as Nat Skinner made his way back to camp but he paid them no heed. His step was light and he whistled tunelessly between his teeth for a sense of triumph swelled within him despite the loss of his dogs. The native's head swung by its hair from his musket barrel and in his coat pocket was a more personal trophy: the scrotum would make a fine new tobacco pouch. Among his peers, the tale of how he had come by the purse would stand him in good stead and he was in no danger of being prosecuted: only a surgeon could tell a man's ball sac from a boar's once the skin was cured. Nor was there any chance of the body being discovered. Even before he left he had heard rustling and growling close by: carrion eaters drawn by the smell of blood. The forest would take back its own.

None of his hearth group ever forgot Touami's return from the Ochre Trail. Frost was thick on the ground and crunched under his feet but even so the women stared as if he were a ghost and the children stuck their hands into their mouths to stifle cries. His hair was matted and long, his chin covered with a growth of beard ragged as lichen and he was so thin, his muscles stood out like cords. A torn wallaby-pelt was draped around his shoulders, cushioning a string made of sinew from which two bulging skin bags hung. The bags were small but, from the tension of the string, heavy. In his right hand was a spear which had doubled as a staff: the butt end was worn by use.

'Aiee . . .' Uné-mawa started towards him then stopped, as if uncertain that this could be her husband. But their little girl, Cuckanahu, who had asked after her father every day, ran to greet him as soon as the first shock of his arrival had passed. At the sight of her beaming face and bright eyes, Touami's heart seemed to dissolve. He lifted the cord from his shoulder and let the bags drop, then swept the child into his arms, pressing his face against hers. She laughed and squirmed as he breathed in the smell of her: warm, sour skin; possum grease; the all-pervading scent of wood-smoke, and it seemed to him that he had never smelt anything so good, or so reassuring.

'Eh, little one,' he murmured and then all he had endured on his journey, the terror, the grief, the privations of the long trail and the sheer physical hardship of digging and carrying the ochre, overwhelmed him. He sank to his knees and wept unrestrainedly while the little girl, disconcerted by his abrupt change in mood, burst into tears and struggled to escape.

Any doubts as to Touami's identity were banished by this outpouring of emotion and the women rushed to hear his tale. Uné-mawa was foremost: she put her arms round husband and child and her relief also found vent in tears because she had begun to resign herself to the likelihood of his death and here he was, alive and whole. But Tealana, who had held back, waiting for Umara to come striding into camp, suddenly pushed forward and pulled Uné-mawa away. She had lost weight since their parting and her eyes blazed from deep hollows as she thrust her face towards her son's.

'Where is he?'

Ever since he had abandoned his father to the white demons, Touami had foreseen and dreaded this moment. Taking a deep breath, he passed Cuckanahu to Uné-mawa while his mind struggled to remember the words he had prepared on the bitter path to and from the quarries. But before he could speak, Tealana read the truth from his expression: she staggered and fell to her knees and her wail echoed eerily though the forest.

Silence followed that cry: even the children made no sound. Touami felt their eyes like fingers pressing into a wound and he shuddered, remembering how, having got the ochre, he had traced his way back to the killing ground and found only bones, crushed by the jaws of *kannenner* and *tarrabah*. There had been no way of distinguishing Umara's remains from the dogs' and so he had scattered ochre in an attempt to appease the restless ghosts and left, though by doing so he had denied his father's spirit peace.

'We came across *num*,' he said at last. 'They had fanged demons with them. I killed those with spears . . .'

'What's going on?' The old man, Meelangana, had been asleep: woken by Tealana's cry, he stumbled across the clearing, blinking in the sunlight. 'Is my son returned?'

Touami groped at his sides. The possum-skin bags were hard beneath his fingers, packed with the pigment that smelled like blood. Its tang cloyed in his nostrils as on every step of the return journey.

'Here is the *ballawiné*,' he said.

9. The Rock.

(Furneaux Islands, 1808).

Only one with an inflated opinion of himself and his place in the world would have designated the jumble of wind-scoured, surf-benighted rocks an island but the Irish deserter and sealer O'Grady was such a man. And while most would have regarded a sojourn there as punishment, to one that had never possessed much more than the clothes he stood up in, a long knife and fleeting tenancy of spirit bottles, it was a kingdom. Especially since he had a subject to lord over: the native woman he and John Bayliss had captured in the south.

Yet the truth was that without her, O'Grady would soon have starved. When all food within easy reach was gone, it was she who dived for shellfish, crays and crabs for despite his years at sea, he could not swim. And she it was who taught him how to gather and eat other food: kangaroo-apples, mutton-birds, the berries, roots and tender tops of plants that otherwise looked inedible though for all these he had to row elsewhere. Wallabies were also to be found on some of the larger islands. However, since O'Grady lacked a dog or musket these had to be traded for and as time passed, their price exceeded the Irishman's means. For the seals which, only a few years before, had been packed so tightly on the rock platforms that there was barely room for a man to walk between, had grown scarce and more wary in their habits and the ships now called but once a year, no longer visiting each island but to the whaling station at George Town. So in addition to his other hardships, a man had to row the few skins he had to sell into port and risk losing his claim to another.

Toualena had endured the years of captivity with a stubborn, unquestioning stoicism. The first, aboard *The Advantage*, had been the worst, confined in the hold with the cargo, chained to the ship lest she take it into her mind to spoil the stores or precious skins and thus jeopardise the voyage. Initially the captain had been uneasy at having her on board but on reflection it seemed better that the men should have a tame *lubra* to hand rather than raid native villages along the coast which not only wasted time but risked greater trouble. Thus she became their slave, to be used as and when the mood took them. On the rare occasions she was brought on deck, blinking in the glare of daylight, the captain marvelled at her strength for she displayed no sign of the pox and when they swilled her down her skin gleamed with health except around her wrists. There the flesh was scarred and thickened from the manacles and her own teeth for once, in a frenzy of rage and despair, she had tried to gnaw through flesh and bone like an animal in a trap. It was John Bayliss who found her on that occasion and, in a rare moment of pity, he had held her tenderly until she slept. But as the voyage progressed, O'Grady had asserted himself as her owner and so when he was put ashore, she went with him.

Having claimed the islet as his own, O'Grady made his home on the most sheltered side where a great faulted crack ran deep into the rock. It was more a wide crevice than a cave proper because there was a thin line of daylight where the fissure opened at the top. But though this meant that water sheeted down one wall after heavy rain, it became O'Grady's chimney. It allowed him to have a fireplace within the cave, the draught through the entrance being more than sufficient to drive smoke out through the top, and with an elephant-seal skin fixed across the mouth, a bed of sand and tussock on the dry side of the cave, even a rock ledge to act as shelf for his store of flour, sugar and other essentials, the place was snug as any slab hut. In addition, it was invisible from the sea, a distinct advantage to the Irishman's mind. Even when the fire was alight the wind dissipated the smoke so rapidly, it could easily be mistaken for mist or flying spume. As a deserter who, if identified, would be sent back into military service or shot, O'Grady trusted no-one and kept his boat concealed: the chaotic pattern of the islet's rocks afforded more than one sheltered mooring. And because the craft was the very means of his survival, he often dragged it ashore though even then he took the precaution of draping it with armfuls of kelp: of that, at least, there was no shortage.

The cave had only one disadvantage as far as O'Grady was concerned: it was so narrow there was only room for a single occupant. On the rare occasions his acquaintance, John Bayliss, called, they sat crammed side by side on the bed. Then, whoever was closest to the fire was in danger of being roasted alive while the other shivered in the draught from the entrance. And when the mood of rut came upon them they had to go outside where the native woman was chained like a dog. O'Grady had made sure the tether was too short to reach the cave's entrance lest one day she take it into her mind to attack him while he slept, though mostly she seemed dull-witted and compliant and to do so would have meant her own death from starvation or thirst since she had no means of freeing herself. But lately his guest had disdained to use her, ignoring the Irishman's taunts that he was going soft

While Toualena sensed that of the two, Bayliss was the more humane, she grew to dread his visits because his continence drove O'Grady to even greatest excesses of cruelty, as if by degrading her, he asserted himself over the whole of humanity. Although he now had her to himself, possession awoke a jealousy in him that was like a raging fire: she had only to raise her eyes to a distant boat to earn a beating. For while when it came to fruitful labour of any kind O'Grady was overcome by a torpor of body, mind and spirit, he had an aptitude for dealing out pain and devised many novel varieties of punishment in which his own gratification was directly proportionate to the woman's suffering. Had he devoted half as much energy to sealing or fishing, he would have been rich: as it was, he wore himself out, consumed by hatred, envy and lust, embittered by the knowledge that without her, his slave, he was nothing: a man alone on a barren rock. Every little humiliation he could inflict upon her therefore became a great matter in his mind and if he could force a reaction it was as if he had succeeded in some magnificent endeavour.

Yet miserable though her existence was, Toualena's spirit remained strong within her. After that moment of despair in the ship's hold she never contemplated suicide though the taking of one's own life was not unknown among the Meelayginnee. If, through some wrongdoing, a person became estranged from their daemon then they might give up, turn their eyes inward and die. But Toualena's daemon had not forsaken her. Although she was far from the forests and heathlands of her own country, *darwalla* often visited her in dreams. And while she had no choice but to submit to her captor's demands, part of her was detached from all that was happening: thus she endured. On the rare occasions he left her to go to George Town or a neighbouring island, she would croon songs of the Meelayginnee to herself and talk aloud in her own tongue to the rocks, the coarse grasses, the seabirds and cruising dolphins, for in her mind these were also people: she was not alone.

One hot summer's day John Bayliss rowed into the little inlet. His reception on his last visit had discouraged him from coming again but this time his intent was more than social. He had had a *lubra* of own but it was O'Grady's he lusted for. Now, with a bottle of spirits in each pocket and money to hand, he believed he possessed the means to buy her.

The boat's prow nudged the shore, sending vortices of fine sand into the swirling water and he took the painter and sprang ashore. The place seemed deserted but he spied the Irishman's boat drawn up above the high-tide mark. Kelp had been draped over in an effort to disguise it and the dry fronds rustled and tapped against the wave-worn wood. The randomness of the sound seemed to emphasise the isolation of the place, the starkness of the black and grey rocks and white sand against the shifting blue-green sea.

Perplexed, for the woman was not in her usual place, Bayliss shouted the Irishman's name and waited. The surf washed around his ankles but his boots had been soaked so often he hardly noticed. Having fastened the painter of his skiff to the line of the other, he stood listening. Apart from the swash and backwash of the waves, there was nothing to hear but the incessant tapping of dry weed on the stranded boat and the squabbling of seabirds over some tidbit on the outlying skerries.

'Must be inside then,' he muttered uneasily. It seemed to him that in such a place a man might easily go mad without the sound of a human voice to remind him what he was. He walked reluctantly towards the cave. He was loth to enter uninvited but the thought of the long row back without achieving or even attempting his purpose, hardened his resolve. He grasped the skin hanging across the entrance, so blotched with weathering it appeared half-decayed, and jerked it aside.

The interior was more like an animal's den, wolf's lair or stinking fox-hole, than human habitation, the bed a heap of filthy rags, the fireplace piled with ash and half-burned bones and shells. An overpowering stench of urine made Bayliss recoil but he had seen enough anyway: the place was empty. As he stepped back onto the beach and let the curtain fall, his mind began to turn over the possibility that the islet was, after all, deserted, that some accident had overtaken the two or else the woman had managed to revenge herself upon her abductor, then swum to a neighbouring island or drowned in the attempt.

He sat on a rounded boulder and delved in his coat for pipe and tobacco, meaning to explore the islet after a contemplative smoke, when he was startled by a shout. Twisting round, he saw the Irishman clambering swiftly over the rock, using hands and feet like a monkey. Indeed, he looked more like some degenerate ape than a human being for his clothes, rotted by sweat and sea, hung in rags from his skinny frame and the matted hanks of his hair and beard framed a face devoid of compassion, the small, cunning eyes bloodshot and yellow-rimmed, the skin weathered to the hue and texture of blackwood bark. It was a visage to inspire fear and even Bayliss felt a kind of instinctive revulsion, sensing that here was a man on the edge of madness. He rose and forced a smile whilst taking comfort from the touch of the leather scabbard against his hip where his skinning knife was sheathed.

'Is that my old friend Bayliss?' O'Grady leapt down onto the sand with a lightness and agility which demonstrated that despite his decrepit appearance, he was still young and quick. He sidled up close and his eyes were bright with expectancy. 'You'd not have come all this way empty-handed?'

'Maybe not.' Bayliss put a hand in the pocket of the kangaroo-skin coat he wore despite the heat and pulled out a squat brown bottle. 'But this time I want something in return.'

'Come to dip your wick at last?' O'Grady winked and pushed

his tongue into the side of his mouth so that his cheek bulged obscenely. 'Well you'll have to wait awhile unless you're minded to swim. She's out yonder.'

He jerked his head to indicate the line of tide-stranded rocks. They looked bare of life save for the ubiquitous lichen which marked the stone like splashes of ochre or bright venous blood. John Bayliss wondered what kind of work required the woman to remain there all day. Whatever it was had attracted the seabirds for they flapped and squabbled around the furthest skerry in a great flock. As he stared, he thought he saw what had drawn them: something long and greyish-brown that glistened in the sunlight, no doubt the rotting carcass of a seal or dolphin. When some of the birds landed and hopped forward to peck, it seemed to move but before he could be certain, O'Grady plucked at his sleeve.

'Let's be having it then.'

They took their ease sitting on the hot, dry sand with their backs against the beached boat. It provided a wedge of shade which spread across their laps and legs as the sun traversed the sky. From where they sat the skerries were blocked from view but the clamour of seabirds was loud in from that direction and Bayliss wondered at their persistence though as the afternoon wore on and the level of the bottle went down, his thinking grew hazy and his speech rambling. Words slipped treacherously from his lips as he told O'Grady of his change in course.

It was his opinion that compared with the bounty of the first years, fur seals were growing scarce and a man had to work five times as hard to justify the trip to George Town. And though prices, it was said, had doubled or tripled, it was not those that did the killing and skinning who profited, but the ship-owners and their masters. So John Bayliss had decided to forgo a life which demanded that a man daily risk his life on the sea or scrabble among the rocks like a shipwrecked sailor. Instead he had applied for a portion of land on one of the adjacent islands. On this he had already built a slab hut and cleared a couple of acres to grow vegetables to sell to sealers and any ship that happened to call in but the *lubra* he had bought to help him died before he finished breaking the ground and there was no other to be got locally. Even in George Town it was becoming difficult to buy a healthy native woman for less than a guinea: most of those on offer were already sick and likely to die as soon as they were set to work.

O'Grady listened as if he had no idea where this speech was leading. He tipped his head back against the velvety surface of weathered wood and squinted into the sun. Then as Bayliss fell silent, leaving his request unspoken, the Irishman's mouth worked and he spat. They both watched as the clot of phlegm and saliva sank into the sand.

'So you thought you'd steal mine?' O'Grady said at last.

Bayliss laughed uncomfortably for he detected danger in the other's quietness. Then he felt in his pockets and brought out a second bottle. 'What kind of man thieves from an old mate?' he asked. 'But without my help in the getting of her you'd be fish-bait, or had you forgotten? I'll give you a good price.'

O'Grady drained the last drops from the first bottle and flung it away. It flashed in a slow arc and smashed against the rocks. His eyes fixed on the one in Bayliss' hand. 'I'll not bargain with a dry throat.'

'Ah, but the grog's part of the price.' Bayliss tucked the bottle back in his pocket. 'That and five shillings is my offer.'

'Jesus Mary and all the bloody saints!' O'Grady exploded. 'That's no offer: it's an insult! Give me a drink or get off my island. Haven't I been generous enough? You'd have paid a shilling a time for a whore in town but not a penny did I take for the use of her. You're a disappointment to me, Bayliss.'

'Eight shillings then.' Bayliss got to his feet and stared with distaste at the man sprawling at his feet. 'Any more than that and I can have a few turns on a white woman and not have to feed her after. As to my land, I can manage on my own until I've saved enough for a proper wife. The seals are finished, O'Grady: with or without that *lubra* you'll have to leave here soon.'

'Oh aye?' The softness of the Irishman's tone sent a shiver up Bayliss' spine and he turned his head to look at the distant skerry where the seabirds still wheeled and cried. Thus he missed the subtle change in the other's expression from open avarice to something more menacing. In this last speech O'Grady had been quick to detect a kind of latent arrogance, the assumed superiority of landowner over landless which, by default, demeaned not only his way of life but implied contempt of him and all his kind. And yet though his blood seethed at the insult, O'Grady concealed his sudden burning hatred for the man standing before him beneath a show of servility: he patted the sand in invitation and as Bayliss, reluctantly, sat down again, launched into a speech extolling the virtues of the woman and how dear she was to him.

When he had finished, they sat in silence for a while. Then O'Grady tipped his thumb in the direction of the other's pocket.

'Give me a drop and I'll consider it.'

Bayliss took out the bottle, thinking the sight of it might be more persuasive than any words. Instead of opening it, he rolled it between his hands, making the contents slosh. O'Grady watched and listened with a kind of agony: his lips moved soundlessly and his hands twitched as if he was in his throes.

'You're a hard man,' he whined at last. 'Ah God, it'd tear the heart out of me to sell her. Fifteen shillings is the lowest I'd consider: who knows where I'll get another that'll suit me as well. And that dram there, sealed.'

'That's more than I can afford,' Bayliss replied, for in truth he was stretched at eight, still having tools and seed to buy. 'Liam — you know she's part mine by right.'

'Ach — you think you're man enough to have taken her alone?' O'Grady jeered. 'An' that big black bugger — didn't you strike him from behind?' He paused, seeing the other's face tighten. 'Now don't get angry: isn't that the truth? And 'tis me that's cared for her and taught her all she knows. That's worth something, to be sure.'

'You can keep the chain,' Bayliss said, with heavy irony. Any affinity he might once have felt with this man had vanished as he realized he was being played like a fish on a line. 'Ten shillings then — and the bottle. That's my final offer, O'Grady.'

'Ten?' The Irishman shook his head and leaned it back against the gunnel of the boat. His eyes were half-closed as if in contemplation but in fact he was watching Bayliss intently, hoping procrastination would provoke a better offer. When none was forthcoming and the other made to put the bottle back in his pocket, O'Grady sighed heavily, opened his eyes and raised his right hand to his face. After scrutinising the rough, dirt-ingrained palm with the intentness of a fortune-teller, he spat in the hollow and held it out to Bayliss. 'Good luck to 'ee.' He ignored the obvious repugnance with which the hand was taken and jerked his head towards the skerries. 'Take her and welcome. Better pay me first mind, in case you slip.'

So glad was he that the bargain had been sealed, Bayliss felt only a vague uneasiness at the Irishman's apparent good humour. He handed over the bottle and delved in an inside pocket for his money pouch. With great deliberation he counted ten shillings into the other's hand. In his excitement O'Grady shook all over as if with the ague and a high-pitched whinnying laugh escaped him.

'You say she's over there?' Bayliss suddenly wanted to be off this islet: the tide was dropping fast and before long his skiff would be grounded. He scrambled to his feet and stood looking towards the far skerry and its screaming gulls. 'Shouldn't she be back by now? What's she doing?'

'Sleeping no doubt, the black bitch,' O'Grady said venomously, unstoppering the bottle and taking a long draught. 'Kick her for me if she is. Oh, and you'll need this, so you will.'

He plucked at his rags and pulled out a string made of sinew from which a small key hung. It took him several attempts to bite through the cord and he cackled horribly as he handed it over. Bayliss waited a moment, weighing the key in his hand then, as no explanation was forthcoming, turned on his heel and strode across the beach.

The sand sank under his feet and water swirled around his thighs as he waded across to the line of rocks which formed one side of the inlet. The skerries were uneven and though the clamour of the gulls dinned his ears as he scrambled over them, he still could not see what had attracted the birds. As he drew near the last of the rocks the birds screamed and dived at him, trying to drive him away. Then he hurried forward, filled with sudden misgiving.

Naked under the burning sun, Toualena lay on her side, chained by the neck to a rusty staple. A rope tied round her ankles ran off the rock into the sea: she was stretched as if on a rack. Her hands were pressed against her face to protect her eyes from voracious beaks but she had been unable to prevent the seabirds pecking at her legs and back which were pocked with bloody holes.

Had it not been that O'Grady was too lazy to procure another, John Bayliss would never have recognised this as the woman the two of them had captured in the south. She was gaunt, her skin dry and grey as desiccated hide, disfigured by scabs and running sores; her head sprouted tufts of woolly hair which crawled with lice. The Irishman had cut a notch in her right earlobe to denote his ownership but the other scars on her body made this superfluous: the cicatrices denoting her tribe and lineage had almost disappeared beneath the marks of his lash and chain. And he had left his legacy also in her womb: from the shape of her belly Bayliss saw she was with child.

Watching the movement of her ribs as she breathed jerkily in and out, Bayliss was consumed by a sense of outrage, not so much at the woman's condition but the fact he had been cheated. He turned and ran back a few paces until he could see the beach, cupped his hands to his mouth, yelled: 'Irish bastard – I'll have you for this!' But O'Grady merely waved in answer and the bottle flashed in the sunlight as he lifted it to his lips.

Bayliss stood irresolute, wanting to smash the little man to pulp. But the woman was his now and even such brief ownership brought responsibility: if he demanded his money and left her here, he guessed O'Grady would likely kill her from spite if she was not already dying. And he imagined the Irishman telling the story in the taverns and brothels of George Town: how he had captured and used a native woman, got her pregnant then strung her out and sold her to an unsuspecting settler, a former comrade who knew no better than to hand over his money without first proving his purchase.

Then, from behind, he heard a moan.

That sound, weak as it was, compelled him to run back. The woman's hands had dropped away from her face, perhaps because his presence had forced the birds to withdraw or else that she was too far gone to protect herself any longer. Her eyelids, swollen and rimmed with salt, remained shut but as he knelt beside her and took out his knife, her mouth opened and her tongue protruded slightly, startlingly pink against fissured, sun-blackened lips.

He pulled on the rope but whatever hung on the other end was so heavy, he could barely move it. When he looked, he saw it was tied to a creel filled with rocks. Seen through the clear water the wicker frame seemed to waver and a small crab with a blue stripe ran over the stones inside. Then he sawed through the rope and flung the loose end into the sea. O'Grady would have to fish for it if he wanted it again.

Toualena lay inert as he undid the rope around her ankles. It had been tied so tightly that the thin flesh had swollen around the bonds. Her hands and feet seemed unnaturally large and bony and old scars formed silvery bracelets around the joints so that it looked as if her own extremities had been chopped off and some-one else's stuck in their place.

The chain was fastened by a padlock the surface of which was so stained and crusted with rust, Bayliss feared the mechanism must be jammed until he realized O'Grady would have locked it earlier that day. Indeed the key shone with grease from the Irishman's body and turned easily enough. At the snick of the lock a tremor shook the woman's body but as he eased the chain away, she sighed and seemed to relax. She had worn it so long, the links had made thick calluses on the knobs of her neck and collar-bones.

Mindful of his promise, Bayliss locked the chain to the staple, then flung the key seawards. It spun wildly around its thong and a great black-backed gull swooped and flew away with it, mobbed by other gulls and skuas. It was a petty kind of vengeance but great satisfaction welled in him at the doing of it. Grinning to himself, he crouched again beside the woman.

From her countenance it was impossible to tell whether she was feigning sleep, sleeping or dying. An existence in which thirst, hunger and pain were the norm had shrunk her face to that of an old woman. Uncertain what to do next, Bayliss reached out tentatively and touched her shoulder. The skin seemed dead as tree bark and she did not react. Discouraged, he withdrew his hand. Some said that the natives of Van Diemen's land did not experience pain like white people but he had not believed it till now. Unless she was so close to death she was unable to feel anything: she must have been lying there all day. He wondered what she had done to earn such punishment, then shook his head disgustedly, realizing the spuriousness of the question. Likely enough O'Grady had put her there for his own amusement.

'You're mine now.' As soon as he had spoken he felt the ridiculousness of the words: even if she had heard them, the woman was unlikely to understand. Yet the saying of them somehow crystallised his sense of ownership: whether she lived or died, she was his property to do with as he wished. If he rolled her off this rock to drown, there was no-one to call him to account; if he spread her legs and took her there and then, no man could say him nay. And perversely, it was as he thought this, his eyes straying to her swollen belly, that pity stirred in him at last. Thus instead of hoisting her sack-wise across his shoulder as was his first intent, he gathered her into his arms, staggered to his feet and bore her like a bride.

Emaciated though she was, Toualena weighed heavy in his arms and her lolling head bumped his shoulder as he made his way carefully back across the rocks. Now, for the first time, he noticed her stench which was rank as putrid meat and made the gorge rise in his throat. Some of it came from the filth ingrained in her skin and hair but there was an underlying foetid odour he could not place. When he reached his boat he had to hold his breath as he laid her gently in the bottom.

Seawater sloshed around his knees as he took off his coat and made a pillow of it for her head. Then he pushed hard on the bows to keep the skiff afloat, aware of the Irishman's mocking gaze upon him all the time. The woman began to shudder, making the boat rock slightly, and Bayliss watched her with dismay. Once, in Port Jackson, he had seen a sailor shake thus after being knifed in the belly: he had jerked his way towards death like a fish out of water. But now she was his, John Bayliss was determined that the woman should not die, at least not because of O'Grady. He leaned close to her head, steeling himself against the foulness of her breath, and hissed 'Live!' and there was no tenderness in his voice: it was a command.

'Eh – it warms the heart so it does, to see you whisper love talk to your darling,' O'Grady called. 'Mind you take good care of her: that's my seed spawning in her belly. See – you got yourself a bargain after all – two for the price of one!'

Bayliss disdained to reply but waded across to untie the painter. He kept his head low so that the other could not see his face which was grim and taut with anger.

'Mind,' the Irishman's tone grew conversational for Bayliss, by necessity, had come within a few paces of where he sat, 'she's not carried any beyond a few months: a good thumping saw to that.' He paused and a look of reminiscence settled on his ravaged features. 'Oh there was one, a few months back but he disappeared so he did. Maybe she killed and ate him for her milk turned sour after. Sucked her dry I did: that's the way to keep 'em quiet. Tup 'em by night and flog 'em by day. Remember that and you'll have no trouble.'

John Bayliss' fingers were clumsy with his eagerness to leave: the knot which should have slipped free resisted his efforts to undo it. Sensing his growing frustration, O'Grady began to laugh.

'Ten shillings!' he crowed. 'Ten silver shillings for that worn-out cunt. Better learn to tie a rope, boy, or she'll be the master o'ye!'

Bayliss' temper snapped. He dropped the line and sprang at his tormentor. O'Grady was quick and agile but the best part of a bottle and a half of raw spirits had slowed him. One look into the other's blazing face convinced him it would be best to run but there was nowhere to go. As he tried to scramble away, Bayliss caught him by the belt and yanked him back. The Irishman put up his hands in a feeble attempt to protect his face: next moment he was down, yelping and writhing desperately to avoid the other's kicks. After a while he went limp. His body jolted and sagged like a sack of flour under the repeated blows and blood spilled from his mouth and nose, forming little grain-crusted clots on the sand.

'I should kill you, you bastard!' Bayliss' breath came in harsh gasps; he licked his bloodied knuckles, then spat on his rival. And then the red tide that had overwhelmed him ebbed: he heard again the slap of wavelets against the hull of his skiff; the hiss of the wind through wiry grasses whose roots clung to crevices in the rock; the distant crying of seabirds, and when he bent to check if O'Grady was bluffing, he saw the Irishman's eyes, yellow and bloodshot, were upturned.

'Bastard,' he repeated and he was tempted to rifle through the other's rags and take back his money. But it seemed to him that such an act would make the bargain void, give O'Grady a claim on the woman. Instead, he cut the painter from the beached boat and made a running noose which he slipped over the unconscious man's head. The other end he tied to an iron ring in the low cliff beside the cave where the woman had formerly been chained. Then he waded out to his skiff, climbed in and began to row, smiling to himself at the shock O'Grady would have when he woke with a rope tight about his neck.

At his feet, lulled by the rocking motion of the boat, Toualena slept.

10. Tea and Damper.

(Derwent Valley, August 1812).

It was winter and the ancient wanderer, Ouniaga, was cold and hungry. For days now a chill rain had been blowing from the south and one night he had been so tired he had fallen asleep inside a hollow tree and let his fire go out. When he had woken long after dawn to discover a pile of wet, charred wood instead of the heap of glowing embers he had expected, a weariness more profound than any he had ever known descended upon him. All his skill and even the magic words he had learned from his great-grandmother failed to coax a thread of smoke from the sodden fuel and in the end he simply pulled his ragged kangaroo-skin tight about his shoulders and huddled inside the tree-cave to wait out the rain. But another day and night passed and it did not stop.

Hunger eventually drove him out. He had survived on leaves and fungi for a week but he knew that if he did not find meat soon, he would grow too weak to hunt. So he settled his spear-bundle on his shoulder and with his waddy swinging from his right hand, set off into the dripping forest. If he was lucky there would be a hearth-group camped nearby who would share their fire and food. But while this would have been a certainty before the coming of the white ones, the valley of the Big River comprising some of the best hunting grounds in Trouwerner and its people the most numerous, many of the Lairmairrener had fled to more remote areas as *num* began to settle there and those that remained had grown wary and hostile and were constantly on the move.

All day he wandered, making his way down through dense growth of blackwood and myrtle, where the gullies were crowded with fern-trees, to the sparser forest on the lower slopes. Here, in the past, the undergrowth would have been kept in check by frequent burnings, the local groups firing the coarser growth to encourage grasses preferred by kangaroos and wallabies. But, Ouniaga noted grimly, vast areas had grown rank and he saw no animals though this was most likely due to the pelting rain.

The light was failing and he had found nothing more nourishing than a few scabby berries and some fungi knobby and hard as wood knurls, when he smelled smoke. No sign of habitation had he seen all day save a deserted camp, the windbreaks so decrepit as to be barely recognisable as structures made by human hands. The fireplaces, blackened patches on the forest floor, were almost lost beneath leaf litter: he reckoned at least three winters had passed since flames had burnt there. And he had walked on, wondering sadly who had made the camp and what had become of them, though he had no way of telling who they were. So disrupted had the seasonal migrations of the Lairmairrener become, they might have belonged to a different tribe altogether.

But there was no denying the scent that filled his nostrils now and he stood still to snuff the air, head uplifted and nostrils flared to make certain it was real and not the product of wishful thinking. Then he hurried on down the wallaby-trail he was following, his weariness and sorrow forgotten. As he walked, his broad, bare feet sliding occasionally in the mud, he pictured the scene that awaited: the clearing with its huddle of tightly-woven lean-toos, each with its own fire to warm the inhabitants, all arranged so that meat could be cooked without need to squat too long in the wet. And hungry though he was, the companionship and security of such a camp was what he craved most, to share food, news and tales then lie down with a full belly in the warm and dry and, in the morning, to wake among friends, to hear the voices of women and the laughter of children, artless and carefree as birdsong.

The twilight deepened and as the rain eased to thick drizzle, shreds of mist wove between the trees and occasional showers of heavy droplets spattered loudly on the soaked ground. The smell of smoke was stronger than ever yet Ouniaga saw no bright spot or even a red flicker amongst the spreading shadows. And because the camp was nothing like he had imagined, he was there before he realized it.

'Camp' was indeed a grand word to describe what was really a bivouac, for the men that inhabited it were outlaws, absconders turned bushranger who preyed upon settlers and lived in the wild, though never far from those who, unwittingly, provided their livelihood. There were three of them, huddled close round a small but fierce blaze. They had made the fire in a shallow pit so that it could not be seen from a distance and their bodies, bulked out by the coats and scraps of oilcloth they wore against the rain, further shielded it from onlookers.

Ouniaga froze. He had blundered within a spearlength before realizing that the hunched black objects were not boulders or worn tree-stumps but *num*, that the fire whose smoke had drawn him there was concealed between them, as if they knew they were trespassing and did not want to be found. And yet though he was keenly aware of their presence, the smell of sweat, wet hair and an unfamiliar odour which was that of wet cloth, they seemed oblivious to his. They were cooking damper on long sticks and such was their concentration, they neither spoke nor looked around.

In his heart, Ouniaga knew he should leave before they realized he was there. Seated as they were, he could see only two of them clearly for the third had his back to him. The fire's ruddy glow lent them a demonic quality for they had the cadaverous, hungry look of predators and their eyes glinted with a kind of feral cunning even in repose. The lower halves of their faces were obscured by tangled beards and the firelight caught in the moisture condensed around their mouths so that it shone like drops of blood.

Beside each man was a long wrapped bundle and a knapsack. There was nothing else to the camp, no shelters nor any of the animals most *num* seemed so attached to. Ouniaga therefore concluded that they must be simple travellers like himself and because they appeared to be weaponless while he had his spear-bundle and waddy to hand; because he was starving and the smell arising from their cooking made his mouth water, he decided to ignore his instincts and reveal himself. With careful deliberation he reached out to the nearest hanging branch and snapped off a dead twig.

The effect was instantaneous. They dropped the sticks of dough, their heads snapped round and one man leapt to his feet, snatching up the long bundle at his side. The eyes of all three probed the darkling bush mercilessly while their hands unwrapped the folds of oilcloth shrouding their firearms but Ouniaga's lean figure blended so well with the striped patterns of bark and shadow that at first they did not discern it.

When at last they saw him, the two still sitting on the ground exclaimed aloud in surprise and relief: they lowered their weapons (a musket and a long-barrelled pistol), and relaxed. But the third, his musket-barrel trained on the old man's chest, spoke sternly and then they raised their guns and looked warily all around though it was impossible to see if others were lurking close by because the cloud had sunk to the level of the treetops and beyond the small circle of firelight it was growing ever darker.

This was Ouniaga's first direct encounter with white men though he had watched their kind from a distance over many years. He knew they could kill him at any moment but he sensed also that they were afraid. And so he did what he would have done on entering any camp where he was a stranger: he bent and placed his waddy carefully on the ground, then lowered his spear-bundle from his shoulder and laid it next to the club, the points directed away from the camp.

There followed a moment of extreme tension as Ouniaga straightened and locked eyes with his opposite, who seemed by his swift action to be leader of the three. Neither moved: they appraised one another suspiciously. Then the musket barrel lowered. In this old man who, despite the wet and cold, went naked apart from a kangaroo-skin tied round his shoulders, the outlier recognised a rare dignity and self-assurance which commanded respect. He looked around, then, sure the aborigine was alone, sat down again, wrapping a fold of oilskin over his musket in such a way it would come easily to hand if required. Once he was comfortable, he waved to Ouniaga (who had not moved), in invitation.

Ouniaga was reluctant to abandon his weapons but he knew he had no choice other than to leave, snatching up spears and waddy and fleeing into the darkness before they had time to fire their death-sticks. But he was hungry and cold and curiosity also drew him. He told himself that had they wished to harm him, they would already have done so. For reassurance, he touched the talisman-bag that hung concealed at his breast and, in thought, called on his daemon, *Menuggana*, to watch over him.

The men drew aside to give him room to sit and they grinned deep in their beards at his naivety. Contingency lay behind their invitation rather than hospitality: Redcoats were patrolling the valley and even a single musket shot might be enough to raise the alarm. Since the old man was alone, they were loth to waste powder and shot in any case, there being quieter and more amusing methods to slay him if it became necessary. But as they picked up the damper-laden sticks and thrust them again into the flames, killing was far from their minds.

None of the three had dealt directly with the aborigines of Van Diemen's Land (apart from a turn on a woman captured by another bushranger group): those they spotted vanished into the landscape rather than risk an encounter. Yet they had lived in the wilds long enough to develop a deep admiration for the natives' bushcraft, the same that a man might feel for a fox's cunning or a dog's fierceness. Now, having invited this one to join them, they became inordinately self-conscious and awkward in his presence. He sat cross-legged, heedless of his nakedness and the rain trickling down his forearms and thighs, his face still and impassive, not looking at his hosts but into the fire, his deep-set eyes unreadable as black stones. Before such massive self-containment, the three were daunted, like ignorant children brought before a mighty patriarch and the fact that an old black man, naked and helpless as a new-born babe, could command their respect exacerbated their uneasiness so that they began to talk and jest loudly to cover their disquiet.

In fact, whilst appearing indifferent, Ouniaga was observing the three closely. His experience of the world was intrinsically intuitive: he could derive even the sense of their speech by nuances of sound and movement. And though his gaze rested on the glowing centre of the fire as if to draw its warmth into his very core, on the periphery of his vision he watched as one man mixed flour and water to make more dough which he moulded into fist sized lumps and skewered on a green twig, while the second opened a little bag and stirred what looked like crushed dried leaves into a pan of water steaming on one of the stones set around the fire. And while he did not understand the purpose of this activity, Ouniaga was fascinated by it, as much as by the third man, the leader, who, resting his twig so that the damper cooked without need for him to hold it, took a clay pipe from his coat and began to smoke, watching the guest with eyes that gleamed red beneath the shadow of the oilcloth pulled hood-like over his head.

To fix them in his mind, Ouniaga named each according to what he saw: the leader, 'Smoke-breath'; the gaunt, pale man who had made the dough, 'Skull-face'; the other, 'Snot-nose' because while stirring the mixture in the pan, he constantly wiped his dripping nose with his fingers.

The first batch of damper was ready. The three lifted their sticks from the fire and blew on the lumps before tearing into them with bared teeth, their lips drawn back to prevent them being burnt. Ouniaga thought of *tarrabah* devouring a carcass for these men ate with similar ferocity. Then the leader pulled a lump off his stick and tossed it to Ouniaga. 'Here: eat!'

Ouniaga caught the bread in a reflex action: otherwise it would have hit him in the face. It was so hot he had to juggle it from hand to hand, much to the amusement of the others who, while still eating, watched him sardonically. Guessing this to be some kind of test, Ouniaga bent his head slightly in acknowledgement and thanks and, when it was cool enough to hold without too much discomfort (he understood now why *num* gnawed it straight from the sticks), he lifted the stuff to his mouth.

The damper was charred to a black crust on the surface which cracked when he bit into it to reveal soggy grey dough on the inside. The flour was coarse and had not been sieved so grit from the millstones made up a sizable proportion and it was infested with weevils which Ouniaga assumed to be deliberate inclusions. The others were so used to contaminated flour they hardly noticed, being too hungry to bother pulling the insects out though some of the lumps were so poorly cooked the weevils were still alive. All four ate voraciously: once he had become accustomed to the bland taste and sticky texture, Ouniaga found that even a few mouthfuls of the stuff were more satisfying to the stomach than an equivalent mass of fungi which, in his experience, was what the damper most resembled.

'Try this.' Having wolfed down his portion, Snot-nose set out three tin cups and poured tea from the pan, tipping it with great care so as to decant the liquid from the leaves. He set a steaming cup in front of Ouniaga. Up till then, having never seen water boiled, the wise-man had dismissed the process of tea-making as a *num* thing, having nothing to do with him. Now he was forced to acknowledge it and so, tentatively, he did what the others were doing: picked up the cup by its handle and put it to his lips.

The tea was black, strong and scalding. Ouniaga had not expected it to be so hot and he almost dropped the cup in surprise. His hosts cradled the tea greedily, savouring the heat (Snot-nose was drinking straight from the pan), and they exchanged glances and grinned at the old man's obvious discomfiture, such ignorance reinforcing their belief that despite their bushcraft, the natives of the island were savages closer to monkeys than civilized men.

Ouniaga sipped the dark liquid with great circumspection. It was bitter as poison and, if the others had not been drinking theirs with relish, he would have thrown it away. But gradually a delicious warmth spread out from his stomach and the blood ran hot through his veins until he felt extraordinarily alert, as if the drink had washed all fatigue from his limbs. He gulped the dregs and held the cup out for more.

The *num* seemed to find his eagerness amusing. Snot-nose said something then filled Ouniaga's cup from the pan while the others laughed quietly. Now that their bellies were full (the damper had the quality of making a man feel as if he had just eaten a satisfying meal though he might wake hours after with his belly griped by hunger), and the tea had taken off the worst of the chill, they looked for entertainment for only Snot-nose felt like sleeping. The leader picked up his pipe again and began to smoke and his eyes never left Ouniaga for he was weighing the value of the old man's body against the risk of capture if they smuggled the corpse to Hobart Town. Medical men would, he knew, pay handsomely for a dead aborigine but this one was aged and a scar on his thigh attested to some grievous injury in the past: he might not fetch a good price. And, if he and his companions were caught, a rope's end would be their future: the idea was tempting but not worth hanging for. Better to remain as they were, preying on isolated farmsteads and living free in the woods.

'Eh, you worthless black bugger, drinking our tea and eating our bread,' he muttered and nudged Snot-nose who was now hunched miserably as close as he could get to the fire without being scorched. 'You're good with dumb animals, Jeb. See if you can get him to sing for his supper.'

'Do it yourself.' Snot-nose coughed wetly and spat a great gob of dark matter into the flames. 'I'm tired: leave me alone.'

Ouniaga watched their exchange and sipped his tea quietly. He did not understand their speech but he felt their change in mood and sensed that it threatened him. Yet at the same time he was keenly aware of his obligation to them: having shared their meal and their fire it was for him to acknowledge their hospitality with some gift, if not something material then in the form of a song or story. And because of the need that had drawn him to their camp he decided to give them the tale of 'The Gift of Fire', when Wyerkartenner, the trickster, had tried to steal fire from Tarner, the first man, and been thwarted by the little bird, *Layngana*.

The rain had ceased but the air was still and fog hung between the trees so that beyond the little circle of firelight the night seemed impenetrable. The silence was broken only by the drip of water from drooping leaves onto the sodden forest floor and the soft flutter of the flames.

'Go on then - you try, you lazy bastard.' Smoke-breath struck Skull-face on the shoulder. 'Or do you think we should feed every black who walks into our camp?'

'This'll send him packing.' The gaunt man reached for his musket but at that moment Ouniaga opened his mouth. So unexpected and extraordinary was the sound that issued from it, the three froze for the old man's voice was strong and vibrant yet so deep it was as if an ancient tree or weathered boulder were giving tongue. And while there were no words to his chant the *num* could understand, there was a resonance to it that was profoundly disturbing. It was as if this old, naked aborigine were reaching to something hidden deep within each of them, something intrinsic to their very being which, hitherto, they had not even known existed.

As the chant possessed him, Ouniaga ceased to be aware of his audience. It was strange not to have others take up the refrain or keep the beat by hitting a hollow log or tapping sticks together, but none of this mattered compared to the power he felt enter him as the spirits of his ancestors gathered, inspiring and sustaining him until he no longer had to think of the words but simply gave himself to their flow. He was Wyerkartenner, matchless in cunning and audacity; he was Tarner, bereft and afraid; he was Layngana, small yet fearless, sent by Droémadeener, the Kindly, to counter the Cunning One's malice. And when the passion building in him could no longer be contained by the bounds of his aged flesh but required movement to release it, he rose to his feet and began to dance.

The chant was hypnotic: so exactly did Ouniaga imitate the quick movements of a little bird, cocking his head and twitching his fingers for wings, that at first the watchers were wholly absorbed, like children watching a conjurer. But then Snot-nose coughed and the spell was broken. Only Ouniaga, involved in his enactment of the tale to the exclusion of all else, was oblivious to their awakening. Now they saw only a wizened old man with a pot belly and skinny limbs, capering about whilst droning interminable gibberish, and because a few moments earlier they had been wholly in his power, they were embarrassed and ashamed before each other. And the same desire stirred in each of them: to humiliate the old man so that he would understand the difference between his kind and theirs.

When he first heard their clapping, which was slow and ironical, Ouniaga thought they were trying to join in but, being *num*, had no idea how. In all his years of wandering and story-telling no-one had ever dared interrupt and to make fun of an elder, a wise-man such as he, was anathema: it did not occur even as a possibility. But the noise had broken his concentration enough for him to hear their voices and laughter: he redoubled his efforts and then, as Skull-face got to his feet and began to hop about and moan: 'Ahheeyyohheeeyyah . . .', he realized they were mocking him.

Experience had taught Ouniaga patience. Therefore, though his anger was fierce and sudden as a summer storm, not by so much as the flicker of an eyelid did he betray it. His dance and chant continued seamlessly and the three *num* (even Snot-nose had joined in), were too intent on parodying him, slipping obscene gestures and words into their performance, to notice the subtle change in his tone as, instead of relating the story, he began to curse. Nor did they perceive that he was gradually moving away from the fire about which they yowled and stamped, the rhythm of their own movements having evolved into a kind of primeval dance which overtook their senses entirely until they forgot it had begun in jest. All three had known the ignominy of shackles and the lash: in the blood-red nimbus of their little fire they pranced and howled defiance of the world and felt themselves invincible and immortal.

A bout of coughing brought Snot-nose to a halt: doubled over, he struggled to draw air into clogged lungs while the other two linked arms and reeled round the fire-pit, staggering and laughing like drunkards. When he had recovered enough to stand upright, the sick man watched the pair uneasily for there was something close to madness in their jerky movements and the glassy stare of their eyes. Then he realized the old man had disappeared. His first thought was that they had been tricked and he fell to his knees and felt frantically around the oilskin bundles. The weapons had not been touched but he unwrapped his pistol and stroked the long barrel lovingly. The coldness of the metal against his skin and the gleam of it in the firelight in some way mitigated the strangeness of the fog-hung night.

The sight of the firearm had an instant effect on the others. They broke apart and stared, their faces shiny with sweat, their clothes, hair and beards dripping moisture. The silence of the forest was immense: it pressed upon them like a muffling hand and the sound of their panting breath seemed loud in the stillness.

'Where is he?' Smoke-breath snatched up his musket and strode in a circle around the camp though he did not stray beyond the reach of the firelight. 'Next time I see him I'll shoot the bastard!'

'What for?' Skull-face wrapped his oilskin close around himself and lay down. 'For God's sake, he was just a frightened old man. Forget it.'

'Aye – did you see his face when he took the tea? Like we were trying to poison him, the poor old bugger.' Snot-nose waved a hand at the looming darkness. 'Think you'll spot him in that?'

Their leader stared grimly into the thick blackness and the futility of searching was obvious. He shrugged and returned to the homely glow of the fire, wrapped his musket and sat down again.

'He was a crafty one for all that,' he admitted grudgingly. 'Took what he wanted then cleared out. Lively old bird an' all, capering about like a young 'un and yowling like a tom-cat.'

'You don't think he was calling others to attack us?' Snot-nose felt the darkness closing in as the fire burned down and looked around nervously.

'Don't be daft.' Smoke-breath quelled his fleeting trepidation by spitting into the fire. 'They only go for those who've stolen their women or children or shot at them. We've naught to fear from them. And that black cunt down at Reese's: it wasn't us caught and chained her. Now, let's get some sleep before this fog clears and the Redcoats start marching.'

They smoored the fire with damp earth and settled down, each with his gun cradled beneath his coat or oilskin, an arrangement they were so used to that the firearms were familiar as lovers in their arms. Before long the sound of snoring rose softly into the gloom.

From the edge of the trees, Ouniaga watched and waited. Their scorn had nullified any obligation on his side. And what he needed most urgently was not tea or damper.

His patience was endless: he did not act until he was sure they were all asleep. They lay like logs, oblivious to his presence. While he waited, Ouniaga tied strips of bark into firesticks and in his mind a new tale took shape: how Menuggana, stealthy as night, outwitted the white ones and stole their fire.

When he moved at last it was with the silent fluidity of a shadow. To reach the firepit he passed so close to the sleepers, he could smell their breath. They did not stir as he crouched and thrust a wad of bark deep into the piled embers and so still was he and so perfect his self-effacement, if any had woken, they were unlikely to have noticed him hunched in their midst.

Once the tip of the firestick was glowing, Ouniaga rose silently and stepped away. Then he noticed the bags piled between Snot-nose and Smoke-breath. He stuck the firestick carefully in his spear-bundle and crept back. The bags were squarish knapsacks of the kind used by soldiers and the buckles were undone. It was too dark to see what they contained so Ouniaga simply lifted out the contents and sniffed them, placing what he rejected on the wet ground. Heavy pouches of round balls with an odd metallic tang and horn containers of some acrid-smelling power he laid aside but in the second knapsack he discovered cloth bags of flour and tea. These he tied together and slung over one shoulder and then he stole away, picking up his spear-bundle, waddy and the precious firestick as he went.

By dawn the rain had started again but Ouniaga was ensconced in a tree-cave big enough to light a fire inside, the hollow trunk acting as a chimney to carry the smoke away. He guessed the three *num* would be angry but he did not fear them: he knew he would hear their coming and could escape before they were aware of him. He stretched out so that the whole length of his body was warmed by the fire for he was weary and his head and joints ached from the exertions of the night. At least now there was no need to go hunting: he could rest and look forward to a meal of damper made by his own hands. As for the tea, he realized belatedly he should have taken a cup or pan to cook water in. He would save it for another day.

11. The Grass Plains.

(Derwent Valley, March 1818).

Every year towards the end of summer the Lairmairrener gathered on the grass plains which lay at the heart of their territory and whose abundance had made them one of the greatest tribes in Trouwerner. It was the last chance for a corroboree before winter: kangaroo drives provided meat for the whole gathering; councils were held at which betrothals and disputes were decided; ceremony was conducted to ensure that the coming cold would not be too severe, that the game thrived, that the children would grow big and strong. Games there were also: wrestling bouts, races and spear-throwing at which the young men vied together with an eye to watching girls. And when the councils and dancing were over and the groups began to leave, the plains were set ablaze so that after winter they would be green with the soft grasses on which kangaroos and wallabies thrived, to provide sustenance for the next gathering.

For the Meelayginnee, the annual journey to the sparsely wooded flatlands was like a holiday, a chance to catch up with kin and friends, for rest and relaxation before the cold season began. Their clan territory consisted of densely forested hills and valleys to the south though in summer they often ventured deep into the highlands where such delicacies as burrowing crayfish and sweet berries that grew nowhere else were to be found: this was the land Tarner, their ancestor, had walked. Thus, because their lives were harder than many of their lowland kin, the Meelayginnee looked forward to the autumn gathering as one of the great occasions of the year and they watched the moon and stars carefully for it was by their position in the sky that they knew when the right time had come.

This year, Toomay, Touami's son, was especially eager to go for he planned to trade spears for dogs. The coming of the white ones had brought many changes to Trouwerner but to the young man it seemed that much of the bad was outweighed by the introduction of an animal that could be used as a hunting partner, that warned when danger threatened and which might grow close to a man as a faithful wife yet never quarrelled or complained. Year after year the worth of dogs had been proven at the autumn gathering and now that Toomay was a grown man, he was determined to buy one despite implacable opposition from his father and great-grandfather, Meelangana. They had never forgotten that Umara, Touami's father, had been savaged to death on the Ochre Trail but Toomay was sure that once he had a dog, they would relent. However, mindful of their opposition he was careful to conceal his purpose, saying that the extra spears were to exchange for ochre though Neeméné, his wife, was angry with him for lying about a sacred thing.

They journeyed slowly, held to the pace of the old ones, Meelangana and Wagarulepu, and Neeméné who was in the last stage of an ill-timed pregnancy. Toomay's mother, Uné-mawa, was particularly protective of her daughter-in-law who, like herself, originated from a different tribe. Uné-mawa belonged to the Toogee; Neeméné to the Nuenone but both were coastal peoples, thus there was a strong bond between the two women. And they were united also against the envy of Tealana, Toomay's grandmother, who had never fully recovered from the death of her husband, a loss for which she partly blamed Touami.

Tealana was long past child-bearing age but that did not prevent her criticising and interfering and she was quick to take offence if the younger women objected. Only the matriarch, Wagarulepu, held any authority over her: a stern word from her was enough to reduce the embittered widow to tears. Touami, who was acknowledged leader of the hearth-group (his uncle, Tumara, who had joined them lately, deferred to him as Umara's son and Meelangana's wits were wandering with age), did his best to comfort his mother and urged the women to make peace for the good of all but he was keenly aware that Tealana had been jealous of Uné-mawa's youth and beauty from the start and as they had all grown older, her spite had transferred from her daughter-in-law to her grandson's wife. And although she was now Tumara's wife, that marriage had never been consummated for he was a quiet self-effacing man, unwilling to compete with his brother's ghost.

Touami had no choice but to leave the quarrelling for the women to sort out among themselves (it was, strictly, beneath the concern of men), but he and Uné-mawa kept a close eye on Tealana lest she harm the unborn babe by her ill-wishes. And it seemed unfair that, of all the women, she was the strongest. It was as if malice sustained her for never did she suffer a day's illness though she complained constantly of headaches and other pains until, secretly, the other women named her 'Monaganurrah', Sickness.

Perhaps because of their concern for Neeméné, no-one noticed Meelangana's decline as the journey continued. The old man had been an elder for many years before Touami's initiation: only Wagarulepu, Tumara and Tealana remembered a time when his fire-scarred body had been straight and his hair and beard dark beneath the grease and ochre. Lately he had grown irritable and even unreasonable, arguing over matters that were usually resolved without debate and stumping off in a huff when his will was crossed though he always returned a little later as if nothing had happened. And because it seemed impossible that the old man was failing at last and that one day he would die, because of the respect due to his longevity, his unjust outbursts and ill humour were tolerated and his opinion sought whenever the elders were in council though they knew that the simplest question often resulted in a mumbled rambling that had nothing to do with the matter in hand but was the outpouring of a confused mind, a tangle of myth and memory leading nowhere.

Touami, to whom his grandfather had come to embody the very law by which they lived, found Meelangana's slow deterioration from powerful wise-man to tottering dotard hard to bear. Of all the group he was most patient in his dealings with the old man though his care was rewarded by little gratitude and much complaint from the rest, especially during the winter when Touami made sure Meelangana got enough to eat though others went hungry. Only Tealana dared voice what was in all their minds: that eventually the old man would become too weak to keep up and would have to be left behind. That thought preyed upon them all and fear of being abandoned tormented Meelangana night and day. Every morning he implored them not to desert him and his pathetic whining drove the rest to distraction. Touami often had to turn away to hide his tears.

On the morning of their descent into the grass plains the old man staggered and fell soon after their setting off: when they helped him to his feet, his throat worked and he stared wildly as if they were strangers or enemies and tried to run away. From that moment it was as if he, Meelangana, had fled his body, only returning at intervals and for the rest of the time a *ragae* or malignant spirit had taken up residence for he acted more like a wayward, vicious child than an elder. At last even Touami despaired. He was forced to strike the old man before he would go with them down the winding trail, and Tealana hissed that now was the time to leave him, before he brought ill-fortune on them all.

They came to a rounded hilltop which afforded a wide view to the north. The great valley opened out into the low undulating ground of the grass plains and rivers glinted on their winding paths across the valley floor. Numerous smoke spirals betrayed campsites, concentrated on the river banks. Beyond the grass plains was a golden haze: there, Touami knew, lay a land of lakes and marshes from which the rivers sprang though he had never been so far. The hills on the other side of the valley veered away sharply, their lower slopes truncated by a deep gorge formed by a tributary of the Big River. Shadows under the trees made the hills appear dark compared with the green and gold expanse to the north and east.

As they looked out, the group was affected by the same kind of visceral excitement that had gripped them in the days when they had over-wintered on the Toogee coast and came within sight and smell of the sea after days of travelling. They breathed deeply, snuffing the air with widened nostrils, and it seemed to them that they could already smell baking meat and friendly hearth-smoke; they listened hard and beneath the soft soughing of the warm afternoon breeze in the trees, thought to catch a deep resonance like a chant, a steady rhythm constant as a heartbeat. Then their excitement could hardly be contained for they knew that down on the flats the gathering had begun, that there would be dancing and singing, tale-telling and feasting and they hurried down the last section of the steep path until the undulating plain, dotted with gums and thorn bushes lay before them. And then they realized that the sound that had drawn them was not the strident uplifting of human voices but the baaing of many sheep.

For Toomay, who could hardly remember a time before *num* and their herds occupied the plains, this was unremarkable. Indeed, as a child, he had often played with the children of a shepherd whose hut was close to the corroboree site though he had been punished for it by his father who wanted nothing to do with the white ones. But Touami and Tumara exchanged meaningful glances when they saw a bunch of the long-tailed, woolly animals trot past for they knew that where *naa* grazed, *num* and their dogs were never far away. And Meelangana pointed and began to gabble a protective charm for instead of startled sheep he saw monsters: saliva drooled from his mouth, his eyes started and only Wagarulepu's timely slap saved him from falling in a fit.

'What are you doing?' Tumara asked, his face full of concern as Touami unslung his spear-bundle from his shoulder and selected a weapon. '*Num* are here by agreement with our people. Don't let your hatred blind you: if you kill or hurt one of them, you will be punished for it.'

It was not the white ones' law he meant but that of the tribes under which a welcome stranger was due the rights of kin. Touami, whose features had hardened at the sight of the sheep, smiled grimly and said, 'That is not my intention but they will know I do not fear them,' and then he hoisted his spear-bundle onto his shoulder and walked swiftly ahead, not wanting the other to see the bitterness in his eyes.

Looking down from the hilltop Touami had seen no sign of *num* across all that vast expanse of grassland save a distant hut with smoke spiralling from one end and he had persuaded himself that this was a shelter such as the Toogee made, the smoke coming not from a chimney but from a fire close to the entrance. It had seemed that the white ones and their absurd animals had vanished from the plains and a wild hope had arisen in him that perhaps they were gone forever, that they had abandoned Trouwerner and returned to their own place beyond the sea. But the sight of the sheep had destroyed this illusion and he was filled with shame for having believed it, a shame exacerbated by that fact that his claim to be unafraid was untrue: in his heart lurked a profound dread of the white demons. He lengthened his stride until even Toomay struggled to keep up and kept his face closed, his jaw clenched so hard the muscles ached. When he saw a thin spiral of smoke ahead he walked straight towards it though he could not tell whether the smoke was from a Lairmairrener fire or white man's hut.

As he watched the lean figure of his father move away, Toomay frowned. As a child he had loved and respected Touami above all others and even after his initiation he had been content within the hearth-group, happy to abide by the decisions of those whose experience was greater than his. But lately he had begun to question his father's judgement, in the matter of the dogs and regarding *num* in particular. Although the circumstances of his grandfather's death and the sealers' attack on his mother's camp were well known to him, it seemed to Toomay that since the white ones were also people, there must be good and bad among them as there were among *parner*. Thus he did not share his parents' prejudice, which he felt was unfair and unjustified, and his wife Neeméné, whose people had had dealings with the white strangers since their first landings, shared his view. Her hearth-group traded regularly with the whaling ships that plied the western side of the channel that was their territory and one of her brothers had even left with the seamen so that he could act as guide and interpreter between *num* and other groups along the coast.

'Don't mind him.' Tumara laid a hand briefly on the young man's shoulder. 'He'll be alright when we reach corroboree. Every year he hopes we'll arrive here to find the white ones gone and every year there are more of them. And he's worried about the old man. When Meelangana's bones go to the fire – aiee – then the old days will be truly over.'

Toomay looked closely at his great-uncle for Tumara himself was well past his prime and his body bore witness to the raid by enemy tribesmen that had destroyed his hearth-group: his wounds and the privations he had suffered after had aged him before his time. But before the young man could reply (it occurred to him that Wagarulepu was even more ancient than Meelangana), they caught up with Touami who was standing rigid and still in the shadow of a tall eucalypt, his eyes fixed on the door of a small hut.

'Yah!' Tumara said softly, not wanting to startle any armed man who was so tense. 'Come on: the corroboree will start without us!' And dismayed by the sternness of Touami's expression, he crossed boldly in front of the building with Toomay at his side.

The hut, crudely constructed from slabs of wood, lacked windows and the door was shut. But smoke wisped from a stick and mud chimney and by the smell of it Touami could tell green wood was burning there: he guessed the fire had been newly replenished. And so as the rest of the hearth-group filed past: Uné-mawa carrying their little girl, Touamyehnna; Neeméné; Tealana; Wagarulepu and Meelangana, he remained behind.

The door of the hut opened slightly. A young boy looked out. His tousled hair was the colour of sun-bleached grass and his blue eyes were startlingly bright against his tanned skin. He watched the two old people until they had passed the hulk of a felled gum tree about a spearthrow from the hut then opened the door and chocked it with a round river stone. He was dressed in patched cloth trousers kept up by a rope belt, and a kangaroo-skin shirt. His feet were bare.

Oblivious to Touami's presence, the boy watched the group pass between the trees. When they were gone he picked up a hatchet from just inside the door and went to the side of the hut where there was a pile of logs. The axe-blade glinted in the sunlight as he began chopping wood, unhurriedly but with great deliberation. It seemed that he was alone, no doubt left to mind the hut and do chores while his father was away.

As he watched the boy, who was focused on his task to the exclusion of all else, Touami was affected by a sense of sorrow he was incapable of understanding. The boy was of an age to undergo his proving, the year-long test of self-reliance all Meelayginnee boys underwent before they were deemed worthy of initiation. No such trial was faced by the children of *num*, nor was their skin marked with their lineage and tribe once they had passed the test, so that at first many *parner*, Touami included, had wondered if the white strangers were really people at all. But this lad, chopping wood beside his father's hut, seemed as at home in the tree-dotted landscape of grass and rivers as Touami himself had been when, as a boy, he had gone into the forest on his first solo hunt. It had been during his proving, Touami reflected, that the white ones had first appeared: now such boys as this were born here and their daemons, whether *num* recognised them or not, belonged to Trouwerner.

Without being aware of it, he had stood so long that the bar of shadow cast by the tree had slid away. He did not notice the sun's warmth on his skin nor realize how it picked out the red of his freshly ochred hair so that he was starkly visible. And perhaps sensing at last that he was not alone, the boy paused in his work and straightened. His eyes went to meet Touami's as if he had known he was there all along.

There was a moment of mutual surprise and recognition in which they stared at each other, scarcely breathing. To the boy Touami seemed an old man but the force of his presence made him awesome: the tension in his wiry body made him appear like a something wrought from the very essence of the land, an illusion heightened by the charcoal that darkened his skin and the ochre in his hair which was the colour of the rich floodplain soil. His shadow wavered no more than the tree's and his very silence seemed menacing though the boy, apart from an initial gasp, had also made no sound.

Very slowly, the boy bent and laid his hatchet on the chopping block. Despite his loathing of all *num* Touami could not help admiring the youngster's courage and his fingers relaxed on the spearshaft. Almost against his will he found himself moving forward, drawn by the boy's apparent lack of fear and a curiosity that was stronger than his hatred.

But as if by his approach Touami had over-reached some threshold of confidence, the boy suddenly darted into the hut, quick as a startled wallaby. In his disappointment, Touami called out and was instantly amazed at having done so. It did not occur to him that the lad might have gone to fetch a death-stick. He stood still, waiting, ensnared by a kind of deadly fascination. Through the half-open door came the smell of woodsmoke mingled with a scent that was new to him: baking flour.

A kookaburra swooped on a cricket and flapped up to devour its prize almost within Touami's reach. The movement shattered the spell that held him and he saw himself as if from the outside: an elder transfixed by the actions of a *num* boy not even old enough to be considered a whole person. Anger and shame shook him like a blast of wind and he trembled. Abruptly, he spun on his heel and strode away.

But before he had gone many paces a call, shrill and strident as a plover's, halted him in his tracks. The lad was running after with a loaf of bread cradled against his chest. Touami's gaze was so fierce, the boy stopped. He held out the bread, talking in a tone similar to the one the women used when they were trying to coerce a stubborn child and, when Touami did not react, broke a piece off and ate it, smacking his lips to demonstrate how good it was. To Touami's eyes the bread looked like the fungus, *pynener*, which was a staple of the autumn and winter and he did not move. A look of disappointment spread across the lad's face but he continued to proffer the bread, pleading for Touami to take it.

'This is not your place: go away!' Touami shouted, exasperated by the boy's earnestness and persistence. His face had become a rigid mask, the eyes bulging and bloodshot: he took another step, raising the spear and then at last the boy turned and fled back to the hut, dropping the loaf in his terror and slamming the door behind him.

Touami stood panting. The quiet of the golden afternoon descended like dust; the smell of the bread made his mouth water. From the direction of the river a dog started barking. He knew he should leave at once but first he walked deliberately to where the loaf lay and trampled it to a pulp though the doing of it left him with a lingering self-disgust. Then he strode swiftly away.

The dog's clamour faded. Soon there was only the sound of his bare feet on the baked earth and the soughing of the wind through sun-bleached grasses. Ahead, spirals of smoke rose from the corroboree fires as they had always done.

Neeméné's child was born just before the corroboree ended. It was a difficult birth which left mother and infant weak, delaying the departure of the whole hearth-group. For the older folk this came as a relief for they enjoyed the sociability of the gathering and dreaded the long journey back to Meelayginnee territory. Only Touami was fretful and restless for he smelt winter when the wind blew from the south-west and longed for the security of the wooded hills and valleys. On the open plains he felt exposed and vulnerable, a feeling that intensified as the gathering gradually dispersed until less than a hundred folk remained. And he was uncomfortably aware that there were many *num* herders now living on the plains.

For Toomay, already anxious about his wife and child, his father's unhappiness exacerbated his own. Every day he went hunting with some young men whose clan occupied the north-eastern edge of Lairmairrener territory, a land of low hills and sparse forest. Each of them had at least a couple of dogs, making up a pack of ten ill-assorted curs. These were, in effect, their weapon, able to bring down a full-grown kangaroo or emu well beyond spear-range: the trick was to beat them off before they tore their prey to pieces. In this Toomay excelled because he was a fast runner and unafraid and the others were content to let him compete with the pack in return for a share of the kill. Yet despite his success, Toomay felt ashamed because Touami's refusal to allow dogs into the hearth-group had not wavered. He seemed unaware that without the dogs and the killing of sheep, the gathering would have gone hungry.

Many of the elders were dismayed by the necessity of taking *naa*, not only because their meat was very fatty but because their loss angered the *num* herders. To the Lairmairrener this made no sense. The shepherds themselves ate sheep yet they were unwilling to share even though they and other *num* killed wallabies, kangaroos and emus in numbers far exceeding their need, often taking the skins and leaving the carcasses for the carrion-eaters. And while these animals, on which the Lairmairrener had subsisted for countless generations, dwindled, *naa* numbers had increased to the extent that in places the grass was grazed to the roots, exposing bare earth which blew away in great clouds when hot winds came from the north for the hooves of the new beasts cut the ground like knives.

It was perhaps inevitable that frustrated by the lack of other game and resentful of the *num* incursion into the Lairmairrener heartland, many of the young men began harrying the flocks for sport, rating their dogs according to the number of sheep they killed. Though the elders disapproved, there was little they could do to prevent it. When he discovered that Toomay's hunting companions were involved, Touami forbade his son to associate with them but once the young man was beyond his sight, he was helpless and though Toomay no longer boasted of *naa* torn apart or driven into the river where their fleeces became waterlogged and they drowned, Touami suspected he still met his associates on the plains. But eventually the northern clans left the gathering and Toomay's friends went with them.

A few days later some hunters noticed *num* gathering close by. Instead of exchanging tea and flour for kangaroo meat as was the custom, they fired their death-sticks as soon as the hunting party was within range, hitting one man in the shoulder. When the group returned (by which time the victim was bragging of how bravely they had fought), dismay spread swiftly through the camp. Tales of massacres by white men whose bushcraft was almost equal to that of *parner*, took on a sudden dreadful significance and many of the elders, Touami included, argued that they should disperse at once. But for the Meelayginnee the *num* camp was directly in their path and Neeméné was still weak. Touami was forced to concede that their safest course lay in fleeing northwards with the rest though every step carried them further from their own country.

So hurried was their departure they did not even fire the grass.

A day and a half later they reached an area of lakes and marshes bounded by a range of mountains whose towering cliffs were like walls barring passage to the north and west. They had travelled as fast as the pace of the children and old people allowed for they were being pursued. Whenever they looked back the same figures were in the distance, never getting closer but always there. Two were on horseback, eight on foot and they kept to the same steady pace all day. At night, when the Lairmairrener hearth-groups sat around their fires, they could see the bright spot which marked the white men's camp and they slept uneasily though when they woke the *num* were no nearer than before.

Although they provided better cover than the grasslands, Touami disliked the marshes. Midges and mosquitoes descended in clouds as soon as they arrived and in places the reeds grew so high it was impossible to see more than a spearlength in any direction. And many of the lakes and pools were floored with mud rather than sand so that a stray step off a path could set a man sinking thigh deep in stinking slime: if no-one was there to hear his cries, he might drown without a trace. Yet for many Lairmairrener this was home, a place abundant in waterfowl and platypus. They relaxed as soon as the rooty smell of marsh settled around them and tried to put the others at their ease but the Meelayginnee remained nervous. Lacking intimate knowledge of the waterways and mires, it seemed to them that the place could become more trap than refuge.

By dusk they were settled in a camping place which had been used over so many seasons, the ground was hard-packed and bare. Shelters of tea-tree boughs thatched with reeds were crowded round a central fireplace for fuel was scarce in this region and one hearth served all. In the space between the shelters and the fire more than sixty people sat or sprawled in little groups. The scene was akin to a fair: self-absorbed knots of people engaged in story-telling and feasting. Every-so-often chanting gave rise to a dance; children and dogs roamed unhindered between the groups; women suckled babes, men boasted and old folk snoozed closest to the fire, the position of highest status.

Drawn into the holiday mood even Touami relaxed but Tumara was restless. Just as the first stars appeared in the sky he rose and wandered into the darkness beyond the edge of camp. Toomay saw him go and assumed he simply wanted to relieve himself. But twilight deepened into night and he did not return. His absence made Toomay anxious and he left his place close to the fire and went to the shelter where he had left Neeméné sleeping and where all their hearth-group's possessions were piled. She was still asleep, the babe huddled against her but one spear-bundle was missing.

Toomay hesitated. He was sure his great-uncle had been empty-handed as he walked into the night: if he had removed his weapons during the afternoon and cached them in the marshes to pick up later, he must have planned his departure. And yet Toomay could not believe he would simply go without telling anyone. He sat back on his heels, his brow creased with perplexity, unsure what to do.

A pair of skewbald dogs trotted past. They looked curiously malformed, their white patches exaggerated in the bright starlight. Their heads were cocked, their ears pricked and Toomay watched them idly at first then with alarm. They paused; their hackles rose: they began to bark.

As other dogs around the camp joined in and the chanting and laughter disappeared beneath the cacophony, Neeméné sat up, startled, and clutched the baby to her breast. A nameless fear leapt like lightning through Toomay's whole being. He caught her wrist and dragged her from the shelter. A dark shape loomed and plunged past as they ran blindly towards the edge of camp.

The night exploded.

For those seated around the fire, the ferocity and unexpectedness of the attack was terrifying. The noise and flash of musket fire was followed by an instant of appalled silence: they stared in shock as four of their number slumped to the ground. Then two horsemen galloped straight across the camp, whooping and brandishing their weapons. Shrieks ripped the night apart as men, women and children ran panicking in all directions, clawing at each other in their desperation to escape. A horseman forced his wild-eyed mount round and round the fire, clubbing down anyone within reach. An old man writhed helplessly in the ashes, his back broken by trampling hooves; dogs barked and howled frenziedly; there were flashes and the sharp reports of pistols; *num* ran among the frantic Lairmairrener, stabbing, hacking, beating indiscriminately at naked flesh with knives, axes, musket butts. Metal gleamed coldly in the starlight and the raiders yelled to one another above the screams, squeals and moans of the wounded and dying in an access of triumph and blood-lust. In the noise and confusion, no-one fought back: their only thought was to get away.

Hidden in a reedbed not a spearthrow from the edge of camp Toomay and Neeméné crouched close together. Muddy water oozed between their toes and the marsh-stink cloyed in their nostrils but they did not move or make any sound. The young woman pressed the babe's face against her breast to keep it quiet but it struggled and its toothless jaws clamped so hard on her nipple she had to bite her lip to keep from crying out. Toomay's arms were around them both and she pressed her head into the hollow of his shoulder and shut her eyes but she could not stop her ears against the sounds coming from the camp. She was so tense, her body rocked with every heartbeat.

Although he did not know it, Toomay was trembling, poised to defend his wife and child with his body if the need arose for he had nothing else. His gaze was riveted on the nightmarish kaleidoscope of images visible between the reeds: it seemed impossible any of it could be real. And this sense of unreality was enhanced when he looked skywards and saw that the stars had hardly moved since the dogs started barking. The feeling that it was all a dream grew so strongly upon him that he watched calmly as one of the horsemen lit a handful of reeds from the fire and rode towards the nearest hut: it was as if he were somehow removed from the danger.

'Toomay! We must go! They'll burn the marsh!'

Neeméné pulled away and stood up. Her body was striped red and black with shadow and firelight as the hut burst into flames. The babe squirmed and gave a little mewling cry and she forced its face once more against her breast to stifle any sound. Toomay had not moved: he was transfixed by the sheets of flame which gusted from the shelters as, one by one, they were set alight. Desperately, she reached out and dug her fingers into his shoulder. 'Come on!'

He rose slowly to his feet, his eyes fixed on the flames. The screams and cries came intermittently now. *Num* on foot made their way about the wreckage, pausing to finish off anyone that moved while the horsemen rode in pursuit of fugitives. Their mounts, frightened by the fires and the smell of blood, leapt and snorted, churning the ground to a morass. To Toomay horse and man seemed one being: wreathed in smoke, glossed with water and sweat, invincible and terrifying.

'Toomay – please!' Tears streamed down Neeméné's face. She plucked at his arm and at last his trance was broken and he realized their danger. Crouching instinctively, they made their way deeper into the marsh, moving until they felt the wind in their faces and knew that, if the reeds caught alight, the fire would move away from them. When they came to a little scrubby knoll upstanding from the mire, they lay down and, in the aftermath of terror, sank into an exhausted slumber.

When Toomay awoke, the eastern sky was grey with dawn and silence hung over the wetlands. He wondered why he, Neeméné and the babe were huddled deep in the marsh for the attack on the camp seemed like a nightmare, vivid and terrible yet unreal. He sat up and yawned and then the reek of burning came to him; he looked down and saw the tracks of tears on his wife's face and the events of the night returned to him with such force that he felt sick and faint. He crawled to the water's edge and bathed his face and the touch and smell of the water restored him to the present.

'Aue . . .' Her husband's soft groan was enough to rouse the young woman. She put out a hand and groped for the infant then, reassured, rubbed her eyes and sat up. The babe whimpered as she picked it up but once it found her breast and latched on, it sucked contentedly and a secret, self-contained smile curved her lips. Here, at least, was one being she could succour and protect.

Seeing her expression, Toomay's heart seemed to melt. He knelt and pulled her close, rocking gently as if she were also a child and the motion calmed him though his senses were alert for any sign of *num*. The unnatural quiet enveloped them, soft, suffocating: even when the babe turned from Neeméné's breast and began to cry, the sound seemed muffled and strange, more like the utterance of some marsh-bird than anything human.

Reluctantly, Toomay detached himself from his wife and child and stood. Lapping brown water and sere stands of reeds surrounded them but smoke rose from the direction of the camp. He knew they must return there but afraid of what they would find he could not bring himself to suggest it. As the light strengthened, carrion birds began to circle above the camp and the air was full of their cries, harsh croaking of ravens, screams of eagles and kites.

Knowing what this signified, Toomay realized they could delay no longer. He jerked his head meaningfully and set off. His face was grim but he moved with a hunter's stealth. Neeméné followed in his footsteps, one hand cradling the infant's head lest she should need to quieten it.

A soft drizzle was falling by the time they reached the slightly raised ground at the edge of camp. Here the screech and squabbling of carrion birds overcame all other sounds. The mingled stench of smoke, burning flesh and marsh-reek caught in Toomay's throat and he almost retched: beside him Neeméné put a hand to her mouth. Her face was almost unrecognisable, haggard and full of dread.

'Stay.' He pushed her to her knees so that she would be hidden from within the camp. Being taller than she, he had already seen bodies scattered between the smouldering shelters. Without looking back, he forced himself to walk into the killing ground. Drowsing dogs with blood-stained muzzles and distended bellies raised their heads as he passed, then relaxed again. He stared numbly at the body of an old man. The marks of horse's hooves were deeply indented in the flesh and the rigid, mask-like face was frozen in an expression of utter incomprehension. At the great gathering, Toomay recalled at last, audiences had been spellbound by the skill and passion of this elder's story-telling: now his eyes had been plucked out and his tongue shredded by the beaks of carrion birds.

The dead lay thickest about the central fireplace. Toomay wandered distractedly from corpse to corpse fearing to find any of his hearth-group. And then his flesh crawled and the hairs on the back of his neck lifted like the hackles of a dog as an eerie wailing arose. Neeméné had left her hiding place to crouch beside the body of a child: she clutched their baby to her breast as she keened. Her wailing, a reaction spontaneous and natural as weeping, maddened Toomay, but it did not occur to him to try and stop her. Instead he tried to close his mind against it and forced himself on, working his way slowly from the centre of the camp towards the perimeter. It was not only the savagery and indiscriminate nature of the killings that sickened him but the desecration that had followed. Many of the bodies were mutilated and others had been arranged in obscene poses to amuse their killers.

Neeméné's wailing drew more survivors from the marsh. When he wandered back, having failed to find any of his close kin among the dead, Toomay found a throng surrounding her. As he approached, women added to the lamentation: they spun with arms outflung, threw themselves to the ground and rolled back and forth in paroxysms of grief. Many of Toomay's hearth-group were there: Tealana writhed in the mud, her voice loudest and most agonised of all; Touami sat in a stupor by one of the smoking ruins, his face a swollen, bloody mask from the blow of a musket butt while Meelangana wandered aimlessly about, stumbling over the bodies, his eyes blank and unseeing. A little later Wagarulepu and Uné-mawa arrived with Touamyehnna. The matriarch's head and shoulders were covered in blood from an axe wound to the head but the others were unscathed. When she saw Touami, Uné-mawa eased the old woman to the ground and ran to him: in the long hours of darkness and fear she had believed him dead.

By midday only Tumara was missing from the Touami's hearth-group. The drizzle had increased to a downpour and the survivors huddled together under any shelter they could find: with the huts burned, most simply held kangaroo skins over their heads. The Meelayginnee were crammed into the charred ruins of their former shelter, sorting through the ashes for the grinding stones, lumps of ochre and flint knives that were all that remained of their possessions: their spear bundles, waddies, woven bags and kangaroo- skin capes had all burned. Though the wailing of the others had not ceased, they were quiet, subdued by the magnitude of the disaster and grieving for Tumara in silence because it seemed wrong to wail for him until they were certain of his death.

As the hours passed and the rain showed no sign of easing, some Lairmairrener emerged and began to collect the bodies for burning. Shock and grief had given way to anger: an emotion requiring release through action. In response to the shifting mood, the women's wailing changed note, becoming low and insistent, full of pain and latent ferocity and the men began to chant epic tales of slaying and revenge which vied with the caws and screams of carrion birds disturbed from their feast.

Leaving Neeméné and their child in the care of Uné-mawa, Toomay went out to help for he could stand the crowded ruin no longer. Tealana followed but she only went so far as the edge of the central fire which still smouldered sullenly in the rain. Here she gathered a handful of white ash to use as a plaster on Wagarulepu's head wound. The old woman did not move or speak as the treatment was applied but Neeméné was astonished by the compassion in her mother-in-law's face. All Tealana's bitterness seemed to have vanished: this demonstration of *num* brutality had at last convinced her of Touami's innocence. She and the others had fled in the night as he had fled on the Ochre Trail, knowing that if they did not escape they would die and her eyes, when she looked upon him, were gentle, full of pity and regret for the years she had held him in contempt, now lost to them forever.

'Eh, Touami,' she breathed. He stiffened at her touch then, as she started to caress him, murmuring words of love and reconciliation in a tone unheard since he was a boy, he relaxed. Uné-mawa looked round jealously, sensing that something had diverted his attention but the old woman did not notice.

'Ah, my son, my love, best of them all,' she crooned. 'What curse was upon me that I did not know *Korerenner's* pride and joy?' And she fell into a kind of ecstasy, murmuring lullabies and hymns praising the return of mighty hunters and warriors as if he was a child again and she soothing him to sleep.

'She has lost her wits at last!' Uné-mawa whispered spitefully, rousing Touami from a happy stupor in which he had indeed reverted to childhood, basking in his mother's love, free from care. Startled and dismayed to find himself still in the ruined hut, his head pounding and his body aching with hunger and weariness, he turned on her, telling her to hold her tongue in so fierce a tone that she scrambled outside, heedless of the little girl's frightened cry. Touami sank into his mother's outstretched arms and laid his head against her withered breasts but no matter how she stroked and whispered, he could not recover his former state of easeful contentment.

The rain was cold upon Uné-mawa's skin but she welcomed it because its sting dispelled some of the lingering terror of the night. Yet there was no escaping the horror of what had happened: the pile of corpses was now larger than a Toogee hut. Those labouring to bring them in were mired with blood and nameless filth and their faces were blank and oddly rigid, as if their daemons had deserted them, leaving them incapable of thought or feeling. When she saw that same immobility in her son's face, Uné-mawa froze and his name, which had sprung involuntarily to her lips, died there for he was staring at her without recognition, as if he had turned blind.

Toomay had just laid a dead child on the pile, a girl of maybe four years. He had held her cloven skull to stop the brains spilling out and cradled her against him as he carried her, trying to still his mind against the thought that this could easily have been Cottruluttyé or Touamyehnna. When he reached the charnel heap he laid her carefully among the others and it was then, as he stepped away, that he felt something alter at the very heart of him. It was as if a fist had tightened on the raw grief and outrage festering there, squeezing and moulding it into anger immutable and indomitable as stone. He stood utterly still, his hands clenched, and a shutter seemed to come down on his sight; when he breathed he could feel the shape of his lungs in his ribcage: the stench of death wrapped him round and he tasted blood.

Then he saw his mother watching him, one hand to her mouth, her face stricken and full of fear. She stumbled forward, calling his name but when she embraced him she found his body hard and unresponsive as if carved from wood: hands fisted at his sides, he let her hysteria wash over him like the rain. Such outpouring was beyond him now and her grief did not affect him. Even when she let go and began to flail at him with her fists he endured it in silence for a while then forced himself to embrace her, stroking the cropped stubble of her hair until she was calm. She clung to him, weeping quietly, but he wished himself far away.

'Toomay, Toomay,' she whispered. 'What can we do? We should never have left our own land. Now *num* are between us and home. Aiee! – they are demons, these white ones: maybe there is no hiding from them!'

In disgust he tried to push her away but she hung on, tenacious as a possum.

'Hiding?' he asked bitterly. 'Is that all you old people can think of?' Since the white ones first appeared we have hidden and done nothing and this is what comes of it. We should have fought them from the start but always the elders have been afraid. If we do not act now, they will take Trouwerner from us and then we shall all die!'

'Toomay, ah Toomay,' she pleaded - and it seemed to him that her fingers had become claws hooking into his flesh: it took all his self-control not to pull away – 'you don't know what you're saying. You were only a little boy when they came to my father's camp and destroyed everything.' Unexpectedly she flung back her head and began to keen, a sound that sent a shiver through him. *'Karteila! Karteila!'* she called at last, piercingly. 'Aiee – all lost!'

The wailing of the women and the defiant chanting of the men had subsided as weariness and hunger overtook them and many paused in their grim work or looked up from where they sat disconsolately in the mud to see the cause of this new outcry. As their attention focused on the pair, Toomay became inordinately self-conscious. He grabbed her shoulders and shook her until she gasped and her eyes, which had taken on the glazed stare of trance, rolled and she saw him. She shuddered from head to foot, her face broke and she began to weep again. 'Aue, their bones have been eaten by the sea and they are gone,' she moaned at last. 'And Toogee spirits will wander in vain searching for them: *num* took them where they will never be found.'

He had no words to comfort her but after a moment she straightened between his hands and stared fixedly into his eyes, a look so penetrating, he was daunted by it. 'You must never leave Meelayginnee country again,' she said passionately. 'Please Toomay, promise me! You belong there: your ancestors will protect you. *Num* have no power in our own places. Please!'

It was in his mind to point out that the Toogee and now the Lairmairrener had been attacked in the very heart of their territories, but at that moment there was a tremendous splashing and disturbance in the reeds. Some of the women screamed while the men, Toomay included, looked frantically for weapons. Then the reeds parted and they relaxed, many laughing in relief, for the newcomer was a *parner.* A spear-bundle was balanced on one shoulder, a dead emu hung over the other. The bird's feet dangled behind his knees and dripped muddy slime from the passage through the marshes. Seeing the piled corpses and the ruined huts, he stopped and stared.

It was Tumara and the sight of him standing there, bewildered and unscathed, was too much for Toomay. Pushing his mother aside even as she let out a cry of recognition, he sprang towards his great-uncle, his eyes hot and fierce, his face set in a snarl. And Tumara, his senses reeling from shock, recoiled: he dropped his spears and the bird, turned and tried to escape the way he had come.

'Coward!' Toomay yelled after him. 'The white demons have gone now – there's no need to run!'

The only response was a violent commotion in the reedbed followed by a loud splash and a wail of despair. Pausing only to snatch a spear from the fallen bundle, Toomay ran after to find his great-uncle floundering in the marsh. When he saw Toomay, Tumara froze and his eyes were full of terror. He had fallen on his back in the muddy water and as he tried to push himself upright, his hands sank into the mire, trapping him. He stared helplessly into the young man's homicidal face and began to shake and whimper like a beaten child, ripples spreading across the water from the movement.

'Where were you?' Toomay held the spearpoint above the wrinkled, cringing flesh of the older man's belly. 'What made you slink away like *tarrabah* before *kannenner* comes? Did you know what was going to happen?'

'I – I –' Tumara stammered desperately. 'How could I? I was frightened but I thought it was just me. Please Toomay, don't kill me!'

Torn between pity and revulsion, Toomay hesitated. From behind came a shriek as Uné-mawa, who had come after, saw what was happening.

'Toomay – no!' she screamed and in that instant he realized that no matter what *num* had done, the law which bound all the tribes of Trouwerner remained intact and while there was still one elder who understood the ancient ways, it would be instigated. For slaying a member of his own hearth-group he would be condemned to a ritual spearing: if he survived it, he would be an outcast for the rest of his life, his beloved Neeméné given to another man. And Tumara's death would achieve nothing: another corpse to add to the already stinking pile; shame and more grief for his kin.

Sensing that if Toomay was going to spear him he would have already done so, Tumara let his head fall back against a knot of muddy roots though his eyes remained fixed on the young man's. 'Toomay,' he pleaded, '*Koonah* called me: what man ignores his daemon? I'm not a coward!'

'No?' Toomay breathed scornfully but so softly as to be inaudible to Uné-mawa who had rushed to join them. Ignoring her son, whose expression frightened her, she bent to help Tumara. He began to writhe and struggle, succeeding in pulling one hand free but it took all her strength to haul him out. Toomay remained aloof, leaning on the spear and watching disdainfully. After the two had extricated themselves and sat gasping for breath, covered with black, stinking slime, he threw the weapon in front of his great-uncle and stalked back into camp, his head held high. When Uné-mawa returned a little later, she was alone.

Once all the dead had been collected the heap was higher than the tallest man and overflowed the hearth area, covering the fire which smouldered beneath and sent up a foul smoke laden with the reek of burnt hair and charring flesh. The rain had slackened to a fine mizzle but there was no more fuel to feed the pyre save the remains of the shelters where wretched folk huddled, racked by hunger, grief and pain: few had escaped wholly unscathed. Yet as the day slipped inexorably towards evening, fear that the attackers might return overcame all other concerns.

Toomay became increasingly restless as the light began to fade. He picked up his great-uncle's spear-bundle and went into the marsh, ostensibly to watch for *num* though it was Tumara's absence that most worried him. Uné-mawa and Neeméné begged him not to leave but he promised to stay within the wetlands and with that they had to be content. But he found that as soon as he was beyond sight of them he had to fight the compulsion to go back, so fierce was his desire to protect those he loved. Only a lurking dread of what might have befallen Tumara compelled him onward.

Tumara's tracks were easy to follow in the wet ground and Toomay moved swiftly, hoping to find him before it was fully dark. The low cloud and smoke meant there would be no moon or starlight and he had no intention of spending the night in the marsh. But while at first the footprints marked the meandering pace of one unsure of his destination, Tumara's stride had gradually lengthened and the imprints of heel and toe became deeply indented as if a sense of urgency had overtaken him as his purpose became clear.

When at last he reached the edge of the wetlands, where the river wound its way onto the grass plains, the young man saw that the trail, clearly visible in the sodden ground, led straight on in the direction of their homeland.

Toomay stood still, surveying the landscape with such concentration his whole body quivered. He could not believe his great-uncle would have attempted the journey alone, especially when *num* were close. Knots of trees stood stark and black in the twilight and the slopes and folds of the grassland were grey, veiled with rain. He could see no distant figure striding away, smell no trace of hearth-smoke nor discern any sign of a *num* encampment. Yet he was uneasy, full of fear lest he should be mistaken. For the first time in his life, he mistrusted his senses.

Like all his people, Toomay lived attuned to his surroundings: the hills and valleys; the trees, birds and animals; the wind and rocks, rivers and pools, even the encircling sea. The sudden absence of this empathy shook him to the core. It was as if something intrinsic to his nature, to the balance of things, to the law that governed all Trouwerner, had shifted. His first thought was to call on *Runnawehnah* but he was afraid there would be no answer, that his daemon had deserted him. He crouched and laid his hands flat on the wet ground, but he could find no solace in the smell of earth and grass that rose to meet him. After a while he rose, easing the spear-bundle on his shoulder. The doing of it reminded him what had brought him there and then the truth came to him.

Before the coming of the white ones, he and his people had lived as their ancestors had done, secure in their knowledge of the world and their place in it. The misfortunes that befell them: wildfires, sickness, hunger, snakebite, a falling branch, were the same as they had always been, to be accepted when they happened and then forgotten because the spirit inhabiting a person never died but simply passed on. Now, Toomay realized, all that had changed: their whole lives were blighted by *num* and the fear of them. And because ancient ceremonies were being disrupted or forgotten, the ancestors were withdrawing from Trouwerner, leaving the people bereft and vulnerable.

As he thought this, a chill crept through him. He was far beyond earshot of the camp: perhaps at that very moment Neeméné was being killed or raped, the rest of his hearth-group butchered. Any idea of following Tumara vanished. He turned and ran back through the gathering dark.

Next morning, a thick polluted fug hung over the marsh. Every sound seemed magnified in the stillness: the wail of a child rang shrilly across the wrecked camp and those preparing to leave shivered, thinking of the ghosts that would haunt this place hereafter. But there was nothing more that could be done for the dead: ochre had been scattered over the smouldering heap and what remained would be left for the carrion-eaters. The survivors wanted only to leave, to hide deeper in the wetlands or to flee to the remote forests where *num* would never find them. And for Touami's group, the yearning for their own country overcame even their fear of the white demons though they dreaded the crossing of the open plain which offered no place to hide.

For three days smoke from the marshes sullied the sky and the Meelayginnee struggled across the grasslands, a distance they had covered easily in half the time before. Touami argued that their slow pace, inevitable because of his own and Wagarulepu's injuries and the need to find food, was to their advantage because *num* would most likely be watching for fleeing fugitives rather than a family group wandering as they had always done, without fear. His words were empty and they all knew it: anyone looking at them would see at once that they were the survivors of some disaster and if they were spotted by horsemen there would be no escape. But they did not speak aloud their fears. As for Meelangana, he stumbled along in a daze, guided by the women, and even Tealana was kind to him knowing the old man's days were almost spent. Because of this, the others looked upon him with a mixture of awe and pity though he was not aware of it. The faces he saw were those of folk long dead and the speech he heard was a meaningless jabber, incomprehensible as the yammer of kookaburras.

On the fourth morning of their journey a line of cloud in the west presaged rain and the hills loomed darkly though to the weary Meelayginnee they still seemed far away. They had woken at dawn as usual and were soon ready to set off, but Meelangana refused to move, grumbling that he was tired and wanted to sleep longer. By the time they had persuaded him to get up and walk, enticing and threatening him as they would have done a recalcitrant child, the sky had darkened and the dampness in the air made them shiver. And as on every day of this journey, when they left at last they walked not strung in a line as was customary, the women and children following the men, but together, so strong was their fear of being attacked.

Late in the morning Touami smelled smoke. He stopped and snuffed the air. It was not simply hearth-smoke for he discerned the taint of burnt flesh. Then his mind reeled: it was as if they had somehow travelled in a nightmarish circle. But instead of the flat marsh, the land undulated, rising gradually to meet the slopes of the hills, and the trees formed a kind of sparse woodland: they were close to the hut they had passed before. Motioning the rest to stay behind, he took a spear from Tumara's bundle and went to investigate while they sat uneasily on the sheep-nibbled grass to rest and wait.

The reeking smoke and the noise of carrion birds warned Touami what lay ahead but he did not relax his guard until he came within sight of it. A heap of black, smouldering slabs was all that remained of the hut and the boy lay face down in front of it. A few paces from him another body was so thick with ravens and eagles, it moved under their assault. An invisible hand seemed to constrict Touami's throat as he moved forward, drawn by the need to know what had happened.

The boy was so obviously dead, lying with limbs asprawl in the dirt, Touami gave him only a swift glance before going to the smoking ruin of the hut. There was another corpse there but it was impossible to tell whether it had been a man or a woman for it was burned to black clinker. It looked more like a twisted effigy than something that had once lived.

Nauseated by the stench, Touami left the hut and squatted beside the boy. He studied the body and the ground around it but did not touch. The rain had darkened the lad's hair to the colour of honey and there was a neat round hole in the middle of his back but though the wound crawled with flies, the blood had all drained into the earth. He must have died almost instantly, Touami realized because though shallow grooves traced where his fingers had clutched at the ground, there was no sign of a struggle.

Touami had no wish to see the face, remembering how the boy had tried to welcome him, and a feeling of regret swelled within him even as he wondered why the carrion-eaters had left the corpse untouched. But then, he reflected with a sudden spurt of bitterness, they had been busy in the marshes and he lurched to his feet and stood staring down, torn between pity and hatred: he saw again the pile of bodies in the wreck of the Lairmairrener camp and trembled as if with fever.

So vivid was the picture in his mind that the noise of carrion birds seemed at once to belong inside and outside his head. He turned towards it, angry that the murder of a *num* child should affect him so deeply. So intent were the ravens, kites and eagles on their meal, they ignored Touami until he ran towards them with a shout, flapping his arms wildly to drive them away. Some flew up with startled screeches but others simply hopped out of reach. These knew he could not harm them and cocked their heads, watching and waiting until he should leave and they could resume their feast.

The body was that of a bearded white man, his clothes and flesh mauled by *tarrabah* and *kannenner*. Touami saw at once why they had chosen this corpse before the others. The skull was smashed and the rib-cage and abdomen gaped open: even the limbs were hacked as if the killer had been frenzied with bloodlust. And recognising this, Touami turned and left, wanting only to be away from that place, to lead his hearth-group to safety where no *num* were.

He found the others sitting on the ground where he had left them and except for Meelangana, their heads moved constantly as they kept watch. Their nervousness reminded Touami of wallabies when they sense a hunter approach and he had to suppress a wild desire to laugh: the relief of finding them unscathed had brought him close to hysteria. Before revealing himself (he had approached cautiously in case enemies were in sight), he waited for the pounding of his heart to subside and listened for the carrion birds to resume their feast. But by some configuration of the ground he could not hear them though when he glanced back he saw that the top of the big gum tree near the hut was thronged with ravens.

Uné-mawa and the rest scrambled to their feet as Touami left the trees and walked towards them but they spoke no words of greeting, daunted by his silence and the grim expression on his battered face. When he picked up the spear-bundle and set off, they followed meekly, Wagarulepu and Tealana tugging Meelangana between them. At last they climbed the long slope that led into the forest: the scents of tea-tree and eucalypt, resinous and intoxicating, wrapped them round; they breathed deeply of the fragrant air and the terror of the grass plains slowly dissipated so that they began to talk and laugh again. Only Touami seemed unaffected by the change in mood. When Neeméné and Uné-mawa dandled his new grandchild before him to demonstrate how, despite everything, the infant was thriving, he told them roughly that the care of children was no concern of his, and turned aside. The women shrugged and went away, wondering at his hardness: Wagarulepu alone guessed the truth.

They had not gone far along the forest track when a tall figure rose before them. It was Tumara. He had made a shelter just off the path and a tiny fire burned before it. The women rushed to greet him but Touami and Toomay hesitated. There was something in the older man's face, a kind of barely suppressed excitement, which filled them with dismay. He ignored the women and came to meet them, limping heavily from a wound in his thigh. His eyes gleamed with triumph.

'See – I'm not a coward!' He grinned and tugged at a cord slung across his chest, then held his trophy out for inspection. It was a small axe. The wooden handle was smooth and shiny with wear but the blade, which had once gleamed brightly in the *num* boy's hands, was dull with dried blood, the colour of rust.

12. Leave-taking.

(Southern Tasmania, Spring 1824).

The swallows had come from the north but snow still clung to the highest peaks when Touami led his hearth-group to the sacred place at the heart of Meelayginnee territory. It was where, long ago, he had been initiated and it was there also that he was most aware of his father's ghost. For Umara's bones had never been burned or brought to the place of his ancestors but left to rot with those of the fanged demons that had killed him. And although the years had begun to tell upon Touami, his memories of that death remained vivid and terrible as on the days after the attack, unlike those of the massacre he had witnessed on the Grass Plains long after. That outrage had taken on the quality of a half-remembered nightmare in his mind, perhaps because his hearth-group had escaped virtually unscathed.

Following those experiences, Touami and his kin avoided *num*: he was suspicious even of other *parner*. His uncle, Tumara, was the sole survivor of a raid by a war-party from a different Lairmairrener clan and their ruthlessness and ferocity had shocked Touami's group. The usual motive for such attacks was the abduction of women for the boundaries of tribal and clan territories were fixed according to ancient tradition. But this time the warriors had taken over Tumara's camp and lived there as if by right and the guardian spirits had done nothing to prevent it.

Several winters had passed since Tumara had joined Touami's hearth-group and during that time they heard of many such incidents. Wagarulepu, eldest of all Meelayginnee, maintained that Wyerkartenna, the Cunning One, had tricked Moinee into leaving Trouwerner and that the spirits of the ancestors had fled with him, abandoning the children of Tarner to chaos and death. But Touami, whilst respectful of the ancient myths, blamed *num* for all the ills that had befallen him and his people and he held them directly responsible not only for his father's demise but the deaths of his sister and Toogee brother-in-law also. For they had disappeared just before sealers had murdered Noné, the pariah, and their bodies had never been discovered.

A grim mood was therefore upon Touami as he led the way through the forest and it was little lightened by the fact that his daughter, Touamyehnna, was to be initiated and betrothed at the forthcoming corroboree. Formerly it would have been unheard of for a girl to marry within her clan but with contact between the Meelayginnee and the coastal bands broken, there was no choice other than to remain unwed. And while she declared she did not care where her husband came from so long as he was a good provider and kind to her and their children (Wagarulepu scoffed at such naivety), Touami worried that this flouting of ancient law would only exacerbate their woes. According to tradition such unions always came to grief.

When at last they reached the camp beside the torrent that descended from the sacred caves, they found several hearth-groups already there. Yet their numbers were far fewer than Touami had expected though it was, Wagarulepu estimated, only a day before the full moon when the ceremonies would begin. The elders sat talking on a shady bank of the river and Touami waved a hand at Uné-mawa and Tealana, indicating that they should establish camp while he, Wagarulepu, Tumara and Toomay went to speak with them.

Over the next few days much ceremony was conducted. Touamyehnna was married and there was dancing, singing and storytelling which sometimes lasted until dawn. But as the days passed, a pervading anxiety overshadowed the celebrations. Formerly there had been little brooding on the past or speculation about the future but now, when nothing else was happening, the clearing was full of groups of people talking. And their talk was all of the white ones. Though few among the Meelayginnee had encountered them first-hand, they had heard disturbing tales from travellers and fugitives: of whales and other creatures killed in unprecedented numbers; of trees cut down and stone camps built;

of wives and daughters stolen or traded for dogs and *num* food; of men wounded and slain: they looked to the wise-ones for explanations and guidance in a world become uncertain and doubted what they heard.

Touami was old and respected enough to hold a place on the council of elders but though he attended the meetings he seldom spoke, aware that despite his years, his wisdom could not match that of his grandfather whose place he had taken. Yet this time he was hard put to maintain his usual control. For most argued that the white ones, like bad weather or a plague of biting flies, had to be endured until they went away of their own volition and then life would continue as it had always done.

Knowing the futility of arguing with men and women whose word, by default, carried more weight than his, Touami sat silent and fuming through long debates that led nowhere while his mind seethed with memories of violence and bloodshed: the stripped carcasses of *karteila*; the terror of the fanged demons; the carnage on the Grass Plains. Every night since their arrival in the sacred place he had re-lived his father's death in dreams and sometimes, waking chilled with sweat, he heard Umara's voice whisper like the night wind, begging to be avenged so that his spirit could come home. Even Uné-mawa could not comfort Touami then for she had borne no live children since his return from that ill-fated journey and in this both saw the judgement of their ancestors, none of whom wished to be reborn with a coward for their father.

One evening, longing for solitude, Touami went alone to the pool at the foot of the waterfall which spilled from the mouth of the sacred gorge. The air was cool and refreshing, laden with the scents of water and ferns, moist with spray, and he felt painfully alive although his pervading mood was one of deep melancholy. And this enhanced the dream-like quality of what followed.

The sun had just set but the stars and moon had not risen and the sky was a luminous turquoise, lending the water and the surrounding vegetation a dark verdancy, when an old man appeared on the rock platform opposite where Touami sat. So silent and smooth were his movements it was as if his form had materialised from the shadows though he was gaunt as a wind-dried carcass. He hesitated and though Touami could not see his face, he felt the old man's glance keenly as the touch of icy fingers.

Whether ghost or living man, so venerable a figure commanded respect and Touami patted the rock in invitation. At this the old man inclined his head and came to join him. As he sat down, the moon rose above the cliffs and its pale light caught in a deep pitted scar from a spear-wound in the man's right thigh. Then Touami knew him. He had never met the wanderer, Ouniaga, before but knowledge that his grandfather, a powerful wise-man, had feared him was enough to make him apprehensive.

For a while they sat in silence, watching the glossy swirl of water in the moonlit pool but though his hand were loose at his sides and his head bent, the tautness of his face-muscles, which threw his cheekbones into high relief, betrayed Touami's tension.

'Do not be angry, son of *Korerenner*,' the old man said at last and his voice was like the sough of wind though dead grass. 'Even the wisest may speak only of what they know. And so when things happen that were formerly unthinkable, they explain them by what has already been. You and I have seen that these *num* are only men yet they come from some place that is not Trouwerner and abide by different laws to ours. And so we cannot understand them.'

Touami drew his knees up to his chest and put his arms about them, feeling oddly self-conscious before the other's quiet authority, like a child brought before a sage.

'*Num* know no laws,' he said bitterly. 'And if they are men and possess spirits, their daemons must be insects: ants or grasshoppers which consume all in their path. So my grandfather told us.'

Ouniaga smiled faintly. 'He was a wise man. But if that is true, what should we do?'

'My grandfather counselled that *num* should be avoided; my grandmother, Wagarulepu, argues we must retreat to the part of our country furthest from them and live our lives as if they did not exist. But it is cold there and food is hard to get. And who can say if any place is beyond reach of these white ones?'

'And so?' Ouniaga spread his hands in a gesture of resignation yet Touami hesitated before answering. He sensed that he was being manipulated for there was expectancy in the other's moonlit face, the expression of one who knows the outcome of a debate before it has begun.

'Is this not the time to act?' The old man's tone was easy, conversational at first but as he continued speaking his passion increased and he leaned forward a little: his gaze held Touami so that he could not look away. 'Every day more of them come and few leave while we watch and fight one another and fall sick and die. Our numbers grow less as theirs increase. Soon it will be too late!'

Touami shivered, realizing that Ouniaga was not simply speaking of Meelayginnee or even Lairmairrener but all the tribes.

'Trouwerner is changing,' the wise-man went on. '*Num* kill us and steal our women and children. They slaughter and do not eat; they are destroying the very forests to make new ground according to their custom: strange plants grow there and the animals which graze upon them are shaped for a different world. And yet it is we, not they, who are dying.'

'How can it be?' Touami was deeply dismayed by the implications of this speech which were wider than anything he had considered before. 'Trouwerner formed us: our blood, our bones, our spirits belong here.' He laid one hand over the cicatrices across his chest which were painted with *ballawiné* in honour of the occasion. 'Does this mean nothing any more?'

The old man looked pityingly upon him and yet he had no answer: these questions had tormented him since he had first seen the white ones in the year of Touami's initiation. In all that time he had become certain of one thing only: *num* would not leave willingly.

'What happens when *loinah* comes to steal *darwalla's* eggs?' he asked ingenuously and Touami started because *darwalla* was his daemon.

'She calls and dances before him to draw him away; her mate comes to help and sometimes others also because *loinah* threatens them all,' he replied automatically, for this formed the basis of one of the most beloved of Meelayginnee myths. 'And while he watches her, the others peck his tail bloody until he goes away to nurse his wounds.'

'Eh – and should we not learn from this?' The wise-man leant back but his eyes remained fixed on Touami's. '*Num* can be killed like other men but they are far from their own place and their spirits will find no peace here. Perhaps they can never be utterly destroyed but it may be possible to drive them away.'

Touami said nothing. He thought of the white boy he had encountered on the Grass Plains, who had tried to give him a gift of food and, later, been killed by Tumara. That boy had seemed as at home in the place of his birth as any Meelayginnee child but he was *num* so where did his spirit belong?

'The white ones are only strong when there are many of them together,' Ouniaga continued. 'Alone, they are weak and easily killed. When they have fired their death-sticks they become helpless as women. And they have things that are good to take.'

Still Touami said nothing but his mind had at last grasped where the other was trying to lead him. He tightened his arms around his knees and his face took on a troubled, brooding look. To kill men, even the white ones, simply because of what they were was anathema to him: in his heart he hated and feared all *num* but he only desired vengeance against those who had set the dogs on him and his father; the gang responsible for the massacre on the Grass Plains. These were personal matters which, according to the laws of the tribes, demanded redress: what Ouniaga was proposing was conflict of a scale and kind unprecedented in Trouwerner.

'I have tried to call lightning and fire-storm on them,' the old man said, 'and nothing happened though in the past I possessed such powers. Maybe the Old Ones are deserting us because we did nothing to stop *num* when they first appeared. Or maybe their sorcery is stronger than ours: perhaps it is true that they come from a land of the dead and are stealing the spirits of our people. For I have heard' - his voice dropped to a whisper – 'that they cut up *parner* they have killed and keep certain parts to work magic on the dead one's kin.'

Touami shuddered and the memory of how he had found his father's remains on his return along the Ochre Trail filled his mind. The scavengers had done their work and Umara's bones were broken and scattered, mixed irretrievably with those of the fanged demons but his skull was missing. Touami had always believed *kannenner* or *tarrabah* must have dragged it away: now, with a start of horror, he realized it might have been stolen and that Uné-mawa's subsequent miscarriages were due to *num* sorcery.

'Why are you telling me this?' His tongue seemed thick and heavy in his mouth and his skin crawled with dread. 'I am no wise-man to know what to do. Even *Lyenah*, who claimed *num* were bad from the start, could not tell me.'

Now it was Ouniaga's turn to be silent. He lowered his gaze and frowned, the moonlight turning the furrows in his brow to long gashes. And Touami waited patiently for though the old man had spoken of declining powers, his reputation was such that no-one in their right mind would dare to cross him.

'Ahh . . .' The wise-man sighed and with great deliberation took the talisman bag from his chest. A light sweat broke on Touami's skin for he sensed some kind of magic was imminent but he forced stillness upon himself. Then Ouniaga began to chant, his voice barely audible above the roar of the waterfall. He closed his eyes, rapt in a profound inward focus. Out of respect, Touami averted his gaze but he could not help stealing occasional surreptitious glances at the wise-man lest some physical change should betray what was happening in his spirit-journey.

Moon-flung shadows slipped across the rock platform: where he had been in awe, Touami began to weary. Ouniaga had fallen silent and his breathing was slow and deep, his mouth and eyes mere slits in his weathered, age-seamed face. His hands, which had been closed around the talisman-bag had fallen open in his lap: had he wished, Touami could have leaned over and taken it without touching the wise-man at all. But even though he had begun to think Ouniaga had simply fallen asleep, he did not dare.

The sound of chanting from the camp sounded above the noise of running water as the corroboree began again but it seemed remote and strange to Touami's ears. He felt as if he and this ancient man had somehow become detached from the living world, removed to a place contiguous with, but distinct from, all that was familiar. Had it not been that he knew himself to be awake (he bit his knuckles to be sure), he would have believed he was dreaming.

Then Ouniaga's mouth opened. It was all ropy with saliva which glistened in the moonlight and a voice issued from it but it was not his. Low and hoarse yet oddly toneless (as if through long disuse the speaker had forgotten the nuances and cadence of normal speech), it was, unmistakeably, that of Touami's father:

'Ah my son, do you not care how I died? Blood claims blood: that is the law. Has *Darwalla* no ears to hear it, no heart to feel? How is it that I wander still?'

As these words left his lips, Ouniaga reached out and grabbed Touami's right wrist, the swiftness of his movement and the ferocity of his grip more like that of one in the prime of strength than an old man. Appalled, transfixed, Touami was incapable of resisting. He watched spellbound as Ouniaga flattened the hand on the rock and then, with uncanny swiftness (so that Touami barely had time to realize what was happening before it was done), slashed the palm with an obsidian knife he had taken from his talisman-bag.

The wound welled darkly as the old man (or the thing that was using him as its mouthpiece), finished speaking and Touami stared at it uncomprehendingly. He felt no pain: he was empty, bereft. Nothing existed but this blood dripping on the bare rock and the darkness closing in.

How long he sat there he never knew. When he woke to himself the moon had sunk and bright stars glittered overhead. Nothing could be heard from the direction of the camp though he listened hard: everyone must be asleep. The only sounds were those of water and leaves whispering in the night breeze.

As memory returned to him, he looked round for Ouniaga. There was no trace of the old man on the rock and the shadows were empty. Yet when he moved his right hand there was a sharp sting across the palm: the encounter had been neither dream nor nightmare. And so his father had really spoken, from whatever void the unquiet dead inhabited.

The moisture-laden air was clammy and chill and Touami shivered violently as he clambered to his feet, cradling his hurt hand against his chest. Grief had lodged like a boulder at the very heart of him: it weighed him down, acted as a drag on his very thoughts. Since the moment he had abandoned Umara to the *num*, Touami had been burdened by guilt but to have his shame acknowledged by his father's spirit was more than he could bear. He moved along the path like a sleepwalker, dazed and heedless of the quoll that scampered in front for a little way; the strident calls of plovers disturbed by another nocturnal rambler: *tarrabah* or someone gone to relieve themselves. When he reached the clearing where the air was full of the gentle snoring of many sleepers, he paused and it seemed to him that he was still caught in the throes of a trance or dream: he saw as if with a stranger's eyes that a sudden flood or firestorm, a raid by hostile tribesmen or *num* with death-sticks could destroy the camp and all the Meelayginnee in an instant. And he realized with a terrible clarity that the laws and traditions which formed the very fabric of their lives were, in truth, as fragile and intricate as a spider's web: once one thread snapped, the whole structure was weakened.

'Touami?' So deep was his introspection he had not noticed Uné-mawa's approach though she had made no attempt to conceal herself from him. He stared blindly until, frightened by the bleakness of his gaze, she reached out and touched his arm. Then he shook his head as if to dislodge his thoughts and saw her standing before him.

'What happened?' Her voice was low and scared. 'Why were you not at corroboree? I stayed awake watching for you. Where have you been?'

He did not answer but looking into her eyes, which were glossy and unreadable in the starlight, breathing in the warm smell of her, he felt weary to the very depths of his being. And she seemed to understand for she did not persist but led him in silence to their shelter. Thankfully, Touami stretched out on the soft, fragrant leaf bed and Uné-mawa slid beside him. The warmth of her body and the calmness of her presence comforted him a little, easing the terrible gnawing loneliness the wise-man had opened inside him until, at last, he slept.

With so many gathered together, hunting was a communal affair: men, women and children taking part in drives which herded game onto the waiting spears of the elders. Soon after dawn Touami and

Uné-mawa set off with the rest but he walked in silence and when the chasers yelled to frighten the quarry, he hung back. Worried and doubtful of his explanation that he had cut his hand on a sharp rock, Uné-mawa lagged also, shadowing him from tree to tree but while her feet were almost soundless on the bare earth and she took care to avoid overhanging branches and dense undergrowth, it was a mark of his distracted state that he did not sense her presence. Normally the empathy between them was so profound that one often knew the other's mind without need for speech.

The noise diminished as the hunt went further away and Touami stood still, head poised to listen. Uné-mawa froze for she was less than a spear-cast from him. But apparently satisfied that he was alone, he squatted and peered intently at the ground. He was so still that anyone chancing past would not have noticed him: his self-effacement was absolute. The shadows of trees slid over him and so well did his figure meld with the patterns of light and shade, the muted greens, browns and greys of the vegetation and earth that even Uné-mawa began to doubt her eyes. It seemed impossible that any living creature could maintain such perfect immobility over so long a period unless they were sick or sleeping.

Then, long after she had begun to weary of the wait, he rose unexpectedly to his feet. Without looking round, he set off towards the camp, moving now with such swiftness Uné-mawa struggled to keep up. It was like trying to chase a fleeting shadow and she was slowed by the need for stealth for she feared what he might do if he discovered she had been spying on him.

As he walked Touami was hardly aware of his surroundings: he was reliving the events of the night calmly and, he believed, objectively. His grandfather, Meelangana, the only man who could have warned him against Ouniaga's powers to persuade and manipulate, was long dead, and it did not occur to him to doubt or question what had happened. Instead he was filled with certainty. His father's spirit had simply put into words what he had begun to believe in his heart: that now was the time for action. And this conviction had been strengthened by the ants he had watched that afternoon. Some animal, most likely an echidna, had broken open their nest and then been disturbed: after their initial panic, the ants had split according to size and nature, the largest and most aggressive swarming to drive off the attacker while others scurried in line along a well-worn groove in the dirt: these bore the eggs and helpless larvae to safety.

He also would send his kin where the very remoteness of the terrain would protect them while he was away.

When he came to the camp the hunt was over. Several wallabies were cooking in the ashes and everyone was in the mood to celebrate. They looked curiously at Touami as he walked towards the river but though some called after, having missed him during the chase, no-one hindered him for the grimness of his face and the blood staining his right hand daunted them. And yet in his heart Touami was no longer downcast: his purpose was set and he was determined nothing would turn him from it. He would grieve no more but seek revenge.

When he came to the river he avoided the trampled watering place and clambered down the bank a little further upstream where a log had jammed between boulders, forming a narrow platform. Here he knelt and drank, bending to suck the water directly from the surface rather than scooping it with his hands. It was cold and slightly bitter to the taste but he savoured it because it came from the sacred gorge and when his thirst was slaked, he washed his right hand with a care that was ritualistic in its deliberation. His blood mixed with the running water and swirled away and joy surged through him as he watched for with the gift of blood and its acceptance by *Liapota* the guilt that had been with him since the day of his father's death was at last lifted: he felt free again.

Once all trace of the blood had dissipated, he climbed the bank. Washing had reopened the gash but this was now of no account so he went to the nearest fireplace and packed ash into the wound to staunch the bleeding. It was only then that he realized Uné-mawa was with him. Beside the river she had hung back, realizing that what he was doing was somehow sacred, but now her eyes sought his with an urgency that would not be denied.

'Touami, what has happened?' she asked.

'Last night my father spoke to me,' he said. 'Not in a dream but through the mouth of Ouniaga, the wise-man. Wagarulepu is right: the hearth-group should stay here, far from *num*, and their lives will be unchanged. But I shall not be with you. It is time for revenge.'

She stared and her gaze seemed to swallow his. 'But Ouniaga is not here,' she said at last. 'He has not been seen in Meelayginnee lands since Touamyehnna was born. You must have been dreaming, love.'

Each of these words was like a blow to Touami's new-found resolve but he shook his head and a slightly pitying smile curved his lips. 'How then did this happen?' he asked, showing her his cut palm. 'My father slashed it with Ouniaga's knife. It was no dream.'

'You told me you cut it on a rock,' she retorted and then something in his expression stayed her anger. She drew herself up and a grave, proud look overtook her features. When she spoke again, her voice was calm and firm. 'My brother and your twin sister were lost when *num* came to Toogee shores,' she said. 'They slaughtered *karteila* and my people sickened and died. If you go, I will come with you.'

'There is no place for women on the war-trail,' Touami replied harshly. 'You and the rest must go into the highlands and deep valleys. It will be hard, but I will return when I can.'

He turned abruptly, trying to escape an argument that could only end in pain but she stepped quickly in front to bar the way.

'Is that what the ants told you?' Her voice was hard and scornful and he stood still, astounded, for he had not known anyone had seen him after he left the hunt, she least of all. 'What do you think you can do alone against the white ones? You couldn't even save your father!'

In all the years they had been together, Touami had never struck Uné-mawa even when she displeased him: he was not by nature a violent man. But at these words, which checked his righteous mood and insulted his very manhood, anger rose in him and he lifted his right hand to strike her out of the way and extinguish the mocking light in her eyes. Yet even as he did so her expression altered to one of expectancy and there was defiance rather than fear in her gaze, as if she were challenging him to do it. And then there was a stab of pain across his palm and blood sprang beneath the ash and he lowered the hand, knowing that whatever he did to her it would make no difference.

'I won't be alone,' he said. 'His spirit will be with me.'

Her eyes did not waver and he looked away, unable to withstand the force of her gaze.

'And I will be there too,' she said.

News that Touami and his Toogee wife were planning to take the war-trail against *num* spread swiftly through the camp. By the time the elders had resumed their council it was known to all and even the children looked upon the couple with a kind of awe. But the rest of their hearth-group were angry and dismayed. When Touami and Wagarulepu went to join the elders, Tealana confronted Uné-mawa.

'Last time we separated I lost my husband to the Ochre Trail, now must I lose Touami also?' Her eyes were wild, her lean face taut with rage. 'Who else is afflicted with this madness? Anyone? Or is it me alone who must bear the curse of a son more bent on revenge than care for his hearth-group, and a daughter-in-law as reckless as a boy?'

'Is it not then a wife's duty to look after her husband?' Uné-mawa retorted. 'We are not asking you to come. Wagarulepu, Tumara and Toomay will make sure no harm befalls you, never fear.'

Neeméné, Toomay's wife, who was sitting nearby with her children, looked up gratefully at this for she knew her husband would be torn between staying and going to fight, but Tealana trembled and her mouth twitched as she worked herself into a frenzy.

'Aiee!' Her cry shuddered through the camp and many looked to see who was in such distress. And once she was the focus of attention, Tealana seemed to lose all sense of propriety. Wailing, she scooped handfuls of white ash from the edge of the nearest fire and began alternately rubbing it all over her scalp, face and body and tossing it into the air so that it hung about her in a fine, choking cloud.

Embarrassed and appalled, Uné-mawa recoiled, not knowing

what to do. Sometimes, especially at a funeral feast, the women would enter a trance through wailing and dancing but there was something more sinister in Tealana's hysteria. Yet though even the elders paused in their debate, no-one moved to help. They simply watched and waited, knowing that whatever the cause, the fit would pass eventually.

Anger and shame rose within Touami like a tide as his mother flung herself down and began to writhe in the dirt and ashes. He remembered how she had mourned Umara long after the usual period, using her loss as an excuse to malinger, never letting him forget what had happened on the Ochre Trail. When she rolled over and, drawing herself into a crouched, kneeling position, began to strike the ground with her fists, he leapt to his feet and strode towards her. Her wailing had subsided to a kind of agonised moan but Uné-mawa saw her eyes flick sideways at the sound of approaching footsteps. Then any pity she might have felt for her mother-in-law vanished: she realized it was all an act. And though she had been prepared to intervene, now she let Touami pass, partly because his face displayed such concentrated fury, she was afraid.

'Be quiet!' He caught Tealana's arm just above the elbow and dragged her roughly to her feet. She let out a sharp cry of protest and flailed wildly with her free arm but Uné-mawa noted she was careful not to strike her son, thus giving him the right to punish her.

'I am not a child,' Touami said tightly. 'You may be my mother but you are foolish and have become lazy since my father died. Would you prefer us to sit idle by the fire while his spirit cries to be avenged? Maybe you want to exchange your great-grandchildren for *num* food or dogs as some have done? If so, go down to their stone camp and let them look after you!'

As he spoke he was marching her towards the lean-to where Toomay and Tumara sat. Tealana's struggles had diminished to an occasional tug or twist but against Touami's strength she was powerless. When they reached the others he let go and she stood rubbing her arm, staring at him through a film of tears.

By now the altercation had drawn everyone in camp. The eldest among them sensed something momentous in the air, a beginning that would become enshrined in myth: *Darwalla* and *Ruwah* preparing for the war-trail. They waited quietly and mothers hushed restless children who wanted to know what was happening.

'My wife and I are leaving,' Touami said firmly and Uné-mawa felt a thrill of pride that he spoke of her as an equal. He swept the crowd with a gaze that was both fierce and challenging. 'We shall take revenge for my father and sister and many of Uné-mawa's kin. My father's ghost came to me last night and told me what to do.'

He paused, seeing the anguish on Toomay's face, and shook his head slightly: the young man rose and walked away between the trees.

'This is our fight: mine and Uné-mawa's,' Touami continued, seeing consternation on many faces and he smiled for a fey, reckless mood had come upon him. 'We two will be enough. The rest should stay away from *num*. Bad things come from dealing with them.'

An uneasy silence fell for many of the younger men were unsure whether he was mocking them. Tumara shifted where he sat and the elders muttered together. But none dared speak directly against Touami because he was acting according to a dead man's wish.

'Those are bold words from one who has only run from the white ones!' Wagarulepu shuffled forward and thrust her face towards her grandson for age had dimmed her sight and she wanted to be sure to whom she was speaking. 'And yet there is wisdom in them. Always I have believed we should hide from *num* though few have heard me until now. Aye . . .' she reached for Tealana's arm, grasping it with such vicious strength that the woman grimaced. 'What will it take before you learn to listen, foolish one? All your wailing will never bring *Korerenner* back: it only disturbs him!'

'I – I -' Tealana stammered, then realizing protest would get her nowhere, she twisted free of the old woman's grip. The crowd parted to let her pass but no-one followed or tried to offer comfort. Their attention was all on Touami and Wagarulepu. The old woman looked searchingly into her grandson's eyes then turned and addressed the gathering, her voice strong and firm: 'Though it is not for any man or woman, even an elder, to tell another what to do, my heart says this: more talk will achieve nothing but the wearing out of tongues. Let this be the last night of corroboree then we shall go our own ways. And the wise will stay away from *num* unless they also want revenge.'

A great tumult arose at the conclusion of this speech as youths who had just been initiated clamoured to go with the couple while many of the elders protested that there was still much to discuss. But to Touami the noise was insignificant as the rush of wind through treetops. He looked upon the wizened, diminutive form of his grandmother and was overwhelmed by a complex surge of feeling in which love, pride and sorrow melded.

'Eh boy . . .' She seemed to sense his emotion because she shook her head, not in denial but acknowledgement as he stepped forward and embraced her. Her skin was dry and loose upon bones that seemed thin and fragile as a bird's but as he breathed in the smell of her, old sweat and rancid grease mixed with the metallic tang of *ballawiné* and the earthiness of clay, he felt like a child again, secure and happy in the belief that while she was there, no harm could befall him.

'Take this.' She pushed him away with a gentleness that astonished him and took the little talisman-bag from around her neck. 'In our own place we'll be safe but who knows what trails *num* will lead you on? You may need *Lyenah's* wisdom.'

He stammered some words of thanks, took the little pouch and hung it round his neck.

'You will return,' Wagarulepu said and whether she had dreamt it or spoke in hope alone, it was with utter conviction. From that moment Touami's resolve purpose burned within him like a steady flame and in the months to come her words became a talisman, a spell to keep him safe.

'*Darwalla* will guide me; *Korerenner* will protect me, *Lyenah* will help me,' he replied. 'How can I fail?'

'Come,' Uné-mawa broke in, jealous of the old woman's power. 'It is time to eat.'

The rest of that evening seemed to drag interminably for Touami, so eager was he to set off, though he was to remember it as the last of a time remote and shining as the Pygeewar. The feasting was quiet for while the participants gorged as usual, their talk was constrained by the events of the afternoon. As was expected of him, Touami sat with the elders at their council fire. Wagarulepu had stayed with their hearth-group though she also was an elder and for a moment he envied her because every-so-often one of the old men would pause to stare at him appraisingly and not always with approval. He endured their scrutiny with a kind of proud diffidence, knowing that whatever they thought of him, his right to vengeance was enshrined in tradition and unassailable.

The children had begun to dance, too excited to wait any longer, when at last the elders finished eating and, one by one, went to join their kin. None spoke to Touami, either to encourage or dissuade, nor did they acknowledge him as they rose to their feet and left. That way, he thought bitterly, whatever happened, they could not be blamed.

He waited until the last of them had gone, leaving him to extinguish the little fire that had burned since the council began, thus signalling its end. He piled stones and earth over the blaze and stamped them down until not even wisp of smoke escaped but as he did so he was overtaken by a profound sense of sorrow and, strangely, of urgency: it seemed to him that if he did not leave now, at once, it would be too late. Then he hurried to find Uné-mawa, hoping she was not dancing. A long line of women was already strung between the fires and their chant, the story of Droémadeener and *Lueena* sounded above the noise of the river and sent a thrill through his blood even as he searched.

Uné-mawa was not among the dancers though Touamyehnna was there with dark shadows under her eyes. But Touami's eyes lingered only a moment on his daughter. Then he turned away from the dance and the circle of watchers and strode swiftly towards his shelter which, he now realized, was the first place he should have looked.

She was sitting inside, her woven bag upon her lap. As he approached she rose and he saw that she had washed the pigments from her skin and removed her shell and sinew necklaces, leaving only the strip of sealskin around her neck that was as much a symbol of her clan as the scars on her breasts and thighs. She looked at him and he saw a clear, calm resolve in her eyes and knew that she also was ready, that the time for ceremony was over and it was better to slip away unnoticed than endure the wails and tears of a formal leave-taking though the grief of parting would be no less.

The sky was red with sunset, red as ochre and its light bathed the forest so that every leaf was limned with gold and the dancing figures seemed clothed in flame. But Touami and Uné-mawa smeared themselves with charcoal and as the sunset faded and twilight spread beneath the trees, they picked up their possessions and stole like shadows into the night.

13. The Raid.

(Black Hills, Spring 1830).

Six winters had passed since Touami left his hearth-group to fight the white demons. He was fifty-one, old enough to be counted among the wise simply from longevity but estranged from his clan, he attended no councils save those of war. Once, he had yearned to return home but the loyalties that bound him to his skin-group had gradually transferred to the young men and women who joined his gang to plunder *num* huts and farmsteads. This had grown to be an end in itself as once unimagined luxuries: food that did not have to be hunted, tea, blankets, even tobacco, became necessities.

Yet in his heart, the resolve that had set him on the war trail had not weakened. His father's spirit no longer haunted his dreams but there were others that had died since, most recently his beloved Uné-mawa, whose blood demanded vengeance. His hatred of *num* remained immutable and uncompromising and it was only through killing or outwitting them that he found fulfilment. Everything else had become a weariness: sometimes, when he was tired or wounded, he longed to die. But then the memory of all he had loved would pull him from the mire of self-pity and, despising himself for his weakness, he would force himself to fight on.

Had Uné-mawa lived, he might have been happier. But with her death, it seemed to him all joy had fled. She had proved as quick and elusive a fighter as any of the warriors; it was she who worked out how to load and fire a stolen musket, and though they regarded it as a clumsy and inefficient weapon, they stole powder and ball thereafter for the fear it inspired in their enemies. And when any of the war-band was hurt or sick, she tended them, for the matriarch, Wagarulepu, who was a renowned wise-woman, had taught her much.

Yet in the end it was her care for others that caused Uné-mawa's demise. She had not died fighting or from wounds or hunger but from the lung-sickness they believed was brought by the demon, Rowra, though it had appeared at the same time as the white ones. It was during winter that the sickness was at its worst for then its effects were exacerbated by hunger and cold and it spread rapidly between people huddled together for warmth. And though at first its victims might deny the symptoms, going out in rain and sleet to find food for those already sick, ignoring the aching of their limbs and head, the sneezing which presaged the beginning of the end, they soon succumbed. Mucus streamed from their mouth and nose, some coughed with such force that their ribs snapped, and they writhed with pain as the fever mounted until at last, their strength used up in their efforts to clear their lungs of the foulness which was slowly suffocating them, they lay lethargic, sank into a stupor and died.

Touami had lost count of the men, women and children he had seen or heard of dying from this sickness (the truth was, more of his companions had died from the pestilence than at the hands of *num*), but after four years he had considered himself and Uné-mawa among the most fortunate: those who had been touched by Rowra and survived. The previous autumn they had both suffered streaming noses and fever but the time of their sickness coincided with a raid on a large farmstead from which they had come away with blankets and enough food to last weeks. This had enabled them to rest and the sickness had gone away; this winter, when Uné-mawa sickened again and died, he was left stricken, disbelieving, bereft. For it meant that of his original gang, only he and a younger man, Longertalenna of the Paradarerme, remained. All the rest had joined later, eager to kill *num,* and though some were motivated by revenge, others simply craved excitement.

Now at last it was spring again, the days lengthening and the sun's warmth lessening the fear of Rowra. This was the time when *num* drove their sheep and cattle to graze on the fringes of the settled area, sometimes leaving their homesteads untended or with only old men, women and children as guard. Once, Touami's group would have attacked the herds but they had learned that the farms made more satisfying targets for when they had been plundered and the inhabitants slain or wounded, the buildings burned easily. One of the few pleasures he still savoured was watching smoke billow from a burning homestead in the knowledge that the owner would see it from afar and hurry back only to find his home and possessions utterly destroyed.

Of late, the white ones had tried to be more cunning as the attacks upon them increased in frequency and ferocity. They set traps, sometimes no more elaborate than a party of Redcoats waiting inside a building, or setting doors and windows so that when they were opened, a gun discharged. But so closely were they watched, Touami and his companions would simply go elsewhere or wait until the owners returned. And sometimes, to add insult to injury, they sprang the booby-traps and stole the weapons meant to kill or maim them. Then they would watch from cover to see what happened and the more anger and despair the white ones displayed, the greater their triumph.

But despite the success of his group, after five years they numbered just seven men. And although only four of the original sixteen had died fighting, Touami blamed *num* for all the deaths. It was after their arrival that Rowra had stalked the land so openly and even the fighter bitten by a black snake had been hiding from Redcoats at the time. And so, while the young men who had joined since were no less trustworthy and, in some cases, better fighters than the first, Touami had learned to distance himself from them, otherwise each loss became harder to bear. While he did not feel guilt (his comrades were, after all, warriors), the burden of leadership weighed heavily on him because he sensed that one day their luck would run out and they would all be captured or killed.

'Ae, *Korerenner,*' he sighed and glanced up through interlaced branches to the sky, ash-grey with dawn, in the hope of glimpsing a brown hawk. Of late he had been acutely aware of his father's spirit watching over him, a vital fierce presence that guarded and guided him when he faced the direst danger or was closest to despair, and he took great comfort from it. But this morning the sky was empty and he looked down and kneaded a scar on his right thigh where a musket ball had ploughed deep into the muscle several seasons before. The old wound stiffened at night and he limped now on setting out and when he was tired.

'Yah – how goes it, Touami?' Longertalenna strode past the shelter where the older man was sitting. Two dogs paced at the fighter's heels, skinny brown and white curs of an ancestry that looked to include hound and terrier for they were long-legged yet rough-haired and their tails curled upwards. Their ears pricked at every sound.

'My bones'll keep a while yet,' Touami replied and the other grinned and walked on. He was without weapons of any sort so Touami assumed he had gone to shit: the dogs would warn if *num* were about.

Kangaroo-dogs having been responsible for his father's death, Touami had at first speared many of those he came across for he feared the fanged demons and was sceptical of their worth in a warband. But one night the camp dogs refused to settle, then barked a warning as a roving party moved to encircle the camp. Recognising that without their vigilance he and his men would have died, Touami became more tolerant of the animals though, despite Longertalenna's pleas, he refused to have one of his own. To Longertalenna, a good hound was a better companion than a woman since it never complained and, in straitened circumstances, could always be killed and eaten. The other members of the gang had at least one each, making up a motley pack.

The camp was stirring: as the brown and white curs trotted back, heralding Longertalenna's return, Touami got to his feet and stretched deliberately. He did this every morning and each time his bones seemed to grate a little more, while his muscles creaked like the boughs of an ancient tree. But only the foolish complain about the inevitable and so he merely frowned and went to join the others at the fire burning at the centre of the camp.

Estranged from their hearth-groups and lands, their very roots, it had become the custom among the fighters to take new names, often the nick-names bestowed upon them. Their tribes and lineage were, of course, marked in their skin but of their true identities only the names of their daemons were revealed to their comrades so that when they died, their spirits could be properly released. Touami and Longertalenna had not subscribed to this name-giving but it had become a fad among the younger men. Their five companions were thus known to each other as Parner-Maydee, (Shadow-man); Magaralenna (Night-walker); Paratibé, (Disemboweller: his favourite weapon was a long *num* skinning knife); Mycowwerer (Full-Belly: he was always hungry), and Rangaré, the youngest, named for his swiftness. These last two had joined in the autumn and had seen no fighting except a few skirmishes with *num* kangaroo-hunters but the others were seasoned raiders.

The camp was situated on the eastern side of a mass of hills which formed a kind of island between two broad valleys to the east and west. These hills were at the very edge of Lairmairrener territory but on the western side they were separated from Touami's homeland by the valley of the Big River, a place of dense *num* settlement where the floodplain was fertile and well-watered. From high on the ridge on the eastern flank it was possible for Longertalenna to glimpse the place of his birth far away but the valley below was patrolled by Redcoats because the track which had been forced through the very heart of Trouwerner ran there. But neither of the two leaders wasted time brooding on people and places they were unlikely to see again. These hills, now isolated from their clan territories, they had made their own, exploring every valley and crag in the knowledge that if *num* ever came in force to try and flush them out, there was no escape. So far the Redcoats had proved slow and so inept in the forest that a child could have outwitted them but many *num* hunters were as skilled as *parner* in bush-craft and Touami feared that one day the roving-parties and soldiers might join forces. And never far from his mind was the knowledge that as their numbers increased, those of his kind diminished.

But now, as he settled himself by the fire and sniffed appreciatively at the smells of baking flour and meat, Touami was affected by a rare and unexpected sense of well-being. When one of Longertalenna's dogs lay beside him, he fondled its head absently and the lines of his face which, over the years, had set in a kind of grim mask, softened a little. Perhaps it was the warmth of the sun's rays filtering through the branches that lent this feeling of contentment he reflected, that and the respect in the younger men's eyes as they sought his gaze and acknowledgement.

Mycowwerer and Rangaré dug in the ashes and divided up the food, serving the leaders first. They ate in silence for the treat of damper and wallaby together was something to be savoured, not spoiled with talk. Touami pushed the dog away when it began to beg and it slunk back to its proper master. Mycowwerer, whose appetite was almost insatiable, scowled as Longertalenna fed the animal but he knew better than to criticise. There was, in any case, plenty to go round.

When their bellies were tight and full they sat and cracked the bones, sucking the marrow with relish while the dogs foraged for scraps. It was unusual to eat so much early in the morning and the younger men guessed something must be planned for later in the day though none was rash or importunate enough to ask either of the leaders. Touami especially was a hero to them and his taciturnity had enhanced his reputation. His men, even Longertalenna who had been with him from the start, both revered and feared him.

Knowing that after so much food they would all feel like sleeping, Touami gave only a brief outline of his plan yet his words were enough to inflame Mycowwerer and Rangaré. They leapt to their feet, eager to set off at once but Longertalenna shook his head in such obvious disdain that they were chastened and sat down again. The group's success so far, he pointed out, had been largely due to their patience: to rush headlong into attack was to act like *num* who had been known to chase after *parner* with such blind enthusiasm that they became lost and were picked off with no more danger to their killers than if they had been wallabies.

Contrite, the two sat with downcast eyes as Touami reiterated the need for stealth for their target was on the other side of the hills: a homestead near the banks of the Big River. It was one of the largest farms yet seen and its destruction so early in the season would send fear through all the white population for they would not only plunder and burn all the buildings but kill every living thing they came across, even, Touami said with a sidelong glance at Longertalenna, the dogs and birds.

No-one dissented and the two leaders lay down to sleep while the others gathered spears into bundles and fashioned new ones.

They could hardly contain their excitement and the dogs (except for Longertalenna's pair which snoozed beside him), became restive: they whined and would not settle. By Touami's reckoning it would be several days before the actual attack: one and a half to cross the hills and another couple watching the farms but the prospect of action made the blood run hot in the young men's veins for they were free of the responsibilities of leadership and yearned to fight.

The sun was high when they set off, each man carrying his own weapons and a firestick, the two youngest bearing the gang's other possessions bundled in stolen blankets. Of these, flour was the most precious. Musty and full of weevils though it was, it precluded the need to hunt and forage and meant they could, if necessary, cover great distances at speed without going hungry. But their stock was very low. Touami had sanctioned its use that morning to give them strength for the task that lay ahead.

As they traversed the hills, it seemed they had returned to the world before *num*. The terrain was rugged beneath tall, scraggy gum trees and the surface was pierced by rocks which stuck through like the very bones of Trouwerner, forming precipitous crags where trees clung in the crevices: there was little water save on a plateau at the top where a great swamp lay. Yet the very harshness of the landscape spoke to Touami for circumstances had also shaped him: scarring and weathering his body, paring his spirit until only his capacity to endure, his immutable resolve remained. He no longer feared death, only that he might die before his purpose was achieved.

Through this forest, formed by extremes of drought, wind and rain, he led his men and only a soaring eagle or hawk would have marked their passing for the habit of stealth was so ingrained by years of war, they moved in silence. There was no sign of *num* or any trace of the hearth-groups that must have once occupied the land: the very fact that the coarse grasses had grown so rank testified to their absence though scorch marks on the trees indicated old burn-offs. Touami reckoned the inhabitants must have hunted mainly on the river flats and been driven away when *num* began to settle there.

That night they found some dry sandstone caves on the side of a vale that was an offshoot of the main Big River valley. Round patches of blackened earth marked old hearths and there were piles of dead leaves in the backs of the caves though these might have been blown there by the wind. *Kannenner* was the most recent occupant: fresh droppings and scattered fragments of bone were strewn around the smallest and deepest cave and the dogs whined and trotted back and forth, eager to hunt down 'child-stealer'. Longertalenna restrained them with sharp words and they lay down but their heads turned at every sound though the scavenger would stay away as long as their scent was in the air.

Paratibé and Magaralenna gathered wood and kindled a fire but they took care to use only dry fuel because Rangaré, who had been scouting ahead, reported that there was a *num* hut tucked in the valley below. He had also discovered a high crag overlooking the Big River. Leaving the rest to find food and water, Touami and Longertalenna went back with the young runner to see the landscape for themselves.

Looking at the long straggle of huts and farmsteads across the floodplain, the agglomeration of buildings on the other side of the river where they had made a settlement, Touami understood at last his enemies' true power. The river flats, which had formerly comprised some of the best hunting ground in Trouwerner, had largely been cleared of trees and was divided up into little plots and paddocks defined by barriers of wood, stone and lines of plants which restricted the movements of animals and people. And close to the buildings were patches of uniform greens, some dark, some bright, where men, women and children toiled, weeding and planting while sheep and cattle grazed the newly fenced pastures without need for people to guard them. Under *num* occupation, the very nature of the land had changed.

'Eh – how can this be?' Longertalenna breathed. His face and words reflected Touami's dismay: they stared at the neat pattern of fields and farmsteads and saw no place for them and their kind.

'One day it will be as before,' Touami said sternly. 'The trees and kangaroos will return and the hunting will be even better. *Num* do not belong here.'

Longertalenna turned his head and looked searchingly into his old comrade's eyes. 'Maybe they will take it all,' he said. 'More of them come all the time, my friend. And what of their children? They know nowhere else.'

'What does it matter? They will never come of age,' Touami replied. 'We cannot falter now. Or would you rather hide in the forest and wait for Rowra?'

'Aie,' the other said softly though not in assent: it was more an expression of resignation. 'We will fight them, Touami: what else is left to us? But when our blood is spent, what then?'

They returned to the caves in silence. Rangaré who, from respect, had waited a little apart while they talked, dared not question them for their faces were closed and grim. And when the others asked eagerly what they had seen, they were non-committal. Neither wanted to admit that their dream to destroy all things *num* had become futile as to try and hold back a river with their hands. For the truth was that for every homestead they had burned in the past, three more had sprung in the valley and these were larger and stronger-looking than before.

For three days they watched the floodplain, noting how often folk used the tracks and how many people were associated with each cluster of buildings. Most of the settlement was concentrated on the opposite, western, bank of the river but the farmstead Touami had picked stood in an isolated position on the eastern side. The river could only be crossed by swimming or boat and the *num* ferry was another obvious target, a little downstream of the farm.

On the evening before the attack, Touami took out the musket he kept hidden in the middle of his spear-bundle, carefully greased and wrapped in a kangaroo-skin. It was the one captured by Unémawa and he handled it with great care though without powder or ball it could not be fired. Mycowwerer and Rangaré looked fearfully upon it, as if by some intrinsic power within the wood and metal it could kill by itself but Touami demonstrated how it worked and allowed them to touch it and their awe faded. Experienced fighters knew that such a gun was only to be feared until a shot had been fired. After that, there was plenty of time to spear its owner before it was ready to fire again.

'Aiee! Then they use them like waddies!' Paratibé exclaimed

gleefully. 'But their reach is short. And the little death-sticks are no better than the long. Watch those with guns most carefully and remember who's fired. Eh – and remember also that when *num* are frightened or angry they often miss!'

Then the excitement that had built up in the young men could no longer be contained. They flung armfuls of dry wood on the fire and by its flaring light began to dance. And because they came from different tribes and clans, this war-dance was an amalgam of many. Touami and Longertalenna began to chant and clap out a rhythm so that what resulted was a meld of all the traditions of the south, the dancers improvising according to what they heard, whirling and stamping as sparks flew towards the stars and the fire leapt: at times they seemed to be wreathed in flame.

Yet although he allowed the chant to sweep him along, Touami was not wholly possessed by it. He knew this demonstration of strength and defiance would help prepare his men for what lay ahead but he did not want them to exhaust themselves. Gradually therefore he slowed the beat and, at last, fell silent and then they flung themselves on the leaf-strewn ground, breathless and laughing, streaked with sweat. As his last act before going to his cave to sleep, Touami gave them each a palmful of *ballawiné* and white clay so they could anoint themselves properly in the morning.

They woke at dawn and because the raid was planned for later in the day, they did not hurry. After breakfasting on damper left over from the night before, they rubbed charcoal all over their bodies, then some went to commune with their ancestral spirits, painting themselves with the sacred pigments (which for added potency were mixed with semen), according to his clan's custom or his own design. Touami always went to fight with his face whitened so that it looked like a skull; Longertalenna painted stripes across his back to endow him with *kannenner's* fierceness and cunning, and because of their success, many followed their example. But of late, some had not even bothered to delineate their tribal marks with *ballawiné*, much to Touami's disgust.

Before leaving the caves, each man lit a firestick. Then they shouldered their weapons and Touami led the way round the hill to a steep gully. The dogs followed closely as they scrambled down into the great valley of the Big River yet though they sensed the men's tension, they uttered not a sound.

At the bottom of the slope they took care to remain within the forest but as they moved towards the river, the land on their right changed from scrub to rough undulating pasture and then flat grassy paddocks. A blustery wind was blowing from the west and cloud-shadows swept over the new-sprung grass.

When Touami came within sight of the farmstead he motioned the others alongside. They knew it was the habit of one man to ride the boundaries of the farm every morning while three others spent their time picking stones in the fields or hoeing the ground near the buildings. Two women had been spotted but they never ventured far from the house. None of these folk carried death-sticks except for the one on the horse. That was why Touami was taking the risk of splitting his band, for he perceived that their greatest danger came not from the place they were attacking but from the settlement on the other side of the river where at least one group of Redcoats was stationed.

Longertalenna, Paratibé and Rangaré he therefore sent to destroy the ferry: once the boat had been sunk or burned, the young runner would report back while the others attacked the ferryman's hut. They slipped away without a word, keeping just within the margin of the forest. Soon even Touami's practised eye could no longer pick them out amongst the patterns of light and shade. The dog pack, naturally camouflaged, loped at Longertalenna's heels but sensing they were on some kind of hunt, they moved with a peculiar tension, eyes fixed on their master.

Then Touami looked searchingly into the faces of his companions: Parner-Maydee, Magaralenna, Mycowwerer. Though he saw trepidation there, each returned his gaze unflinchingly and pride swelled in him at their steadfastness. 'Come on.'

Strung in single file they made their way to a rough post and rail fence which marked the boundary between scrub and field. The split wood was already weathered silver-grey but the fence was stoutly constructed and when Parner-Maydee and Magaralenna tried to push it down, it did not budge.

'Don't waste your strength: it'll hamper them more than us,'

Touami said shortly and he handed his spears to Parner-Maydee and unwrapped the musket. 'Remember: keep your eyes open and be quick!'

They ran along the fence-line towards the farm. This was the most dangerous part of the mission for they were clearly visible from the house and yard and each felt horribly exposed. A pair of plovers flew up with strident calls as they passed and sheep grazing in the middle of the paddock raised their heads to stare but did not startle. Even a woman hanging out washing in the garden behind the house was oblivious to their approach: though she paused in her work and looked to see what had alarmed the birds, she did not notice the dark figures moving in the scant shadow of the fence. Once she spotted the plovers swooping to land in one of the river meadows, she turned back to pegging out sheets. They billowed like white sails in the wind, half-blinding her as they flapped back and forth.

The first building beyond the fence was a timber-slab byre. Touami and his companions paused behind it to catch their breath. From their look-out in the hills they had noted the lay-out of the buildings and even been able to guess their purpose so that now, with a hunter's memory for landmarks, they knew exactly how to cause most damage in the shortest possible time with the least risk to themselves. So detailed was their planning there was no need for speech. Touami gave his firestick to Mycowwerer, whose task it was to set the place ablaze, and, with the musket held across his body, nodded to the others to follow him and climbed over the gate into the yard.

The washerwoman was completely unaware as they crept behind her. They passed almost within touching distance but her attention was focused wholly on her task. The door into the house was open: she had chocked it with a stone. They entered the kitchen and there on the table was a metal bin of flour and a mound of dough covered with a cloth.

'Get the food.' Touami ordered and he snatched a spear from Parner-Maydee and set off to explore the rest of the house for he was mindful that the powder and ball he needed was more likely to be stored there then in any of the outbuildings.

The house comprised two storeys, the upper half being reached by a stair in a narrow hall between the kitchen and a room cluttered with furniture. Having glanced in there and seen nothing of use to him, Touami leapt up the stairs. His keen ears and nose had already picked up the crackle of fire and the acrid smell of smoke: it could not be long before someone raised the alarm.

The stair led into the middle of a single room which was divided by a couple of blankets hung to make a curtain. An iron bedstead with polished brass knobs almost filled the space to his left. Pillows and a quilt were stacked neatly upon it. To one side was a rail from which a few dresses and petticoats hung; on the other was a wooden stand with a basin of dirty water on top. Sunlight streamed through a small window, catching gyres of dust-motes in its rays.

Touami considered taking the quilt because it was brightly coloured and would be warm but it was also bulky so he dismissed it. Then he thought he heard movement on the other side of the curtain. He slung the musket on his shoulder to leave both hands free for his spear, stepped forward and ripped the blankets down.

To Touami, the woman standing before him looked like something from the spirit-world. She was draped in a voluminous white nightgown and her gaunt face was the colour of bone. Her expression seemed hardly human: the eyes, sunk in purple hollows, were wide with horror, her mouth an oblong gash. She raised her hands and he saw her throat work but she uttered only a strangled whimper and then her gaze went to a wooden crib by the wall. A baby was sleeping there under a woollen blanket, fists curled close to its mouth. Its downy hair was the colour of dry grass.

Touami hesitated. A shrill scream came from downstairs, followed by the noise of breaking china and splintering wood as the place was ransacked. Then the woman began to plead, tears streaming down her face, wringing her hands, and all the while, though it seemed impossible that the racket from the drawing-room and its mother's distress should not have disturbed it, the child slept.

Touami's eyes left the woman and probed the rest of the room. A man's clothes were folded in an open wooden box and a pair of high black boots stood in a corner. He unslung the musket and shook it in the woman's face, then jerked his head towards the trunk.

'Please.' She shook her head and her hands plucked frantically at the ties of her nightgown until it fell open, revealing turgid, blue-veined breasts. 'Don't hurt us. Please.'

The semi-translucency of her skin and the smells of fear-sweat and sour milk revolted Touami. He waved the gun again, angry at the time she was forcing him to waste and when she shook her head and began to back away, he smashed the butt into her face. She fell without a sound, blood streaming from her crushed nose, and lay moaning, half-stunned. Touami stepped over her and began to rifle through the trunk, pulling out clothes and throwing them aside until, at last, he found what he was looking for: a bag of shot and a powder-flask. He loaded the musket with great care then laid it aside and bundled his finds in a fine linen shirt which he knotted and tied round his waist.

From below someone shouted his name: he guessed Rangaré had returned from the ferry. The woman's groans grew louder, interspersed with a word: 'John, John'; the baby woke and began to scream. The noise maddened Touami. He leapt to his feet and plucked away the blanket, grasped the infant by its ankles (he thought its shriek would burst his ears), and dashed its head against the window-frame. The woman screamed and struggled to rise. He dropped the baby and speared her through the stomach, driving the weapon home with such force that she was pinned to the floor-boards. A high-pitched whine came from her: she writhed and drew her knees up as if for sex or childbirth while her hands clutched at the shaft but he felt no pity. Compared to Uné-mawa she was pale and soft, more like a grub one finds in rotting wood or under a stone than a woman. He picked up the musket and turned to leave for the crackle of fire had turned to a steady roar: the air was thick with smoke. And then he stopped, transfixed.

His father's face stared out of the wall. Set in a visage white as a bleached skull which was framed by a cap of freshly ochred hair, the bulging, bloodshot eyes held his so that he could not look away. He opened his mouth to scream and the other mouth opened in the same moment, a gaping red hole in a mask of death. The sound of panting filled his ears: he could not tell whether it was his own or came from the woman. Icy sweat bathed him. He whispered '*Korerenner?*' and the thing mimicked him as if in mockery.

He realized he was seeing his own reflection.

An ungovernable rage possessed him: he wrenched the mirror down and flung it at the woman. Her eyes had taken on a dull inward stare but she jerked spasmodically as the glass smashed into long, glittering shards within a handsbreadth of her face. The blood that had pooled beneath her spread in a long red tongue towards Touami's feet. He shuddered then, as shouting and an explosion burst from outside, leapt down the stairs. He raced through the kitchen where a pile of cloths and broken furniture was smouldering: the door was open, he was almost through –

On the other side of the doorway, facing the house, stood a man. He was wearing a heavy coat and there was a pistol in his right hand: his face was shocked and pale. Touami blundered straight into him. Both recoiled but of the two, Touami was quickest. As the *num* brought the pistol against his chest, Touami jabbed the musket butt into his stomach, sending him reeling back. The washer-woman's body sprawled across the path and the man's feet came against it. He staggered.

That moment was all Touami needed to bring the musket stock crashing on the man's head. He fell, stunned, and Touami snatched the pistol and pressed the barrel into the slack-jawed mouth. But the weapon would not fire: in disgust Touami flung it away. He was loth to waste his own powder and ball so he picked up the chock-stone and used it to crush the man's skull. Then a hand gripped his shoulder and pulled him away.

'Where were you?' Longertalenna's face was striped with blood, sweat and dust, taut with anxiety. 'Paratibé's hurt: he' - he jerked a thumb at the dead man – 'rode him down when we tried to spear the horse. We sank the ferry but there are Redcoats coming across the river: *num* must have seen the smoke. And Mycowwerer was shot but he'll live. I sent them back to the caves with the others. We must leave!'

Touami grunted in assent and followed his old comrade across the yard. Here the heat from the burning buildings was so fierce they had to shield their faces with their hands. Two more bodies lay there: a man stuck through with several spears and a boy who lay on his back, his face battered beyond recognition. Despite the danger, Touami paused to look closer for though he wore a ragged shirt and trousers, the youngster was of their own kind.

'He wanted to stop us,' Longertalenna said briefly. 'Parner-Maydee tried to talk to him but he didn't understand.'

'Then he was already lost,' Touami replied.

Dead animals also lay scattered in the yard. Two dogs had been speared and hens and geese clubbed or decapitated: pathetic bundles of feathers lying in the dirt. And when they reached the gate, Touami saw that the carnage extended into the paddocks. The bearded man's grey horse stood in the middle of the field, its head hanging and blood pumping steadily from a spear-hole in its chest while partially disembowelled sheep lay dead or dying on the grass or scampered panic-stricken over it, pursued by Longertalenna's dogs.

'Good,' was all Touami said when they reached the boundary fence and paused to look back. A great plume of smoke rose high above the farmstead and flames licked from the windows of the house. The screams of pigs and another horse trapped in the burning buildings sounded an excruciating counterpoint to the bleating of terrified sheep and the dogs' excited yelping and Longertalenna grimaced: he hated to cause pain to any animal. But Touami grinned for he was watching the river crossing and a group of *num* had just come into view.

Even from that distance, their voices could be heard. Four wore the bright red coats of soldiers and two of these aimed muskets at the rampaging dogs while the rest hurried towards the farm. The sound of shooting seemed to split the air but the dogs were unharmed. Longertalenna made a high-pitched yipping noise and they sped towards him as Touami raised his gun to his shoulder and fired back.

The Redcoats were well beyond the musket's range and Touami knew it but he still felt a rare flicker of satisfaction as they turned and ran to hide behind a tree. This was why he bothered to carry the gun: not because of its killing power but for the fear it inspired in *num* to whom it seemed an outrage that their own weapons could be used against them. But Longertalenna, crouching to fondle the blood-stained heads of his dogs, frowned. To him the act seemed reckless for if they were pursued there was little chance of escape with two of the gang injured and all of them tired. Yet he did not criticise for there was something so awful in the other's intensity it was as if he were possessed by a malignant spirit.

'I'm going back,' was therefore all he said and he rose and walked into the forest, the dogs, calm now, pacing at his heels. But Touami lingered, his eyes fixed greedily on the towering smoke and the flames still gusting from the windows and door of the house, willing them higher so that all trace of the woman and child and the shattered thing which had shown him himself, would be utterly destroyed, turned to ash and blown away to wherever they had come from. A kind of ecstasy took hold of him as he squatted in the shadow of the trees. He rocked, leaning on the musket for balance, while a keening sound issued from his lips, a song of death and triumph. And then, close by, he heard a tiny scratch of claws on bark and a chirrup: he looked round and *darwalla* was perched on a twig almost within his reach. The little bird cocked its head and its eye was knowing and bright as it looked at him, then it spread its fan-like tail, chirruped in warning and flew deeper into the trees.

His trance broken, Touami shivered. Recalling the face staring out of the wall, the shock of recognition, he saw a kind of madness in those bulging eyes and the frenzy from which his daemon had rescued him. If Uné-mawa had still been alive they would have slipped away and lain together on a bed of leaves, seeking relief from the horror and danger in each other's arms. But she was gone and he had no way of reaching her, for after he and his men had burned her body, they had been forced to move on and so far he had been unable to return.

The bleating of the sheep had died away. There was a great crash and a huge gout of black smoke erupted as the roof of the house collapsed but the flames were subsiding. An immeasurable weariness overwhelmed Touami: it seemed to take all his strength to stand. For a moment he contemplated waiting until an enemy came within musket-range but after this they were unlikely to go about alone and to take on more than one would mean certain death. And while part of him welcomed the thought of an end, pride and faith were stronger: he could not abandon his comrades, the living and the dead, so selfishly. So he gritted his teeth and climbed slowly and laboriously up the slope.

When he reached the caves the sun was sinking towards the horizon and his limbs shook with weariness. All his men were there except Rangaré. Mycowwerer was propped against the cliff with his wound packed with ash; Magaralenna tended the fire while Longertalenna and Parner-Maydee sat beside Paratibé who lay swathed in blankets, shuddering.

'Eh, I was about to come looking for you.' Longertalenna looked with pity upon his old comrade who seemed shrunken and wasted beneath the layers of war-paint, dried blood, dust and sweat. And seeing the question in Touami's eyes, he added hastily: 'Rangaré is at the look-out. We've not been here long: we had to carry Paratibé.'

'Ae.' Touami laid the musket carefully on the ground and dropped the shirt bundle beside it. Then he knelt beside the wounded man and lifted the blankets. He could felt the eyes of the others upon him, knew they were awaiting his decision and a howl swelled within his chest because he was old and tired and the responsibilities of leadership seemed suddenly too much to bear.

Paratibé's face was bruised and bloodied from the blow of a musket butt but though his nose was crushed and his eyes barely visible in a mass of bruised flesh, his most grievous injuries came from the trampling of the horse he had attempted to bring down. Looking at the unnatural ballooning of his abdomen, the indentation where one side of his ribcage had caved in, Touami felt sick. From his pallor and the clammy coldness of his skin he guessed Paratibé must be bleeding inside, knew also he might take another day to die and that there was nothing they could do to relieve his suffering. He tucked the blankets back and sat on his heels, his mind blank with exhaustion.

'Here,' Longertalenna handed him a fistful of dripping moss. 'Drink. Food'll be ready soon: you'll feel better when you've eaten and rested. Our bones won't go to the fire yet.'

'No.' Touami tipped his head back and squeezed a trickle of droplets straight into his mouth. It seemed to him that he had never tasted anything so good: a liquid coolness that was like the essence of the forests of his boyhood. When he had finished, he used the moss to wipe the sweat, clay and blood from his face and arms. Then he forced his mind to the present and gave orders for he realized the attack was unlikely to go unavenged: 'Parner-Maydee, eat, then take a firestick and make little fires a little way into the forest where *num* will see them. With luck they'll waste their time attacking false camps. We must go deeper into the hills before they come here.'

While the younger man took a lump of half-cooked dough from the ashes and blew on it to cool it, Touami turned to Longertalenna who was squatting on the other side of Paratibé, and added quietly, 'We shall have to leave *Lunna* behind. Find a hollow tree where *num* will not find him.'

Longertalenna bowed his head and put out a hand to touch the wounded man but he withdrew it before making contact. By calling him by his daemon's name Touami had effectively declared Paratibé dead but he had fought with them for many years and Longertalenna was loth to abandon him.

'Eh, we are all becoming *ragae*,' he muttered but he got wearily to his feet and went to search, his dogs trotting a little ahead.

Barely had Parner-Maydee left, bearing two firesticks in one hand, his spear-bundle balanced on his shoulder, when Rangaré returned. His eyes were bright with excitement and his skin shone with sweat for he had run all the way from the look-out. Looking at his lean eager face as he squatted by the fire and waited to give his news, Touami felt the aching of his joints and the heaviness of his limbs all the more. Yet, with an effort, he forced a smile (unaware it was more a grimace, his mouth pale and seamed like an old scar), and motioned the young man to speak.

'They're coming!' Rangaré said. 'More Redcoats crossed the river on a raft. They talked for a long time and sat about watching the burning while others killed the wounded animals and put the people on a cart. Then some went along the riverbank and others came to the edge of the forest. They did not enter until another two came across the river with a strange *parner* in *num* clothes. They talked again then went into the forest and began to climb the hill so I came back here.'

Touami thought a moment, cursing inwardly. He had heard that *parner* from another place were helping the white ones and he guessed that the bush-craft of such a man would be comparable to his own. But a single tracker could only follow one trail at a time: quickly he told Rangaré what Parner-Maydee was doing and sent him after, to lead the pursuit away and help lay false trails while the rest of them moved deeper into the hills.

Rangaré's eyes gleamed as he realized the importance of his task, the trust laid upon him on this, his first day of fighting. Mycowwerer watched jealously as his young comrade picked up a spear-bundle and left, slipping between the trees with such balanced grace he seemed more like a shadow than a man, but he had no time to brood on his ill-luck. Magaralenna returned from the creek below, his arms dripping and his hands full of wet moss, and when Touami told him they must prepare to leave, he laid his precious burden on a strip of bark and went to help Mycowwerer.

The young man gritted his teeth as he was hauled to his feet but the pain of his wound was far less than he had expected: it was the stiffness of his muscles that hurt most. The musket ball had passed straight through his side without touching any vital organs or blood vessels and the hole was packed with ash to staunch the bleeding. Once an initial wave of dizziness had passed, he was able to help the others move their plunder into the smallest cave. Keeping aside only a bag of flour, a tin pan and a pouch of tea, a couple of blankets and Touami's ammunition, they hid the rest, piling stones to block the entrance and strewing bark and dead leaves on top. Then, with a handful of dry grass they obliterated their prints. Whilst there was little point in attempting to conceal their occupation of the other caves, they had no intention of leading enemies directly to their cache.

While they were occupied thus, Longertalenna returned. He shook his head resignedly when Touami told him Rangaré's news and the dogs wove around his legs, sensing his unhappiness.

'I've found a place,' he said, his eyes upon the swathed form of Paratibé. 'But it will be hard to get him there.'

'Then we'll go now.' Even as he spoke, Touami worried that this was the wrong decision, that he was endangering them all for a man who was dying anyway. But he knew there was, in truth, little choice. Leaving Mycowwerer to carry the flour and other necessities, he and Longertalenna lifted Paratibé between them, using the blanket in which he was wrapped as a stretcher. Magaralenna, who was carrying the weapons, water and a firestick, walked behind as they left the flat area in front of the caves and he covered their tracks as best he could.

While they tried to carry him smoothly, the need for speed, the roughness of the terrain and the weariness of his bearers meant that some jolting was inevitable and Paratibé gasped and moaned. Touami and Longertalenna tried to close their minds to the pain they were causing him and the stench that arose from the blankets. He was no longer in control of his bodily functions and they were damp with urine, excrement and blood.

At last they came to the base of a steep rocky slope and Longertalenna called a halt. Paratibé was young and slender in build but to the two old men his weight had become insupportable and after laying him down they bent over, panting. Mycowwerer also laid down his bundle and leant against a tree, his hands pressed to his side. The exertion had made his wound bleed again and his face was grey and beaded with sweat. Yet he made no complaint and when Magaralenna offered a handful of dripping moss he drank gratefully.

'Up there.' Longertalenna pointed to an ancient blue gum at the top of the slope. 'It's hollow at the base. The white ones won't bother to climb to it unless they see us. Come on.'

Looking up, it seemed impossible to Touami that they would manage to get Paratibé to the tree at all but he knelt beside the wounded man and told him what they were about to do, begging him not to cry out however much they hurt him. And Paratibé, whose face was tense and hollow with pain, managed to gasp his thanks and then his eyes rolled back into his skull, his head lolled and they knew that this was their best chance, to move him while his spirit was out of his body.

It took all four of them to lift and drag the long, heavy bundle up the slope and Paratibé regained consciousness before they were halfway: they felt his body contract every time he banged against a rock or tree-root. But he uttered no sound other than short, harsh gasps, hardly audible above the sound of their own breathing, and when at last they laid him down, a long groaning sigh.

'Eh, it's over, old friend,' Touami whispered to him, 'we're here,' and while Magaralenna went to fetch their gear, he sat with his hand resting gently on Paratibé's shoulder in an effort to comfort him. Mycowwerer sat close by, his eyes set in an oddly unfocused stare, his lips drawn back from clenched teeth. But he said nothing.

When Magaralenna returned, they drank, squeezing every drop from the saturated moss. Touami dripped water into Paratibé's mouth and the wounded man revived a little: he opened his eyes and muttered words none of them could understand because they were in his own northern dialect. When no-one responded he became agitated, plucking at the blankets and struggling to rise. Dismayed, Touami and Longertalenna, who had been piling leaves into the hollow tree as a bed, held him down but it was only when he had freed himself of the blankets that Paratibé quietened. Then Touami cradled the wounded man against him and told him they would not let the white demons find and defile his body but would themselves return one day and carry his bones to the land of his birth so that his spirit could be at peace. And Paratibé relaxed. He closed his eyes and a serene expression overtook his ravaged features: he did not speak again.

Mycowwerer, who had known the dying man least, took away the soiled blankets while the others lifted Paratibé for the last time and laid him carefully inside the tree-cave. There was no room for him to stretch out so they curled him in a foetal position with his head towards the entrance so that he could see the stars. Lastly, when each had said farewell in his own way, Touami and Longertalenna pulled a heavy branch across the entrance to conceal what lay inside and prevent carrion eaters dragging the body out for *num* to find.

'When he is ready, *Lunna* will come for him,' Touami said. He spoke for Mycowwerer's benefit for the young man had just returned and there was accusation and horror in his eyes as if he could hardly believe what they were doing. And then they picked up their scant possessions and made their way back down the slope, Touami bringing up the rear because as the eldest it was fitting he should be last to leave.

By the time they reached the wallaby track at the base of the slope it was growing dark but Touami knew they must put as much distance as possible between them and their pursuers if the delay caused by Paratibé were not to prove fatal.

Then, faint with distance but unmistakeable, they heard a scream. It shrilled like *tarrabah's* and was followed by the crack of musket-fire. The reports echoed in the hills and valleys, triggering a cacophony of other sounds as startled birds cried their alarms. And when all this had died away the screams continued, pulsing like a woman's. From experience Touami knew this was the noise white men made when they were speared: an agony and situation that seemed beyond their capacity to bear.

'Should we go back?' Mycowwerer asked anxiously. Touami and Longertalenna exchanged glances for this question revealed his inexperience but when he turned to reply and saw the worry in the young man's eyes, Touami pitied him for his naivety. And so he replied roughly but not unkindly, 'Parner-Maydee has fought *num* for many years: he can look after himself and Rangaré. Those are a white one's screams. They fear death more than we, being far from their own place.'

At this Mycowwerer looked abashed; he shifted from one foot to the other and fiddled with the blanket tied across his chest. Longertalenna looked at him searchingly then made a soft whining noise deep in his throat and walked away with the dogs pacing close on his heels. Humbly, Mycowwerer waited for Touami to precede him but the elder gestured him to go ahead, not from kindness but because he wanted to keep an eye on him in case, being wounded, he began to flag.

They climbed through deepening twilight, and with every step they felt safer for these hills and gullies were unknown to *num*.

Every-so-often they paused to listen but there was no sign of their enemies and the dogs seemed untroubled. Then Touami relaxed a little though he knew he would not be at peace until the other two returned.

As he plodded along the path, eyes fixed on the shoulders of the young man in front, Touami sank into a kind of trance. It seemed to him that he was walking in a dream, that this journey would not end until his flesh and bones crumbled into dust and were consumed by the forest or blown away on the wind. At times he saw the four of them from above: shadows in the forms of men drifting along the winding path: the stark shapes of the trees with their strips of pale bark seemed more substantial than their transient, ghost-like figures. And the dogs also seemed unearthly: they trotted silently at their master's heels as if they were but an extension of his will, formed by the power of his mind. Even when Longertalenna stopped in a small clearing next to a tiny spring-fed pool, Touami could not dispel the haze of weariness that detached him from reality. It took the touch and taste of cold water to do that and then he looked at his surroundings, the tongues of flame flickering to life under Magaralenna's hands, the slender trees and the ruins of old shelters, with a kind of wonder for he last recalled leaving the tree where Paratibé had been left to die.

'Eh, Touami how are your bones?' Parner-Maydee slipped out of the darkness, Rangaré at his shoulder. 'We gave those *num* such a fright they'll be scared to go out after nightfall. They almost shot each other! There's no need to worry about them: they've gone back to the river with their wounded. They were in such a hurry they left their dead behind. Aiee – it was easy!'

'Yah – even their *parner* ran away!' Rangaré added. His smooth musculature and the grooves of his ribs were picked out sharply in the flamelight so that to the elders he seemed the epitome of a young warrior: his teeth and eyes gleamed as he grinned in triumph. 'Who can withstand Touami's fighters?'

The two leaders exchanged glances and Magaralenna, who was mixing damper, looked warningly at the young man but said nothing. And then Rangaré, daunted by the unusual silence, realizing that Paratibé was missing, crouched to see clearly into the elders' faces. 'They'll never beat us,' he said fervently. 'You'll see.'

Touami was too tired to argue, nor did he wish to quash the young man's enthusiasm with bitterness. So, with an effort, he praised Rangaré's swiftness and daring, the strength of his spear-arm, and later, when they had eaten and drunk, joined in the celebration as the younger men danced. But while their victory chant rose towards the stars, his heart wept.

14. The Deceivers.

(Southern Midlands, Tasmania, 1832).

The woman was small with the quickness and bright eyes of *darwalla*. Her skin marked her as Nuenone but of a clan unknown to Touami. She stood at the edge of the hilltop camp and waited while the dogs inspected her. When they backed away, hackles raised and growling, she smiled and there was a strange look of triumph in her eyes as she stepped forward. Longertalenna, to whom the dogs had crept for comfort, frowned. He had learned to trust their instincts long ago and he sensed at once that they not only disliked but feared her.

'Yah!' Touami gestured towards the fire where he and his men were sitting, inviting the woman to join them but she hesitated, her eyes roving the camp with an appraising, almost critical, intentness. He watched her uneasily while the younger men jokingly assessed their chances for she was young and pretty, her skin gleaming with health, and there was a kind of teasing provocativeness in her stance. Then he saw movement in the shadow beneath the trees and realized she was not alone.

The dogs alternately whined and growled as two more appeared: a woman, older and more heavily built than the first and a man. The latter, like the women, was well fed and his eyes, deep-set beneath a fringe of heavily ochred hair, were steady and piercing. He carried no weapons but that, Touami thought grimly, might be because his skin-marks defined him as an enemy of the Lairmairrener whose territory they were in. His companion bore the cicatrices of a Toogee clan and Touami wondered how three people from such distant tribes should be travelling together. There was something in their manner, a kind of arrogance, that made him instantly defensive and from Longertalenna's face, he knew his old companion felt the same. But whoever they were and whatever their purpose, the strangers still had a right to a place by the fire and a share of whatever food and shelter was on offer and so, reluctantly, Touami invited them to sit down.

As if the presence of the others had given her confidence, the little Nuenone woman was the first to accept. She settled herself opposite Touami and sat with one heel shielding her pudenda. The other woman sat close to her and, unusually, the man took his place between them. This instantly made him the centre of attention and those who up till then had appeared uninterested were drawn to the fire for in their experience no man who was in his right mind would sit with the women. And when he saw the young woman's expression alter to the smugness of one whose expectations are fulfilled, Touami realized the whole encounter had been planned to the last detail, that the man's impropriety was deliberate, and his distrust of the three deepened.

Although it was customary for strangers to declare themselves (though a host had no right to demand it), he therefore decided to speak first, to make it clear that here he was eldest and leader, whoever they were. They listened politely as he told them who he was but though his reputation had spread far amongst the remnants of the tribes, they did not react. Angered by their coolness, he added, 'We are all fighters here,' and waited.

Perhaps realizing that this grim old man and his warriors would regard a reply from a young woman as an insult, it was the man who answered. He was already the subject of speculation, not only because of his apparent shamelessness in sitting on the woman's side but the fact that his skin, smooth and sleek as that of the Toogee in former years, was unmarked by *num* weapons. Every member of Touami's gang bore scars from shot, cutlass or knife somewhere on their body and had it not been for the stranger's fine physique and proud demeanour they would have scorned him as a coward, a sodomite, a nothing, and driven him away.

'I am Woorady,' the man said calmly. His gaze went from Touami to Longertalenna and he smiled as if he knew exactly what they were thinking. Then he gestured towards the woman who was squatting like a toad on his right. 'This is Dray. And this,' he waved towards the other who was staring rudely at Touami instead of lowering her eyes as propriety demanded, 'is Truganana.' He hesitated before adding firmly, 'My wife.'

A murmur ran round the assembly and the two leaders exchanged dismayed glances for these names were well known among the groups of fugitives scattered around the periphery of the usurped areas. Since the terror of the Black Line, where *num* soldiers and settlers had joined forces in a great drive intended to capture the remnants of the Lairmairrener and Paradarerme, these three had accompanied a white man called Robinson in journeys all over Trouwerner. His mission was to persuade *parner* to leave their own territories for a place where they were promised security, food and shelter. But while he had heard of some that had gone willingly, Touami had never known any return and thus he resolved to remain on his guard no matter how cunning or tempting their words might be.

'We have heard of you,' he replied, glowering at Woorady. 'But we have no dealings with *num* or their friends except to kill them. What do you want?'

The three seemed immune to his hostility. Woorady's face remained impassive while the women smirked. And their calmness inflamed Touami: he felt the blood beat in his temples like a drum and his hands clenched. It took an immense effort to hold himself still, willing the dignity proper to a great warrior and leader to shield him from the strangers' guile.

'Our father, *ny rae num* Robinson has long wished to meet you,' Woorady said. 'In peace, for he means you and your people no harm and expects none in return. He is camped nearby. But knowing your reputation he sent us to arrange a meeting. He offers help and protection: that at least is worthy of consideration.'

'I want nothing from *num* except that they go away,' Touami replied harshly. 'And any white one who dares show his face near this camp will die. There is nothing to discuss.'

He rose, signalling the end of the meeting and Longertalenna did likewise, the dogs winding uneasily about his legs. But the strangers did not move. The two women looked at each other and exchanged sly smiles while Woorady sat stone-still, his eyes bent on the fire, knowing the elders would not leave while he remained.

And Touami, who had never imagined such effrontery, hesitated and turned back frowning, aware that all his gang had gathered round and were waiting to see what he would do.

'*Num* will never go away,' Woorady's tone was flat, that of one reiterating a simple truth to a stubborn, unbelieving child. 'Even as we sit here they are planning another Line, stronger than the last. This time they will capture or kill everyone who is not under *ny rae num's* protection. What will you do when they come here, when they surround this hilltop and fire their guns? Unless you have the power to fly like *korunah*, they will take or kill you and if you are captured, they will lock you in a stone hut in the cold and dark. Have you heard of the great one, Manalargenna? He has agreed peace and travels with us: many of his people have already gone to a place set aside for us, where *num* provide food and shelter and there is no fighting. If you stay here, you will all die before another winter comes.'

'We are fighters,' Touami growled, but a soft murmuration arose from the circle of his men and a cold hand seemed to grasp his heart for he sensed how these words had shaken them.

'You know I speak truth,' Woorady said quietly, and his gaze locked with Touami's across the smoking fire. 'Perhaps it would be better if we talked alone. Wisdom is not always found where there are many voices.'

At this, Longertalenna, who was listening intently whilst affecting indifference, tensed and jerked his head, signalling the rest to come closer for he guessed that the strangers were working a strategy they had long practised. But Touami narrowed his eyes and looked suspiciously at Woorady, saying, 'Raids and ambushes I command: for the rest, the lives of these men are their own. They come and go as they please. We will debate this together or you will leave. If you refuse, we will kill you and take your women.'

'Come then.' Woorady waved his hand in a languid gesture and the preposterousness of the invitation took the two leaders aback. They exchanged helpless glances, knowing that they were being manipulated but unable to retaliate without resorting to violence. Then they resumed their places and their men sat beside them though they took care to leave wide spaces between themselves and the strangers. An expectant silence fell in which the distant caw of a raven seemed loud and intrusive.

'Speak,' Touami said at last, uncomfortably conscious that he was acting against his will. And in an effort to maintain his authority and self-respect, he added forcefully: 'And when you are done, take your women and leave at once. You are not welcome here.'

A shadow fleeted across Woorady's face at the deliberate snubbing of his companions but he was too skilled and experienced a negotiator to allow it to distract him. He breathed deeply then spread his hands in the manner of a wise-man and looked searchingly into the faces of his audience while a low hum escaped his lips. So penetrating was his gaze and so mesmerising his voice that even Touami and Longertalenna succumbed though the former was gripping his talisman-bag with knuckle-whitening tightness to protect against sorcery.

Yet contrary to their expectations, Woorady did not begin by explaining Robinson's mission. Instead he talked of Trouwerner as it had been before *num*: how the tribes had lived lives unchanged since their fathers' fathers' time, sometimes warring and raiding but mostly in peace; how in the burning season the sky was dark with smoke, signalling mass migration to the coast, then in the spring, when they returned to their own territories, new grass lured kangaroos, wallabies and emus out of the forest and there was plenty for all. As he spoke, a great nostalgia took hold of his audience though most were too young to recall those days which now seemed a distant dream, remote and shining as the Pygeewar. And the longing for what had been, which was now lost, was like a fist squeezing the entrails. A kind of dizziness affected them and they swayed and moaned as if mourning their beloved: instead of the stark, wind-flayed gums and clumps of coarse grass on the hilltop, they saw the subtle greens, greys and browns of lush forest and endless grasslands and the sough of the morning breeze through the treetops became the distant murmur of the sea.

Seeing that his audience was wholly captivated, Woorady bent his head and Dray took up the tale. In contrast to his tone, which had been calm and sad, her voice was deep for a woman's and harsh so that the listeners' mood of sorrowful contemplation was replaced by a sense of dreadful anticipation. And yet though her spell was different, her words were no less powerful than Woorady's. In language vivid and terrible as the events she was describing, she told of the coming of *num*, their insidious, unstoppable advance like a plague of creeping insects, stripping away all that the people held dear, stealing women and children, killing and harrying at will. And of Rowra she spoke also, how the demon spared the white ones but took both weak and strong among the tribes until only a remnant of Trouwerner's people remained and *tarrabah* and *kannenner* grew fat upon the dead.

'Aiee,' breathed Woorady and the circle of fighters echoed him, transported by the woman's voice (which itself seemed wrenched from pain), into an ecstasy of sorrow. Even Touami, his defences breached by that collective outpouring, felt tears prick his eyes and, unashamedly, let them spill over and run down his cheeks: when he came to himself and stole a glance at Longertalenna, he saw that he too, trusted comrade and friend, was affected the same way.

'Eh, why do you weep like women, my friends,' Woorady asked gently, 'when you are still alive and strong? You fought and your blood wetted the earth like rain but when change comes, men are like ants struggling to climb a sandhill. The end of the Pygeewar was such a time maybe, when the Great Ones bequeathed Trouwerner to the children of Tarner. That we believed was all, our place and the place of our ancestors, bounded by water without end: we did not know there was anywhere else. But now these white ones have come and they have different Great Ones, yet they are also men with their own ancestors and another place, far from here.'

He paused to allow these words to sink in and Touami cuffed his tears away: his face had grown hard and closed. But such was the lingering power of Woorady's speech, he did not intervene but waited and beside him one of the dogs whined softly.

Then Woorady stretched his arms out to either side and tipped his head to stare into the sky where wisps of cloud stretched like strands of gossamer against the clear, infinite blueness. And having adopted the traditional posture used by storytellers and wise-ones, he began to chant.

This was so natural, it was some time before the listeners

realized the words were almost wholly unknown to them, bearing no affinity to the tongues of the tribes. Confused, the little band of fighters looked askance at one another, unsure whether he meant to insult them by using the ancient chant usually reserved for great myths as a vector for what they gradually recognised as *num* words. Many, Longertalenna included, glanced round to check that their weapons were still at hand lest the chant was a spell to beguile them while enemies crept close, and when they looked again at the three they saw that the women's lips moved to form the same words; their eyes were closed and they stretched out their arms until their fingers touched, swaying slightly back and forth like a line of saplings rocked by the wind.

All this time, Touami had not let go his talisman. Now, angered by the audacity of these strangers who dared demand a hearing only to utter an incantation of the white ones, he fingered the bone beneath the worn kangaroo-skin and begged his grandfather's spirit to help him withstand the magic being summoned by the three. And as if in direct response to the hardening of his resolve, the chant changed, becoming more urgent, and now *parner* words were mixed with the *num*, fragments of meaning interspersed with nonsense, like a new landscape glimpsed though gaps between the fingers or a star-crazed sky seen between thick branches. The effect upon the listeners, whose knowledge of *num* language was sparse, was profound. A fierce longing awoke in them to understand the full meaning of this chant for they belonged to a people whose very being was expressed through song and story and they recognised its power from the passion of the speakers.

'For ever and ever.' As they reached the climax of what, Touami realized after, was a carefully staged performance, the three strangers opened their eyes and gazed round at their audience with peculiar fervour. Their eyes shone with joy; they gripped each other's hands and raised them so that many of the watchers looked up, half expecting some terrible manifestation of *num* power to appear there, then, like a battle-cry they yelled the last word: 'Amen!' and leapt to their feet. As the echoes of that cry died in the folds of the hills the young women, whose neck was adorned with so many circlets of sinew that they formed a thick collar, stepped forward and began to speak.

Her voice was as different from Dray's as the sweet piping of a wren from a raven's croak and her demeanour also for while the older woman was stern and grim, Truganana gazed upon her listeners with a candour that was almost seductive. She explained gently that the purpose of the chant was to demonstrate how *parner* tradition and *num* law could be made into something new and good with neither side being the loser. And the last part was a prayer to the white ones' god who, unlike Moinee, could be persuaded to help men through the right words and promises. It was largely because of their faith in this god, she said, that *num* had succeeded in changing the very face of Trouwerner: from him came much of their power and because the tribes were ignorant of him, they had been punished with misery and death.

Hearing this, Touami shivered. If Meelangana had been there, he would have judged the truth of this assertion and Wagarulepu, wisest of Meelayginnee, could have looked deep into the young woman's eyes and seen her real nature. But the old man was long dead and the ancient matriarch far away in the wild mountains to the south-west. If she lived, she would be older than any of her people since the Pygeewar, but she could not help her grandson.

'Eh, my friends,' Truganana continued, 'so much death, yet it does not have to be that way. Our father, the white man Robinson, has pleaded with his god on our behalf and the government has made a place for us where those who mean us harm cannot go. There is all the food and tea you could desire; they have built huts and furnished them with blankets: in that place there is no need to hunt for meat or dig for roots or to shiver in the cold. Already many of our people have gone there: they scorn you who stay away, fighting and dying miserably in the forest when you could be with them, living in ease and plenty without fear.'

Looking at the young woman, her face bright with enthusiasm, her flesh plump yet firm, Touami was reminded of Uné-mawa as she had been in their youth, vivacious yet self-contained, possessed of wisdom and self-assurance far beyond her years. And the birth of their son, Toomay, had enhanced rather than detracted from her beauty: he remembered her laughter, like the sound of water in a parched land and suddenly he felt lost, old and weary, worn down by a loneliness he had only just realized.

Perhaps something of his doubt and uncertainty was reflected in his face because Truganana fell silent and laid her hands demurely in her lap. She looked like a young bride awaiting the arrival of her husband and her gaze seemed to reach deep inside him so that he thought with horror: 'What does she want: is she part of the bargain too?' and clutched his talisman-bag so hard, the charred bone crumbled between his fingers.

'You have spoken of what *num* offer, woman: what do they want in return?' Longertalenna's voice came like the screech of a cockatoo, harsh and strident, shattering the spell of the strangers' eloquence. Then the fighters stirred uneasily and their eyes grew hard and watchful for they were ashamed at how easily they had been seduced.

'After all you have suffered, we do not blame you for being mistrustful even of your own kind,' Woorady replied smoothly. 'Peace is all they ask: an undertaking that you and your kin will never again attack farms and huts or harry herders and their animals. And you must leave Trouwerner and go to the place Truganana has spoken of. That is for your own protection and you will be allowed to return when it is safe, when both sides forgive the wrongs inflicted upon them rather than seeking vengeance. Then *num* and *parner* can live together in peace.'

'That's all?' Touami could not conceal his astonishment at the simplicity and generous nature of these terms. It seemed incredible that after so much killing, so soon after the marching of the Black Line, *num* should want a truce. He leant forward and stared fiercely into Woorady's eyes, seeking the slightest sign of duplicity but the young man returned his gaze steadily and the faint smile that curved his lips was one of sympathy and understanding.

'You need not decide now,' he said. 'We are only messengers and our words are crude compared with our father, Robinson's. Nor do we have the power to speak on behalf of the *num* chiefs: that also lies with him. Let us bring him here and then you can decide. But do not forget that Manalargenna, who is a wise and great one for all our people, has already agreed.'

'But if *num* want peace, we must be winning!' one of the young men broke in excitedly. 'Why should we agree to their terms? We should make the demands!'

A murmur of agreement arose and Woorady's eyes narrowed. Then he took a step back and swept his arm to indicate the crowded squalor of the hilltop camp and beyond, to the valley far below where the *num* road ran and the land had been cleared and settled.

'Look about you,' he said. 'Are your eyes blind? They offer peace because they are tired of killing. But if you stay and fight, they will not stop: each raid makes them angrier. In the end they will hunt you down and when you are dead they will cut off your heads and take them to the Governor.'

'Enough!' Longertalenna bared his teeth in a grimace that was like a snarl. 'We are not children: we know what the white ones do and we are not afraid. Whether here in the hills or in some other place, one day we shall die. Even *num* cannot change that!'

A look almost of pity settled upon Woorady's face. 'You are wrong, my friend but it is for *ny rae num* to speak of God's mercy and the rewards of heaven. Will you not at least hear him?' He paused and seeing lingering doubt in the faces of the two leaders, consternation and puzzlement in the eyes of their men, spread his hands in a gesture of resignation. 'You will lose nothing by such a meeting: he is but one white man. And by it you may gain more than you can dream of.'

His persistence and fervour filled Touami with disgust: he longed to be rid of these strangers who had somehow made him unsure of himself and his purpose.

'My dream is a land free of *num*,' he said shortly. He rose and walked away between the trees without looking back and it seemed that the strangers were unprepared for such abruptness. They looked at one another in dismay and when Longertalenna also made to rise (he had delayed only because of the stiffness in his joints), Woorady and Dray put out their hands to restrain him while Truganana looked on with a supercilious smile as if to covey that such ignorant folk were not worthy of salvation.

'Wait!' Woorady had not dared touch the old man (to do so

would have breached the most basic of courtesies: the right of an individual not to be handled against their will), but there was desperation in his tone. 'Many of your kin have gone already. If you will not speak with our father you will never see them again and they will never know your tale. Great fighters you may be but if you stay here, you will be forgotten before your children's children come of age. Is that a fitting end? Think well before you refuse us.'

Slowly Longertalenna got to his feet. The dogs pressed against his legs but for once he ignored them. He stood straight and still, looking searchingly into the faces of the three and only Woorady could withstand his gaze: there was such fierceness there that the women were daunted and dropped their eyes. But from his comrades, the young men with whom he had shared so much, the aged warrior heard a low, urgent muttering and he understood, with a dull sense of sorrow, that while they would not openly contest his will, neither he nor Touami had the right to speak for them. And the bitter truth was that without them, the two old leaders could not last long. They would starve in the barren hills or be slain by a roving party eager for revenge and their bones would moulder far from their own lands.

'At dawn tomorrow you may bring the *ny rae num*,' he said and tried to ignore the triumph with which the three nodded in acknowledgement then turned to walk away. He watched until they had disappeared among the trees and as the voices of his comrades rose around him, he thought to hear distant laughter, raucous as kookaburras' and as heartless.

15. Wybalenna.

(Flinders Island, April 1835).

The two old men coughed as they toiled up the hillside, bent almost double against the steepness of the slope. Above them the sky was a clear, rain-washed blue and in the distance the sea sparkled. The wind was from the west and there was a cool edge to it that presaged the onset of winter though even through the thickness of their clothes they felt the sun's warmth on their backs.

The slopes surrounding the compound had been largely cleared for grazing but just over halfway up there was a craggy outcrop of grey rock to which a few wind-bent tea-tree bushes and wattles clung. The eyes of the two ancients were fixed on this feature with the single-mindedness of swimmers spotting land and they did not speak as they struggled towards it, all their strength being concentrated on reaching their destination.

'Eh – far enough!' Touami gasped when they came to the trees. He sat down on the nearest slab of stone and was racked by a bout of coughing that left him speechless and gasping. His companion sat beside him, hawked up a great gob of phlegm and spat it forcefully in the direction of the settlement below. Then, when he had recovered his breath he began to peel off the layers of clothing: woollen jacket, knitted cardigan and thick cotton shirt. This revealed a frame spare as a skiff's for he was hollow-chested and his bent spine protruded like a keel. His skin, seamed with many scars, the cicatrices of his ancestry and battle-wounds from long years of raiding, was the hue and texture of blackwood bark, so furrowed and dry it looked dead.

'Ah – that's good.' He bared his teeth in a smile that was like a snarl and stretched out his arms, luxuriating in the contrast between the sun's heat and the wind's cool caress. And then, with a swift glance down the slope to make sure none of the *num* overseers were looking (a glance he hoped Touami had not noticed), he hauled himself to his feet and stripped off his trousers, revealing legs that were little more than sticks of bone, the muscle reduced to flaccid strings.

The wasting of his body, which had more to do with age and inactivity than lack of food, seemed not to concern Longertalenna who, away from the confines of the settlement, was determined to enjoy himself, but to Touami it served as a reminder of his own mortality. So far as he knew he was older than his brother-in-arms but he had never visualised himself in anything like Longertalenna's state of decrepitude. And so rather than expose (and thereby admit), his degeneration even to his closest friend, Touami, though he also longed to feel the sun and air on his skin, continued to sit hunched in his clothes, the hampering layers of cloth that in his first years on the island he had refused to wear and traded to visiting sealers or the convict-servants of the officers for extra tea and tobacco. A look of puzzlement settled upon Longertalenna's face but he knew better than to question Touami when he was brooding and so satisfied himself by leaning back against the sun-warmed rock with a sigh of deep contentment, one hand pulling idly at his foreskin.

Looking upon his old comrade, Touami was filled with envy. He had long ago lost the ability to live wholly in the present with no thought of the future or regret for the past. Longertalenna, whose hearth-group had been slaughtered by bushrangers, had no living kin to care for or worry over; deemed too old and frail to participate in the settlement's regime of work and schooling, he was free to take his ease and do more or less what he pleased; his dogs, the main recipients of his affection, demanded little more of him since they scavenged food from everyone else. Thus, in a place where many had grown embittered and resentful in exile, he seemed at ease, apparently as happy as in his ancestral lands.

By contrast, Touami could not sleep at night for thinking of those he had left behind, his son Toomay, his daughter-in-law Neeméné and their little boy (who by now would have grown to manhood), most of all. He clenched his fists as he sat there in the warm autumn sunshine and his face grew grim and closed. Under his breath he muttered lines from a battle-song so ancient that its origins were lost even beyond knowledge of so great a sage as his grandfather, Meelangana. For there was something at his very core, hard and immutable as stone yet fierce as flame, which precluded his final submission to the fate that had brought him here: acceptance.

'What's wrong?' Unable to relax completely while his companion was so disquieted, Longertalenna propped himself on his elbows and peered intently into Touami's face. 'Do you miss *num*?'

'Them!' A spasm of distaste crossed the other's features and he leaned to look down towards the compound, his hands crossed on his knees. The thinness of the arms poking out of the frayed sleeves of his jacket and the misshapenness of the joints suddenly struck Longertalenna as pitiful: those hands, gnarled and weathered as ancient tree roots no longer possessed the strength or suppleness to fashion a spear or knap a stone. And this realization effaced his contentment like a dark cloud moving across the sun.

'Had we stayed, our bones would lie scattered in the forest,' he said sombrely. 'Perhaps it's time to rest at last. There is nothing we can do for those we left behind – if any are still alive, that is.'

Touami glanced up in surprise for it was rarely that Longertalenna was despondent or, at any rate, expressed it. And in old friend's eyes he saw such sorrow and compassion that he was abashed and looked quickly away, afraid of what the other might read from his face.

'Eh, maybe we have lived too long,' he murmured and for a moment, imprinted on the sere brown slopes and the huddle of buildings below, he seemed to see the figure of a bent old man shuffling away between towering stringybarks and swamp gums. That had been his last glimpse of his grandfather, Meelangana, alive. Towards the end of his life, the ancient could hardly recognise his kin, but his periods of forgetfulness were interspersed with instances of piercing lucidity. And one night not long after their return from their last, fateful sojourn on the Grass Plains, he had been called by his daemon, *Lyenah*. Such dignity had clothed him when he bade farewell next morning, no-one sought to change his mind: they watched him make his slow way into the deep forest and though they waited for a day and a night, he did not return. Now Touami, who had gathered the old man's bones and burned them, was filled with admiration for the manner in which his grandfather had recognised his time to die, and he felt his own tenacity in clinging to life as a failure.

'Ach, what are we: men or old crows sitting on a branch, waiting to drop off?' Longertalenna asked suddenly, with a flash of his old wit. 'You have kin still alive and close: had you never come here she would believe herself alone.' He sat upright and pointed seawards to where smaller islands were lined like the humped backs of whales. 'Look hard and maybe you'll see her hearth-smoke.'

Touami's eyes followed the pointing finger automatically but he was loth to acknowledge what lay behind Longertalenna's words. Less than a moon ago, a party of sealers and settlers from neighbouring islands had descended upon Wybalenna, bringing their women (most of whom had been stolen or bought from the tribes), and children with them. There had been much rejoicing at their arrival, old enmities forgotten in the novelty of meeting new people and kin thought lost. Dancing and singing had followed, the visitors enjoying a day's holiday while their *num* masters traded seal-skins, mutton-birds and vegetables for flour, clothes and rum at the soldier's cantonment. The two old men had joined in wholeheartedly, the celebration providing welcome relief from tedium, until one young woman had begun to take unusual interest in Touami. She stared rudely at the cicatrices on his body (the exiles had all stripped to dance or chant), and kept sidling close only to scurry away when he returned her gaze. She was short in stature and her skin was of the coppery hue common among those of mixed parentage yet there was something in her meld of shyness and audacity that reminded him sharply of his twin sister. So discomfiting was this similarity (for it was long since he had thought of Toualena, who had been lost when Toomay was still a little boy), that Touami took to turning his back whenever he caught her watching. And then someone must have told her who he was.

Even now, memory of that meeting brought unwanted tears to the old man's eyes. Only when the visit was nearly over had the young woman gathered courage to approach him and her speech had not been in Meelayginnee language but a mixture of English and island-dialect he barely understood. Indeed, having begun, it was as if a river had burst its banks: overwhelmed by the flood of words, he had listened without fully comprehending until a white man with a grizzled beard and stern, weathered features came to the fence and jerked his head, calling 'Sarah, time to go!' She had obeyed at once, not even bidding Touami farewell, and left him bereft and wondering. Since then he had spent most evenings trying to come to terms with tidings that had shaken him to the core.

It had been hard, discovering that his twin sister had died only a season or two before his departure from Meelayginnee lands. Long after her closest kin had mourned her death, she had borne a daughter by one of the sealers that had kidnapped her whilst living with another who had rescued her from the brutality of the first. That this could have happened without his knowledge was incomprehensible to Touami: he could not understand why *darwalla* had not revealed the truth in a dream or signs. And the sight of the young woman with his sister's eyes and high cheekbones set in a face of *num* shape had been profoundly disturbing, a feeling exacerbated by her diffidence. For a look of doubt and disappointment had settled upon her features as soon as she knew his identity so that he wondered what she had expected.

Bitterest of all had been the revelation that Toualena had died of the same lung-sickness that had killed his beloved Uné-mawa. The unfairness of his sister succumbing to Rowra after suffering so much at the hands of the white ones aroused all the old hatreds deep within him so that now, staring down at the compound, he ground his teeth and had to choke back the bile that rose scalding in his throat. And his heart cried out to *darwalla*, the little bird that had, it seemed to him, betrayed them both. For, his sister-daughter said, her mother had often told tales of her people but spoke as if they were all dead: after all she had endured, she dared not believe that any of her hearth-group had survived and her daemon had never enlightened her.

'Eh, Touami my friend . . .' Frightened by the look on his companion's face, Longertalenna sought to bring him to the present for Touami's eyes were fixed and staring, his face rigid. 'It's not for us to die with the dead. She won't forget you: how could she? Maybe that is to be the way of it from now: the blood of *parner* and *num* will mix and our peoples become one. Would that be so bad?'

Touami took a deep, shuddering breath and forced calmness on himself for he was filled with the urge to strike out, to kill his conflicting emotions with action, however futile and unjustified. And then, from the paddock behind the lean-to that served as church, came a tumult of squawks and cackling and the high-pitched voices of children as they chased the hens and geese they were supposed to be tending; from the scrub on the opposite slope a currawong called and Touami saw himself at last for what he was: an old man clinging to the past because he was too proud to admit defeat and refused to acknowledge, even after years of exile, the likelihood that he would never see his own lands again or discover the fate of his kin.

'Ach - how should I know?' he replied with difficulty. 'Old I may be but I'm no wise-man to scry what will be.' He jerked a thumb to where the children were now being scolded by the *num* catechist. 'They'll be the ones to find out.'

'Aie! You think so?' Longertalenna suddenly clasped his hands round his knees and began to rock with laughter. It was a sound dry and mirthless as the rustle of the wind through sere branches but his eyes, milky with age, gleamed with a kind of sardonic amusement. 'Listen, old crow, did a *ragae* steal your spirit? You never used to give up so easily. Our lands are still there even though we do not see them and one day we'll return: wasn't that the agreement? All this work and god-talk they give us is what women do with children: keeping them occupied so they won't cause trouble. But one day, when all the *num* have agreed peace, Father Robinson will take us back. Then we'll do ceremony so the spirits know we've returned and our daemons will speak to us again and Rowra will go away. And our people will be strong.'

Touami looked closely at his friend. There was no trace of irony in that lean, scarred face: it was animated by fervour akin to a fanatic's, full of wild hope. And for a fleeting moment he was touched again by a swift and bitter envy for he could not bring himself to have such faith in any white man. Yet rather than arguing, because he loved and esteemed his old comrade, he satisfied himself by growling: 'But we are not children.'

It seemed, however, that Longertalenna did not hear these words. He stretched out his arms and eased himself back against the rock, luxuriating in the sunshine. On his face was the knowing smile of one secure in his convictions and his eyes had taken on the blank, unfocused, stare of the blind.

16. The Coming of Night.

(Green & Flinders Islands, October 1835).

After Rowra claimed his comrade, Longertalenna, it was only the thought of returning to Trouwerner that gave Touami strength to endure. For he had promised that when the time came, he would dig up his friend's bones and carry them to Paradererme land. Estranged from his kin and his daemon, *tiennah*, the old man had died in great distress and that memory haunted Touami. He was determined to live until his obligation was fulfilled and Longertalenna's spirit was at peace. Then he could go to Meelayginnee country and himself find rest.

Meanwhile it was mutton-birding season. These were now scarce on Flinders Island so the exiles were escorted to neighbouring Green Island. Here, the mass of flying birds darkened the sky every dawn and dusk and there was plenty for all.

The soldiers soon joined a group of sealers who were harvesting the young birds not for meat but feathers, and at first the aborigines were content. They set up windbreaks of heath and driftwood in any spot sheltered from the gales and feasted on *yolla* eggs and chicks pulled from their burrows while the parent birds were at sea. But there was little else to eat save what could be gleaned from the island's rocky shores and after three weeks even Touami, for whom mutton-birds were a treat, began to tire of their strong-tasting, oily flesh and longed for other meat or even a piece of damper. As fuel became scarce, they watched hopefully for a boat that would carry them back to Wybalenna and with worsening weather, their need grew dire. Of late, no supply ships had come to Flinders Island and many had traded their clothes and blankets for convicts' rations. Now they huddled half-naked around feeble fires, and wondered if *num* had abandoned them for good.

Then one morning Touami was woken by excited voices. Like most of the others he had moved into a hollow on the western side of the island, the only place where fresh water was to be found, and at first, from the shrillness and volubility of the speech he thought there was trouble: that someone had fouled the pool or usurped another's hunting area. If so, it was for him, the eldest, to sort out but as he clambered stiffly to his feet and wrapped his ragged coat close about his thin frame, a gust of wind struck with such force, he staggered. A young man, dressed only in a tattered shirt, caught his arm and steadied him.

'Eh, father, don't worry!' he laughed as Touami instinctively pulled away. 'He's here!'

'Who?' Looking into that joyful face Touami's heart twisted painfully with the envy of the aged for the young. 'What do you mean?'

'*Ny rae num*!' the young man replied triumphantly. 'He landed last night. We're off to see him: are you coming?'

A day of great excitement and celebration followed for the whole group traversed the island to find Robinson and his son at the boat harbour, along with his old companions and a group of new exiles who watched the proceedings with bewilderment. But to the disappointment of all, the *ny rae num's* stay was brief. After two days, he sailed for Wybalenna, leaving behind his comrades, Woorady, Truganana, Dray and Manalargenna to join in the mutton-birding.

After that, a mood of joyful anticipation settled upon the exiles. Even Touami, who did not wholly trust any white man, could not conceive why the *ny rae num* should have come unless to restore them to their homelands. And though they spent several more weeks on the island, frequent news from Wybalenna reminded them that they were not forgotten. As the weather improved, boats plied back and forth with supplies, while the 'Mission *num*' as the exiles called Robinson's old companions ('*num*' referring to a state of mind and dress rather than mere skin-colour), entertained them with tales of their travels and exploits across the whole of Trouwerner.

Touami was enamoured as the others of Woorady and Truganana's stories and though he did not join in the dancing that always concluded the corroborees, he chanted with the rest and was filled with hope. But the old wise-man, Manalargenna, did not participate. After landing, he had parted from his son and daughter and hidden himself away as if he were sick or sought a place to dream and although it seemed impossible that anyone could remain concealed on so bare and populous an island, no one had seen him since. His absence worried Touami who, every morning, found it a little harder to rouse himself, to bend stiffened joints and force life into his body again. (Sometimes when he coughed, pain racked his chest and stomach though he convinced himself this was not due to Rowra but the inexorable advance of old age). For apart from Manalargenna, there was no-one else among the exiles who had attained so many years or whose memory stretched back so far.

It was not until the day came to leave that the old wise-man re-appeared. Everyone had gathered at the harbour, most with sticks of mutton-birds to take back to Wybalenna, and they watched the approaching boat with anxious eyes. But then a woman cried out and pointed at the cliff-path where Manalargenna was descending with unsteady, stumbling steps. And many of his kinsfolk moaned in pity and dismay for his head was shaved like a woman's or outcast's and his shoulders were bowed as if the weight of his tattered greatcoat had become insupportable.

To see the once proud and upright wise-man reduced to a shambling wreck was profoundly disturbing even to those that, like Touami, were his enemies by tribal tradition. Some thought he must have been abused by the sealers. When he reached the crowd he looked neither left nor right but walked straight through until he reached the water's edge and there he sat on a rock, bowed over, his arms resting on his knees and his hands dangling loosely in front. And those closest to him felt a chill for the old man's face was sunken, grey-hued, and his eyes seemed blind to the throng of people and the swirling water at his feet.

'Eh, he claimed to be like *num*!' Truganana said cheerfully, for the crowd had begun to murmur with a growing sense of outrage. 'On the way here, when we sailed past his old places. He took a spyglass and paper and used them just like the captain to tell where he was. 'See, now I am just like you!' he said, and *nymenner* smiled and clapped him on the shoulder' – here she thumped Woorady affectionately to demonstrate how it had been – 'and maybe that's why he did the cutting: no more *comenner*, no more *ballawiné*, just like *ny rae num*!'

Most of the gathering seemed satisfied with this explanation: they laughed and looked sardonically upon the hunched, silent figure. But Touami did not smile. Manalargenna was no kin of his, nor did he count him as a friend but his heart was wrenched by pity as those who had previously feared the wise-man's powers now copied Truganana's portrayal, putting their birding sticks to their eyes in imitation of telescopes and capering about as if trying to keep balance on a rolling ship. And when the old man did not respond, their mood became crueller, the boldest mocking openly, calling him dotard and woman until his kin began to remonstrate. Fearing the ugly mood would turn into a fight, Woorady and Dray intervened, aided by the arrival of the boat. This provided an immediate distraction and Manalargenna was forgotten in the scramble to board: his kin formed a kind of guard around him all the way back. But the old man seemed oblivious to them and his surroundings, like someone snared in a dream, and when they finally reached the settlement he took a blanket and wandered off alone.

Over the next few days an atmosphere of barely suppressed excitement grew at Wybalenna. This was partly due to the issue of new blankets and clothes and the arrival of plentiful supplies of flour, tea and sugar but of greater significance was the announcement of a fête to be hosted by the outgoing governor, in which a great treat was promised. There was not one among the inhabitants, Touami included, who did not believe that the occasion was designed for the proclamation that would end their exile. Even the arrival of more captives could not suppress the joyful mood and Manalargenna, who had returned refreshed from his lonely sojourn in the hills, was also affected by it, pursuing a young woman with such eager intent that she took refuge with the parson.

The day of the celebration dawned bright with only a light breeze blowing from the sea: it promised to be warm. Tables and chairs had been set up by convict-servants in a clearing between Wybalenna and the governor's house, a spot well known to the exiles who held corroborees and secret ceremonies there. Happy that such a propitious place had been chosen, they walked there in a long, straggling line and their chatter and laughter rose like the noise of a flock of lorikeets. Even the sick came: the weakest being carried in blankets, and these laughed and joked with the rest.

Manalargenna was accompanied by his son and daughters and others of his people but there was something in his demeanour, a kind of febrile tension that made Touami uneasy. He was reminded of Longertalenna just before he fell sick, when he had spent days on the hillside above the settlement in constant watch for Robinson and his party. Touami wondered afterwards whether his old comrade had felt Rowra's approach and so become desperate as his hopes of returning home turned to despair.

But this day there was no time for brooding: the holiday mood was infectious. To honour the exiles a lunch of mutton and plum pudding was served by the Governor's lackeys and all the adults were given wine. Touami, like many of the others, thought the taste unwholesome, like stale water in which leaves have fermented, but he liked its effect which was to engender a feeling of carefree well-being akin to that which came in dreaming.

After eating, the older folk sat in the shade, taking their ease and talking nostalgically of the past while some of the *num* officers organised cricket, a game at which many young *parner* excelled. The activity released some of the energy that had been building in them whilst replete under the trees the elders fell asleep. A flock of currawongs, seeing the tables unattended, swooped in search of scraps and were chased away by the servants: even the birds' strident protests as they flapped back to the safety of the branches did not rouse the slumberers.

The shadows lengthened and the slight chilling of the air at last woke the sleepers. They moved into the sunshine and began to talk and laugh again. High tea was served and the atmosphere of anticipation, quelled in the afternoon by a surfeit of food and wine, was re-kindled for the important white folk sitting at the top table also seemed excited: the climax of the event was imminent. When the Governor's wife and then the Governor himself stood and made speeches, everyone listened politely and clapped but it was Robinson the exiles were waiting for. He sat staring across the clearing, apparently oblivious to the proceedings until the Governor, who had finished speaking some moments before, coughed meaningfully. Then, with apparent reluctance, he got to his feet.

He began by thanking divine providence for granting such a day which was, he said, ample reward for his labours and justification for everything he had strived for since embarking on his Mission. To see the same people who, but a short time ago were among the most wretched on earth, brutalised and hunted like beasts, living in ignorance of civilization and the Christian faith, sitting at table with no less decorum and appreciation than many of their white peers, was more than he could have hoped for and was proof, if such were needed, that the natives of Van Diemen's Land were less ignorant than those who claimed them debased almost beyond human condition: such people, he claimed, knew only those individuals so abused by the whites they had reverted to a state of savagery as will any creature fighting for survival.

Touami and the rest listened impatiently though by now they were used to Robinson's hyperbole and long digressions of which they understood little and cared about even less. He thanked the hosts, praising their kindness and generosity so fulsomely that they blushed. And then at last he turned back to the rows of men, women and children he had brought here, all of whom were watching him intently. The tension was almost palpable. He smiled, inclined his head slightly in acknowledgement and gratitude for their good behaviour, and sat down.

There followed a moment of silence in which most of the assembly simply stared, dumbfounded. After all the hope and expectation of the day, the disappointment was like a physical blow. Then a murmur arose like the soughing of the wind. Some, thinking there had been a mistake and Robinson had forgotten the main purpose of the occasion during the course of his speech, clapped and shouted for more but he merely looked up and smiled then turned and began an earnest conversation with the Governor's wife.

Sitting amongst the elders, Touami was silent as the hubbub rose all around. He, like the rest, was profoundly disappointed but the fête was not yet over and it seemed from the demeanour of the white folk that the great treat was yet to come. After a while the holiday mood resumed but now there was an hysterical edge to the laughter and when some of the young men got up and danced, their movements and chanting betrayed a barely contained fierceness like that of warriors on the eve of fighting.

The sun set. During Robinson's oration some of the officers had been busy at the far end of the clearing and in the paddock beyond, fixing packages to trees and fencing. Now as the soft darkness under the trees spread and the first stars appeared overhead it was the *num* who were most excited: they kept glancing at the objects and when bright points of light moved between the trees, lackeys bearing tapers, they nudged one another and called for the dancing to stop though the *parner* leaping and stamping in the centre of the clearing were deaf to anything but their own chant.

The points of light bobbed and paused and for a moment the burning fuses glittered like stars pinned to the tree-trunks. Then the night exploded.

Touami was not alone in leaping to his feet and looking wildly for a weapon: his first thought was that they had been betrayed, that the fête was a trap and a massacre had begun. But though the noise and smell of gunpowder, the flashes and flaring light reminded him of the night of terror in the marshes when the Lairmairrener had been attacked, he realized suddenly that no-one was hurt, that the Governor's wife was laughing and pointing in delight at a whirling shower of purple and green sparks, that the bangs and flashes, blooms of light and colour in the sky were meant for enjoyment. He resumed his seat seething with shame and exchanged rueful glances with his neighbours. Gradually the wild beating of his heart steadied.

Apart from some very young children who wailed and cried throughout, once the exiles were certain no harm was intended they began to relish the display, clapping enthusiastically after each firework for they had never seen or imagined anything like it. And when at last the show was over and the Governor stood to thank everyone for coming, they applauded and praised him without reservation. Despite their earlier disappointment, they were sure now that they must be important in the eyes of the Government to merit such an occasion.

Throughout the afternoon and evening, Touami had watched Manalargenna, for of all the 'Mission *num*', he was closest to Robinson. Attended by his kin, the patriarch had eaten and drunk with apparent relish though whenever he thought no-one was looking, his smile faded and he looked ill and worn. When the fireworks were at their climax, he rose and went alone to where Robinson sat with the Governor. The three spoke briefly, then Manalargenna turned abruptly and walked heavily back to his seat. In the intermittent, hectic radiance from the fireworks, Touami could not see his face clearly but it seemed to him that the old man was weeping.

The assembly broke up: a straggling procession wended along the trail which was now lit by flaring torches. Most were animated, talking happily about the grand event; the children slept in their mothers' arms. Being of a people in whom the habit of living day to day was deeply ingrained, with full bellies, the novelty of the fireworks and the generosity of their hosts, most had forgotten the expectations they had harboured at the start. But Manalargenna did not speak all the way back and he stumbled often and would have fallen had it not been for the support of his daughters who walked beside him.

That was the last Touami saw of the old wise-man: after that night, Manalargenna did not venture from the hut he shared with his kin. And yet in the first days after the fête he was hardly missed for the *ny rae num* kept everyone busy from dawn to dusk, helping in the little gardens, reaping the harvest or clearing a new track through the scrub which was to be his private walkway. But this frenzy of activity did not last long and then the disappointment of that night re-manifested as a general mood of despondency. By now it was clear that instead of making arrangements for their departure, Robinson was entrenching his position as the new Governor of the island and it did not go unnoticed that while he was happy to supervise their labour (as if they were convicts and he their overseer), he rarely visited the settlement and avoided the hut where, it was rumoured, Manalargenna lay dying, although without the wise-man's contribution his mission would most likely have failed.

A kind of superstitious dread kept Touami away though as an elder it was incumbent on him to offer help and comfort to those in need. He had already witnessed too many suffer the agonies inflicted by Rowra but more than that, it was a sense that to acknowledge the ebbing of so great a life was to admit the end of something even more significant, a failure that went beyond mere physical defeat but marked the destruction of the very essence of a people: their stories, their traditions, the laws by which their lives were possible. For without knowing what had become of the rest of the Meelayginnee, those he and Uné-mawa had left behind long ago, with Manalargenna's passing he, Touami, would be the only living link with the time before *num*. And this he was unwilling to accept.

During the day Touami was able to deny the fact of Manalargenna's decline, but his nights were haunted by memories of others that had succumbed to Rowra and in sleep he was tormented by dark dreams. When long shadows crowded in as the fire sank, he thought to glimpse the figure of his comrade, Longertalenna, pacing the length of the room as at the height of his illness, his eyes wild and his skin glossed with sweat; the weight of the dog which shared his bed was like that of his beloved Uné-mawa when, after a night of agony, she sank into a stupor of exhaustion while he lay awake, listening anxiously to her quick, shallow breaths; in the sigh of the wind through the grass thatch he thought to hear their voices as they begged their daemons to end their suffering. And when at last he managed to sleep, nightmares thronged his mind: he watched helplessly as the *num* surgeon slid a blade into his friend's arm, releasing a pulsing stream which did not stop until Longertalenna's face had shrunk to a grinning skull; ravens circled as his long lost sister crawled brokenly through a patch of scrub, pausing now and then to cough up a bloody vomit that stained the earth like *ballawiné*; his father's remains, mixed with those of the kangaroo-dogs that had killed him, reassembled into a monster with dog's skull for head and a crooked spine which ran on two legs like a man and chased him through a forest where the flapping shreds hanging from the trees were not bark but human skins.

Touami would wake from these dreams shuddering and slimy with sweat and though he was comforted a little by the warm fug of sleeping people and dogs in the room, the sounds of their breathing and the flutter of flames in the hearth, he could not wholly escape the horror. Some seemingly endless nights he slipped outside where the air was cool and fresh against his skin and stars glittered high and remote in patterns familiar to him all his life. Tales of the ancestors were written in those constellations and their spirits dwelt there also, far removed from the pain and grief of their flesh and blood descendants who were still bound to Trouwerner. But while he took some solace from such things (even now, the scents of tea-tree and damp earth sent a thrill through his blood, reminding him of the forests of his boyhood), Touami was increasingly aware of a sense of dislocation, as if having spent so long away from his ancestral lands he was of no consequence, an anachronism, a relic whose existence had no relevance.

At such times, when loneliness rose like a howl through the very core of him, he would clutch the little bag containing his grandfather's bone (now crumbled to dust), and implore *Lyenah* to send some sign that he was not alone. But the nightmares returned night after night and when one afternoon he climbed laboriously to the crag he and Longertalenna had visited so often, stripped off his clothes and smeared himself with ash and charcoal before lying down to dream, the state of trance eluded him and he returned to Wybalenna ashamed at his failure and painfully self-conscious lest anyone had seen him. After that, he felt even more isolated for it seemed that even his daemon, *darwalla*, had forsaken him, yet something indomitable in his nature refused to submit to despair, that final degradation of spirit that meant the end. Despite everything he clung to the belief that *ny rae num* would keep his word and he would see Meelayginnee country again.

Manalargenna died at last on a bright summer morning and the wail of lamentation rose eerily against the chatter of rosellas and the distant crying of seabirds. Touami watched from the hillside as the old man's kin bore the long, wrapped bundle to the store-house where the surgeon performed autopsies on all the settlement's dead.

He did not grieve for the dead man but it felt as if a cavern had opened beneath his ribs, leaving him hollow and empty, as if he also no longer belonged among the living. So strong was this sensation that he bit his knuckles until his jaws ached but the pain was fleeting and insignificant. Only the sight of Robinson leading a band of Lairmairrener men to the cemetery to dig Manalargenna's grave brought him back to some sense of reality for as soon as the *ny rae num* turned to walk away, they stripped off their jackets and shirts and began the dance that marked the passing of a great one. The sound of their chanting echoed through Touami's bones: he rose painfully and made his way down to join them but when he reached the fence, it seemed to him that he was witnessing something from the past and that the dancers were merely aping what had gone before. Half-clad in white man's clothes, without the pigments which opened the path to spirit-being, their dance was nothing more than a performance, like the chanting of the catechism to please *num*. And so Touami did not linger or join in the chant as he had intended but walked heavily to his hut, filled with shame not for himself but the dancers, men of his own tribe, many of whom had never been properly initiated and could therefore have no real understanding of the ritual they were enacting.

The funeral was held next morning. All the exiles waited in the yard, talking in subdued voices for without Robinson, the surgeon and the catechist, the burial could not proceed. When at last they came, the *ny rae num* pale and stern, the churchman reeking of rum, the coffin was lifted onto the shoulders of the dead man's fellow tribesmen, his son foremost, and carried to the graveyard, the exiles walking behind in solemn silence.

The cemetery was no more than a small fenced paddock: sheep grazed there except on the occasion of a funeral. The rows of graves were unmarked by stone or plank: the thickness of the grass being the only indication of when their occupants had been interred. The mound where Longertalenna lay was already covered over though pocked with hoofprints where the sheep had nibbled the tender new growth. At the end of the row was a heap of raw earth, red against the green, and a gaping rectangular hole. The Lairmairrener had dug deep.

When the coffin had been lowered, there was a long silence. The catechist stood picking his teeth, humming tunelessly and staring into space. The mourners looked into the grave from which the rising smell of damp earth was mingled with the resinous odour of the coffin; from the settlement came the sound of frenzied barking for the dogs had been shut away for the duration of the funeral. As the moments drew out, the children became bored and restless and Robinson began to chew his nails, directing swift, poisonous glances at the drunken churchman who seemed oblivious to where he was and where his duty lay.

Finally Robinson's patience broke. He stooped and picked up a handful of earth which he tossed into the grave. It pattered like hail on the coffin and the catechist started and looked around as if amazed at where he found himself. Then without further ado, he launched into a monologue on the virtues of the Christian faith, an oration so tedious and rambling that even Robinson, himself given to flowery discourse, began to shift from foot to foot. The exiles stood impassively, paying the speech no more heed than the sound of the sea. By now the children, bored beyond endurance, had fled and were engaged in a game of chase around the graves: their shrill voices seemingly as carefree and ignorant of grief as those of magpies and wrens.

The shadows, which had stretched long over the graves at the start of the ceremony, shrank; the sun rose to its zenith and at last the voice trailed into silence. For a moment there was complete stillness, then the catechist picked up a clod and flung it into the grave. Even it thudded against the coffin, he turned on his heel and stumbled away, startling a kookaburra which flew up with loud cackling laughter. And the assembly was affected by a profound sense of wrong, though none could have expressed it in words. Even Truganana and Woorady were affected: they looked questioningly at Robinson who stood staring into the grave with an expression of profound sorrow and then, as if he felt the intentness of their gaze, he stirred.

'Ah, there are few men like he who has now departed,' he said slowly. 'But he is now in a better place.' He paused and took a deep breath and those close to him saw that tears glittered in the corners of his eyes. 'But, my friends, join me in the church this afternoon and I will give tidings to comfort you on this day of loss.'

With that he turned and walked away in the opposite direction to the catechist yet it seemed to Touami that his demeanour belied his speech for his shoulders were bowed and his tread slow and heavy. It was as if he had no idea of the effect of his words which was to re-kindle the old hope and excitement in the hearts of all that heard them. Indeed, in the minds of many (especially among the Lairmairrener), the thought took shape that perhaps the *num* Government had made their return conditional upon Manalargenna's death, fearing the wise-man's power not only over his own tribe but all the peoples of Trouwerner.

The half-faced shack that served as church and school was packed that afternoon. Men, women and children stood in expectant silence and their dogs sat or lay beside them as they waited. A sick babe whimpered and its mother sang to quieten it but that was all. This time, they were sure, their faith would be justified and *ny rae num* would give them the news they had yearned for since setting foot on the island. And there was not one man or woman who did not think of their homeland (the earth and rock, air and water from which not only their bones and flesh had sprung but those of their predecessors), with such intensity that tears came to their eyes. Some murmured their daemon's name like a charm while others clutched talisman-bags or surreptitiously traced the cicatrices marking their identity and lineage through the layers of cloth that covered them. And when at last *nymenner* came, their eyes devoured him, reading meaning into his every look and gesture: their hearts beat fast in anticipation and some felt a kind of ecstatic dizziness and swayed where they stood.

Robinson took off his hat and smiled a smile in which sorrow and compassion were melded. He began to praise the dead man so fulsomely that the congregation moaned in sympathy: it was clear that Manalargenna's death affected him as deeply as any of them. And then he paused in his eulogy and his eyes seemed to shine with joy though they were full of tears. 'Our friend, like you, suffered greatly because of the usurpation of his country by white invaders,' he said – and the listeners held their breath – 'but now he will go to heaven. God will tell his angels to carry his soul to heaven and he will see God face to face as I see you and he will never be sick any more, never hungry any more but he will be happy, happy forever. Eh, my friends, he will like it so much that he would not like to go back to his own country again. He will have no desire to return there. If you could say to him: will you come back to your own country again he would say "No". No. He would be displeased with you, he would not like to hear you ask him, he would say "No. I like this place. I like it better than my own country. . ."'

Touami, like the rest, at first heard these words with a kind of blank incomprehension, as a man in the dock might listen to sentence of death being passed upon him. So inured were the exiles to the religious nonsense of the catechist, as soon as the words 'God' and 'Heaven' were uttered their attention wavered, they detached themselves from their surroundings and, in their minds, wandered far away. Thus it was that when Robinson spread his arms and began to pray, they copied his gestures automatically, the rhythm of prayer lulling them into a trance-like passivity. He blessed and thanked them for their understanding, then left, walking quickly across the yard towards the surgeon's quarters.

The congregation dispersed. To many as they came out into the bright afternoon it was like waking from a dream. They stood around uncertainly and glanced towards the heap of raw earth in the graveyard and it dawned on them that they had been cheated though they were not sure what they had lost. But Touami gazed up the hillside to the little clump of trees that had been a sanctuary when Longertalenna was alive and realization of the truth was like the coming of night: he stood in the sunshine and the blackness of despair overwhelmed him.

There was a raven perched in one of the trees. It spread its wings and gave a harsh, grating croak. Touami turned and walked with dragging steps towards his hut. Now at last he understood Manalargenna's decline. Sailing past his homeland, he also must have begun to realize that the *ny rae num's* promises were empty and that, unwittingly, he had betrayed his own people. Robinson had deceived them from the start: there had never been any intention of returning them to their own country.

People called out as he passed, wanting his opinion of *nymenner's* speech but Touami did not hear them and they fell silent when they saw his face, daunted by the grim line of his mouth and the bleakness of his gaze. No-one followed as he entered the hut but a low murmur arose after he had gone inside for in their doubt and confusion many had hoped he would guide them in Manalargenna's stead.

Alone in the dank semi-darkness of the room Touami stretched out wearily on his bed of grass and leaves and turned his face to the wall. He thought of his promise to Longertalenna, a pledge that would never now be fulfilled and the bitterness of betrayal was swamped by a wave of futility and hopelessness he could no longer fight.

Outside, the sun sank towards the west, turning the distant grasslands and forests, the mountains of Trouwerner to gold and the sundering straits to liquid fire. But Touami lay in darkness: the passage of time no longer had any meaning for him. There was a fluttering inside his rib-cage as if a wild bird, *darwalla*, was trapped there. It struggled for a while, then was still.

The author lived in Tasmania for many years. In addition to shorter fiction, S. Pitt has published several novels, including *Korunah's Gift* which takes up the story of the Meelayginnee in the early 21st century.

Also by S. Pitt:

The Boy who found Salt

The Cove

Fen-wolf

Cromwell's Promise

Four Wonders

Find out more at:

<www.spittbooks.com>

www.ingramcontent.com/pod-product-compliance
Lightning Source LLC
Chambersburg PA
CBHW021650110726

47902CB00007B/1897